COMMITMENT

Nancy Ann Healy

ISBN: 069230388X
ISBN 13: 9780692303887
Library of Congress Control Number: 2014917539
Bumbling Bard Creations, Manchester, CT

Chapter One

Friday, December 5th

Alex Toles sat at her large wooden desk sorting through carefully placed piles of financial reports and detailed inventory assessments. It was becoming familiar territory. In less than a year, the former FBI agent's life had changed dramatically. The life Alex had resigned herself to for so long had vanished. She set down the paper in her hand and rubbed her temples lightly. Closing her eyes, she inhaled deeply before looking at the small clock on the corner of her desk. Her eyes traveled to the pictures just inches away, and a soft chuckle escaped her lips. The former Army Captain, NSA and FBI agent had been a confirmed bachelorette. She had been a woman who needed no attachments, only puzzles to solve. Alex gently lifted the framed photo of a beautiful fair-haired woman and a little boy. Attachments it seemed, were something she now cherished. The ringing of the phone snapped her from her private thoughts.

"Ms. Toles?" the voice inquired.

"Yes, Marta?" she answered.

"Your wife is on line two. I know you had a call scheduled. Are you available?"

"Of course. You know, you can always interrupt me for family. Thank you, Marta. I'll pick it up now," Alex responded. She pressed the blinking line and closed her eyes. "Hi."

"Alex?" Cassidy spoke softly. "Hey, are you all right?"

"Yeah. You know me and desks." Alex said, sounding slightly dejected.

"In fact, I do," Cassidy said lightly. "You still making the trip home tonight or are you going to stay at your mom's?" Cassidy asked. Alex huffed. This was one of the changes in life that frustrated her. Her father's sudden death six months earlier put Alex in the unique position to assume the helm of his company. Unfortunately, that meant longer periods away from home than Alex cared for.

An investigation that had begun with her wife's ex-husband, Congressman Christopher O'Brien, had taken many unexpected twists and turns in the last months. Turns that led her to meet the woman with whom she now shared her life. Twists that led her to discover an underground collective within the intelligence community whose agenda she still could not fully discern. Change, it seemed was inevitable, and it permeated every facet of her life. Learning of her father's long term involvement and his company's role within the intelligence community was only the tip of a behemoth iceberg. The assassination of President John Merrow, her former colonel and friend, changed the intelligence game completely. His career as a CIA agent had made his occupancy of the Oval Office a major boon for a group known as The Collaborative. Alex was certain that President Merrow's decision to maintain a greater loyalty to the people he was elected to serve than to his intelligence roots led to his murder.

The stakes were high for Alex. Few knew the truth; that a small boy Alex Toles now called her son was, in fact, the former president's biological child. It increased the risk to Alex's family, and that only furthered her resolve to protect them. Since assuming the helm at Carecom, Alex had uncovered even more disturbing realities. Her father's company was a front for both sanctioned and unsanctioned CIA operations and funding initiatives. Nicolaus Toles had dedicated his life to the *agency*. Alex still remained unsure where all of her father's loyalties had been placed.

Alex's position at Carecom was accompanied by the establishment of extremely unlikely alliances and a new identity of sorts. To most of the world she was now Alexis Toles, President and CEO of Carecom. Within the world of intelligence she was Alex Toles, CIA agent, a covert operative, the spider; a spy. This was a world where trust was a precious commodity, not readily given. It was a world Alex found both intriguing and mind numbing. But, as much as her new found career often consumed her time and attention; it paled in importance whenever she heard the sound of her wife's voice. Home was a place Alex longed to be and home was not the halls of Carecom. She pinched the bridge of her nose and answered her wife's question definitively. "I'll be home tonight. I have a call in fifteen minutes. I'm leaving after that."

"Alex, you sound tired," Cassidy answered in concern.

"I'll be home, Cass."

Cassidy licked her lips and shook her head. "I have an idea."

"Oh?" Alex perked up slightly.

"Not *that* kind of idea," Cassidy chuckled.

"No?"

"Well, maybe that kind of idea," Cassidy confessed. "That wasn't what I meant. Just do me a favor and go to your mom's when you are done. You and I both know that you will not be leaving there anytime soon." Cassidy could hear Alex's breath catch as she mounted a protest. "Alex...just go to your mother's."

"Cass, I don't want to be apart again tonight. This has not been the easiest time for you." Cassidy took a deep breath and nodded on the other end of the phone. "Cass?"

"I'm here. No, it hasn't. But, you will be much better after you get some sleep. Your back is not going to cooperate with a two and half hour drive after working all day. You'll be miserable all weekend. The weather is supposed to be good tomorrow, and we promised Dylan we'd get a Christmas tree. I need you to be able to help with that."

Alex let out a frustrated sigh. "I hate this."

"I know. I do too. Please, just humor me? I'll call you later," Cassidy promised.

Reluctantly, Alex acquiesced. "Okay. I love you; you know?"

"Of course, I know," Cassidy said softly. "I love you too. I'll talk to you later."

Alex set down the receiver slowly and glanced at the photo on her desk again. "Marta?" she called her assistant.

"What can I do for you Ms. Toles?'

"Oh for heaven's sake will you please call me Alex? It's been close to six months!"

"Whatever you want Ms. Toles."

"Marta!" Alex shook her head but smiled. "Can you please get my mother on the line?"

"Certainly, Ms…"

"Alex, Marta…Alex."

"Certainly."

Alex began readying herself for her last call of the day when her cell phone rang. "Toles," she answered.

"No meeting," the voice responded.

"Nice of you to call, Pip," she poked at the man on the line.

"Seriously, no meeting," Jonathan Krause answered.

"Okay? What's going on?" Alex asked.

"I need to see you," he answered.

"When?"

"Now," Krause said.

Alex rubbed her face with her palms. "Where?"

"Can you get downtown?"

"Yeah. At this time of day, it is going to be a couple of hours. Where?" she asked.

"How about a winter stroll? Maybe a little shopping?" he suggested.

"Fine. I'll meet you in front of the hall."

"I'll be there," he answered.

***

"Dylan, slow down!" Cassidy called to her son as she walked through the door of her mother-in-law's home.

Helen Toles took the bag from her daughter-in-law's hand and sighed. "Cassidy, you look exhausted. Are you all right?"

"Yeah; I am." Immediately, she saw the skepticism on Helen's face. "Honestly, I promise."

"This custody battle is wearing on you," Helen observed. Cassidy rubbed her forehead and closed her eyes. "All right; what do you say we go sit and have a cup of tea?" the older woman suggested. "Alex just called. You were right. She'll be later than she expected. Said she got called to an unexpected meeting." Cassidy just nodded. "I know," Helen said sympathetically as she placed her arm around Cassidy.

"I just miss her," Cassidy confessed.

Helen took a deep breath. After years of tension and a lengthy separation, she had grown closer to her daughter over the last few months than she had ever dreamed possible. One thing that Helen Toles understood clearly; the woman she now guided to her kitchen table was the driving force in the evolution of that relationship. She was eternally grateful to Cassidy for that. Alex had been spending several nights a week at her parents' home since taking over her father's company. It was a welcome turn of events for the older woman, but she knew that the distance was taking its toll on both her daughter and her new family. Alex had recently confided in her mother that she was making plans to change the situation as quickly as possible. It was something she wanted to surprise Cassidy with as a Christmas gift. Looking at her daughter-in-law now, Helen was tempted to break her silence. She opted for a softer approach. "She misses you too," Helen assured Cassidy with a solemn smile.

"I know. I'll be glad when things are settled…at least when *something* is settled," Cassidy chuckled.

"How are things looking…if you don't mind my…"

"Oh, not at all. Custody should be settled sometime shortly after the first of the year. You know…Chris…he just, well…he has no interest in seeing Dylan, but he seems to have every interest in making my life hell." It was a fact. Congressman Christopher O'Brien found every excuse he could to postpone court appearances, dodge requests for information or signatures, answer phone calls, or meet with a mediator. Just as Cassidy had predicted, her ex-husband had no interest in resolving custody of Dylan in a timely, much less amicable manner. He had not called Dylan in several months. He had begun making pointed accusations about Cassidy to the press. The saving grace for Cassidy remained the fact that Dylan was not only unfazed by his father's absence; he seemed to be relieved by it. "I'll just be glad to have it over with," Cassidy confessed.

"How about work?" Helen asked.

"Oh….it's good. The kids are great," Cassidy smiled.

"You miss teaching full time, don't you?" Helen inquired knowingly.

Cassidy shrugged. She did miss teaching full time. There had been a great deal of press coverage since her abduction the previous spring. Most of it focused on her relationship with Alex. Then, there was the ongoing custody battle with the congressman. That increased her visibility again. The combination of everything made finding a full-time slot problematic. She had settled for a tutoring position. It was the kind of program Cassidy believed in. She spent three afternoons assisting teens who had dropped out of high school or had been forced out of a traditional classroom setting in preparing for their GED.

Cassidy sighed. "Sometimes. Sometimes I miss it. You know, with Dylan in school and Alex away so much lately…"

"I understand. I remember those days," Helen interrupted her daughter-in-law. Cassidy looked at Helen inquisitively. "Oh, well," Helen began as she filled the tea kettle. "Nicolaus was away so much. When Alexis and Nicky finally were in school, well…there were days it certainly felt a bit lonely." Cassidy offered her mother-in-law an understanding grin. "Well, it won't be forever," Helen winked.

"Helen?"

"Hmm?" Helen responded. Cassidy gently shook her head as if to clear a thought. "Cassidy? What is it?"

"It's nothing."

The older woman made her way to the table and pulled out a chair to face Cassidy. "It is something. What is it?"

Cassidy closed her eyes and took in a deep breath for courage. "It's not just the distance."

"Go on," the older woman urged.

"I….."

"Listen, Cassidy….whatever it is that is bothering you. Well, I think of you as a daughter. I know you have Rose, and I…"

"Alex and I have been…No one knows…but we've been trying for a while…"

Helen's smile grew. The only surprise in Cassidy's confession was that Alex and Cassidy's efforts to conceive seemed to be something they wished to keep a secret. "I see," Helen smirked slightly.

"We haven't told anyone. We agreed, actually. I can't believe I am telling you."

"Are you worried? Cassidy, a few months…that is not long," Helen reassured as the kettle's whistle blew.

"No. I don't know. It's just…every time she seems so disappointed. Then she's away. I don't want to disappoint her," Cassidy sighed.

Helen put down the tea in front of Cassidy and reclaimed her seat. She took a sip from her cup and gently set it aside. "I'm going to tell you something and I want you to listen to me."

Cassidy looked up with tears in her eyes. Helen was determined to calm the younger woman's fears. The past months had been filled with an odd mixture of great joy and incredible sorrow. Cassidy had been held against her will and come close to death. The president had been assassinated. President Merrow was one of Alex's closest friends, and it had been a devastating blow for her daughter. Alex was shot, which Helen suspected motivated her daughter to make a formal commitment to Cassidy and Dylan as soon as she could. And, after a wonderful celebration at their wedding; the family faced the untimely passing of her husband, Alex's father. Helen sighed and offered her daughter-in-law a sad smile. "You have been through a lot, both of you. I never; I never thought Alexis would want a family. She has a family. I don't think you could disappoint her if you tried," she said, grasping Cassidy's hand gently.

"I probably just did," Cassidy said tacitly.

"No," Helen giggled. "From your mouth to God's ears. I know nothing. I am curious why you both want to keep it a...."

"Part of it is the custody battle. Part of it...well, I think she wants it to be a big surprise to everyone," Cassidy explained.

Helen's laughter filled the room, and Cassidy looked up sheepishly. "I'm sorry, dear." Helen wiped her eyes. "Surprise?" Cassidy's confusion was evident. "Cassidy," Helen tried not to start laughing again. "Your mother started a family pool on your wedding day." Cassidy's eyes flew open. "Frankly, I hope it does take a little longer. I bet February for an announcement." Cassidy opened her mouth to speak, but nothing came out. "Oh, come now; you know your mother," Helen reminded her. Cassidy chuckled. "I love my daughter, but I hate to break it to her, this is not exactly earth-shattering news."

"Don't tell her that if it happens," Cassidy said with a half-hearted smile.

"It will happen when it is meant to happen. That's how life is," Helen said plainly.

"I hope you are right," Cassidy said softly.

"Just don't be surprised if my daughter's reaction is not what you expect *when* it happens."

"What do you mean?" Cassidy asked.

"Well, don't ever tell her this," Helen said as she bit her lip. Cassidy nodded her agreement. "Her father fainted when he found out I was pregnant. Dropped like a sack of potatoes," she laughed.

"You're kidding."

"No. I'm afraid I'm not." Helen laughed heartily at the memory. She shook her head, and her voice dropped to a whisper. "He seemed to know. He was convinced it was a girl from the moment I helped him off of that floor." Cassidy watched as Helen grew pensive. "He loved her." Cassidy tried to conceal her misgivings, but Helen immediately saw the younger woman's doubt. "Oh, I know. He could be hard; so hard, particularly on her." She let out a strong sigh and stood. "Give me a minute," she said as she excused herself from the room.

Cassidy sat silently pondering her mother-in-law's words. She had only met Nicolaus Toles twice before his death. He was cordial but hardly warm. Cassidy had watched Alex struggle to comprehend her father's sometimes vicious and always pointed criticisms. It was incomprehensible to her how any parent could be so cruel. She sipped her tea and pondered her memories of Alex's father. She was lost in her silent contemplation when she noticed an envelope being placed in front of her. "What's this?" Cassidy asked.

Helen let out a sigh and shrugged. "I don't know," she answered, sighing at the perplexed expression on Cassidy's face. Helen reclaimed her seat and pointed to the envelope. "Alex found a letter addressed to me in her father's desk. That was with it."

"Does Alex know?"

Helen shook her head. "No. I don't see how she could. It was inside, addressed to you." Cassidy looked to Helen hesitantly. "He said in his letter that I should give it to you when I thought the time was right."

Cassidy tugged at her bottom lip with her teeth as she pondered the paper in her hand. "Do you know what it...."

"I have no idea what it says, Cassidy. It's his writing. It is addressed to you. Evidently, he felt there was something he needed to say."

"I don't understand," Cassidy whispered.

Helen smiled. "Nicolaus was a complicated man. He wasn't always that way." She paused and shook her head. "You know, we were apart for the first few years of our marriage; almost entirely. I was so relieved when he came home, supposedly for good." Cassidy studied the woman across from her. Helen's eyes had taken on a faraway glaze. "When Alex came, well, I thought that would settle him." Helen closed her eyes and exhaled forcefully. "It did; for a while." Cassidy sensed the sadness in the older woman's voice and instinctively took Helen's hand. "Oh, Cassidy. Things sometimes change. You love someone, well...you learn to accept those changes; even when you don't understand them. He always had other commitments. My commitment was always to him." Cassidy offered an understanding smile. "I don't know what is in there," Helen said. "I expect there are many things I don't know." Helen saw Cassidy's expression darken slightly. "Oh," Helen chuckled. "I know more than he or Alex, or even you might think. You live with someone long enough, well...There are no perfect secrets, Cassidy."

"Why give it to me now?" Cassidy asked.

Helen took a moment to regard the younger woman before her. She took a deep breath and then gently touched Cassidy's cheek. "Oh, Cassidy. You and I are very much alike; I suspect. Alex will always have other commitments. She is very much like her father in that way." Cassidy swallowed hard. "And you, well, your commitment is to your family. So is hers. She just has a different way of showing it. She is her father's daughter, even if she would like to deny that. I'll leave you for a while. Read it or wait. I have no idea what it says. I know two things. Two things I have always known. Nicolaus loved me," she paused.

"And?" Cassidy gently urged.

"And, he loved his children. No matter what he said or what he did." A tear trickled down her cheek. "He loved them."

Cassidy felt Helen place a gentle kiss on her forehead and watched her leave the room silently. She loved the older woman. Helen was quite different from her mother. She was more reserved and quiet, but Cassidy had grown to understand Alex's mother. She giggled inwardly. "She's a lot like you too," Cassidy mused aloud. She often marveled at how much Alex looked like her mother. Cassidy had come to learn that Helen was also extremely sensitive and thoughtful. They were qualities Alex shared with Helen. They were qualities not everyone took the time to see in Alex. Cassidy loved the sensitive side of Alex. It gave her wife a sense of vulnerability. In its unique way, that made Alex the strongest person Cassidy had ever known. "Well," she sighed. "Let's see what you have to say."

***

"Where are you off to?" the congressman asked.

"Why? Will you miss me?" Claire Brackett laughed. "You have that pretty blonde waiting for you at home. What's her name, again? Shelly?"

"Cheryl."

Claire Brackett shrugged. "You like those blondes; don't you, Congressman?"

"Jealous?" he quipped.

"Hardly. Don't flatter yourself."

"So? Are you going to tell me or not?" he asked.

"I have a meeting with my father," she answered as she buttoned her blouse.

"Do you think he suspects?"

The redhead let out an animated guffaw. "Suspects? What? That I am working with Dimitri?" O'Brien nodded. "No," she continued. "I don't think he *suspects.*"

"Your father is no fool, Claire."

She turned to him slowly with a smile of satisfaction. "He doesn't suspect. He knows."

"And that doesn't concern you?" O'Brien was puzzled by his lover's apparent lack of concern. Admiral William Brackett was considered by many to be the most powerful presence in United States intelligence circles.

"Concern me? No. Why should it?"

"Think you might be a bit over-confident," he chimed.

Claire chuckled. "Not at all. It's useful to me."

"If you say so," O'Brien answered.

"Christopher," she said, smiling as she slipped her arms through her leather coat. "I am no more on Dimitri's team than I am on my father's." He looked at her skeptically. "I don't care about their agendas."

"So? Then why? Why side with Dimitri?" he asked.

"There are no sides, Congressman. You sound as if you think this is cops and robbers," she mocked him. "No one is in this to protect anything or anyone but themselves."

"I'm not certain your father would agree."

"Developing a conscience?" she laughed. O'Brien's expression hardened. "Be careful with that, Christopher. Don't go getting heroic ideas now."

"I know my role."

"Yes. I suppose you do. I'll see you," Claire said as she reached for the door.

"When?" he asked.

"When it suits me," she answered, closing the door behind her.

***

Alex walked down the stairs of Government Center and stretched. This walk always reminded her of her father. In spite of all that she had learned these last few months, heading into Boston with the man she once revered as a hero still held fond memories for her. Now, those memories now made her heart ache. She reached in her pocket and pulled out her phone. She walked slowly, drawing out her pace as she waited for an answer.

"Alex?" Cassidy answered.

"Yeah."

"Where are you?" Cassidy asked.

"I got called to a meeting in the city," Alex responded. "Guess it was a good thing you twisted my arm into staying at my mom's."

"What's wrong?"

Alex sighed. "Nothing; I just got off the T and..."

"Started thinking about your father; didn't you?" Cassidy asked gently as she allowed her fingers to trace the envelope in her hand.

"Yeah. I did, but then I started thinking about you. I only have a minute, but..."

"You started thinking about me? Really?" Cassidy asked.

Alex chuckled softly. "Cass, I know we are supposed to get the tree, and all. And, we can, but...do you think maybe you and Dylan could come up to my mom's tomorrow?"

Cassidy tried not to laugh. "Any particular reason?"

"Well, you know...my mom loves you guys and maybe since it is supposed to be nice.... Maybe we could come in here...to the city. The lights are up..."

Cassidy smiled and shook her head on the other end of the phone. They had only made the trip into Boston a few times together over the summer. Cassidy had noticed that each time the short trek seemed to transform Alex's lingering sadness over her father into a sense of peacefulness. It seemed to be the one place Alex could remember the man who raised her fondly. "I think that can be arranged," Cassidy smirked.

"Good. Maybe Mom will come back home with us. I know she wants to see Nicky. Then I could leave my car here. And, you know she would love to decorate the tree with you and..."

"I'm sold," Cassidy responded. "Is it going to be a late night for you?"

"Nah. I doubt it. Unless your buddy Pip wants to go shopping."

"You're meeting Pip?"

"Yeah," Alex answered.

"I doubt it is about shopping then," Cassidy observed quietly.

"Well, he did mention it," Alex replied playfully as she caught sight of the topic of their conversation.

Cassidy took a deep breath. She was all too aware that meetings between her wife and Jonathan Krause were seldom of a social nature. The potential realities of those meetings always unsettled her, but she had accepted Alex's life as part of her own and she was determined to be calm and supportive. "Alex, Pip hates to shop almost as much as you do," she offered as a weak attempt at humor.

Alex laughed. "I won't be late. I'll call you when I get to Mom's. Cass?"

"Yes?"

"I called," Alex stopped in her tracks, just shy of her destination. "Well, I just hope our kids love coming here with me as much as I..."

Cassidy closed her eyes and inhaled deeply. "They will."

"I hope so," Alex said quietly.

"I'm sure Dylan will convince you tomorrow."

Alex laughed. "Talk to you in a bit."

"I'll be waiting." Cassidy hung up the phone and contemplated the envelope in her hand again. "I think this will wait until we are home," she said.

***

"So?" Alex asked.

"Nice to see you too, Alex," Jonathan Krause answered as the two began to stroll through Quincy Market.

"Yeah, well. Not that I don't love spending time with you," Alex shot back, "but no offense, I can think of places I'd rather be right now."

"How is Cassidy?" he asked.

"Tired," Alex sighed. "Truthfully, I'm a little worried about her."

"The custody hearing?" he asked with genuine concern. Alex shook her head. "What?" he asked.

"Just, well...we've had a few rounds of trying and nothing. She just seems; I don't know...like she feels guilty about it or something. The second time I couldn't even be with her." Krause stopped their progression. Alex pinched the bridge of her nose and continued. "Jesus. What the hell? I didn't want to tell her I was relieved. I mean, I know I am not technically responsible, but I'd like to be there when my kid is conceived. Crazy, huh?"

Krause smiled. "You didn't tell her that?" Alex shook her head. "You should. I know Cassidy enough to know she would appreciate that. I'll bet you she felt the same way."

"You think so? She seemed so disappointed," Alex said.

Krause laughed. "She probably doesn't want to disappoint you."

"She could never..."

"I know that. Maybe you should tell *her* that," Krause suggested.

Alex nodded as they resumed their pace. Jonathan Krause was not someone Alex would ever have imagined regarding as a friend. It was strange; she thought. There was an effortless nature to their relationship. They seemed to understand each other intrinsically. At first, Alex chalked up her inclination to trust the man to the devotion she knew he held to her wife. Over the last few months, she had begun to realize it was more than that. Jonathan Krause was a literal genius. He was as articulate as he was cunning. He was also fiercely loyal to those he cared for, just like Alex. Everything in Alex told her to trust Krause, and she did. She loved Brian Fallon, and she felt a deep sense of loyalty to her NSA roots and Michael Taylor and Steven Brady, but Krause was different. She could read his expressions, and he could anticipate her actions. It was uncanny. Sometimes, when Alex allowed herself a few moments to dissect their relationship, she would begin to question her sanity. After all, Jonathan Krause was a ghost she had hunted for years at the NSA. Now, in what she often considered the strangest turn of events in her life, he had somehow become not only her partner, but her closest friend.

"You didn't call me here to discuss my family issues," Alex said. "What's going on?"

"Got a lead on the Cesium Brackett took," he explained.

Alex stopped abruptly. "When?"

"Matthews contacted the admiral last night. Bucharest. Final destination? Unknown. But, Matthews seems to think it is headed toward The Russia-Ukraine border."

"Jesus. Whose play?"

Krause shook his head. "I don't know. I don't like it. The admiral called in the sparrow."

"What the hell would he call in Claire for? He knows she's in Dimitri's pocket," Alex said in disbelief.

"I don't know. Maybe he thinks he can rattle her somehow. Shake something loose," Krause offered.

"She's got plenty loose already," Alex rolled her eyes.

Krause chuckled. "I don't know, Alex. Just be ready for anything. Any luck on the ASA shipments from Carecom?"

Alex shook her head. "Not much, no. It looks like my father cut off the funnel to ASA sometime just before he died. The trail just stops. Completely."

"That doesn't make sense."

"I don't know," Alex admitted. "Does Matthews think someone is planning on using it against our interests?"

"We both know if anyone uses it....no matter where, it will be against our interests. Shit, Alex. Its origins are American. Count on the fact that they will play that hand," Krause told her.

"Where does that leave us?" she asked.

"Waiting. Nothing else we can do until there is some more movement. Matt has put some assets near the border. The admiral is pushing Strickland to send some *diplomatic* assistance to the embassy in Moscow."

Alex followed Krause into Faneuil Hall and stepped into a line for coffee. She shook her head again and pursed her lips. General Matthew Waters was someone they both trusted. Admiral William Brackett remained an entity that Alex still regarded with considerable skepticism. This tangled web concerned her for a number of reasons. Russ Matthews was more than simply the American ambassador to Russia. He was a friend. He had worked closely with President John Merrow from within The Collaborative, seeking to shut down operations both regarded as imprudent and dangerous quietly. She was certain the Russians suspected his involvement in thwarting several exchanges of technology and weaponry. Living in Moscow increased the risk to the ambassador. Alex suspected his dealings would not play well with President Lawrence Strickland, either. "Krause?" she began.

"What?"

"What about Russ?"

Jonathan Krause nodded. "Yeah, that thought crossed my mind. I'm surprised they haven't acted before now. Kargen and Ivanov clearly know he is not on team Russia."

"Yeah," Alex said under her breath.

"Wait." He stopped and leaned into Alex more closely as she stepped away from the counter. "You're not thinking they might implement the Cesium in an attack aimed at Russ?" he asked, his stress visibly increased.

"I don't know what to think, but I'm confident that crossed your mind as well," Alex shook her head slightly and handed Krause a coffee. "Maybe it's time I made a friendly call to my old friend Ambassador Daniels in London."

"Under what pretense?" Krause asked.

"Carecom works closely with several British corporations. All of them have ties to ASA. I'll find an opening."

Krause laughed as he watched Alex head toward a bakery counter. "Hungry?" he joked as Alex pointed to several desserts. "You sure *you* aren't eating for two?"

"Cute," she drawled out sarcastically. "Cass and Dylan are coming up tomorrow." He nodded his understanding as she accepted her bag from the cashier. "Why don't you talk to Callier? See if he has any clue why my father would stop the flow to ASA," Alex suggested.

"I will do that. He's been preoccupied lately. Worried about something. I can see it."

Alex listened carefully to the tone in Krause's voice. He held affection for the Frenchman. That was evident. "Well, seems there is plenty to worry about."

"Yeah, Alex...about that..."

"What?" she asked.

Krause took a deep breath. "What are you going to tell Dylan? I mean...are you going to tell him about his father?"

Alex remained silent for several moments as they weaved through a slight crowd. "That's up to Cassidy."

"What do *you* think?"

"I think sooner or later he will learn the truth," she answered. Krause nodded, and Alex could see the slight grimace on his face. "You know, he's grown quite fond of you," she said, receiving a nervous chuckle from Krause. There were a few things Alex understood about her new partner. Jonathan Krause adored Cassidy; he loved John Merrow, and Dylan was a part of them both. Krause had been put in the strange position of claiming Dylan as his own within their professional circles, and Alex knew part of him desperately wished that were true. She continued softly. "I hate keeping it from him, but if it keeps him safe. Well, I will do anything to keep him safe. I know you will too."

"Yes. I will. I take it you are staying at Helen's?" he asked.

"Yeah," Alex's voice dropped as she spoke the word.

Krause considered the woman beside him for a moment. He admired Alex, a sentiment he never intended to share with her. It was not simply because Alex commanded Cassidy's heart. Some days he hated to admit that he understood why the teacher had fallen for Alex. He suspected he would always love Cassidy McCollum. But, Cassidy McCollum was a girl he knew many years ago. Cassidy Toles was a woman. Krause was certain Cassidy was the strongest and most compassionate person he had ever met. The reality was that she loved Alex. What surprised him the most, was that Alex had come to command his heart in a much different manner. After John Merrow's death, Krause was convinced he would never trust anyone again; not completely. He trusted Alex completely. More than that, he cared about her. The misssion that he and Alex had embarked on had taken a toll on both his partner and the woman he had loved for many years. It was odd; he thought. He had always been convinced that avoiding any attachments was the safest course in life. Now, that seemed an impossibility. "I'll see Edmond. Work on the Daniels angle," he said.

"What about Claire?" Alex asked.

"I'll follow up with Fallon on that," Krause replied. "I'll make sure he is cautious but more aggressive in his surveillance before I leave."

Alex's face grew concerned. "Maybe we should call Taylor in. Fallon is not..."

"I trust Fallon," Krause interrupted her. Alex shook her head. She hated that her former FBI partner and friend, Brian

Fallon, was embedded in this life, but she had to agree. Fallon was smart; he was resourceful, and most importantly he was trustworthy. "He'll be fine, Alex."

"Yeah. Is that your personal guarantee, Pip?" she raised her brow.

"No."

Alex let out a chuckle. "That's what I thought. Tell Fallon to be careful."

"Watch yourself, Alex. Daniels is…"

"A viper. I know," she said as she began to walk away.

"Alex," Krause called after her, causing Alex to stop abruptly and turn. "Tell her."

Alex shook her head with a smile and then nodded. She scanned her surroundings silently and recalled a similar December afternoon with her father many years ago. "Yeah. Maybe I will," she whispered to herself.

***

Chapter Two

"Mr. President, Prime Minister Kabinov is on the secure line."

"Thank you, Robert," President Strickland replied. The president waited for the door to close and slowly lifted the receiver to his ear. "Sergei. What, may I ask, compels you to call?"

"Ah, Mr. President. Has it been that long that we are no longer friends?" the Russian prime minister answered.

"Am I supposed to believe that this is an extension of friendship?" the president inquired.

"Lawrence, you know the position. Your ambassador, his interference is unacceptable."

President Lawrence Strickland drew in a full breath and released it slowly. "Ambassador Matthews is not the issue."

"Ah, no. But, he is part of the equation; is he not? It's time. Ivanov is ready," the prime minister answered.

"I have diplomatic assistance en route. I can't pull them back now, Sergei. It would raise too many questions," Strickland interjected.

"Unfortunate for them. Perhaps an added assurance for us," Kabinov answered.

"How soon?" Strickland asked.

"It is in motion. You will know when the sparrow flies. The president will call formally."

President Lawrence Strickland closed his eyes and swallowed hard. Sergei Kabinov was a man he had crossed paths with many times over the years. Kabinov was considered by most to be moderate in his political ideology, far more so than Russian President Yegor Markov. Strickland shook his head gently as he considered his reply. "You understand...once this transpires, there will be no turning back," Strickland warned.

"Mr. President, am I sensing hesitation?"

"You sense my comprehension, Sergei. Comprehension of what we will soon face."

"Sometimes, Mr. President, fear is the greatest motivator. It ensures control. Something we have both lost," Kabinov reminded the American president. "They need an enemy, Lawrence. One they can taste. We will provide that for them all. Blurred lines have created chaos. It is time for clear divisions again."

Strickland closed his eyes. He had resigned himself to this course. Control equaled power and power was something he had sought his entire life. The news was riddled with conspiracy theories about President John Merrow's assassination, stories of corrupt politicians and election officials, insinuations of over-arching and intrusive eavesdropping. Terrorists were not an enemy that could be leveraged for economic or even political gain. They were mostly invisible and difficult to portray. With an unseen and undefined enemy, the enemy had slowly become the state. Kabinov was not wrong. The same was true in Russia. This new world of blurred geographical lines had been a boon for many, but it had unintended consequences for those attempting to lead nations. The digital age consumed far more than it produced and somehow it needed to be slowed. Years in legislative life instructed the president that more drastic measures were required. Sometimes, the answers to the future are found in the past. The past was precisely what Kabinov was about to recreate. "I'll await President Markov's call. We will proceed as planned."

"*Chto sluzhit nam, sluzit vsem* (What serves us, serves all)," Kabinov said as he disconnected the call. The president gently placed the receiver on its home and threw his head back. There was nothing to do now, but wait.

***

"Claire. Sit down."

"You could have at least invited me for dinner," was Claire Brackett's snarky reply.

Admiral William Brackett frowned and shook his head slightly. "Why would I do that, Claire? I doubt very much that the type of evening my company would provide would rank very high on your social calendar."

Claire Brackett leaned back into the large chair and propped her feet on the table in front of her. "That hurts, Daddy. Don't you remember all those bedtime stories you used to read me?"

The admiral cleared his throat. It pained him to look at the woman his daughter had become. Claire Brackett was beautiful and clever. She was articulate, and she was brilliant. She was manipulative, like any agent that hopes to survive and rise to the top of the intelligence echelon. But, Claire Brackett was also unfocused, unruly, and uninhibited; by anything. She was a pure, unadulterated opportunist without any cause or meaning informing her actions. He had told her many stories, taken her many places, introduced her to diverse cultures; all hoping that she would become as centered as she was cunning and as dutiful as she was driven. He often wondered now where he had failed in that endeavor. He loved her, but he feared he could not save her from herself. "I'll leave the evening entertainment to Dimitri and your congressman," he said dryly.

"Guess I won't expect you to pay for the wedding," she quipped. Admiral Brackett chuckled. "So...then, what is it, Daddy? No dinner. No stories. What is it that you called me here for?

He smiled and took a seat on the edge of his tall, wooden desk. "Seems your friends misplaced something that you took for them," he said. Claire Brackett's expression became tauter, but she did not respond. "Oh, what?" her father asked. "You give me credit for knowing your relationship with Dimitri, but you think your efforts with Agent Anderson would somehow escape my notice?" He nodded with a sarcastic smile. His daughter remained silent, but he could see the stiffening of her posture. It would be difficult for most people to read Claire Brackett, but for her father she remained largely an open book. It was the Achilles Heel that Claire still refused to acknowledge. He rose from his makeshift seat and paced the room slowly as he continued. "I wonder how Dimitri will feel when he realizes that his nuclear material is missing." He let his statement lie for a moment and then turned to face his daughter. "Do you think he will blame you?" Claire remained stoic. "No. Of course not. You simply liberated it from Carecom, and that was months ago...and right out from under Agent Toles, I might add. Now, *that* is something." His compliment was caustic at best, and he saw the almost imperceptible twitch of his daughter's eyelid. "Well, knowing Dmitri and his uncle, my bet is that he *will* blame you. You and Agent Anderson...and, if I were a betting man, that very nice man who charged you with such an enormously difficult task."

"Is there a point to this?" Claire finally asked.

"You are my daughter, Claire. Contrary to your beliefs I would prefer you stay alive."

"I'm sure," she said with a roll of her eyes.

The admiral studied his daughter from across the room. "I would suggest you find it, but I'm certain Agent Toles and Agent Krause are already on that." He watched as the young woman's pupils dilated.

"So your point in this meeting was to bait me with Alex Toles?"

"No. Not at all."

Claire Brackett stood indignantly. "Well, thank you for the enlightening chat. You always were focused on my education," she offered smugly.

"Education is the best investment anyone can make in themselves, Claire.... Particularly in your line of work."

She smirked and moved toward him, slowly leaning in and kissing his cheek. Softly she whispered in his ear. "Nice move. I'm not your pawn to play," she hissed.

The admiral stood perfectly still and unwavering in expression as he watched his daughter leave the room. He waited several long beats before lifting the receiver of his phone. "Yes.... She just left....Hook, line, and sinker.....I am certain. She'll contact him any minute....Just be cautious. She may light the way down the path, but don't expect that path to be clear...... Watch yourself."

***

Alex walked through the door of her mother's house and collapsed against it momentarily. She set down a small bag in her hand, then her briefcase. She tossed her keys on top of the case and pinched the bridge of her nose. The house was quiet. She suspected her mother had retired early, and she felt herself wading through a mixture of disappointment and relief that she was alone. It had been a long few days. She glanced up the staircase in front of her and gently massaged her temples. The weight of her conversation with Jonathan Krause was sizeable. Alex learned early on in her career that when she felt a twinge in her gut she needed to pay close attention. Right now, she felt ill. Everything within her was telling her that Russ Matthews was in trouble. She feared that whatever retaliation Viktor Ivanov and the former Russian contingent of The Collaborative chose to take; it would have a larger purpose on a much grander scale.

Worse, at least for Alex, she was concerned about Cassidy. Cassidy was under constant pressure dealing with Christopher O'Brien. Alex knew that Cassidy was determined to distance Dylan from the man he knew as his father. It was all taking a toll on her wife. She wondered if perhaps they should take a break from attempting to grow their young family. It was an added stress, even if it was with the most loving and hopeful of intentions. Alex felt incredibly guilty for her frequent absences over the last few months. She knew they added to the strain. She had missed Cassidy. She had missed Dylan. The physical distance was something she needed to close, and soon. There would always be trips she would need to take, many times without warning. That was unavoidable and all the more reason that her daily work needed to move closer to home. She kneaded her temples, threw her head back against the door and sighed.

"Alex?" a voice softly called.

Alex's eyes were startled open. She strained to focus on the sight in front of her. "Cass?"

"Yeah," Cassidy giggled as she began to close the distance between them. "Surprised to see me, I guess." Cassidy smiled as she reached Alex.

"What are you doing here?" Alex asked, almost as if she was unsure Cassidy was real.

"I missed you too," Cassidy laughed and placed a gentle kiss on her wife's lips.

Alex kept her eyes closed and took a deep breath. "You have no idea how happy I am to see you."

"Um-hm. You might *see* me better if you opened your eyes," Cassidy joked. Alex just sighed and kissed her gently. "Alex?"

"Hmm?"

Cassidy tried to suppress her laughter. The relief she felt in Alex's arms was indescribable. It lightened her spirit. "You look exhausted," she observed. "Did you eat?" Cassidy asked. Alex opened her eyes and shook her head. "Alex, you have to stop and eat." Alex turned slightly and handed Cassidy the small bag she had placed on the floor, sporting a cheesy grin. Cassidy narrowed her gaze playfully and peeked in the bag. She rolled her eyes and nodded. "I see," she said. "Cupcakes were not exactly what I was referring to."

"They're vanilla," Alex chimed in, widening her toothy smile.

"Umm."

"You love vanilla," Alex observed.

"Yes, I do," Cassidy admitted. "Are you trying to tell me you want dessert before dinner," Cassidy flirted.

"I like dessert," Alex offered.

"Yes, I know that too." Cassidy's next thought was immediately interrupted by a passionate kiss. "What was that for?" she asked as Alex pulled back slowly.

"I'm just glad you are here. Where's Dylan?"

Cassidy patted Alex's cheek. "I wondered how long that would take." She watched Alex's eyes widen hopefully. "Your mom took him upstairs about an hour ago. Go on," she encouraged. "He'll be thrilled to see you."

"I don't want to wake him," Alex said a bit sadly.

"Honey…."

Alex sighed. "I hate this, Cass."

"I know. Do you want to eat something?"

"I'm not hungry," Alex replied.

Cassidy stroked the agent's cheek tenderly. "Okay, let me put these in the kitchen. Go up. I'll be right there." Alex kissed Cassidy on the forehead and followed her direction. She reached the top of the stairs and stopped. She didn't want to wake Dylan, but she couldn't resist looking in on him. She opened the door to the bedroom and peered inside. Dylan had the blankets tucked tightly around him. Alex laughed. "Some things never change," she said, recalling how her mother always tucked her in protectively. She tip-toed to the bedside and kissed Dylan carefully. Cassidy reached the door and just watched. "Sorry, Speed," Alex whispered. "I promise. I promise, pretty soon I won't be away so much. I love you, Dylan."

Cassidy swallowed hard. She could hear the tension and the heartache in Alex's voice. "Alex..." Alex ran her hand gently over the sleeping boy's head and looked at the ceiling as if to implore an answer to an unspoken question. Cassidy closed her eyes and let out a sigh before she continued. "Come on. He'll be bouncing into our bed in the morning." Alex nodded and followed her wife across the hall. She shut the door behind her and immediately collapsed onto the bed. Cassidy stood at the end of the bed and began removing Alex's shoes. "Alex, I'm worried about you."

"I'm okay, Cass. Really. It's you I'm worried about."

"Me?" Cassidy asked in confusion.

"Yeah, you," Alex answered.

"Why?"

"What do you mean; why?" Alex asked. "All this chaos with O'Brien, and then...well, you know...the whole thing with the baby...and..."

"Alex," Cassidy said gently as she climbed onto the bed. "I am all right, honestly."

Alex let out a sarcastic chuckle. "Jesus. I wasn't even with you the second time... I mean..."

Cassidy bit her bottom lip gently. She sensed the conversation was about to move into a territory neither had honestly explored. "You couldn't help that," she said.

"Why doesn't that make me feel any better? Cassidy, you are dealing with everything alone. Bad enough that I'm not there to handle that jackass O'Br...."

"Alex," Cassidy called to her wife in a comforting whisper.

"No, seriously. I'm not even there when you go to...I mean when we're trying to have a baby? God," Alex said exasperatedly. Her voice dropped. "I felt so horrible...worse that I was relieved when you weren't..."

Cassidy tilted her head in surprise. "You were relieved I wasn't pregnant?"

Alex put her face in her hands. "I didn't mean....no....but, well, yes...I mean...I know I'm not...but I'd still like to be there when…you know." Cassidy's smile grew as her eyebrow raised in amusement. Alex looked at her wife curiously. "What?" Alex asked. "I'm rambling."

Cassidy kissed the agent's cheek. "I thought you were disappointed. I was worried that I, well…that you…"

"Never, Cass."

"Hmm. Quite the pair, aren't we?" Cassidy mused.

"Sometimes, I guess we are."

"Alex, I want you there. Of course, I do. I swear, I am all right. It takes time sometimes. I just, well if it doesn't…"

"It will happen when it's meant to," Alex said with a reassuring smile. Cassidy grinned. "What?" Alex asked.

"Nothing."

"Cassidy? Come on; what?" Alex urged.

"You're going to be mad."

"At you?" Alex asked. "I doubt that."

Cassidy let out a heavy sigh. "That's what your mother said when I talked to her earlier."

"You told my mom about us trying to have a baby?" Alex asked. Cassidy nodded sadly. "You told *my* mom and not *your* mom?" Cassidy looked at Alex sheepishly. Alex laughed.

"You're not mad?" Cassidy asked.

"Mad? No."

"But, Alex…we agreed. I know you wanted this to be a…."

"Cass, you needed someone to talk to. I surely didn't make myself the best candidate for that; did I?

"Alex…."

"No. It's true. I haven't been there like I should."

Cassidy kissed the agent gently. "You are always there for me. Even if you are in another state or another country. I know that."

"It's not the same."

"No, it's not," Cassidy admitted.

"Cass, things at work…there are some things…I just…"

"Alex, I know. Not specifically, but I know you. There is something I want to ask you."

"What is it?" Alex asked.

"Would you....if this month....if it's not...What would you think if we waited to try again until after the holidays?" Cassidy suggested in a whisper.

"You want to stop trying?" Alex asked for clarification.

"No," Cassidy said emphatically. "I just...I think if we start again after the holidays and the custody is settled....It's just with you away so much and..."

Alex kissed her wife. "I think that's a perfect idea." Tears had begun to stream down Cassidy's cheek, and Alex felt her heart sway in her chest. "Why are you crying?"

"I don't want to disappoint you, Alex. I want this baby as much as..."

"I know that," Alex said as she wiped away her wife's tears. "You could never disappoint me, Cassidy Toles. Not ever. Stop worrying now, okay?" Cassidy shook her head as her tears continued to gain speed. "Cass? What is this about?"

"What if I can't, Alex?"

"What if you can't get pregnant?" Alex asked. Cassidy nodded. Alex sighed and pulled Cassidy to her. "Then I guess we look at other options...if you still want to have a few more."

Cassidy laughed through a sob. "A few more? Alex, we might have to consider other options if what you are looking for here is a football team."

"What do you have against football?" Alex joked. She felt Cassidy's laughter mix with her tears and kissed the top of her head. "As long as I have you and Dylan, I will be happy."

"I love you so much," Cassidy said through a few remaining tears.

"Well, that's a good thing since you are married to me," Alex said lightly. "*Je t'aime plus que tout* (I love you more than anything). It will all work out; you'll see. We'll be in the Super Bowl before you know it." Cassidy laughed and closed her eyes. She didn't care if they fell asleep exactly as they were. She was home. Home was wherever she could be with Alex and Dylan, and it was the one place she never intended to leave.

***

"Edmond."

"Jonathan, how are things in the states?" Edmond Callier inquired.

"Tense," Krause replied.

"And the family?"

Krause took a deep breath. "They are not my family, Edmond. They are Alex's."

"Mm. And, Alex?" Callier continued.

"She's all right. Wondering why her father would suddenly stop the flow of funds to ASA," Krause replied.

"Interesting. What do you mean he stopped the flow?"

"It seems he stopped funneling the usual amounts to ASA shortly before his death," Krause explained.

"Anywhere else that she has noted that action?" Callier asked cautiously.

"Not that she mentioned, no."

Edmond Callier rubbed his chin and released a heavy sigh as he headed to the bar at the far side of his office. Slowly, he opened the bottle of scotch that sat atop it and poured himself a glass. "Nicolaus Toles was an enigma, Jonathan. The Broker.... well, he had access to the inner workings of everything in The Collaborative; as it once stood. If we were the ship, he was the engine room."

Krause considered the statement carefully. "Edmond?"

"Yes?"

"You still haven't told me much about Mr. Toles."

"What makes you so curious?" Callier asked. Krause did not immediately reply. Edmond Callier let out the hint of a nervous laugh. "You're worried."

"Of course I am worried. We are on very shaky ground..."

Callier interrupted. "No. You are worried about your family. Why is that so hard for you to admit, Jonathan?"

"I told you. They are not *my* family."

Callier laughed. "Families can be complicated." He took another long sip of his scotch and savored it for a moment. "Come to Paris."

"Why?" Krause asked abruptly.

"You have questions that you want answers to. I may not have the answers you seek. And, the answers I have may not be what you want to hear," Callier explained.

"I don't have expectations," Krause replied.

"Good. Then I will see you soon."

***

The door to the warehouse rolled up slowly and then swiftly closed. Claire Brackett walked deliberately through the spacious room that was filled with boxes and pallets toward the singular door that resided at its opposite end. She pressed a few numbers into a keypad and the door opened. She stepped through into the narrow corridor that led to yet another door and stopped abruptly, waiting as the camera scanned her presence. She pressed her thumb against another small pad and watched as the steel door opened automatically, granting her access to a world most people only see in movies. The walls were covered with large screens, each depicting real-time footage of various places around the globe. Long tables lined the room adorned with endless, smaller flat screens. Claire Brackett was always surprised by the veritable silence in a room that was filled with constant activity. It both intrigued and unsettled her. She preferred her life working in the field. This was a coward's version of the spy game, safely tucked away, peering into people's everyday lives; most of whom Claire Brackett regarded at insignificant and uninteresting. She shuddered slightly in disgust.

"Sparrow," a man's voice greeted her in the distance. "What brings you here?"

"We may have a problem," she answered.

"We always have problems," he laughed.

Claire Brackett did not share in his humor. She was uncertain how much validity to place in the information her father had given her. One thing she did know; it was unwise to dismiss anything Admiral William Brackett said as unimportant. "I am glad you are amused. My father seems to think that certain assets we secured are…well…"

The man before her reared his head in laughter. "He is a clever old coot."

Claire Brackett regarded the man before her cautiously. "Are you telling me that my father is setting me up again?" she asked.

"I can't say what the good admiral's agenda is. Perhaps he was given false information," he said simply, but Brackett could see his eyes twinkling in amusement. "Or, perhaps he just knew you would run here to me."

"You're not concerned?" she asked

"No. The package is at the border already. And, I think this would be a good time for you to visit our friend Dimitri."

"You want me to go to Moscow?"

"No, I want you to see Dimitri," he answered.

"I don't understand."

"Well, Claire….if your father is expecting you to provide a pathway…"

Claire Brackett's frustrated reply came swiftly. "You think he is using me?"

The man shrugged. "You don't?" He watched her expression harden. "You have used him, yet you expect him to do less?" He shook his head. "Dimitri will be in London Tuesday. Meet him there. Meet Agent Anderson at the coffee shop Monday at noon. You'll get the details there."

"And then what?" she barked.

He smiled as he turned to take his leave. "Just follow the directives, Sparrow."

The redheaded agent watched as the man walked across the large room and through a set of glass doors. "Follow," she began to muse. "That's not what I was raised to do," she whispered to herself. "We'll see who follows."

***

Jonathan Krause picked up his phone and lifted it to his ear. "Krause."

"It's Blevins. I need a ride."

Krause inhaled deeply. "Flat tire?" he asked.

"No, lost my keys," the response came swiftly.

"I'm not close. I'm afraid you are on your own. Perhaps you should call a cab," Krause suggested.

"All right," the voice answered. "It would have been more convenient for you to pick me up."

"Yes. Sorry about that. Is the car secure or do you need a tow?" Krause asked.

"It should be fine."

"Good. Sorry, I can't help you," Krause offered.

"I know how to call a cab," the man responded.

Krause chuckled. "See you soon. Let me know if you find those keys."

"Will do," the voice said as the call disconnected.

Krause rubbed his hand over his head in frustration. The last thing he wanted to do was disturb Alex's weekend. The call, however, was enough to convince him that a brief visit was necessary. Brian Fallon would not make such a call if he were not certain that they were compromised in some way. Fallon had been tailing Claire Brackett for months. Both Krause and Alex had been waiting for a break where the younger Brackett was concerned. As reckless as the young agent's actions could be; she was adept at covering her tracks. Krause began running through possible scenarios with the young, cocky Brackett at their center. The fact that the she had been responsible for the retrieval of the Cesium he and Alex had been attempting to track down for months concerned him. Tensions of late were higher than the usual off the charts strain embedded within the intelligence complex. It would have been an understatement to say that the situation had become volatile. The protocol that he had established with Brian Fallon was something he had hoped would never be needed. Dealing with Claire Brackett as the fringe operative she appeared was one thing; managing her as an agent whose ties remained secretly and deeply embedded in the agency or NSA could prove to be a nightmare.

It was clear to Krause that the admiral's plan to call in his daughter and plant a seed of worry had worked. She ran to someone. It was where she found that someone that now concerned Krause the most. The warehouse in Baltimore had long functioned as Krause's home base. The facility housed what was once the nerve center of the agency's most secretive operations. It was comprised of a collection of NSA, CIA, and DOD experts and analysts. It had been The Collaborative's living room. It was, until this moment, a location he had met with both Brian Fallon and Alex Toles.

Krause shook his head and groaned. He was anxious to get to Paris and speak with Edmond Callier, and this time he was determined to be unrelenting. It was time for some answers, long overdue answers. He had grown tired of researching The Collaborative's money trail. That provided clues, many clues, but to date it produced no actionable intelligence. There was one question that was nagging at the back of his mind; was this focus on the money trail deliberate? Had the admiral and Edmond Callier merely been stalling his efforts with Alex? It left a bitter taste in his mouth. Alex needed to know if Fallon was compromised in any way. He silently cursed the need to disrupt his new partner's life again and the need to delay his flight overseas temporarily. "Sorry, Alex," he sighed as he turned the key in the ignition.

***

Chapter Three

Saturday, December 6th

Alex woke up and rubbed the sleep from her eyes. She felt the space next to her and shifted to Cassidy's side of the large bed, inhaling the faint scent of her wife's perfume on the pillow. Cassidy reached the doorway and smiled at the sight before her. Normally, Alex was up well before her wife. On the rare occasions that Cassidy vacated the bed while Alex was sleeping, she often returned to find the agent hugging her pillow tightly. "Miss me?" Cassidy called playfully.

Alex made no effort to move and mumbled her response, still clinging to the pillow. "Why are you up?"

Cassidy giggled and made her way into the room with a cup of coffee. "It's 9:00 a.m." Cassidy laughed a bit harder as Alex reluctantly pulled herself to a sitting position, holding Cassidy's pillow to her chest and pouting like an overtired child. "You are going to have to let go of squishy me, if you want this," Cassidy winked and gently pried the pillow from Alex's grip, replacing it with a cup of coffee.

"Squishy you?" Alex asked.

"Thought I didn't know about that, huh?" Cassidy raised her brow. Alex suddenly found the contents of the cup in her hand fascinating. Cassidy could not help but laugh. She had gotten up one night after Dylan had come into their room. When she returned, she found Alex cuddled up to her pillow. Listening to Alex mumble, she decided to ask her wife what she was doing. In Alex's sleep induced haze she had muttered, "cuddling squishy you." Cassidy kissed Alex's cheek and whispered in her ear. "I'm not sure how I feel about being called squishy, but I think you are adorable."

Alex gave a slightly embarrassed groan and took another sip of her coffee. Cassidy took the opportunity to sprawl across the bed and put her head in Alex's lap. "Where's Speed?" Alex asked.

Cassidy closed her eyes, feeling Alex's hand instinctively begin to comb gently through her hair. "Looking through boxes of ornaments with your mother. It was a great diversion to keep him from coming up here to pounce on you."

"You could have let him…"

"Mm-hm…I know," Cassidy replied. "You needed the rest, honey."

"I guess I did," Alex admitted. "I take it you asked Mom about coming back with us later today."

"I did."

"What did she say?" Alex asked.

Cassidy cuddled a little closer. "I think she is looking forward to it."

The sound of the doorbell caused both women to sigh. They both chuckled at Dylan's enthusiastic greeting when the door opened. "Uncle Pip!"

Alex exhaled forcefully, and Cassidy felt the stiffening in her wife's body. "I take it this is not a social call," Cassidy said softly.

"Probably not," Alex admitted, placing a gentle kiss on Cassidy's head. She carefully extracted herself from underneath the weight of her wife and watched as Cassidy threw the pillow she had been holding over her face. "Hey, be careful with squishy you," Alex admonished. Cassidy kicked her feet slightly in frustration, and Alex laughed. "I'm sure it is nothing earth shattering," Alex assured her.

Cassidy sighed and threw the pillow off of her. "I just would like a couple of days…just for us to be…"

Alex smiled. "I know," she said. "You know....You love Pip, and so does Dylan." Cassidy's brow furrowed. "You do," Alex laughed. "And he loves you both. I'm sure an excuse to see you figured into the equation."

Cassidy contemplated the look in Alex's eyes. She had watched the evolution of Alex's relationship with Jonathan Krause. They were alike in many ways. There was little doubt in Cassidy's mind that Alex had genuine affection for Jonathan Krause, though it was something Alex never spoke of directly. "Well, whatever it is, it had better not change our plans," Cassidy said more firmly than she had intended.

The tension in her wife's voice did not escape Alex's notice. She offered Cassidy an apologetic smile. "It won't." She kissed Cassidy on the forehead and headed to retrieve some clothes.

"Mom! Alex! Uncle Pip is here!" a voice bellowed up the stairs.

Alex finished buttoning her jeans and pulled a blue sweater over her head. "Come on," she said as she pulled Cassidy to her feet. Cassidy collapsed into the agent's arms, and Alex held her close.

"Promise?" Cassidy asked weakly. She hated being needy, but the truth was, she did need Alex.

"I promise, Cass," Alex replied with another soft kiss. "Come on, the sooner we get down there; the sooner we get on with our weekend."

"I hope so," slipped almost inaudibly from Cassidy's lips. It did not go unnoticed by her wife, and Alex made a silent commitment to close the physical distance that had kept them apart far too often as soon as possible.

"I promise," Alex whispered as they made their way down the stairs.

***

Dylan was excitedly showing his Uncle Pip some of Alex's childhood Christmas ornaments when Alex and Cassidy reached the room hand in hand. Immediately, the boy found his feet and ran to his parents. "Alex, look!" He held out a Big Bird ornament with a great big smile. "YaYa says this one was yours!"

"Yep, I believe it was, Speed." Alex winked and swept Dylan up onto her. His feet gripped her waist, and his arms flew around her neck tightly. "I missed you, Dylan," Alex said, her voice hoarse with more emotion than she expected.

Dylan just smiled. "Mom says we are getting our tree tomorrow!" He turned back to the man that was sitting on the sofa and continued. "YaYa's coming too. She's going to let me take some of her ornaments and help us with the tree," he said. "Why don't you come, Uncle Pip?"

Jonathan Krause's lips curled into a warm, genuine smile. Something about Dylan always seemed to remind him of his youth. He could see so much of Cassidy in the youngster. He looked like his mother. He was intelligent and compassionate just like the woman Jonathan Krause had always loved. Dylan's eyes twinkled with the mischief of the best friend Krause missed every day. "I'm sorry, Dylan. I wish I could."

"Why can't you?" Dylan asked.

"I have to take a trip. But, I'll bet Alex would take some pictures and send them to me."

"Of course," Alex said.

"Not the same," Dylan pouted. Cassidy looked at her old friend and winked. Jonathan Krause had quickly become Uncle Pip after Alex's father's funeral. It was a relationship that Cassidy oddly welcomed. Dylan had three strong men in his life, Uncle Nick, Uncle Brian, and Uncle Pip. At first, Alex appeared a bit nervous about the bond Dylan seemed to form with her new partner, but Cassidy had watched that fade more and more with each passing day. She looked at Alex and saw the understanding expression in her eyes. With

Alex's absences over the last few months, and the departure of Christopher O'Brien from their everyday lives, Cassidy wondered if Dylan would feel insecure. He had battled some fears, but Alex's constant reassurance coupled with the presence of male role models that enthusiastically engaged with her son, seemed to ease the majority of Dylan's anxiety. Cassidy was grateful for that.

"I know it's not the same, Dylan," Cassidy spoke up. "When are you leaving?" Cassidy asked her friend.

"Late this evening," he replied.

"Well, could we entice you to at least stay for breakfast?" Cassidy suggested.

"Depends," he answered.

"On what?" Alex asked.

"On whether or not you or Cassidy is doing the cooking," he quipped.

Cassidy covered her mouth to stifle a chuckle as Helen answered. "Alex will not be coming near my stove. My kitchen, my rules."

Dylan had climbed back into the tall CIA agent's lap. "Alex makes the best cereal," he said.

"Really?" Krause asked him with a tickle.

Dylan laughed. "Yes."

"Are you sure?" Krause asked again with another burst of tickles.

"Yes!" Dylan cried through his laughter.

"Well, maybe there is hope for you yet," Helen smirked at her daughter. Alex rolled her eyes. "Dylan, why don't you help your mom and me make some pancakes for Alex and your Uncle Pip."

"Okay," he happily agreed, taking his YaYa's offered hand and following her to the kitchen.

"I'm sorry," Krause said, looking at the two women before him. "I didn't want to bother you. I just need to talk to Alex for a few minutes."

Cassidy sighed and felt Alex's arm drape around her. "It's all right. As long as you don't sweep her away to Beijing or Brussels or wherever you two..."

"No sweeping," Krause promised.

Cassidy nodded. "And," she began when she saw Krause's concerned expression. "And, you promise to come see that tree when you *don't* need to talk to Alex." The surprised expression on her friend's face amused Cassidy. "You heard Dylan," she said.

Alex nodded and kissed Cassidy's head. "I told you," Alex winked at her partner.

Krause was not used to such sentiments. His only reply was an uncomfortable grin that held the promise that he would comply with Cassidy's orders. Cassidy shook her head. "I'll leave you two to do whatever it is you do," she said. "Don't let it take longer than those pancakes," she cautioned. "Helen takes hot food very seriously."

Alex laughed. "Consider us warned," she whispered to Krause as Cassidy exited the room.

"Oh, I will," Cassidy called back. "She's your mother. I'm not saving either of you if you make her wait."

Alex shook her head. "She should be a spy. She'd be a secret weapon. She hears everything," she joked to her partner.

"And don't you forget it," Cassidy's voice called back.

"Never," Alex laughed. "So," Alex shifted the playful banter. "Not that I don't enjoy your company, but...."

"Fallon called last night." Alex was perplexed. "He called in as Blevins. Said he needed a ride," Krause explained. Alex took in the information and pinched the bridge of her nose. "Brackett was at the warehouse, Alex."

Alex looked to the ceiling and tightened the grip she had on her nose, gradually moving her fingers to her temples. "After the admiral spoke to her?" she asked. Krause nodded. "Shit. Any idea who she was seeing?" Krause shook his head. "Fabulous," Alex said sarcastically.

"Alex, if someone in that facility is Claire's contact..."

"Fallon is compromised," she finished his thought. "We need to pull him."

"I'm not sure that's the answer," he said cautiously.

"You want to try and leverage this?" she asked.

"Think about it. They don't know that we know."

"You can't be sure of that," Alex said.

"No, but you can't be certain that they do know. And, Alex, if we pull him now, we might make it worse for..."

Alex hated to agree, but Krause was right. Pulling Brian Fallon now might not only tip their hand and compromise their efforts, in might put her former partner at greater risk. "Any ideas?" she asked.

"None that I could call concrete."

"Whoever it is; they have to be at a high level," she observed.

"I agree," Krause said. "I needed you to know before I head to France. In case..."

Alex nodded her understanding. "Krause?"

"What?"

"Let's have Brian bring this information to Tate."

Jonathan Krause's expression immediately gave away his surprise. Alex had always shown great restraint where Agent Brain Fallon was concerned. She was protective. He agreed wholeheartedly with her assessment of the situation, but he wondered why she would suddenly shift so drastically. "Alex, you and I both know Tate is agency. He may be at the FBI, but we don't know what his allegiance is."

"So, you don't agree?" Alex asked with the raise of her brow.

"I didn't say that. Assistant Director Tate is still an unidentified entity. It's a risk. A risk to Fallon. Why now?"

Alex looked toward the kitchen and closed her eyes. She exhaled forcefully and returned her attention to the man seated next to her. "We both feel it," she said. "This volcano is going to erupt at any moment. If Joshua Tate is the friend he has suggested in the past, well....maybe, just maybe he will prove to be a valuable resource; at least for Fallon."

"If he's not?"

Alex nodded. "Then, if we play our cards right; he leads us down the path we have been searching for."

"You want to spy on the spy," Krause chuckled. "Fallon will be at greater risk either way."

"I know," Alex said. "We don't have a choice. Maybe Callier can…"

"I will press Edmond this time," Krause said. "We can't go to OP TECH with this one. Not as usual. Don't put Tate in play until I speak with Edmond. Perhaps that will give us a clearer direction."

"You trust him?" Alex asked.

"I trust you," Krause deadpanned. "Getting Fallon killed is not on my to-do list."

Alex nodded again. "Is he still tailing Brackett?" Krause confirmed the question with a smirk. "Good. Any more news on that Cesium?"

"No, but the admiral's plan worked, Brackett led us at least part way down the path we needed to find," Krause said. He noted the pensive expression on Alex's face and the way her thumb pressed into her temple. "What?" he asked.

"We can't wait to put Tate in play," she sighed. "If whoever Brackett went to….Krause, if they suspect we know….anything...Brackett could be their decoy."

That thought had crossed Jonathan Krause's mind as well. Hearing Alex verbalize made it real. "Are you thinking of involving Taylor?" he asked. "Fallon will need help if he hopes to plant anything at all on Tate," he said.

Alex closed her eyes. Michael Taylor was one of her closest friends. In this new life, she was reluctant to involve him, for a host of reasons. While she was certain that Michael Taylor suspected her continued involvement; officially she had left intelligence circles. She was hesitant to give any definitive indication otherwise. "What about Jane?" she suggested. Jane Merrow seemed the safest option. She had the contacts, including her brother General Waters. "Maybe Matt can..."

Krause agreed. "I'll make the call before I leave."

"PANCAKES!" an excited seven-year-old called.

"Alex?" Krause grabbed hold of his partner's hand. Alex turned. "It's someone at that..."

"I know," Alex said. Whoever Brackett had visited, it was someone they knew intimately. Neither Krause nor Alex had ever seen Claire Brackett anywhere near the Baltimore facility. Whoever Brackett's contact was, he or she likely knew the whereabouts of both Agent Toles and Agent Krause. It increased the likelihood that it was someone in their loop. Alex had experienced her father's betrayal; little could surprise her now. "We'll find out," she said. "Let's go. Double agents will be the least of your worries if my mother's pancakes get cold." Krause chuckled. The absurdity in life could be unnerving. It was absurd. One minute his life consisted of issues that could lead to massive loss of life, the beginnings of a war, the oppression or enslavement of thousands of people, and the next he was discussing breakfast food. Alex caught the glint in his eye. "Madness always looks better after pancakes," she winked.

***

Sunday, December 7th

Cassidy sat on the couch sipping her tea, watching as Alex strung lights around the Christmas tree that Dylan had chosen. He was prattling on about Santa Claus visiting in a few weeks, and Cassidy found herself pondering how many more Christmases she would get to enjoy that innocence. She was feeling the most relaxed that she had in weeks, and she was content just to sit back and take in the scene before her. "Penny for your thoughts," Helen whispered, taking a set next to her daughter-in-law.

Cassidy smiled at the older woman. "I was just wondering how many more Christmases we will get to bake cookies for Santa and leave carrots for Rudolph," she answered.

"It does pass quickly," Helen mused. "Alexis was only Dylan's age when she put the pieces together." Helen laughed at the memory. "She was always unbelievably curious. Needed to understand how Santa could fly a sleigh with reindeer." Cassidy chuckled, not surprised that Alex would see even the magical myth of Santa as a puzzle to solve. Helen continued as she watched Alex coach Dylan on the correct way to position lights on the large tree. "But, she never said anything. Nicky, he believed until he was nine. Alexis convinced him Santa was real every year. One year, she was about ten, I think...so Nicky was six....I heard her get out of bed very late. I saw her leaning out her window. I couldn't imagine what she was doing with the window open in December. The next morning she woke Nicky up all excited to show him the glitter the reindeers had left on the awning below her window." Cassidy listened to the sweet story and glanced over to catch her wife whispering in Dylan's ear. "I would imagine Dylan will be the same with whoever might come along," Helen suggested.

"I hope so," Cassidy said quietly.

Helen patted the younger woman's knee. "I would count on it. And, if Alexis has anything to say about it; I'm sure Dylan has a few years left in him," she winked.

The rest of the afternoon was enjoyable. Cassidy had to admit that she was tired of hearing *Grandma Got Run Over By a Reindeer*, but the song seemed to bring endless laughter from both her son and her wife. It was a small price to pay for the sound that she had missed over the last few weeks and months. By eight o'clock, Dylan had become punchy. He was overtired and continued to fight his need for sleep. When she gently suggested it was time for bed, Dylan uncharacteristically began to argue. "Dylan," Cassidy cautioned.

"I'm not tired," he complained.

"Speed," Alex urged. "It's late. We're all tired. Even me." Dylan looked at her skeptically. "Come on, I'll go up with you." Dylan stared at Alex but made no move to accept her hand.

"Dylan," Cassidy's voice became firm.

"I want to stay with you," he said plainly.

Alex looked to Cassidy and immediately understood. The day had been filled with playfulness. It was the first day that Alex had set all work aside in several weeks. The first day that they had simply been together, without any interruptions, in longer than Alex cared to admit. She scratched her head and sat back down next to the boy. She had been looking forward to some alone time with Cassidy, but it seemed to her that something else was more important right now. "How about this?" she began. Dylan looked at her carefully. "Pajama party in our room." Alex looked at Cassidy, who winked her approval. "But, that means no more arguments, Speed. You go brush your teeth and get your pajamas on. Mom and I will be up in a few minutes."

Helen beckoned her grandson to follow. "Come on, Dylan. This old lady needs her rest too. I'll go up with you while your mom and Alexis finish down here."

Dylan began following his YaYa and stopped. "Can you tell me more about the reindeer?" he asked Alex hopefully.

"Sure," she responded. "Go on, we'll be there before you know it." He scampered up the stairs, and Alex pulled Cassidy to her. "I know we were hoping…"

Before Alex could continue her thought, Cassidy silenced her with a kiss. "Are you going to sprinkle glitter on the roof?" she asked.

"She told you that, huh?"

"I love you, Alex."

"I'm sorry, Cass."

"For what?"

"For not being here. For being distracted so much. You don't deserve that. Neither does Dylan."

"Alex, you haven't done anything wrong. We just miss you. Both of us."

"Yeah, well....I didn't intend to tell you this now," Alex sighed.

"Tell me what?" Cassidy asked, feeling a lump of worry form in her throat.

Alex chuckled. "No, it's not what you are thinking."

"I'm not sure what I am thinking," Cassidy's voice broke slightly.

"It was supposed to be a Christmas present."

"What?"

Alex sighed. "I'm moving my office in January. Actually, I am moving the executive offices completely." Cassidy searched Alex for her meaning. "I can't be this far from you anymore, not daily."

"Alex, what about Marta and..."

"We'll keep purchasing and marketing in Natick. The executive offices are moving to New Haven. We already have a small office there..." Before Alex could continue, Cassidy was kissing her passionately. "I guess that means you approve?" Alex asked. Tears had begun to escape Cassidy's eyes. "It's okay, Cass."

"Alex, are you sure? This is your father's...it's..."

"I told you before. You and Dylan are the most important things in my life. I wish I could have done it sooner. It's taken some time to figure out the logistics. I promise; this year will start differently."

"Thank you," Cassidy whispered hoarsely.

"Thank you for putting up with me," Alex said as she rose to her feet. "Do you want to go tell Dylan?"

Cassidy shook her head. "Tomorrow," she suggested. "Tonight reindeer and glitter stories, tomorrow we'll tell him when he gets home from school." Alex nodded her understanding. Dylan needed rest, and the news would no doubt excite him. "You are going back with your mom Tuesday?" Cassidy asked gently as they climbed the stairs.

Alex sighed and stopped their progression. "I think my mother is going to go see Nick for a few days."

"Alex, you left your car at..."

"Well, guess you will be stuck with me a few days longer."

"Are you sure?"

Alex resumed their trek toward the hallway above them. Dylan was running into their bedroom with his stuffed rabbit in hand. She laughed. "Positive."

***

Monday, December 8th

"Mr. President," Congressman Christopher O'Brien greeted the man before him.

"Take a seat, Chris."

"What is it that I can do for you?" O'Brien asked.

"I want you to see your son."

"Excuse me?" O'Brien asked for clarification.

"I thought I stated that clearly," the president responded.

"I haven't seen Dylan in several months, Mr. President."

"Yes, but for now, you still have that right; don't you?" the president asked. He watched O'Brien shift uncomfortably in his chair. "You have a mediation meeting; I understand. One that Dylan is supposed to be at. Stop postponing that."

"All due respect, Mr. President; I'm not sure my family situation has any bearing on..."

"It presents an opportunity, Congressman. Two words. Alex Toles."

O'Brien's disgust was evident. "What does that have to do with me?"

"Your son gives us unique access, Christopher."

"What exactly are you suggesting?" the congressman asked. The president nodded to a tall figure that was standing at the far side of the room. The man slowly approached the seated pair and opened a small box in front of the congressman. "What is it?"

"What does it look like?" President Lawrence Strickland quipped.

"It looks like a toy."

"Yes, it does. A peace offering; shall we say? An apology from a father to his son," the president smiled.

"I don't understand."

Strickland laughed. "An apology with ears."

"He may not even want it," O'Brien said stoically. "Not from me."

"Then I guess you will need to use your powers of persuasion to convince him."

"How do you know she won't suspect…"

"It's benign. She'll no doubt be curious about your motives. I'm sure your ex-wife will share that sentiment, but I doubt she will suspect the actual purpose."

"What do you hope to gain from listening in on their personal…"

The president reclined in his chair. "Alex Toles has one weak spot, O'Brien. That is her family; who just happen to be your former family. I intend to leverage that. She'll be far more open at home than is wise. She's proven that already."

"If she finds out…."

"Then make sure she doesn't," the president responded. "Oh, and Chris? Make certain you have those accounts well in hand. Dimitri will be in touch soon." O'Brien retrieved the box that held the toy car and nodded his understanding. He mumbled under his breath as he paced out of the room. He had successfully avoided Cassidy for months. That game had been brought to a conclusion by an unlikely source. He chuckled at the silent admission that spying on Alex brought him a certain degree of satisfaction. "I wonder if Claire has any clue," he mused, feeling an odd sense of empowerment in his newly assigned task. His lover often mocked his relevance in their initiatives. He had unique access; perhaps he had been hasty in his decision to distance himself from his ex-wife. A more amicable approach might make him a greater asset. He smiled at the thought. "We'll see who is the more relevant, Claire," he smirked.

***

Brian Fallon sat at a corner booth sipping his coffee and turning a napkin endlessly in his hand. He was only moderately surprised when Alex contacted him. The idea had already sprung into his mind that this might be a good time to assess what FBI Assistant Director Joshua Tate's motives truly were. Fallon was walking a tightrope. He was positioned within the FBI under Tate, but he was officially immersed in the NSA under Michael Taylor. Unofficially, Fallon reported all that he was able to uncover to Jonathan Krause and Alex. He was acutely aware that in this game of international economics and politics, there were truly no agencies. Names were merely facades. Individuals had agendas. There were groups within groups, and discerning the true motives of any person meant painstaking research, intrusive observation, and the acceptance of constant risk. Tate had been his mentor early on at the bureau, and Fallon had always respected the man. He hoped that his trust would be proven a wise decision. If it was not; he would not hesitate to use, expose, or even silence Joshua Tate. It was a shift in his life that sometimes sickened him. There were ugly truths he had seen now. He could not close his eyes to them.

"Agent Fallon," a deep voice broke through the agent's musings.

"Assistant Director," he returned his superior's greeting.

The appearance of a familiar waitress momentarily froze any further discussion. "Usual?" she asked.

"Indeed," Tate responded.

She winked. "Coffee, cream, no sugar and a cinnamon bun."

He returned her wink and awaited for her departure to continue. "We both know I love the coffee here, Fallon," he said dryly. "What gives? Taylor is not giving you enough work these days?"

Fallon nodded. "NSA, FBI, all the same thing; isn't it?" he responded.

"Not always," Tate answered. He smiled at the waitress as she placed his order on the table. He sipped his coffee until she was out of sight. "So, then, agent....what is it you need from your former boss?"

"Last I checked you were still my boss," Fallon responded.

"On paper," Tate replied.

"I guess the question is whether or not I can still trust you," Fallon said plainly. Tate silently sipped his coffee. "Claire Brackett," Fallon began. Tate shrugged. "Seems Agent Brackett has some friends that no one was aware of."

"The notion that Claire Brackett has any *friends* at all is a revelation," Tate said.

"She gained entry to a facility in Baltimore," Fallon explained evenly.

Tate's expression remained the same. "How *is* Alex?" he asked, noting the question in Brian Fallon's eyes at his response. "She's wondering where I will fall," Tate laughed. "I don't know why Claire would be at that facility. Why were you?" he asked. "And don't insult me, Fallon. I'm not talking about you trailing Agent Brackett." Fallon nodded but was unsure how to respond. Tate sighed. "You think I know? Who she met? I know who you met. Tell Krause and Toles to be cautious. I will see what I can find out. Brackett's been traveling in the company of NSA for months. Be careful, Fallon. I can't cover all the tracks. There are too many now."

"Assistant Director," Fallon began. "You think her contact is NSA?"

"I think Admiral William Brackett is the CIA, Fallon. If she is not in step with her daddy, then it has to be someone that covets his authority. Believe me, there are many; CIA, NSA, DOD, FBI, and it does not end there. President Merrow had grown cautious of everyone. He involved only a handful of people that I am aware of. That included myself, your new friend Agent Krause, an ally in Russia, an old family friend, and Agent Toles; which involved you by extension. Other than that, I don't know of anyone that he entrusted with anything of importance. It's a small circle. A miniscule circle in a massive organization. I'll play some poker, Fallon, but I can't make you any promises. Tell Alex and Krause; they are wise to test me," he smiled. "Watch the admiral. Closely." Tate rose to his feet and stopped to whisper into Brian Fallon's ear. "They are the pair he fears, Fallon. Agent Toles and Agent Krause. They were never supposed to find one another. It's changed everything. Be careful," he cautioned.

Brian Fallon stared at the table for a long moment. Nothing Joshua Tate had said surprised him up until his parting words. "What the hell does he mean by that?" Fallon muttered. He picked up his phone and dialed a familiar number.

"Fallon?" Alex answered.

"How is my former partner?" he asked lightly.

"Relaxing at home for a change," Alex answered.

"I'm jealous," he admitted.

"And you?" she asked.

"You know, coffee with the boss," he replied.

Alex understood. Tate was in play. "And how is my former boss?" Alex asked.

"The same. Wanted me to tell you he misses you," Fallon laughed.

"I'm sure."

"I was thinking about a visit," he replied. "Before the holiday craziness."

Alex took a deep breath. If Fallon felt the need to see her in person, something was troubling him. "Dylan and Cass would love to see you," she said. "I suppose I could manage." Fallon couldn't help but chuckle. "When were you thinking? I'll be back in Massachusetts Thursday and Friday."

"I don't want to impose on your family time," he said.

"No, no. Cassidy has a meeting with O'Brien, their lawyers, and a family counselor tomorrow afternoon. O'Brien hasn't cancelled....yet. I want to be there. How about Wednesday for dinner? You sure you want to fly up for just a day?"

"Yeah, in fact maybe I can get my flight back out of Logan Thursday," he offered.

"That way your old partner can take you to the airport, huh? I suppose I could manage that. I'll tell Cass. See you Wednesday."

"Great. See you soon, Alex."

Alex disconnected the call and put her face in her hands. "What is it?" Cassidy asked with a soft grip on the agent's shoulders.

"Fallon's coming for a visit Wednesday."

"Is that a bad thing?" Cassidy asked curiously.

"No. I just worry about him." Cassidy nodded and kissed Alex's head. "Cass?"

"Hmm?"

"Do you think he'll cancel?" Alex asked.

"Brian?" Cassidy asked. "Didn't you just..." Cassidy saw Alex's expression darken. "Oh....Chris." Cassidy let out a heavy sigh. "I don't know. Doesn't look like it. He can't put it off forever."

"Why does Dylan have to be there?" Alex asked.

"Like it or not, Alex, until the paternity is settled, Chris is Dylan's father; at least on paper. They want to see the interaction."

"He hasn't even called Dylan."

"I know," Cassidy responded. "But, Alex...he has to submit willingly to the paternity..."

Alex sighed. "I hate this. I swear to God. I thought my father was...Jesus. I hope to God I am never that kind of..."

"Alex, you are a terrific parent," Cassidy looked at Alex intently.

"What is it?" Alex asked.

Cassidy bit her lip and held up her finger. "Hold on." She left the room for a moment and returned to place an envelope in front of Alex.

"What is this?" Alex looked up to her wife, and Cassidy shrugged. "This is addressed to you, not me." Cassidy nodded. "Cass? Is this my…is this from my…."

"Your mother gave it to me the other day. I guess it was in something you found that was addressed to her." Alex looked at Cassidy with a fear in her eyes that broke Cassidy's heart. "I didn't want to open it without you."

Alex swallowed hard. "It's not for me," she said.

"Do you want me to open it?" Cassidy asked. She could see the answer plainly as she accepted the letter back into her hands. "Alex, no matter what this says…"

Alex just nodded. Cassidy broke open the seal and retrieved the handwritten note from inside. She opened her mouth to begin reading when Alex stopped her. "You read it first…to yourself, Cass."

"Alex…"

"Please," Alex closed her eyes. "Read it first and then read it to me."

"All right."

***

Chapter Four

Cassidy watched as Alex scanned the paper in her hand continuously. She patiently and silently observed the myriad of expressions that washed across her wife's face. Something in her told her to give Alex as long as she needed. When Alex was ready, she would break the silence. Her deductions proved right. "I don't understand," Alex said softly. "How could he have....why would he say those things? Meet O'Brien and then..."

"I don't know, Alex."

"He knew. All along, he knew."

Cassidy licked her lips. Nicolaus Toles' words were not what she had expected. "Obviously, John trusted your father, Alex."

"Why? What would make him think he could trust my father with that information? Cassidy...My father, my father's efforts paved the way for some of the most heinous things I have ever encountered. He funded warlords, wars...even genocide."

Cassidy took a deep breath. "But, you were his daughter, Alex. No matter what, you were his daughter."

"I don't understand, Cassidy. He made every effort to pull me away from you; pull you away from me. Why the hell would he want to ensure that O'Brien was removed from our lives? On John's say so? This is crazier than..."

Cassidy moved from her seat and knelt in front of Alex. "Maybe he finally realized that nothing he did was going to pull us apart."

"How could John know? Cassidy? How could John have known that Krause would…"

"John knew that Pip and I were old friends, Alex. Beyond that, I…"

Alex looked at the letter again as Cassidy watched her carefully. She began to read it aloud.

My Dear Cassidy,

You must have so many questions. I'm certain that you will be surprised by this turn of events. I imagine that I am the last person you expect a letter from, or would want a letter from. There are many things I wish that I could explain to Alexis. She has always followed her own path, never the one I sought to guide her down. I've no doubt that many discoveries await her, about me, about herself.

She has made many choices that I did not agree with and would have paid with my life to prevent. Despite what you might think; you are not one of those. Not long ago, a good friend came to me. He was confident that Alexis would raise the son he never knew; your son. There are realities, Cassidy, to your son's identity, and to whom you choose to love that put you all at risk, Alexis included.

Fate seems to play a role in our lives at times. Christopher O'Brien is a pathetic excuse for a human being, much less a parent. Nonetheless, his presence creates an even greater threat to you all. I suspect you already know that as well. I promised Dylan's father I would ensure his safety. I promised myself I would keep my children protected. The proof you need of Krause's parentage is in a Carecom facility in Stockholm. It will readily provide DNA coding for Dylan that proves Krause is his father. This was the last wish passed to me by a man we both regard as a friend. It is your choice whether or not to honor that. Should you decide to follow this course, you will find directives in Stockholm. A good friend of mine at Technologie Applique in France will assist you.

Cassidy, there is much that Alexis will discover in this life she has chosen. She has an insatiable curiosity and a need to pursue the truth. Much of it will be painful. My time is limited. That is a foregone conclusion. I will not attempt to explain nor excuse my actions. I have followed the path that I believed best for us all; most of all for my children.

My children are exceptional human beings. They are intelligent, discerning, and they possess a sense of loyalty that I cannot claim comes from me. When they fall in love, there is no deterring them. You seem to have a unique capacity in that department. You have Alexis's heart and her devotion. That is clear to me. She stood before me confidently protecting her family, and I have never been more proud of the woman that she has become. In her presence, I am humbled. I am thankful that she has you now.

I hope you will consider the course that has been prescribed. It will, I believe, shelter you all in some way.

Take care of my family. They are yours now in more ways than you might imagine.

With gratitude,

Nicolaus

"Alex?" Cassidy called gently.

"What do you think about this?" Alex asked.

"About what your father said or about pretending Pip is Dylan's father?"

"Both," Alex answered.

"Honestly? I don't know. We agreed. No secrets. I don't know. Your father kept so much from you; even if he thought he was protecting you; look what that has done. I don't know, Alex. Maybe it would be easier right now, but it doesn't feel right," Cassidy said truthfully. Alex closed her eyes with a defeated nod. "Is that what you think we should do?" Cassidy asked carefully.

Alex was slow to respond. She weighed her words and exhaled sadly. "No. It's not," she said. Cassidy watched as tears pooled in Alex's eyes. "But," Alex continued, "part of me is tempted, Cass. I won't lie to you."

"You honestly think it would be safer for Dylan? Long-term?" Cassidy asked. She suspected there was something else behind Alex's statement.

"Maybe. Maybe not."

"Then why?" Cassidy pressed gently.

Alex let a nervous chuckle escape. "It'd be easier. It would clear the way..."

Cassidy smiled. "For you to adopt Dylan." Alex nodded. "Oh, Alex."

"Selfish. I know. Guess I have some of my father in me after all."

"I am certain that you have a great deal of your father in you," Cassidy began as Alex looked at her regretfully. "But, you are not selfish to want that, Alex. I want that too. And, if I hear you correctly, as much as you want it; you have no intention of following this idea."

"No. I don't want to do that to Dylan. I would never ask that of....I couldn't ask that of Pip. I've asked enough of him already," Alex said quietly. "But..."

"But what?" Cassidy asked.

"I think maybe we should see what exactly is in Stockholm and how Edmond Callier figures into this."

"Edmond?" Cassidy questioned.

"Yes, he's the head of Technologie Applique."

"I know," Cassidy said. "I've met him."

Alex snickered. "When you were in France?" Alex wondered. Cassidy nodded. "That's where Pip is headed now."

"Alex, what about the other things he said?"

Alex pulled Cassidy onto her lap. "It's hard for me to accept anything he said as the truth."

"I know," Cassidy said as she laid her head on Alex's shoulder. "He thought enough to write it, Alex."

"Maybe."

"You don't honestly think he had some ulterior motive?"

"I don't know," Alex replied. "It's just another piece in this puzzle that he seems determined to keep me from solving. What is he hiding, Cass? All these veiled innuendos. Protecting me from what? I just...maybe it isn't me that he wanted to protect."

Cassidy had to agree. She suspected that there was a great deal of truth and emotion in Nicolaus Toles's letter. Even she could see that it appeared what Alex's father feared most was what Alex might uncover; not her physical safety. "I'm sorry, Alex."

"Don't be."

"Are you all right?" Cassidy asked with concern.

"Where my father is concerned, I'm not certain I will ever be able to forgive him. But yes, I am all right." Alex chuckled softly.

"What's funny?" Cassidy asked.

"Well, we do agree on a couple of things," Alex said. Cassidy opened her eyes wider in encouragement. "Christopher O'Brien is a pathetic excuse for a human being..."

"And?"

"And you most definitely have my heart," Alex smiled.

"Good to know," Cassidy winked and gave Alex a tender kiss. "Are you going to show it to Pip?"

"It's your letter, Cassidy."

Cassidy shook her head. "No, I think we both know your father wanted you to see it."

Alex sighed. "I think it's wise," Alex answered. Cassidy agreed. "No matter what, Cass. I promise Dylan will stay safe. We all will."

Cassidy shuddered slightly and allowed Alex to pull her closer. "I know," she answered.

***

Tuesday, December 9th

"Jonathan, how are you?" Edmond Callier greeted the younger man on the phone.

"Tired, Edmond; if I am to be truthful."

"Long flight?"

"Long life," Krause chided.

"How about dinner at my residence tomorrow then?"

Krause was surprised by the invitation. The Callier residence was rarely a place utilized for business. He had only visited a handful of times over the years. "I would be delighted," he answered.

"Good. What do you say seven o'clock? I have been meaning to show you my wine cellar for some time. Perfect excuse," Callier offered. "You know how to find your way?"

"I believe so," Krause replied.

"I look forward to our meeting."

Krause pondered the short conversation. He wondered what Edmond Callier might deem important enough to invite him to such a private affair. The ringing of the hotel phone snapped him from his thoughts. "Yes?" he answered.

"Sir, there is a message for you at the desk. Would you like it delivered or…"

"No, I will be down shortly. I'll retrieve it there. Thank you," Krause answered.

***

Cassidy watched as Alex fidgeted with the glass in front of her. "Alex," Cassidy whispered. "Relax, honey." Alex gave her wife an uncomfortable smile and Cassidy sighed quietly. She was not looking forward to seeing her ex-husband either, but she hoped this meeting would bring them a step closer to moving forward with their lives. Still, nothing that Christopher O'Brien might say or do would surprise her, and she shared Alex's apprehension. The door opened slowly, and Cassidy lifted her gaze to see her ex-husband making his way into the room. She sensed the tension rise in Alex and gently rubbed her wife's back to calm her.

"Cassidy," Christopher O'Brien greeted his ex-wife cordially.

"Chris," she responded evenly.

"Hey there, buddy," he called as he made his way to Dylan. Dylan had been sitting quietly next to Alex drawing a picture. At the sound of his father's voice, he positioned himself closer to Alex and placed his head against her shoulder.

Alex could feel the anxiety pouring off Dylan. She carefully, but deliberately put an arm around his shoulder and kissed the top of his head, taking the opportunity to whisper assurances to him. "It's okay, Speed. Mom and I are right here."

"Well," a woman's voice broke through the evident tension. "Now that everyone is here, I'd like to get started."

Cassidy kept a close watch on Alex and Dylan. It was strange; she thought. Alex typically took on the role of protector, but she could see a vulnerability in Alex's eyes that both moved her and incited a fierce need to protect her family. Cassidy listened as the counselor and lawyers spoke calmly, answering unemotionally to the questions they posed to her. When she heard her ex-husband finally speak, she instantly felt a red-hot anger well up within her.

"Of course, I want to see my son. I simply don't want to cause more friction for him," O'Brien said. "This situation," he paused and Cassidy could see the smug expression in his eyes. "This situation is less than ideal. I may not have been a perfect husband or father, but Dylan's best interest has always been my primary concern. I love my son."

It took every ounce of self-control that Cassidy could muster not to respond violently to her ex-husband's words. He was a master. While she could taste the insincerity dripping from him; she was not convinced the counselor would be as perceptive. Alex felt Cassidy's grip on her hand tighten and instinctively squeezed Cassidy's hand gently in reassurance. As always, their relationship was a dance. They moved in time with the needs of the other. Cassidy bit the inside of her cheek to restrain the words that clamored for escape.

"Dylan," the counselor's voice softly called. "How do you feel? Do you want to see your father?"

All eyes turned to Dylan except Cassidy's. Her steely gaze remained fixed on the man who once shared their lives. Dylan looked at the table and toyed with the picture he had been drawing. "It's okay, Speed," Alex said gently. "You just be honest. No matter what," she told him. Dylan pressed harder into his hero and shook his head 'no' softly.

"Is that how you really feel, Dylan?" the counselor gently asked. He nodded.

"You've done a marvelous job of turning my son against me," O'Brien shot. Neither Alex nor Cassidy responded. "Dylan," he called with as much concern as his voice could portray, making his way toward the boy. "I am sorry." Dylan looked up at the man who was now squarely in front of him. His small eyes held the hint of a tear, but his face gave away his anger as the congressman continued. "I am still your father."

Dylan considered him for a moment. He felt Alex's lips brush against the top of his head, and he looked up to her. Alex flashed him a reassuring smile. He looked back at his father and shook his head. "You hate Alex."

"Dylan," the congressman began to reprimand his son.

"Mom and I love Alex."

"Dylan," he repeated.

Again the counselor interrupted. "Dylan, you don't have to choose between Alex and your father," she said. Dylan felt his father reach for him and took the opportunity to climb into Alex's lap. "Is there anything you want to say to your parents?" the counselor asked him. He looked at Alex and Cassidy and then at the gentle woman who was asking him the question and nodded. "Go ahead. You can say anything you need to," she encouraged.

Cassidy held her breath. Alex tightened her grip on the boy in her lap slightly. Dylan looked back at Alex and then to his mother. He stopped and touched the necklace that hung around Alex's neck and turned to the man he knew as his father. "You said Alex is not my mom. She calls me every day when she has to be away. She takes care of me and Mom and Grandma and YaYa."

"Dylan," he said firmly.

"Go on, Dylan," the counselor encouraged as she shoot a stern look of warning to the congressman. "It's your turn to talk."

"You never call me. You didn't come to my party."

"Dylan, I had to work...."

"Mr. O'Brien," the counselor warned again.

Dylan snuggled into Alex and felt his mother's hand tenderly rub his back in encouragement. Cassidy's heart was breaking. She was acutely aware of the pain and disappointment her ex-husband had caused in Dylan, but he had never articulated that to her fully. The anger, disappointment and frustration radiating from her son was palpable. Alex pulled him to her protectively. Dylan was unsure of what to say. "It's all right, sweetie," Cassidy's voice cracked slightly.

"Dylan?" the counselor called to him. "Do you want to spend time with your father?"

"No," his hushed reply came.

O'Brien seethed. He swallowed his anger and painted on the winning smile of a polished politician. He gestured to his lawyer, who handed him a small box, wrapped with a bow. "Well," he said. "I am sorry that you feel that way, Dylan." He gave his son the box under the scrutinizing gaze of one extremely protective agent. "I know this doesn't make up for me being away, but I hope you will accept it," he said. O'Brien reached out to ruffle his son's hair, and Dylan jerked back. "I see," O'Brien said as he rose back to his feet. "You certainly are persuasive," he shot at his ex-wife. Cassidy shook her head in disgust and reached for Dylan, who gratefully climbed into his mother's lap. "It's not over," O'Brien bent over and spoke into Alex's ear.

Alex fought her desire to lay him out flat with one punch. She took a deep breath and smiled at him. Silence had suddenly enveloped the room as Dylan's frustrated tears fell on his mother's shoulder. "It's all right, Dylan," Cassidy comforted him.

"I don't want to go with him," Dylan cried louder than anyone would have expected.

Cassidy felt her body begin to tremble. She could feel Dylan's fear and the contempt it bred in her for the man a few feet away made her sick inside. "Shh," she whispered, kissing his head and whispering comforting assurances to him.

O'Brien headed for the door and looked at the counselor. "You see how they have corrupted him?" he asked harshly. "She's not his mother," he said.

"Yes she is!" Dylan exploded.

"Dylan, honey," Cassidy pulled him closer. His body was shaking violently, and Cassidy suddenly felt helpless. It was extremely uncharacteristic of Dylan to have an outburst.

"You can't take her away!" he yelled again.

"No one's taking anyone away," the counselor promised.

"He said so. He said so," Dylan cried.

Alex looked across to the congressman. She was tempted to address him directly. It was clear to her that at some point, Dylan had come to believe his father would take Alex away from him. She closed her eyes to calm her temper and leaned into Dylan and kissed him. "It's okay, Speed." Alex found her feet and calmly walked across the room. She looked at the counselor and stepped directly in front of the congressman. "No one will ever take me away from my family," she said calmly. "No one. Now, you have upset my son enough for a lifetime."

"Your son?" O'Brien began.

Alex made no reaction and placed her hand on the door to the small conference room. She opened it slowly and gestured to him. "Yes, Congressman."

He stared at her coldly and then looked back at Cassidy. "Cassie…Dylan and…"

"Just go," Cassidy implored, continually rubbing her son's back in small circles.

O'Brien began to walk through the door and leaned into Alex. "You're not as smart as you think," he chuckled.

Alex shook her head and shut the door behind him. She looked at the counselor, immediately seeing the sincerity in the woman's apologetic eyes. Alex smiled sadly and headed for her family. She bent over and looked at the box on the floor. She wanted to kick it, but she thought that a more mature approach was called for and picked it up, handing it to Cassidy as she gently extracted Dylan from his mother's protective hold. Dylan clasped onto Alex. "If you don't mind; I'd like to take my family home now," Alex said pointedly.

"Of course," the counselor said, opening the door for the agent. She placed her hand on Cassidy's shoulder and stopped her momentarily. "We'll figure it out. I promise," she said. Cassidy nodded and accepted Alex's hand. Dylan had barely spoken of his father in months. Now, she understood that he had overheard many things; things he had not shared with her or Alex. She grasped Alex's hand tighter as her tears threatened to escape.

Dylan laid his head on Alex's shoulder, and Alex could feel him beginning to succumb to sleep. "I love you, Speed," she said. He mumbled something and tightened his hold on her neck. "I promise, no one will ever take me away." Cassidy heard the declaration and sighed. Her thoughts were suddenly traveling to the letter Alex's father had written, and for the first time her heart was genuinely torn.

***

Wednesday, December 10th

Jonathan Krause sat quietly sipping the scotch Edmond Callier had poured him. They had spent the last hour in casual conversation, discussing business deals and associates in a benign and amicable manner. Krause studied his mentor carefully. There was a sense of tension emanating from the older man that was not customary. It was Krause's intention to leave this visit with a clearer picture of who Nicolaus Toles was, and who exactly was pulling the strings in what was left of The Collaborative. "So, Jonathan. A nice dinner calls for a pleasant wine; don't you think?" Krause nodded his agreement. "I've never shown you my wine cellar; have I?"

"I don't believe so, no."

"Excellent. Why don't we take a walk? I promise you, if you cannot find an appropriate wine there; one does not exist," Callier bragged with enthusiasm. Krause tipped his head in acknowledgement and followed his host dutifully through the expansive mansion until they reached a door. A narrow stairway led them to a cool, dry basement. The historic stone walls and the soft lighting made Krause grin instinctively. Callier continued making casual remarks about the home, its history, and of course, wine. The Frenchman had always impressed Jonathan Krause. It was clear that he was being led to a safe haven of sorts; a place without ears or eyes. Callier smiled and pressed a button on the wall. A door slid gently open and, Krause could not hide the bemused gleam in his eye when he heard a recording begin to play behind them. He shook his head. Most people thought these types of things the imagination of novelists and filmmakers. They were, in fact, Jonathan Krause's reality. It was a reality he could not deny he found exhilarating. "So Jonathan; I'm certain you did not follow me here to discuss my expertise in fine wine."

"No."

Callier sighed and sat on a short wooden table. "First, tell me what has you so concerned for your family." Krause's hand reached the back of his neck, displaying his discomfort with the question. "Oh, come now, Jonathan. Your curiosity about Nicolaus Toles is not simply about financial transactions," the older man keenly observed.

"No, it isn't."

"Mm. Your concern is for your family. I've known you a long time, Jonathan."

"They are not my family, Edmond," Krause said. Edmond Callier stroked his chin in thought. He nodded and slowly made his way to a cabinet on the far wall. He pulled it open and retrieved a small photo, placing it in Krause's hands. "What is this?"

Callier smiled and resumed his seated position. He pointed to the picture. "Look at it." Krause studied it closely. "Your father never wanted his children in this business, Jonathan." Krause lifted his gaze from the photo in confusion. "That surprises you?" Callier asked.

"My father groomed me for this my entire life. I still remember the disappointment in his eyes when West Point rejected me."

Callier smiled. "You haven't really looked at that picture."

Krause returned his gaze to the small black and white photo in his hand. "It's my mother. I don't recognize..."

"Look closely," Callier instructed. The older man took a deep breath. "Jonathan...In my life, I have had two best friends. One, I lost long ago. The other," his thoughts trailed. "We did not all share the same vision for our children." He laughed and shook his head. "And, our children often did not share the vision we had." Krause felt his mouth suddenly go dry and looked at the man before him, a sense of foreboding of what was to come. "Your father engineered your rejection to West Point. He paved the way for your education at Stanford. He devised the organization that would ensure you were put in a suit quickly rather than left in the field. All of it to keep you removed. To keep you somehow, safe."

"From what? My brothers...My father..."

"Benjamin Krause?" Callier grinned. "He raised you."

"What are you saying?" Krause asked.

Callier took the picture from the younger man's hands. "He never wanted your sister or brother in this game either. He put more roadblocks in her way..."

"I don't have a sister," Krause interjected.

Callier's eyebrow raised with a smile. "I think you already know that is not true."

Krause uncharacteristically put his face in his hands. "Alex," he whispered.

"Mm. Not that surprised; are you?" Krause could not answer his mentor's question. "You are very much alike. Down to whom you fall in love with," Callier chuckled.

"Why would my mother…"

"There is so much you don't know, Jonathan. Nicolaus, Anthony, and I; we agreed. Many years ago, we agreed. Anthony was adamant that John would serve. No matter how hard John fought that," Callier paused and closed his eyes. "And, Elliot? Well, there was no stopping him. God knows I tried. I am only grateful his sister allowed me to guide her down a different road. Nicolaus and I…This is not an easy life. Not one made for attachments. Not one that can ever guarantee any happiness."

"No one has that guarantee," Krause observed harshly. "You had no right…"

"Oh? You don't think so? And, what of Dylan? What would you do to protect the boy?" Callier asked pointedly.

"You still haven't answered my question," Krause replied.

"Did you ask one?" Callier nodded again. "Haven't I? You wanted to know who Nicolaus Toles was. I told you. I told you before that I may not have the answers you seek and that the answers I had may not be what you expected."

"You know what I was asking," Krause answered.

"If you want to know who Nicolaus was, in any capacity, I have given you the key to it all."

"A father who; what? Abandoned me?" Krause snapped.

"Hardly," Callier replied. "Hardly. You think that your father; the father you knew was your link to this life." Callier let out a heavy sigh. "He was not. Though he would love to make that claim. Nicolaus was not always simply a money broker. For many years, many….he worked in the field when his father was still alive. He had a partner; just like you."

Krause shook his head in disbelief. "My mother," Krause guessed. Callier nodded. "What about Alex's…"

Callier smiled. "Helen is an amazing woman."

"You know…"

"I was at their wedding."

"Alex doesn't know…"

"No. I've not seen Helen in many years. We were young, Jonathan. Hard to believe; I am sure," he chuckled. "But, once upon a time, we were young. Nicolaus and I attended Harvard together. He studied law. I studied economics. Our paths were carved for us," he paused and considered his next words. "Your father, Alex's father, he loved Helen. He always loved Helen. The field is a strange place. You know that. Your mother was his confidante. In many ways his true best friend. Life….and death move us sometimes. There was never any regret on either of their parts. Your mother left her position. Married the father who raised you. And, there were no regrets for that either; not that I am aware of."

"Does she know?"

"Who?" Callier asked.

"Helen? Does she know?" Krause asked softly. He could not understand the emotions coursing through him. He'd grown fond of Alex's family. A sense of guilt seemed to creep over him.

Callier sensed his young friend's distress. "You are not as cold as you would like to believe," he said. "You want to know…Does she know who you are?" Callier asked. Krause nodded. "I don't know that answer. I don't believe Nicolaus ever told her that." Krause hung his head slightly and sighed. "But, she knows he had a son, yes." Krause looked up in shock. "Jonathan, I told you once before that you are like my son; as was John. As Alexis is much like a daughter to me, more than you realize. She is my goddaughter. My oath was given long ago to protect her."

Krause bristled. "You made the call to have John…"

Callier sighed. "No. Things are not what they seem. The walls hear everything; all the walls that surround us, every minute. This room is my only sanctuary. It took years for us to devise a safe method of communication. There is one in this home. There is one at Carecom and one...one that resides off the basement of a townhouse in Arlington."

For months, Krause had blamed himself. He had tried to warn John Merrow about the impending assassination attempt. He had planted deliberate chatter for the NSA and Secret Service. He had hired a sharp shooter to make it look good in case anything went awry; a shooter that never showed. Now, Callier was telling him that there was nothing he could have done to save his best friend. "He knew it was coming. Before I told him...before..."

"Yes," Callier answered.

Krause attempted to absorb all of the information he had been given. He was surprised to find tears had begun to sting the back of his eyes. He had felt it; a connection to Alex. A soft buzz in his pocket startled him. He shook off his thoughts with an audible exhale and looked at his phone. "Shit," he mumbled. He looked to his mentor. "I assume there is a safe line in here?" Callier nodded. "I need it," he said, barely masking the urgency in his voice.

"Alex?" Callier asked. Krause nodded. "This way."

***

Chapter Five

Alex kept a close eye on Cassidy as Cassidy puttered about the kitchen. It had been a long night. Dylan slept for hours after their afternoon visit with his father. When he did awake, the scene had turned emotional. It took Alex and Cassidy more than an hour to calm him down. For Alex's part, she felt utterly helpless and unbelievably guilty. Dylan would not share what he had overheard his father say. Cassidy was not certain if his father had directly made accusations or threats regarding Alex. He just kept begging not to have to leave his parents, and for Dylan, that meant Alex and Cassidy. Alex could tell by her wife's demeanor that Cassidy had been pushed beyond her limits. It was rare for Cassidy to shut down. When Alex attempted to approach the subject gently late in the evening, Cassidy had simply said she was tired. Now, they were awaiting the arrival of Brian Fallon. Alex was fairly sure that a visit from Uncle Brian would cheer up Dylan, but where Cassidy was concerned, she remained at a loss.

"Cass?"

Cassidy continued her work at the kitchen counter, putting together a lasagna for their dinner. "Yeah?"

"Are you all right?

"I'm fine."

Alex pinched the bridge of her nose and made her way behind Cassidy. She leaned over and placed her arms around Cassidy's waist, gently turning her wife so that she could look at her. "Please tell me what you are thinking."

Cassidy closed her eyes and pressed her lips together tightly. "Honestly, Alex...I'm not sure what I am thinking. I need some time to just..."

"I know," Alex said. She kissed Cassidy's forehead and breathed a small sigh of relief when Cassidy welcomed the embrace fully. "I promise that we will figure it out," Alex said as she continued to hold Cassidy close.

Cassidy leaned fully into Alex, feeling her emotions begin to surface. Being with Alex was the safest place Cassidy had ever known. It was also the place where her heart controlled all reason and action. She sniffled slightly and pulled back. "Let me get this finished," she said, avoiding Alex's eyes. She was relieved when the sound of the doorbell pierced through the silence that hovered between them. "Go get that," Cassidy said, placing a kiss on Alex's cheek.

"Cass?" Alex turned back.

"Go on," Cassidy said, offering Alex the faintest hint of a genuine smile. Alex nodded.

"Uncle Brian's here!" Dylan called excitedly.

"Guess someone beat me to it," Alex chuckled and moved toward the hallway.

"Hey, Speed, why don't you go see if you can help Mom for a few minutes?" Alex suggested.

"Okay, but we are going to play pool later, right?" Dylan asked.

"Promise," Fallon answered. "It's time Alex was reminded who the dynamic duo is," he winked.

Dylan scampered off toward the kitchen, and Alex shook her head. "So, is this a conversation for the living room or do I need a jacket too?" she asked. Fallon just raised his eyebrow. "That's what I thought. Good thing there's no snow on the ground," she chuckled. "Help me go get some of the firewood out back?" Fallon nodded and followed Alex into the kitchen.

"Hey, Cassidy," Fallon greeted.

"Hi, Brian." Cassidy wiped her hands on a towel and moved around the counter to take her friend into a hug. "I'm glad you are here," she said genuinely. "Aren't you staying?" she giggled, gesturing to his coat.

"Thought I would put him to use," Alex chimed. "Take a walk down back and bring up some more wood for the fireplace. Seems like a perfect night for it."

Cassidy smiled and turned to see Dylan liberating himself a cookie from the counter. "Sneaky," she squinted at him. "Can't imagine where you get that from," she looked to Alex.

Alex shrugged innocently. "Only one, Speed," Alex directed. Dylan smiled and headed off into the living room. "We'll be back in a few," Alex said as she led her friend out the back door.

Cassidy shook her head in amusement. She was tired, and she was frustrated, but the arrival of Alex's former partner lifted her spirits. Brian Fallon had been a good friend to them both and Dylan adored the man. If nothing else, the visit provided a momentary diversion for Cassidy. It was a diversion she desperately needed.

***

"So, believe me," Alex began, "I am very glad you are here. Yesterday was unbelievable."

"I'm sorry that O'Brien is such a..."

Alex laughed. "There are lots of words I could use for him. But...what's going on? You said on the phone last night you thought Brackett was heading to London."

"She is. No maybes," he answered.

"Hmm. I called my good friend Ambassador Daniels this morning. Told him we needed to discuss some of the orders coming in from our clients in London. He seemed as if he was almost expecting my call."

Fallon was puzzled. "You called him because of Brackett?"

"No, that was incidental. My father cut off most of the usual payment transfers to ASA about a week before his death. No reroute. Just stopped them cold. The accounts at ASA are closely associated with two of Carecom's major accounts in Britain. There doesn't seem to be any delay in the transfer of goods to those entities. It doesn't make sense. If he wanted ASA shut out, he should have tamped down on the orders from these two British subsidiaries."

"I don't get what that has to do with Brackett," Fallon answered.

Alex shrugged. "Could be a coincidence; her heading to London. I doubt it. The orders that Carecom filled were just fronts, Fallon. The supplies we were sending did not equal the cash that was deposited into Carecom, then routed to ASA. It's just a mechanism to move money."

"Okay? I still don't..."

Alex sighed. "The real items that were being traded were biological technology and nuclear components. The money; that part... Look...Stillman and BGA are two of the largest distributors in Europe for military medical supplies. Both are headquartered in London. They ordered; we shipped the dummy goods; the funds came to Carecom's account and then it was carefully funneled through diversified funds to reach its final destination at ASA. It had been that way for more than fifteen years. It took me two months to discern all the accounts, and Krause nearly an equal amount of time to backtrace through European banks. Once we had it nailed it was clear. Then it stops. The trail goes stone cold right before my father's death. Why? I don't know. I'm not sure on whose direction he stopped it, or if it was by his own accord. It happened just about the time I," Alex stopped and took a seat on the woodpile. "Right about the time I broke into Carecom. Coincidence?" she paused. "I don't think so. Just like I don't think Brackett in London is by chance. Too convenient. Particularly given the fact that Krause got a lead on the Cesium Brackett liberated in the spring."

"Where?"

"Near the Russia-Ukraine border. Doesn't know whose play or the final destination," Alex huffed. "We should have thought that through more clearly and at least tagged it."

"Well, you can't go back now," Fallon offered. "So, if it's in..."

"Whoever she went to in Baltimore; well, I suspect they *want* us to follow her to London," Alex surmised. "What about Tate?"

"I don't know, Alex. More of the same. Cryptic."

"What's your gut tell you?" she asked.

Fallon shook his head. "I don't know. Something tells me he's on your side. Something he said just keeps rolling in my..."

"What did he say?"

"Something about you and Krause...You're their fear; that you were not supposed to find each other."

"That is interesting; not that surprising though. Could just be a smoke screen," she said.

"What about Brackett?" Fallon asked.

"We'll tail her. I'll talk to Krause. I imagine Mitchell will be more than happy to assume that task. I am curious about Daniels' role in all of this. London is not just a diversion or coincidence; not with what these accounts seem to be indicating. They may want our focus there as a distraction, but there is more to it than that."

"You think the Cesium is in London?" Fallon asked.

"No, but I suspect the money is, meaning whoever paid for the package. The question is where it is being moved to," she said as she bent over to start picking up some wood. "Let's let this play a bit. Stick with Tate, see if he comes up with anything on Brackett's mysterious contact."

"What about our contact protocol? I assume the warehouse is off..."

"Everything stays as it is for now," she interrupted him.

"Alex, if Brackett met someone there, chances are they know about my involvement."

"Exactly, and until we know who that someone is that she met; you are safer if we pretend we don't know she met with anyone at all. Nothing changes," Alex said. "If need be I will visit our accounts in London, and pay a friendly visit to the good ambassador while I am there."

"Alex, Tate was worried. I could see it…about you and Krause."

Alex laughed. "Pip and I can take care of ourselves. I'm curious what he meant, but I don't really see that it is a relevant issue. We both know people. We both possess certain…. well; I could understand why people might prefer we did not speak, much less work together," she chuckled again. "I'll keep my eyes open; I promise. Now help me get some of this wood."

***

Cassidy took a deep breath and stretched her neck. She listened to Dylan as he engaged in some pretend battle in the living room and shook her head softly. She and Alex had opted to let Dylan take the day off from school. It hadn't required much discussion. He needed to feel secure and for Cassidy that trumped every other consideration. Hearing him now, she felt assured that they had made the right decision. She closed her eyes and let her head fall forward, relaxing for the first moment in twenty-four hours. "Why am I not surprised?" she rolled her eyes at the sound of her cell phone. "Just one minute's peace?" she directed her question toward her phone. She laughed and lifted it, not immediately recognizing the number displayed. "Hello?"

"Cassie," the voice responded.

"What do you want?" she answered coldly.

"I think we need to talk about things; don't you?" her ex-husband answered.

"No. I don't."

"Well, I suppose that is your choice, Cassie. Like it or not as far as any court will be concerned, Dylan is my son. I am not satisfied with this arrangement."

Cassidy toyed with her lower lip between her teeth and attempted to keep her voice even. "You've done enough to upset Dylan. What is it that you hope to gain?"

The congressman sat in his home office, reclining casually in his large leather chair. Dylan gave him access to Alex, access he knew was prized. It made him more valuable than a simple pawn. It gave him leverage. "Oh. Well...I don't think the environment you are providing is healthy. I've spoken to my people. Either you can meet me half way or I will make the arrangement permanent."

"What the hell are you talking about?" Cassidy seethed.

"Dylan living with me, of course," O'Brien replied.

That was it. There was no turning back. "Christopher," she began. "You are the most selfish, despicable human being I think I have ever met." Cassidy's voice began to rise louder and louder with each syllable. "There is no way in hell that Dylan is ever living with you. Don't call here. Don't come near *my* son. Do you understand me?"

"I understand you. You are the one who is not understanding," he returned her sentiment. "As I recall he has been my son for seven years. That bitch is not Dylan's mother. I don't know what has happened to you. It's sick. He needs to be protected, and I am not..."

Hearing his mother's voice as it rose steadily, Dylan cowered slightly in the doorway to listen. "That's it, Chris. I am through with you. Stay the hell away from my family. Alex is my wife. She is Dylan's parent, not you. What part of that are you not understanding? There is nothing to discuss. I am done with your threats. Done with your lies. Done with you. You are not taking Dylan from anyone, ever. That much I can promise you. This conversation is over," she slammed her phone onto the counter.

Dylan ran into the living room crying. Cassidy heard a sudden crash that sounded like a wall had fallen down. "I hate you!" Dylan yelled. Cassidy ran.

"What the hell was that?" Fallon asked as he and Alex approached the back door. Alex dropped the wood in her hand and sprinted through the door towards the sound of Dylan's screams. Cassidy was holding him on the couch, rocking him gently.

Alex looked at the television screen that had cracked straight down the middle and then at the box that lay crumpled on the floor. It had split open, and the flashing lights from a toy truck could be seen spilling through. "What happened?" she asked fearfully. Cassidy just shook her head.

"I'm not leaving," Dylan whimpered.

Alex looked at Cassidy in confusion. She thought they had successfully quelled Dylan's fears from the previous day. "I got a call," Cassidy said and raised her brow. She turned to her son and took his face in her hands. "No one is taking you anywhere, Dylan. No one is taking anyone away. I promise you. I promise you."

Fallon scooped up the box and retrieved the toy from inside. He went to hand it to Dylan and Dylan threw it again. "I don't want it!" It struck the table and let out a slight whine before the blinking light faded completely.

"Dylan," Alex lowered her voice. "Calm down." She bent over to pick up the toy and several pieces of plastic and metal that had broken off and froze.

"What is it?" Cassidy asked, seeing the expression on Alex's face.

Alex offered her wife a sheepish grin. "Nothing," she said with the raise of her brow. She gestured to Dylan. "Listen, Speed." He looked up to her with swollen eyes. "I know you are very angry with your father. I know you are scared. I know." Dylan looked down. "You can't throw things no matter how upset you are, okay?" He nodded. Alex sighed and reached out for him, placing the broken toy on the table. "You listen to me. Mom and I promised you. I promise you he will not call here again. Okay? You don't have to see him. You don't have to talk to him. You need to trust me."

"Alex?" Dylan whispered.

"What is it, Speed?"

"What if he hurts you?" he asked. Cassidy froze and looked at Alex in astonishment.

"Why would you ask that, Dylan?" Alex asked gently.

"He said he would. I heard him. He said you and Mom would pay. Cheryl told him to stop…and he…"

"What, Dylan? He what?" Alex urged quietly.

"He hit her," Dylan whispered. "I saw him."

Alex nodded as Cassidy pulled Dylan closer. "No one is going to hurt you, or Mom or me. I'm sorry that happened, Speed."

"Dylan," Cassidy began. She felt as if someone had ripped her apart. "Why didn't you tell us this?" Dylan just shrugged. The pieces were coming together now for Cassidy. She did not like the picture she was seeing clearly for the first time. Her ex-husband had raised a hand to her once when they were in college, never making contact. It was enough that Cassidy had decided to study abroad for a semester. When she returned, she found his attitude had changed. She brushed Dylan's bangs aside and wiped his tears.

"Why don't you go get cleaned up," Alex suggested. "Uncle Brian and I will get that wood inside and we will put this all behind us, okay?"

"I'm sorry," Dylan said quietly. "I broke the T.V.," he cried.

"I know," Alex said. "It's okay. It's all right," she reassured him through his tears and hugged him tenderly. Dylan looked at his mother who nodded. "It's okay," Alex repeated. "Go on up and wash up. Mom will be right behind you."

"Can we still play pool later?" he asked hopefully, trying to mask his sadness.

"That's why I'm here," Fallon added lightly. Dylan smiled and headed up the stairs.

"I'll be right there," Cassidy called. "Alex, we have to do something," she continued. Alex pressed a finger to her lips and lifted the toy from the table. "Alex?" Cassidy questioned with equal parts confusion and urgency coloring her voice.

Alex turned over the toy and pointed to its bottom where a piece had broken off then pointed to her ear. Cassidy was still puzzled. "I think what's important now is that we *listen* to everything Dylan has to say," Alex pointed to the toy again. "He needs to know we *hear* him clearly." She lifted her brows as she handed the car to Fallon to inspect.

Understanding dawned on Cassidy, and she covered her mouth in disbelief. Alex nodded. "You're right," Cassidy replied. "Let me go get him all set. Maybe after pool, you and I can have a talk with him," she offered.

"Yeah, I think that's a good idea," Alex said. Fallon studied the toy, the anger in his eyes becoming more evident by the moment. Alex clasped Cassidy's hand in reassurance and watched as her wife left to tend to Dylan. "Let's get that wood," Alex suggested to Fallon.

***

Alex stopped in the kitchen and retrieved a phone from a locked drawer. She passed by the logs that had rolled free on the patio and headed for the woods behind the house. As soon as she felt she was at a relatively safe distance she sent the message. She waited for a numeric response and looked at Fallon. "I need to talk to Krause."

"Alex, if they are listening in there then your cell..."

"We have a method. Whoever gave O'Brien that toy is..."

Fallon shook his head in aggravation. "How do you know O'Brien didn't want to listen for his own..."

"No. It's high tech. Whoever it is doesn't have access to the ears that are already here," she explained.

"Are you telling me that your house is bugged?"

Alex shrugged. For the last few months, she and Cassidy had taken Krause's suggested precautions in dialogue. Alex and Krause had located the "ears" in the house fairly easily. She was able to render them useless when needed, but she was still vigilant. She and Krause were on the radar. That meant devising numerous ways to hold conversations that seemed entirely mundane that in fact, were dealing with matters of great interest to anyone who might be listening. "It comes with the package, Fallon. I have it under control. What concerns me is who wants to listen in on my life that does not have access." Alex had two needs now. The first was to ensure Dylan was safe in every way, and the second was to determine who O'Brien's puppeteer was. She had wondered why he had begun to show a sudden revitalized interest in Dylan. Now, it made sense.

"Alex, how are…"

"Krause will call in twenty-five minutes." She began walking back toward the house and stopped at the patio. "Do me a favor?" she asked. Fallon nodded. "Bring the wood in and tell Cass I realized I forgot to pick up dessert. I'm just going to run downtown and get something."

"It's not important," Fallon said as Alex opened the back door for him.

"No. I know," she said stepping into the kitchen and retrieving her keys from the counter. "I think after what just happened, Dylan and Cassidy could both use something to sweeten their day. I'll be back by the time Cass has dinner ready. Just tell her….and start that fire, will you?" Alex laughed.

"Sure thing," Fallon replied. "You sure have taken to the role of boss," he joked as Alex opened the door to the garage.

"I was always your boss," Alex mocked him playfully as she took her leave. "You just weren't paying attention."

"Probably so," Fallon muttered. He looked at the toy on the table and sighed wondering what else could befall his friend and her family.

***

Alex accepted a small bag from the clerk and nodded her thanks. She looked at the phone in her hand as the message appeared, "3-21". She smiled back at the young girl behind the counter and began to head for the door when a voice called to her. "Miss Toles?" Alex turned back. "Sandy says your brother is on the phone. She's in her office if you want to grab it there."

Alex smiled. "Thanks, Jeannie." It had been the perfect plan. Nick and the owner of the pastry shop in town had been friends for years. They had attended culinary school together, and Alex frequented the bakery. She was considered family. The cordial relationship provided a terrific means of communication for Alex and Krause. It was a contingency plan they had yet to utilize, and Alex was grateful they had concocted it now. She moved past the young woman and into a small side office.

"Hey, Alex," Sandy greeted. "Sorry, that you missed Tony. He just left." Alex smiled. "Take as long as you need. Hope everything is okay."

"Yeah, I probably have last minute requests," Alex joked. She waited for the door to close and picked up the phone. "This is Alex," she said lightly.

"Better get extra cupcakes," Krause replied.

"Yeah. Well, that might be a good idea, actually. Seems we have extra company," she answered.

"Who?"

"Not sure," she said.

"Where?"

"O'Brien sent home a present with Dylan," she responded.

"Is he all right?" Krause asked immediately. Alex let out a sigh. "Cassidy?" Alex let out another audible breath. "Alex?"

"We need to talk." Now it was Krause's turn to release his tension in a sigh. "You with Callier?" she asked.

"Yeah," he responded. "Can you tell?" he asked. "Can you tell whose it is?"

"It's not CIA or NSA issue. If it is, I've never seen it. God knows I've seen enough of them. It's subtle. Most people would never have noticed it."

"How did you…"

"Dylan threw it. Toy truck. Broke it in a couple of places. Just in the right place. A tiny shiny piece behind a wire that doesn't quite match," she paused. "Listen, I don't like this. Brackett is on her way to London. Tate said something to Fallon about you and me; something to the effect that people didn't want us to find each other." Alex listened to the marked silence filling the line. "Now, O'Brien shows his face all of a sudden, making overtures toward Dylan…"

"What kind of overtures?" Krause asked.

"Threats," Alex answered. "We both know that this is not about Dylan."

"Shit…Alex…Callier just told me that Dimitri is headed to London as well."

"Great." Alex pinched the bridge of her nose and released it. Her father's letter was plaguing her thoughts, and if she was right, it was at the center of Cassidy's now as well. "There's something else….my father….Pip, he…"

"Alex…."

"He left a letter for Cassidy," Alex whispered through the line.

"What?" Krause asked.

"Yeah, I know…listen we need to talk face to face."

"I agree," he said quietly.

"You think you can get Mitchell on Brackett; subtly?" Alex wondered.

"Yeah. They want us to follow her to London," he observed.

"So, where don't they want us?" Alex asked.

Krause looked over toward Callier, who was leaning against the wall. "Good question. Can you get here this weekend?"

"France?" Alex asked.

"Yes."

Alex let out a heavy sigh. "I don't…."

"Dylan?" he asked. There was no response. Krause was hoping to bring Alex to Callier, but the lack of response from his partner told him everything he needed to know. "I'll be back Saturday. The train station."

"All right," Alex agreed.

"Alex, leave it on…don't let them know you found…"

"I won't. I think we should give them something to think about," she replied.

"You want to plant false information," Krause surmised.

"Yes, I do."

"All right. I'll see what more I can learn here. Alex…."

"Yeah?"

"In that letter was there anything about…."

Alex closed her eyes. "We'll talk when I see you Saturday," she said softly.

"Yeah. Just be careful," he reminded her.

"You too," she said, disconnecting the call with a sudden feeling that there was something more Jonathan Krause wanted to say. Alex mentally stored the conversation away and walked back to the counter. 'Never too cautious' was her motto now. "Seems I'll need another couple of cupcakes," she explained.

***

Chapter Six

Alex shut off the light and pulled Cassidy into her arms. "How are you doing?" she asked.

"Better now," Cassidy sighed.

"I want you to go with Dylan to your mom's. I'll pick you up there Saturday night."

Cassidy propped herself up on her elbow. "Are you worried he might try something with Dylan?"

"No, I'm not," Alex assured as she pulled Cassidy back into her arms. "I'm curious about who he is trying to impress though. And, I have a few things to take care of," she whispered. "It will be easier if you are there; no curious eyes. I am worried about you and Dylan." Feeling Cassidy tense Alex quickly clarified her meaning. "I'm not worried about your safety, Cass. I am worried about both of you emotionally. I just think it would be good for you both."

"Alex..."

"I know. School. I know. It's only two days, Cass." Alex felt Cassidy tighten her hold. "What is it?"

"I've been thinking; about Pip....about your father's..."

"Yeah. I know. Me too," Alex admitted.

"I know it's not," Cassidy sat up slightly to regard Alex in the faint light. "I can't believe I am about to say this."

Alex nodded her head in quiet understanding. "It's not my first choice either. It does solve the immediate problem. And," Alex stopped abruptly.

"And what?" Cassidy urged.

"Right now, I want Dylan to feel safe. It's the best alternative. If we can show that O'Brien is not Dylan's..."

Cassidy blew out a heavy breath and laid back on Alex. "What do you think he'll say?"

"Pip?" Alex asked and felt Cassidy's affirmative nod. "He loves Dylan as much as he loves you. John was like his brother. On some level I think he feels he is betraying that," Alex said plainly. "That's why I hate asking him. Doesn't really make sense if I think about it, though."

"Why is that?" Cassidy asked, tracing light patterns over Alex.

"John apparently agreed to this," Alex paused. "And, Pip has proven it more than once. He'd do anything for you."

"Mmm," was the only response.

"What?" Alex asked.

"I think you are missing something in that statement," Cassidy offered.

"I don't think so. It was John's idea. We both know Pip would do anything for..."

"Yes, I know that," Cassidy admitted. "It isn't just me that he would do anything for."

"Well, of course not. Dylan is..."

"No, Alex. You don't see it," Cassidy said.

"See what?" Alex asked.

"You and Pip. You can't see it. You're too close."

"What are you talking about?" Alex asked somewhat defensively.

Cassidy chuckled softly. "Honey, I don't know how it happened, but I've never seen you so comfortable with another person."

"You," Alex answered.

"Yes. That's not what I meant, and you know it," Cassidy scolded playfully. "You care about him." Alex squirmed slightly beneath Cassidy and Cassidy giggled again. "Like it or not, Agent Toles, you and Pip are friends." Alex sighed. She had admitted it to herself long ago, but she had never voiced it to anyone else. Cassidy heard another uncomfortable sigh escape her wife. "Why is that so hard for you?" she asked.

"I don't know," Alex confessed. "For years at the NSA Jonathan Krause was on my radar as a player. There's no logical reason I should trust him. Well, other than the fact that he would die before he let anyone hurt you."

"But?" Cassidy encouraged.

"I don't know. I just do."

"Just do what?" Cassidy asked.

"Trust him," Alex answered.

"And?"

"Should there be more?" Alex laughed.

"You care about him," Cassidy said plainly.

"I...."

"Alex, he's your friend. Just like Brian...like Nick, like everyone you love, you worry about protecting him."

"He can take care of himself," Alex observed.

"Everyone needs someone to take care of them sometimes, even Pip," Cassidy said softly.

"You've never told me much about your time in France," Alex said.

"No. I guess I haven't," Cassidy admitted. She exhaled forcefully and closed her eyes. "It was not exactly the best time in my life." Alex stroked Cassidy's hair and waited for her to continue. "I needed to get away. Studying abroad was the perfect solution."

Alex could feel the tension rising in Cassidy. "Get away from what?" she asked.

"From Chris."

"Cass?" Alex was certain she could feel the heat of Cassidy's tears through her T-shirt. "Please tell me he never hurt you."

"No. Not physically."

"Go on," Alex encouraged.

Cassidy shifted nervously and sighed. "It was right at the end of my junior year. Chris had already hinted at an engagement. I was," Cassidy closed her eyes and struggled to continue.

"What?" Alex asked softly. "You don't have to tell me, Cass."

"It's not that. I just…I don't know, Alex. Looking back now, I just…sometimes I can't understand why I stayed with him; why I married him at all."

"What happened?" Alex asked gently.

"Oh, well…at first I was excited. He was already working in a large firm in San Francisco; making quite the name for himself. He can be quite charming; you know?" Alex remained silent, and Cassidy giggled. "No, I guess you don't." Cassidy patted her wife's stomach. "You've only seen a glimpse of that. It's the real Christopher O'Brien that you know."

Alex shook her head. "Cassidy…."

"No, it's true. I should have obeyed my instincts then. I went to visit him, unannounced of course. I thought it would be a surprise; you know? A romantic weekend before the summer break. I was excited. I had just gotten a job for the summer in this great little bohemian café. I had roommates lined up to share a small apartment in Haight-Ashbury." Cassidy grew whimsical for a moment as her thoughts strayed. "I thought it would be perfect for me. I always had this crazy notion I would write a novel about two couples who met in the sixties and whose lives took different turns." Alex smiled silently. She loved hearing Cassidy's stories. She heard a dramatic sigh escape Cassidy's lips and knew it signaled a change in emotion. "Anyway, I was excited to tell him. I thought that he would be happy for me. I would stay on the west coast for the summer instead of returning home," she chuckled sarcastically.

"But?"

"Well, he flipped out. No wife of his was going to work in a dingy, liberal café. What was I looking to find? Men?" Cassidy took a deep breath. "I pointed out that we were hardly married and that I would do whatever I pleased." Cassidy felt the slight jiggle beneath her and knew that Alex was chuckling. "Is that funny?"

"No," Alex answered. "I just can't imagine anyone telling you what you could do."

"Mm. Well, I never enjoyed that. But, I wasn't always the person I am now, Alex." Alex understood that as well. "I was furious. I mean, really angry. He was angry. I don't even remember everything he said. I do remember," she stopped as she felt the knot in her stomach begin to make its presence known at the vivid memory. "He said that he would never marry a common whore." Alex flinched at the words as they rolled off her wife's tongue, but she remained silent and listened, knowing there was more. "I told him if I had become a whore then it was because he made me that way," Cassidy's voice dropped. Alex heard the soft whimper from Cassidy's tears as they continued to fall. "I went to leave. He grabbed me. Hard. I screamed for him to let me go. He did. Then he swung his hand back. I kicked him in the shin, grabbed the door knob and ran out of his apartment." Cassidy nestled closer to Alex. Alex held her gently; feeling the trembling in her wife's body. "He shouted that he would never marry a whore anyway. I just kept going. I decided that next week to go to France. Didn't take his calls. Didn't see him until he showed up at my mother's right before I left for Paris."

"I'm sorry, Cass."

"Yeah. Me too. I should have known."

"He never tried to hit you again?"

"No. He had some harsh words now and again. But, no. The truth is, Alex, we hardly saw one another. It was…well," Cassidy stopped briefly. "I guess, in some ways we used each other," she admitted quietly.

"I don't think you are capable of that," Alex reassured.

"Knowingly? Maybe not. He was my first Alex. He offered me the world on a silver platter. I just…"

"You were young," Alex said.

"I was selfish and stupid."

Alex sat up slightly and brought Cassidy to face her. "Cassidy. You may be many things; opinionated, strong, even temperamental," Alex said as Cassidy raised her brow. "You are neither selfish nor stupid. There is not a soul who knows you that would describe you that way. Believe me."

"You're bias," Cassidy said.

"No, I'm not."

Cassidy shook her head. "Well, there is one person that I think would…"

"That asshole is no judge of anyone's character. He has none himself," Alex said bluntly. Cassidy smiled. "So, that's why you went to France to study?" Cassidy nodded. "But you went back to him." Cassidy shrugged. Alex let out a heavy sigh and pulled Cassidy into her arms. "No one has the ability of hind-sight, sweetheart. If they did they would never learn anything," Alex said. Cassidy laughed.

"What?" Alex asked.

"That's something like what Pip said when I told him the story."

"Pip knows?" Alex asked.

"Chris kept calling and I didn't want to talk to him. I got drunk one night and unloaded it all on him; in French no less," Cassidy chuckled.

"Can't imagine he was too thrilled by that story."

"No. Probably not. I don't remember much more than that," Cassidy confessed.

"Cass?"

"Hmm?"

"Chris was your first? I mean, like the first person you…"

"Yeah."

"And, John was just….that's it; isn't it? I mean other than me?" Alex asked a bit sheepishly.

"Does that surprise you?" Cassidy asked. Alex just kissed her head. "Alex? Does that bother you?"

"No," Alex answered. "I just know how lucky I am."

"What are we going to do about him?" Cassidy's voice was tinged with apprehension.

"Whatever we have to," Alex said definitively.

"Pip?" Cassidy whispered.

"If it comes to that, yes."

"I wish you were the first," Cassidy barely whispered. "Sometimes I feel like you were."

Alex understood perfectly what Cassidy meant. "As long as I am the last," she said, lightening the mood.

"Promise," Cassidy answered.

"It will be all right. I promise," Alex said as she closed her eyes.

***

Saturday, December 13th

Alex walked along the train tracks until she finally reached the cracked cement of the old platform. She was grateful that nature had chosen to hold the frequent New England snow at bay. This walk was no picnic in the best of conditions. It took the agent nearly forty minutes hiking through dense woods to reach the destination. She had to admit that Jonathan Krause had found the perfect meeting place. No one came here. Once in a while this place might see some kids that wanted to party or the occasional addict, neither of which posed any threat to what she and her new partner needed for privacy. Should anyone see them, they would likely surmise that the pair were law enforcement looking for a drug dealer and scurry quickly. She laughed softly as she approached the large room where she was certain to find her unlikely friend. "Waiting long?" she asked.

Jonathan Krause turned and offered her a wry smile. "No longer than any of the other men in your life I suspect."

"Ouch," Alex answered playfully. She sincerely doubted that most people would believe Jonathan Krause had a sense of humor at all. It was one of the things that drew her closer to the man, even if his sense of humor was often at her expense. She understood the jabbing. It relieved tension for them both, and she could dish it back just as quickly when the mood struck her. "Well, don't tell me you invited me to such a lovely place to discuss my track record with men," she supplied.

"Hardly," he laughed. His features seemed to soften slightly as his voice followed suit. "How are you?" he asked with concern.

Alex squinted with curiosity. It was not that it was unusual for Krause to ask the question, but she was certain she denoted something different in his demeanor and tone; something she could not quite put her finger on. "I'm all right." Before Krause could ask another question, she continued. "Dylan and Cassidy are fine."

"Good. I had an interesting meeting with Edmond," he said.

"Anything more on my father? Any clue why he cut off those funds to ASA?"

Krause forced a smile and shifted a bit. "No. Edmond was unaware that your father had done that. He didn't seem overly concerned, but I don't think he knows exactly why."

"And my father?"

Krause nodded. "Some. Seems he was not always just a money broker," he explained. Alex studied his face closely as he continued. "He was in the field for quite some time when your grandfather was still alive."

"My father was a field agent?" she asked in disbelief. Krause nodded. "A spook?"

Krause could not help but smile and shake his head slightly. "Alex, you are a spook." She huffed a bit and nodded. "There's more," he said.

"What?"

"His partner...."

"Shit...just don't tell me his partner was related to O'Brien or something. I swear..."

"Seriously?" Krause mocked the idea. He stopped and then turned stoic. "No. Alex, his partner was my mother."

"You're not kidding," Alex said seriously. "Are you?" she asked. "Are you kidding?" she repeated. Krause shook his head.

"Well, that explains them not wanting us to meet," she surmised. She looked over to notice that the man before her seemed to find his shoes suddenly interesting. "Okay? What? That's not all; is it?"

Krause looked up and smiled half-heatedly. "You know there is always more to every story," he answered.

"Mm-hm. What about this new development with O'Brien?" she asked. "I assume you told Edmond. Did he have any clue who might be listening?"

"No. He did seem moderately concerned. Which, for Edmond, is rare. This spilt between the Russian contingent in The Collaborative and the rest; it's not good, Alex. They are seeking to compete now with our interests."

"He thinks the Russians..."

"Maybe. Claire is in Dimitri's pocket. And, Alex...there is money missing from O'Brien's campaign."

Alex bristled. "What are you talking about?"

"Right before he died," Krause paused and sighed. "O'Brien went to your father."

"I already knew that."

"No, not about you. The Broker set up the funnels for PAC donations. Masterson Marketing, CBC Consultants are CIA fronts; just like Carecom. A payment schedule with a list of services to purchase was outlined for the campaign. The campaign director was chosen."

"Okay. So, just like with Carecom services were purchased on paper that need not be rendered and the money filtered through..."

"Exactly. Except it hasn't been. O'Brien fired the campaign director we placed. Those funds have never been transferred.

Without our person inside, well....Edmond can't be certain where the funds are being diverted."

"What does that have to do with bugging my house?" Alex asked. "You think they are hoping I will give up the ghost? Give up something there about Carecom's accounts? Somehow get access to our pipeline?"

Krause nodded. "Exactly."

"I don't know. That doesn't make sense to me. I would never..."

"I know, but *they* still don't know. They know I have been there, Alex. We have no reason to hide those conversations from the CIA. It makes some sense."

"Maybe. I have a feeling there is more than that," Alex said. "So, you think O'Brien is skimming for himself?" Krause shrugged. "Nah," Alex said. "I agree. He is too much of a coward for that. Someone else is syphoning that money. The question is where. What if we had that conversation?" she asked with a gleam in her eye.

Krause laughed. "Dummy accounts?" he offered. Alex raised her brow. "I was hoping you'd say that," he smiled. "Follow the funds," he said. Alex's jaw tightened slightly, and she sighed. "What is it?" Krause asked.

"Pip," she began.

"Oh, this is not good," he said. "You only call me Pip when you want to give me a hard time or something is wrong."

She let out another audible breath. "My father, in his letter to Cassidy," she stopped and retrieved it from her pocket and handed it to him. "Maybe you should just read it for yourself."

Alex watched as Krause read over the paper in his hands slowly. His expression remained remarkably calm. It was a trait that all great agents possessed. She noticed that he stared at the paper for a few seconds longer after finishing before very carefully folding it and handing it back to her. She was surprised when a gradual smile appeared on his face. "So? When do we leave for Stockholm?" he asked.

"Pip…I…"

"It's all right, Alex," he assured her. Alex started to protest, and he held up his hand. "I'm not surprised by the letter," he said as he noted the questions in Alex's eyes. "Edmond told me many things, Alex. I blamed him. I blamed him for John, for his death. I blamed myself."

"I know," Alex said softly.

"The thing is; John knew. He knew even before I did. Before I even called him, before I called and set up the chatter for NSA. He already knew it was coming. Days before, actually."

"What?" Alex asked.

"He had time to think things through, Alex. More time than I did," Krause said, his voice tinged with a mixture of sadness and anger.

"Look, I can't ask you…"

"You didn't ask," Krause said flatly when the sound of Alex's phone startled them both.

"Hello? Cass?" Alex looked at Krause, and he smiled. "Everything okay?" she returned to the phone call. "What? When?" Alex shook her head silently. "No, I heard you. I'll be there as soon as I can. Okay. See you soon."

"Everything okay?" Krause asked.

"Mm. Barb just went into labor," she explained. "Look. I know this is…"

"Alex. You need to go be with your family now," he said. "I will do whatever you need for Dylan. Besides, I suspect you are as curious as I am about what is in Stockholm."

"You could ask Edmond," she suggested.

"I could. That's not as much fun though," he smirked. Alex nodded her understanding. "I don't think we should both go. Brackett is still on her way to London," Krause continued. "Edmond got the word while I was there that she's set to meet with Daniels on Wednesday. Let me go to Sweden."

Alex nodded. "I'll book a flight when I get home."

"Ian is tailing her there. Just…"

"I have it," Alex said. "I already laid the groundwork with Daniels. Just....whatever you find in Stockholm....it's your decision," she said.

Krause nodded. He knew that both Alex and Cassidy would be reluctant to make an official claim that Dylan was his son and he both understood and respected that. The truth was that he loved Dylan. He remained silent for a long moment, looking intently at Alex; an understanding he had been reluctant to allow until this moment overtaking him. "Let's worry about that when I get back. Go on," he said.

"Pip?" Alex turned back and looked at him compassionately.

"Go," he said. "Wish Nick and Barb the best for me."

Alex nodded. "I will," she answered, turning to leave.

Krause watched her as she exited and closed his eyes. He shook his head and attempted to process a truth he knew he could not deny. Alex was, without any doubt in his mind, his sister. He wondered how he could tell her. He wondered if she would believe it. He rubbed his face vigorously and jumped at the sound of his cell phone. "Krause," he answered. "Are you sure? Where?" Krause licked his lips and shook his head. "I'm leaving the country shortly. It needs to be soon. I'll let you know," he hung up and chuckled sarcastically. "No one can hide forever," he mumbled as he made his way out of the train station.

***

Joshua Tate walked calmly and deliberately through the large oak doors. He had been here many times at the direct request of the president. He had never before taken it upon himself to seek the man who held the Oval Office. His efforts over the last few days to uncover what the young Claire Brackett was truly involved with had led him down a path he was reluctant to believe could exist. His suspicions had led him here. It was the perfect opportunity. President Lawrence Strickland had recently made contact with the Assistant FBI Director; inquiring about an investigation that his division was spearheading. It was a convoluted case that centered on the possible bribery of several federal judges. Tate was positive that the president's true interest revolved more around the potential parties that might be implicated if, in fact, an indictment was made. The fact was that informants had named several high-level advisers at the White House. It surprised Tate that the trail had not gone cold abruptly. He was no stranger to the inner workings of government. Few decisions were ever made on the bench that were not influenced by politics, and politics meant money. What was unusual was the lack of caution, almost hubris, in the trail that had been left so clearly marked. He suspected that someone within the new president's administration might be attempting to compromise or even implicate the president himself. Often, those initiatives were created within the agency Tate had served now for many years. He had found no evidence of a CIA plot to dethrone the newly crowned American king. Tate was all too aware that Lawrence Strickland regarded himself as exactly that; a king.

"Sir," a voice greeted Joshua Tate and directed him to follow.

Tate nodded and followed silently. He accepted a seat in the waiting area and closed his eyes. Anyone who passed by would have assumed that the assistant director was resting. In fact, he was concentrating on the voices that surrounded him, pulling pieces of conversations that to most would seem benign into his consciousness, and sorting the trivial from the potentially revealing silently.

"Director Taylor was here earlier," a man's voice said softly. Tate mentally pulled the voice into his focus and listened. "One thing, Strickland sure can piss him off. I don't know what happened, but I'm sure I heard Taylor call him a naïve fool," the voice finished. Tate smiled inwardly. It confirmed a closeness between the NSA Domestic Affairs Director and the new president, a familiarity that Tate suspected had deeper roots. The sound of approaching footsteps roused him, and he smiled at the man who now directed him to follow the path to the president's location.

"Joshua," President Strickland greeted the assistant director. "I was pleasantly surprised to hear you would be visiting."

"Mr. President," Tate returned the greeting, accepting what he regarded as a weak handshake from the president.

"So, I take it you might have some news for me," Strickland began. He nodded to his aide to close the door and leave them in privacy.

"Well, I have to tell you that I am somewhat surprised at the carelessness of some of those implicated," Tate answered.

"My staff members, you mean?" Strickland questioned cautiously.

"Yes."

"Do you think that it was a ploy of some kind? A directive from elsewhere?" Strickland asked. The president was keenly aware that most who had been loyal to President John Merrow regarded his administration as little more than a nuisance. He did not have a military background; he was not tied to intelligence; he was, in short, a politician through and through. Some saw that as weakness. Strickland was aware that meant there would be initiatives to remove his authority and relevance.

"It's possible," Tate answered. "I'm wondering if we should involve NSA. Perhaps it would be wise to seek Director Taylor's…"

"No," Strickland answered. Tate felt a familiar tingle travel through his body. It was the sensation he remembered from his days as a detective in New York City interrogating suspects. The president had responded much too quickly. Tate lifted his eyebrow in question as the president rose from his seat and paced across the floor. "I don't think it is wise to involve any intelligence service," the president explained.

"I see," Tate said. "Sir, the FBI is limited in ways that…"

"I understand, Joshua. Look, John turned to you more than once. I need this handled."

Tate nodded. His suspicions were confirmed by the president's reaction. "Mr. President, I will handle the investigation to the best of my ability. If this is someone attempting to compromise your administration, the best course will be to get closer." The president's expression tightened dramatically. "Sir, the NSA is far better equipped to handle this piece of the investigation. Domestic Affairs is..."

"Director Taylor is not an option," the president responded harshly.

Tate remained expressionless and stared stoically at the man across from him. He studied the older man's demeanor and posture. "Very well. I would advise you to keep an eye on Mr. Stearns." The president flinched slightly at the name. Gregory Stearns was a trusted adviser on domestic economic policy. He also has been one of Strickland and Merrow's most successful fundraisers during the last campaign. He was savvy and smart and able to penetrate and motivate the largest corporations into falling into line with the previous administration. He had hoped that the man's unique talents would serve his own as well.

"Understood," the president answered. "Stearns has served many senators and congressmen over the years," Strickland observed. "I can't see what he would gain by compromising this administration."

"Perhaps nothing," Tate answered. "I would have brought this to Director Taylor; that would have been my preference. It seems that you think that is inadvisable. It is best that you know where to keep your eyes focused," he explained. Strickland nodded, but Tate could see the pensive crease taking shape in the president's forehead. "Well, I'm sorry I don't have more for you," Tate continued. "I did not want to call in other resources without your approval," he finished.

"I appreciate that," Strickland acknowledged. The president had read many notes from his predecessor regarding his trust in the Assistant FBI Director. One thing that Lawrence Strickland knew about John Merrow was that his trust was carefully and cautiously placed in very few people. He hoped that Joshua Tate would prove an ally.

Tate rose as the president led him to the door. "I'll be in touch," he assured the president.

"Thank you, Joshua," Strickland replied. "I hope you understand..."

"You are the Commander in Chief," Tate said. "You owe me no explanation."

Tate watched as the president's eyes took on a slight gleam, and his lips turned upward into a notable smile that barely masked its underlying arrogance. "Good to see you," Strickland said. Feeling emboldened by the assistant director's statement, he patted Tate condescendingly on the shoulder.

Tate made his way down the narrow corridor fighting the urge to physically brush off the feel of the president's hand on his shoulder. Lawrence Strickland was no John Merrow. The mere presence of the man caused bile to rise into Tate's throat. He stopped outside the large white doors as he waited for his car and took note of the younger man in the suit that stood, apparently waiting as well. "Need a ride?" the assistant director asked.

"Oh," the younger man turned abruptly. "I apparently missed my ride earlier" he answered.

Tate smiled. He recognized the younger man immediately. "So," Tate began. "How do you like working at the NSA?" The man looked at Tate in surprise. "It's all right son," Tate said. "Joshua Tate, FBI."

"Oh, I'm sorry," the man extended his hand. "Agent Marcus Anderson."

"Your boss left you behind?" Tate asked with the raise of an eyebrow. Marcus Anderson was known to the assistant director.

His traveling companion over the last few months was another young agent Tate followed closely and with great interest. It was imperative that he play this coolly. Anderson was no rookie. While young, any agent assigned to work with Claire Brackett was hardly a novice. What piqued Tate's curiosity more was the other company the agent apparently had been keeping. Traveling with Michael Taylor was normally an honor that was reserved for more senior agents; particularly travels to The White House. "I'm happy to give you a lift."

"I don't want to impose. I'm certain they will send someone," Anderson said.

"Well," Tate shrugged. "If you haven't called yet; there is no sense in causing anyone that inconvenience. After all we are all on the same team," he winked. Anderson nodded his assent. "Excellent," Tate offered. He looked at his driver as the man came to open the door. "I'm afraid we will have to make one extra stop," he joked. "Seems we have picked up another stray." Tate laughed at the incredulous expression on Anderson's face and got into the car. "Relax, agent. That's what we do at the FBI mostly, but don't tell anyone."

Seeing the NSA Agent relax again slightly, Tate directed the driver to drop Anderson wherever he needed to go. He didn't expect much meaningful conversation, and he didn't need it. They rode in silence until they reached Anderson's destination; the younger agent thanked Assistant Director Tate and Tate offering the typical response. Tate watched as Agent Anderson made his way toward the Lincoln Memorial and smiled. He leaned over the seat to the driver. "Drive up to C Street and let me out," he directed. A few minutes later he exited the vehicle and positioned himself to wait patiently. Tate had greeted Anderson's story that he was already running late for a meeting with his partner at the Lincoln Memorial with a sympathetic smile; telling Anderson he remembered 'those days' well. He was relieved that Anderson clearly had no idea who he truly was. To Anderson, Tate was an FBI Assistant Director, in some ways a dime a dozen in these circles. Knowing that Anderson's recent company was Claire Brackett, and all too aware that Agent Brackett was currently on her way to London; Tate surmised quickly that the agent's intended destination was likely elsewhere. His suspicions were confirmed when the agent casually passed him walking up 23rd Street. "Visiting State, are we?" Tate smiled. "Well, let's see who you are really meeting," the assistant director mused.

***

Chapter Seven

Alex walked into the waiting room and saw Cassidy sitting beside her mother talking quietly. Cassidy looked up and caught sight of her wife approaching and smiled. "Hey."

"Hey yourself," Alex answered softly. "How's she doing?"

"Nick came out about half an hour ago," Cassidy said. "It will be a while."

Alex nodded and took a seat beside her wife. "Where are Dylan and Cat?"

"With Mom at Nick's," Cassidy answered. "She'll make the trek when things are closer," she explained. Alex nodded again quietly. "You all right?" Cassidy asked.

"Yeah," Alex answered softly.

"I'm going to go get some coffee," Helen interrupted as she reached her feet. "Anything you need?"

Cassidy shook her head. "Coffee would be great," Alex answered. "Don't you want some?" Alex asked Cassidy.

"No, not right now," she said. Helen smiled at her daughter-in-law and took her leave.

"Cass? Are you okay?" Alex asked, momentarily forgetting the unsettling feelings hospitals always brought on for her.

"Yeah, why?"

"I don't know. Just surprised. No coffee? You look like you could use some."

Cassidy laughed. "Is that a polite way of saying I look like crap?"

"No!" Alex chimed. "Just tired."

"Well, I am tired. But, it'll be a long night no matter what. If I start now, I will only need more later," she explained. "So, how was Pip?"

"Okay," Alex said.

"Alex?"

"He's going to check things out in Stockholm," Alex said nervously.

"And?" Cassidy prodded.

"I'm going to head to London for a couple of days," Alex said tacitly. She saw Cassidy's nearly imperceptible nod of understanding. "Only a couple of days."

Cassidy smiled. "It's okay," she said. "You showed him the letter?" Cassidy asked. Alex nodded. "How did he take it?"

Alex laughed. "I told you. He would do anything for you."

"Um-hmm."

"I don't want to talk about that now," Alex said, shifting nervously.

Cassidy took hold of the agent's hand gently. "I know you hate hospitals," she said. Alex shrugged. "Are you going to be all right here; waiting?"

"Yeah," Alex answered, relaxing slightly. "So, what do you think?"

"About?" Cassidy asked.

"Think it's a boy or a girl?"

Cassidy took a deep breath and sighed. "Well, I know Barb would not so secretly love a little girl, but for some reason I have a feeling we will be greeting another nephew."

"Yeah? How come?"

Cassidy shrugged. "I don't know. I was sure Dylan was a boy. No one believed me," she chuckled. "I just have a feeling."

Alex smiled and stroked Cassidy's hand. She closed her eyes for a moment and let her thoughts stray from her surroundings, wondering if Cassidy would have *feelings* when they finally conceived. Her smile steadily grew wider in contentment, and she heard Cassidy giggle. "What?" Alex asked without opening her eyes.

"What are you grinning about?" Cassidy asked.

Alex decided to leave her private thoughts exactly as they were. "Nothing in particular," she fibbed and then yawned. "Going to be a long night, you said. Just trying to make the best of it."

"Uh-huh," Cassidy answered in disbelief. She shook her head at the realization that Alex had, in a moment, drifted off to sleep.

"She sleeping?" Helen asked as she took a seat. Cassidy nodded. "In a hospital?" Helen couldn't believe it. Cassidy shrugged. "Miracles never cease," Helen said with a roll of her eyes.

Cassidy looked at her mother-in-law and winked. She studied her hand as it entwined with her wife's. "No. They really don't," she whispered.

***

Jonathan Krause stepped out of the taxi and made his way into a small coffee shop. He scanned it quickly and took note of the man sitting in the far corner. He approached casually and moved into the opposite bench. "So? Not like you to want coffee at this hour," Krause said lightly.

Brian Fallon smiled. "No. That is usually your department. I took the liberty," he said as their waitress approached and set a steaming mug in front of each of them. Fallon nodded his thanks. "How are you, Agent Krause?" Fallon asked.

"Curious," Krause answered as he lifted his coffee slowly to his lips.

Fallon sighed. "I got an unexpected call to meet with my boss this afternoon," he offered.

"Which boss?" Krause inquired.

"Fair question," he said. "In that you and I are sitting here now, I guess we both know that rules you out," Fallon joked. He took a deep breath as his voice became more tentative. "Tate," he answered.

"Really? And what did the good assistant director have to offer?" Krause wondered.

"Look, I don't know what to make of this," Fallon began. Krause merely raised an eyebrow in question as he continued to nurse his coffee slowly. "He visited the president today and ran into a stranded NSA agent," Fallon said. Seeing the vein in Jonathan Krause's neck begin to pulse, Fallon quickly but carefully continued. "It was Anderson, apparently keeping company with a certain NSA Director."

Krause nodded and very slowly placed his coffee back on the table. "Continue," he said.

"Krause," Fallon's voice became strained. "He followed him. Followed him to State." Jonathan Krause listened intently but with no visible change in emotion. The CIA agent's ability to remain so remarkably collected in any situation and to maintain an unreadable expression often unsettled Brian Fallon. Fallon continued slowly. "Did you know that Ambassador Daniels was here; in the states?" Fallon watched as the muscles in Krause's neck visibly strained. "Gets worse. He thinks," Fallon paused and took a breath for courage. "He suspects Director Taylor is working with Brackett. He thinks…"

"He thinks Taylor is Brackett's contact," Krause surmised. Fallon nodded. Krause took another sip of his coffee before steadily easing it back to the table again. He turned to Brian Fallon and nodded his understanding.

"Krause, you don't actually think that Michael Taylor…"

"I don't know. Either Tate is trying to throw us off his trail, or there is a good chance your other boss is not who we believe him to be," Krause answered. "Those are the only two possibilities." Krause stopped and considered what course to take next. "Look, I am headed to Stockholm this week. Alex will be headed to London. If Daniels is here, it's something that was decided quickly. Daniels is set to meet with Sparrow on Wednesday....back in London."

"Do you want me to..."

"No," Krause said. "No. Alex is headed in that direction."

"What about Taylor? She'll want to know..."

Krause stopped Fallon's thoughts. "Nothing to Agent Toles yet, Agent Fallon; not about Taylor. You've still been drilling into O'Brien's accident for the NSA?" Krause asked. Fallon nodded. Fallon had been investigating a car accident that very nearly cost Congressman Christopher O'Brien his life. Officially, every agency and the Metropolitan Police Department had ruled the accident just that; an accident. Alex had been certain it was anything but an accident; after months of investigation, even the most promising trails seemed to lead to a dead end. "Nothing new?" Krause inquired.

"No," Fallon said.

"There will be. There's money unaccounted for in O'Brien's campaign. I'll send you the information. Bring it to Taylor. Alex and I are going to leverage those little ears the congressman sent home with Dylan. Let's see where they lead us," Krause offered.

"You think we can flush him out. Whoever it is?" Fallon asked.

"I think one of your two bosses knows far more than he is saying. You're close enough to both to water the seed that we plant and then watch it grow," Krause said.

"Krause, Taylor is Alex's..."

"I know," Krause said. "People are seldom who we think they are Fallon," he paused and attempted to swallow his personal reality. "Sometimes not even ourselves," Krause said softly. Fallon studied him as the CIA agent rose to take his leave. "Stick as close to Taylor as you can. Give him the information on O'Brien that I send. And, Brian?" Krause stopped and put his hand on the man's shoulder. Fallon looked at him inquisitively. "Watch yourself."

***

Sunday, December 14th

Alex shifted uncomfortably in her chair, still groggy from her impromptu nap. She heard Cassidy's voice speaking softly. "What time is it?" she mumbled.

"It's almost four o'clock," Cassidy answered, taking a moment to gaze at Alex's sleepy state affectionately.

"Still no baby?" Alex asked in amazement.

"No," Cassidy chuckled. "Your mom went in a bit ago and she's definitely getting closer. They're giving her something now to try and help coax the baby a bit," Cassidy explained. "I called Mom; she'll be here with the boys shortly. I guess they haven't slept anyway. Cat is too excited."

As Cassidy finished her statement, Helen appeared around the corner. "Oh, look who decided to keep us company," she poked at her daughter.

Alex growled slightly. "I'm sure you two didn't even notice," she said.

Helen laughed. "Well, I am sure after all that rest you could use a stretch," she said.

Cassidy snickered, and Alex looked at her mother in confusion. "What are you talking about?" Alex asked.

"I thought, perhaps, you and Cassidy could take a walk and say hello," Helen suggested.

"You mean in her room?" Alex asked warily. Cassidy covered her mouth in an attempt to hide her ever-widening smile. "Nick is there," Alex dismissed the suggestion.

"Yes, he is," Helen repeated the obvious.

Cassidy stood and offered her hand to Alex. "What?" Alex asked again with a look of concern on her face. "I'm sure Barb doesn't want to see…"

"Actually, Alexis," her mother began. "She specifically asked if Cassidy would come in." Alex huffed slightly and took Cassidy's hand. "I should think this would be a fantastic opportunity for you," Helen said. Still tired, Alex looked at her mother completely perplexed. "Think of it as homework," she winked at her daughter. "You are married to a teacher."

"Great," Alex mumbled. "You've been spending too much time with Rose. I'm cutting you off. And...I don't have any homework yet," Alex replied. Helen just took her seat and grinned, catching Cassidy's muffled laughter as she led Alex off.

"Alex, you don't have to go in if you don't want to," Cassidy said when they reached the door of Barb's room. Alex just shrugged. "I know you hate these places, but Barb isn't sick."

"I know," Alex sighed. "I just feel...I don't know...out of place."

Cassidy nodded her understanding and encouragement. She raised her brow to signal her final question and Alex nodded for her to proceed. Cassidy opened the door gently and peered inside. "Hey, you up for a visit?" she asked her sister-in-law.

"Please!" Barb answered, sounding slightly exasperated.

Alex followed closely behind and made her way to her brother. "How are you?" she asked him.

"Exhausted," Nick whispered.

"Ow! Dammit that hurts," Barb winced. Cassidy smiled and took her hand.

"Maybe you should get up and walk around some more," Nick tried to suggest gently to his wife.

Barb shot him a look of disgust. "It's four in the morning; I have a needle in my arm, a bowling ball in my stomach, pain in my back...and you want me to walk?"

"Well, it might help, you know...speed things up," he said.

"Alex?" Barb directed her question to her sister-in-law. Alex pointed to her chest, and her eyes grew wide. "Do me a favor and take your brother for this walk he seems so interested in. Ow! Ugh, my back." Alex looked at Cassidy, who was desperately trying to hide a Cheshire cat-sized grin at the expression on both Nick and Alex's faces. Alex nodded and pulled her brother's arm. "And, Alex?" Barb called. Alex spun on her heels. "Piece of advice. There are moments when silence is your ally," she finished. Cassidy chuckled and turned to Barb, who had also begun to laugh softly as brother and sister sulked slightly and left the room.

"How are you doing?" Cassidy asked once Alex and Nick had left.

"I'm okay," Barb said, making a futile attempt to get comfortable. "I just want it over, you know?" Cassidy understood completely. "I love Nicky, but I wanted to throttle him about an hour ago; watching him sleep like a baby in that chair."

Cassidy smiled. "Alex slept for the last six hours. I'm surprised she can walk with her back."

"Well, she better not fall asleep on you when you are in this position," Barb said.

"I'd better not be in that position at this hour," Cassidy laughed.

"Yeah? You know something about communicating with… Ow!"

Cassidy sat with Barb for the next twenty minutes, supporting her and keeping her company. Barb had long been referring to Cassidy as the sister she had always wanted, and Cassidy felt the same way. She remembered her labor with Dylan vividly and completely understood Barb's need for a break. A change of scenery was not an option at this point, so a change in company sometimes was exactly what the doctor ordered.

Alex walked Nick to the cafeteria to find some coffee. They sat at a small table, and she watched as Nick stretched his neck and rubbed his temples. "Are you worried?" she asked.

Nick shrugged. "Yeah. No….I don't know. I just feel helpless."

"Was it like this with Cat too?"

Nick nodded. "Pretty much. Just nothing I can really do, you know? Just wait."

"Everything is okay though; right?" Alex asked nervously.

"Yeah. Seems to be," he answered with a yawn. "We should get back though," Nick said. "She wanted some time with Cassidy. I know that, but she won't be happy if I'm gone too long."

Alex grabbed the coffee she had purchased for Cassidy and gave her brother an encouraging pat on the back. She had missed Cat's birth while she was overseas working on a case for the NSA. She hated to admit that the underlying sense of anticipation and seeing Barb in the hospital bed had unsettled her. She led Nick down the long corridor until they reached the elevator. They rode together in silence, watching the floors tick by until a surprisingly loud "ding" startled them both. Reaching the room, Alex could hear the curse words flying from Barb's mouth clearly. As Nick opened the door, she instantly saw that Cassidy was holding one of her sister-in-law's hands while she rubbed the woman's back gently with the other.

"Jesus, I forgot how much this hurts!" Barb yelped in frustration as her contraction passed. Cassidy rubbed slow circles on her friend's back and looked across to Alex, who had turned quite noticeably pale. She leaned into Barb's ear and whispered something, and Alex watched Barb's lips turn into the hint of a smile. "All right, Alex. You saved me from Nurse Nick's walking remedy. You are free," Barb declared.

"We can stay," Alex began.

"No, no," Barb said. "Cassidy tells me the boys will be here any minute. You two will have your hands full, for sure."

Cassidy placed a soft kiss on Barb's forehead. Barb smiled at her, and she made her way to Nick, clasping his hand. "Hang in there. I'm sure it won't be that long now," Cassidy whispered.

Alex handed Cassidy her coffee as they walked out the door. "Thanks," Cassidy said. "You all right?" Cassidy asked her wife. Alex shrugged, and Cassidy could see the worry on Alex's face. "She'll be fine, Alex," Cassidy assured. "She's just uncomfortable, tired, and ready for it to be *over.*"

They made their way slowly back toward the waiting room. Alex stopped abruptly before opening the door. "Was it like that? I mean, for you?" Alex asked her wife.

Cassidy smiled. "You mean when I had Dylan?" Alex nodded. "A bit, I guess. I've had more pleasant experiences," Cassidy laughed.

Alex shuddered slightly as she opened the door. An excited seven-year-old bounced toward them, and Alex scooped him up. "Hey, Speed," she greeted him with a bear hug.

Cassidy leaned in to kiss Dylan's head and took the opportunity to whisper in Alex's ear. "If you had started to wonder," she said. "It was worth every single second."

Alex turned to regard the twinkle in Cassidy's eye. She felt Dylan's head rest on her shoulder and smiled softly. "Yeah, I believe it," she said.

***

A black sedan pulled up outside the long stretch of townhouses and Christopher O'Brien stepped into the back. "Let's take a drive," the older man in the back seat commanded the driver. He made no move to turn to the congressman as he continued. "So, what exactly have you done this time?" the man asked.

The tension emanating from the man beside him made O'Brien shift slightly in his seat. "I'm not certain I know what you mean," he answered.

"Well, Agent Krause and Agent Fallon both paid personal visits to Agent Toles last week. That's not a very usual scenario. Both in one week," the man said.

"I don't see what that has to do with me," O'Brien answered more pointedly than he had intended.

"Really? I suppose it is some coincidence that you met with her last week, and suddenly Fallon appears in Connecticut followed by Krause?"

O'Brien shifted again. "I couldn't put off that meeting any longer."

"So, that's why you called your ex-wife and threatened to take Dylan away the other day," the man asked without turning. O'Brien's surprise was evident. "What?" the man asked, finally moving to face the congressman. "I don't recall instructing you to interfere in their lives."

"He's my..."

"No. I think we both know he is not. So, where did this idea come from? Or...did you think up this whole scam in the little thing we loosely refer to as your brain?" the man inquired.

"I was told to make that meeting," O'Brien reconsidered his answer momentarily. "I assumed the directive came from you."

"Well, that was your first mistake."

"Excuse me?" O'Brien replied.

"Assuming," the man answered. "And who should I thank for this debacle?" O'Brien swallowed the lump in his throat. He had assumed that the president's request had, at the very least, been approved by the man beside him. "Do you care to enlighten me?" the man asked. "Or, should I guess?"

"I was called to a meeting...."

"Strickland," the man mumbled in disgust. "Well, I shouldn't be surprised. And what exactly did our ingenious leader ask you to do?" O'Brien hesitated. "I don't want to ask again."

"He wanted me to get closer. Gave me something for Dylan."

The man's sardonic laugh momentarily pierced the tension. "Strickland? Interested in a seven-year-old?" He shook his head. "I see. Dare I ask the motivation?"

"Just a way to listen," O'Brien's voice dropped. "He said it would be imperceptible."

The man laughed harder. "Well, he apparently does not know Alex Toles or Jonathan Krause very well. You back off."

"I don't think that is possible now," the congressman said.

"Why is that?"

"I had my lawyer file a..."

"You idiot." The car stopped, and the older man grabbed hold of the congressman's jacket. "I have better things to do than clean up your mess. You figure it out, Congressman. Now, get the hell out of my car."

Christopher O'Brien offered no argument. He stepped outside the vehicle and watched it pull away slowly. "Shit," he grumbled, pulling out his cell phone. "I need a ride," he said.

***

Alex couldn't believe there was still no baby. It was almost ten in the morning. "How long does it take?" she wondered.

Dylan had fallen asleep in between his two snoozing grandmothers. Cat, however, remained wide awake, watching a cartoon in the waiting room. "How much longer Aunt Cassidy?" he asked.

"I don't know, sweetie. It's one of those things. Your little brother or sister is just not quite ready yet," she answered him softly.

He shrugged. "I wish he would hurry up," Cat groaned.

Cassidy laid her head on Alex's shoulder. "Tired?" Alex asked.

"Yeah."

"You should have had that coffee I got."

Cassidy just sighed. She had given the coffee to her mother when she arrived with Dylan and Cat. "Yeah, because it was so effective for her," she gestured to the three sleeping bodies across the room. Alex started to reply when the door opened, and a fatigued, but broadly smiling Nick appeared. Cassidy sat up immediately and crossed the room to wake the sleeping trio.

"So?" Alex asked.

Cat made his way to his father and looked up with expectant eyes. "Boy," Nick said. "Seven pounds, twelve ounces, twenty inches."

"You have a little brother, Cat," Cassidy said with a pat on his shoulder.

"Can I see him?" Cat asked excitedly.

Nick nodded. "Yes, you can. I will come and let you know when she's ready for some more visitors," he said to the room.

"Take your time," Helen said. "How about we all head down and get some breakfast? By the time we're all done, she should be ready."

"Can we bring you something back?" Rose asked Nick.

"No," Nick responded. "But, I know Barb is dying for a cup of decaf. And not the kind the nurses are offering."

"Consider it done," Rose replied.

Nick wandered out of the room with Cat at his side. Dylan groggily made his way to his parents. Alex lifted her son, and he grabbed hold of her tightly. "You are tired," she observed. He rubbed his eyes and put his head on her shoulder. "Tell you what...Why don't you and Mom rest here for a bit and we'll bring you something back."

"Alex, are you sure?" Cassidy asked.

"Yeah. No offense, you look beat. Just relax. I'll take the grannies here with me."

"Grannies?" Rose asked.

"Well?" Alex replied.

"Your babysitting fee just increased," Rose said as she made her way out the door.

"Inflation," Helen said following her.

"Yeah, whatever," Alex rolled her eyes.

"You keep adding all these kids; you won't be able to afford us," Rose called back.

Cassidy laughed at the banter as Dylan cuddled up next to her. She heard Alex's reply in the distance. "Hey, I haven't added anything," Alex argued.

Cassidy heard Helen snicker. She stroked Dylan's hair and closed her eyes. "Mom?" Dylan whispered.

"Hmm?"

"Can I have a little brother?

Cassidy smiled. "Well, Dylan…I'm not sure I can promise that. What if someday you have a little sister?"

He huffed. "I guess. As long as she likes cartoons. She could be Wonder Woman or," he mumbled as he drifted off to sleep."

"I suppose, she could, Dylan. If Alex has anything to say about that; I suppose she could."

***

Alex stretched out on the bed and closed her eyes. It had been an extremely long twenty-four hours. She could hear Cassidy faintly outside the door talking with her mother about something. She laughed. "How does she do it?" she asked herself.

"How does who do what?" Cassidy asked as she opened the door.

Alex laughed harder. "That. I could hear your voice outside the door, but I couldn't make out any of the words, well except boys and baby. How do you do that? Hear things so clearly?

Cassidy shrugged. "I don't know. Never gave it much thought. Just always could."

Alex watched as Cassidy undressed and moved to replace her sweater with an oversized T-shirt. "You were great today," Alex said.

Cassidy kissed Alex's cheek and snuggled against her. "I didn't do anything, Alex," she yawned.

"Yeah, you did. You wrangled everyone out of Barb's hair for one thing."

"She was tired. It was time," Cassidy said softly.

"Jacob…I would never have imagined they would pick that name," Alex laughed.

"I like it," Cassidy offered.

"You do?"

"I considered that name for Dylan."

"Huh. He's so tiny," Alex said with a sense of wonderment.

Cassidy closed her eyes and smiled against Alex's chest. "They usually are," she joked. When Alex made no response, Cassidy lifted her head in concern. Alex had her eyes closed, but Cassidy could see the myriad of emotions play across her face. "Alex? What is it?"

"I missed Cat being born," Alex said.

"I know," Cassidy replied. Alex opened her eyes and caressed Cassidy's cheek. "What?" Cassidy asked.

Alex seemed at a loss for a moment. She took in a deep breath and kissed her wife. "Just watching you today. First with Barb, then with the boys....then...Well, holding that baby. I just..."

"I know," Cassidy whispered. She understood completely what Alex was feeling. She suspected it was quite similar to the emotions that seemed to course through her all day. They had culminated in the afternoon when she and Barb were finally able to coax Alex into holding little Jacob. Cassidy watched as Alex tenderly held the baby, studying everything about him. She had felt a powerful surge of emotion when Dylan climbed onto the chair and took up residence in Alex's lap to visit his new cousin. She closed her eyes for a second and opened them at the feel of Alex's hands brushing her hair back.

Alex started to speak softly. "Cass...I..."

Cassidy stopped Alex with a gentle kiss and pulled back slowly. "Show me," she said as her heart began to race. There were moments that Cassidy had accepted could not be put into words. She often wasn't certain that anything could convey the depth of love she felt for Alex. In those moments she craved Alex's touch. Her need to be closer, to be a part of the woman she loved, could overwhelm her. The day that they had shared would have left most people drained and exhausted. For both Alex and Cassidy, it was an event that reminded them of all they had come to cherish and all that they hoped to have in their future.

"*Tu es tellement belle* (You are so beautiful)," Alex breathed in Cassidy's ear. Cassidy simply closed her eyes and reveled in the gentle explorations of her lover. Alex held her close and trailed soft kisses along her neck, gradually increasing in ferocity as they moved over Cassidy's chest. Alex's hand drifted sensually lower, kneading and caressing until she finally reached her destination.

Cassidy moaned and directed Alex's face back to hers. "Please, Alex… " Cassidy struggled to breathe.

Alex fought to control her emotions as she felt Cassidy submit to her fully and willingly. Making love with Cassidy always astounded Alex. The world fell away when Cassidy's arms surrounded her. No one else existed in these moments, and at times, Alex selfishly wished she could disappear into this world and never return. She felt Cassidy begin to fall over the edge and pulled her closer, whispering promises of forever repeatedly. She was startled when she heard the first tears escape her wife. "Cass?" Cassidy's sob mixed with a giggle. "Did I do…"

"You are perfect," Cassidy laughed and cried at the same time.

"Why are you crying?"

"I don't know," Cassidy confessed as her tears began to subside, replaced by genuine laughter.

"What's so funny?" Alex asked.

Cassidy propped herself up and kissed Alex's lips. "I'm just happy, Alex."

Alex smiled and wiped away the last traces of Cassidy's tears. "Someday it will be us, Cass."

Cassidy sighed and placed her head on Alex's chest. "I know."

***

Tuesday, December 16th

Jonathan Krause followed the tall man down a winding hallway. His thoughts drifted to the life he had long accepted;

a life that centered on duty. His duty had always been to follow orders. It had never felt like a choice to him. It was simply the destiny he had been handed. He watched as the man leading him turned to the left and felt the blood pound forcefully through his veins. That life had been a lie. Krause was no stranger to lies. He was no innocent when it came to manufacturing secrets. He had, more than once, constructed an elaborate web of lies in order to conceal the agency's efforts. He didn't ask questions. That was not protocol. Now, he approached the room that he suspected held answers; answers he was unsure he wanted at all.

The door opened, and Krause nodded to the man holding it. "If you need anything else," the man began.

"No, thank you," Krause replied.

"There is an intercom on the wall. Just call when you are finished," the man said as he closed the door gently.

Krause retrieved a paper from his pocket and scanned it quickly with his eyes. He made his way to the drawer marked 1975. Taking a deep breath, he punched in the code on a small number pad and waited for the tell-tale click. He retrieved a small box from inside and laid it on the table at the center of the room. More slowly that he imagined possible, he lifted the cover. Two things immediately grabbed his attention, an envelope in handwriting that was as familiar as his own and a picture. He rubbed the back of his neck and closed his eyes, steadying himself before retrieving both. Krause could feel the perspiration gathering on his brow as he opened the envelope.

Alex,

If you are reading this, then I must assume that I am gone, and your father has led you here. I am certain that you have many questions. You always have questions. Some I can answer, others I am afraid it is best I leave for you to discern yourself. I suppose it is no secret to you now why I sent you to Cassidy. I couldn't risk their safety, Alex. Not my son's, and not his mother. I never expected you to fall in love with her. Perhaps, I should have.

There are many things you need to know. I know you, how honorable you are. I know Cassidy enough to realize that she is as honest as a person can be and still survive in this world. You will both be reluctant to do what I am suggesting and allow Jonathan to act as Dylan's father. It is not a disservice to me, nor do I believe will it be to my son. Jonathan has always been my best friend. I am certain you will doubt his motives after so many years following the fragments his missions left behind. He, like me, followed the orders he was given. He is a good man. I can promise you that. He may not believe that himself, but he is. He has always loved Cassidy. From the moment he saw her at Stanford; he loved her. He understands the risks that Dylan faces, both from who Dylan truly is and from the father he has always known; most of which I believe you will find in the latter. I cannot shield them anymore, Alex. I cannot protect them. You and Jonathan can.

Every few months, I am required to donate my blood; in case of some medical emergency. I'm sure you are aware of that contingency plan. Things now are strained at best within the circles that I travel. My efforts have been significantly compromised over the last few months, and I am still unsure where the damage originates. My time I fear is limited. I've asked your father to use Carecom's connections and to secure some of the blood I have donated safely, for your use. You, of course, will need to switch it with Jonathan's. That, I believe, should assist you in mitigating the O'Brien problem. Edmond will assist you when you are ready. Everything he will need is on the drive enclosed. Your father has promised me that the sample you need will be safe in an obscure Carecom facility. I have also included a map of sorts. It's taken me nearly six years to develop. It lists players, mostly through the money trail I have been able to uncover. It is widespread, Alex; an infection. They call themselves The Collaborative, but Alex, they have become more disjointed than ever. There are hidden agendas, rogue operations, and splinter factions. It's not about safeguarding anything; it's about money. You need to be cautious. These people fear very little and control more than you might dare to imagine. Jonathan has a reputation, not only for his brilliance, but for his unique abilities and relationships. They will be hesitant to act against his personal interests. They regard me as soft. They regard him as ruthless. He can help you, and I believe he will.

Whatever you think right now, Alex, I have always loved you. There is nothing that I can do to change the past or my role in it. The more you uncover, the more of that you will understand. I cannot forgive myself for walking this path blindly as long as I did. I can only look to the future; the future of my children, all of them. There's a great deal you will learn, of that I am sure. While I am tempted to divulge much of what I know; I am not certain it is my place. I've enclosed a photograph for you. Your father gave it to me some time ago. Your father, my father, and Edmond Callier. They are the only men whose help I dare seek now. Trust Jonathan. I trust him with my life, with the life of my family. I trust him with your life. You are not the unlikely allies that you may believe. Keep searching, and you will come to understand. Please, Alex, take care of Jane and the girls. They love you as much as I always have. Take care of Dylan and Cassidy. You deserve happiness. You always have. I'm sorry I can't be there to share it.

Always in my heart,

John

Jonathan Krause set down the letter and closed his eyes. A tear washed over his cheek as he lifted the phone in his pocket to his ear. He waited. "Alex?"

"Pip? Is that you?" Alex asked. She waited for the silence to break. "Pip? Are you in Stockholm?"

"Yeah."

Alex had never heard such evident emotion in Jonathan Krause's voice. Her voice softened. "Jon? What is it?"

"I'm fine, Alex," he responded. Alex could hear her partner struggling to regain his composure. "Are you in London?" he asked.

"Yeah. Just landed about twenty minutes ago. Listen...."

"Alex, just be careful. Daniels...I don't trust him."

"What about you?" Alex asked.

"I'm headed back tomorrow."

"Stateside?" she asked.

"Yeah. I have some seeds I want to plant," he said. "Have to plant them before we can water them."

"Fallon?" she asked for clarification.

"He is the soil, yes."

"All right. Pip, do me a favor?" Alex asked.

"Yeah?"

"Check in on Cass and Dylan."

"Why? You worried?" Krause asked

"You are worried about Daniels. I don't trust O'Brien."

"That makes two of us. I'll take care of it," he promised.

"Thanks. Gotta go."

"Understood," he said. Krause let out a heavy sigh as he placed the contents of the box and his cell phone back in his pocket. "You knew," he whispered aloud. "John, you knew Alex was my sister. Why the hell didn't you tell me?" He shook his head in confusion and disbelief and pressed the intercom. "All set." He retrieved the small picture from his pocket as he waited. "Jesus Christ, John. Who was going to tell us? How the hell am I supposed to tell her?"

***

Chapter Eight

Wednesday, December 17th

"Well, Sparrow. You are looking well."

"Does that surprise you somehow?" Claire Brackett asked.

Dimitri Kargen laughed. "Not at all, Sparrow. I assume you have taken care of the matters we discussed?"

"Don't I always?"

"Mm. Perhaps not always as prescribed. The money is secure?" Kargen inquired.

"Of course," she answered.

"Is that so?" another voice called. Ambassador Daniels confidently made his way into the large office. "I hope it is, Claire," he said.

"I had O'Brien replace his campaign manager with your agent. I assumed he had all the necessary information," she answered.

"Yes. He did," Daniels replied. "The funds should arrive in the Swiss account by Christmas."

"Why so long?" Kargen asked.

Daniels cocked his head and narrowed his gaze at the SVR agent. "You don't want those funds traced back to you; do you, Dimitri?" He watched as the Russian's posture stiffened considerably. "No, I shouldn't think so. Buying and selling nuclear material is not something your government needs in the press. If we want this to work, it has to leave no trace."

"I thought the point was to tie the..."

"Yes. It is. First we erase. Then we create," Daniels responded.

"What does this have to do with me?" Claire asked.

"Perhaps I just appreciate your," Daniels paused and allowed his eyes deliberately to scan the length of Claire Brackett's lithe body. "Company," he raked his eyes over her again.

Dimitri Kargen smirked slightly. "Sparrow, you certainly are well traveled," he teased her.

"Easy, Mongoose," she winked.

Daniels bristled slightly at the interaction before him. His advances toward the young Brackett were intentional. Claire's propensity for utilizing her physical attributes was legendary. "Claire, President Strickland has arranged for some diplomatic assistance to arrive in Moscow. The exact time has been kept in a very tight circle. The route not disclosed. Someone sees the need to be extremely cautious."

"And?" Claire asked with a roll of her eyes.

"And, I want you to find out when this trip is planned, who, and how," he answered.

She looked at him for a long moment and then smirked. "And how would you propose I do that, exactly Mr. Ambassador?"

"Use your charm," Dimitri offered.

"Are you suggesting I seduce the president?" Claire looked at the ambassador directly.

"Well, I know he isn't exactly Colonel John Merrow, Sparrow," Daniels chuckled. "I don't care who you seduce or how you seduce them. Just get the information. Either get it from the embassy in Moscow or get in Washington. Just. Get. It."

***

Alex waited patiently in the small café. She sipped her cappuccino and pondered the paper before her. "Looks like interesting reading," a voice roused her.

Alex looked up from the paper at the handsome man before her. MI6 agent Ian Mitchell was as imposing as he was good-looking. At 6'4, his broad shoulders, dark sunglasses, and the slight scruff of his face served to embellish his natural commanding stance. "Ian," Alex greeted.

The MI6 agent relaxed and removed his glasses to accept a seat across from Alex. "Agent Toles. What brings you to my fair city?" he asked.

"Where the sparrow flies," she began.

"Ah, yes. She left her meeting with your good ambassador about forty minutes ago. Booked a flight to Minsk for Friday," Mitchell noted the concern and question in Alex's eyes. "No worries for now. She is entertaining a guest. I suspect she and Mr. Kargen are in for the evening."

"Why Belarus?" Alex asked.

"I'm not certain, to be honest. A neutral meeting place of sorts? I have it on some authority that your president is moving some assets into Moscow."

Alex nodded. "That's what Agent Krause indicated, yes; at General Waters' behest. You think it has something to do with that?"

"Perhaps," Mitchell shrugged. "If they are moving that Cesium, well…."

Alex shook her head in frustration. "You think Daniels is pulling her strings?"

"At the moment. He's into something outside our scope. British Intelligence has been watching the ambassador closely of late, more closely than our normally collegial relationship would warrant. He's had more calls from representatives of Markov's administration than any diplomat I have ever encountered."

"We both know that the only thing diplomatic about Daniels' presence is his immunity," Alex said.

"True. We both know there are very few diplomats," Mitchell winked. "He knows something, Toles. I would lay odds it involves that Cesium we have been chasing."

"All right, stick with our friend Sparrow," she replied as she folded the paper in front of her and pushed out her chair.

"What are you planning?" Mitchell asked.

"Are you worried about me, Ian?"

"Alex," his tone changed. "Daniels is no novice."

"You let me worry about Paul Daniels. I know his weakness. Trust me. He wanted to shift our plans to dinner. Business first at the embassy, then dinner. I know exactly what his game is where I am concerned. I can handle Paul. You just follow Claire." Alex stood to leave and turned back. Mitchell had reached his feet, and Alex extended her hand. "I don't expect any issues, but if you don't hear from me....Agent Krau..."

He shook his head and offered her a smile. "I will expect your call late this evening."

Alex made no verbal response. She smiled and removed her hand from his grip, nodding her agreement as she left.

***

"Ambassador," Alex smiled at Paul Daniels.

"Alex. I thought we passed all those formalities when you visited in the spring," he said.

"I suppose so."

"So, let's get the business portion of our evening put to bed," Daniels winked. The words were not lost on Alex, and she fought to suppress a chuckle at his arrogance. "I'd much prefer catching up. You certainly have been busy since our last meeting. From investigating to negotiating," he commented.

"I suppose that's one way of looking at it," Alex admitted sarcastically.

"What is it that I can do for the head of Carecom then?" he continued as he offered her a seat on the sofa.

"Stillman and BGA," she answered.

"What about them? I know there is concern about tariffs and port restrictions, but Alex, while I can argue the administration's case here; even plead that it is not in the best economic interest for either of us...I cannot compel..."

"No, the restrictions are not an issue for Carecom, easy to navigate. What concerns me are their orders, Paul."

"I'm not sure I follow you," he asked for clarification.

"There are....inconsistencies. Inventory records don't match payments Carecom received..."

"Sounds like an accounting issue," he dismissed her.

"Perhaps," she responded. "I would still appreciate..."

Daniels smiled. "Your roots are showing," he winked. "You think Carecom was laundering. You want me to check the government orders to Stillman and BGA. See if they match the original orders placed," he surmised. "I have one question."

"That is?" Alex asked.

"Do you hope it was your father or do you hope it originated here?"

Alex pursed her lips and then smiled. "I just want it rectified, Ambassador. I want Carecom in the clear. That's my job."

"Of course, it is," his statement dripped with insincerity. "I'll see what I can do. I'll need some information."

"I've already had the documents sent to your attention," she assured him.

"Why doesn't that surprise me? Long trip for a five-minute conversation," he observed.

"A good excuse to visit," she winked. "I have other business in the area."

"Then I am glad you found a reason to fit me into your schedule. Now, what about dinner? I took the liberty of making a reservation at your hotel for seven-thirty," the ambassador said.

"That's not for another hour," Alex said with the raise of her brow.

"I expected your needs might take a little longer. How about a drink beforehand?" he suggested. Alex just smiled. "Wine, was it?"

"That's Cassidy's drink," she replied evenly.

"Yes, I recall that now. I prefer a good scotch. Interested?" he raised his brow.

Alex tipped her head in acknowledgement. She accepted the first drink and sipped it generously. She pretended to listen with great interest as the ambassador continued offering what she could only describe as scantily veiled sexual innuendo at every turn. This was a scenario that she had grown accustomed to over the years. It was part of being a woman in a business dominated by egotistical men; men who were used to getting their way in every conceivable way. Inwardly, she gloated. She understood the power of seduction; the allure of conquest. In fact, she'd mounted more than a few conquests of her own throughout the years. For Alex, affairs of the heart and the bedroom had always been purely for personal satisfaction. That reality had proved her ace in the hole many times during investigations. She could play the game as long and as convincingly as any man who cared to engage her, and she could end it so abruptly as to leave the most polished silver tongue stunned into silence.

Paul Daniels sat on the arm of a chair, sipping his third glass of scotch, making little effort to conceal his intentions as he leered at Alex. Alex sipped her drink slowly and watched him carefully. "We probably should be getting to that dinner," she suggested, deliberately holding the ambassadors gaze as she stood.

He pulled her toward him and she raised her brow. "No rush. I'm sure you have many interesting stories."

Alex leaned into his ear and took a moment to scan the top of his desk more closely. "Which stories interest you, Ambassador? You mean my time in the military? No..." Alex took a step back and opened her eyes wider.

"We have a great deal in common, Alex. We both know it," he said, lifting his scotch to his lips before placing it on the side of his desk. Daniels pulled Alex closer, and she allowed it for a moment, focusing on one area of the desk behind him intently. "You and I have similar needs, similar interests," he said cockily.

Alex rolled her eyes over his shoulder and retrieved the scotch carefully. She gently pressed him away and smiled. Seeing her expression, Daniels grew bolder and reached out greedily with his hand. Alex took the opportunity to place the scotch in it and deliberately closed the ambassador's fingers around the glass. She placed her lips closely to his ear and whispered her reply. "I suppose we do…have much in common, Paul." She pulled back and lifted the hand he held his scotch in toward his lips. "We both enjoy a good scotch. We both know the other is not exactly who they claim to be. And, as I recall from my last visit, you were quite interested in my wife." She patted his cheek and took another deliberate step back. "Since she is not here, I guess we will both just have to settle for dinner." Alex turned gradually on her heels and headed toward the door. "Finish your scotch, Paul. We'd better get something to fill you up. You look a bit pale."

***

Friday, December 19th

Cassidy opened the front door and felt a breeze blow by her. "Hi, Aunt Cassidy," Cat managed as he flew past her toward the sound of Dylan's voice up the stairs.

Cassidy shook her head and laughed. "Glad you could make it, Cat," she mumbled. "Dylan's upstairs," she called to him playfully.

"I know!" he called back.

"Sorry about that," Nick said.

Cassidy led him through the door. "Nothing to be sorry for," she said.

"Are you sure it's okay? I mean, Cat spending a couple of nights?" Nick asked.

"Of course," Cassidy said in confusion. "Why wouldn't it be okay?"

"I don't know," he said, moving to place Cat's backpack near the stair. "I know Alex has been away and..."

"It's more than okay," Cassidy assured him. "Alex will be home tomorrow afternoon."

"That's what I mean. I know she's been traveling and she..."

"Come on, let me get you a coffee," Cassidy offered. "She has been away more than I would like. I admit it," Cassidy said as she moved about the kitchen, readying the coffee pot. "But, it's not forever. Barb needs the break. Helen needs to go home. We'll bring him back after dinner on Sunday. Don't worry about us."

"She's moving the offices; I heard," Nick said as Cassidy placed a cup of coffee in front of him.

Cassidy nodded and took a seat beside her brother-in-law. "Yeah. Seems to be her focus this coming week," she explained. "Good thing my mother and your mother love to shop or I would have had to take care of Santa's list all by myself," Cassidy joked.

"How are you doing?" Nick asked softly.

"Me?" Cassidy asked. Nick nodded. Cassidy let out a small sigh. "I'm fine, Nick. Honestly. It's been a rough few months dealing with the custody and Alex being away so much. I won't deny that. But, that will all pass. I'll be glad when it does," she admitted.

"You know, I can swing down Sunday, so you and Alex don't...."

"No. No. Don't fool yourself. She'll be chomping at the bit to see that baby. We'll bring Cat home."

"Well, then at least come for dinner," he said.

"Nick, the whole point of this is to give you two some quiet time," Cassidy reminded him.

"It's just dinner," he said.

"All right. We'll pick pizza up on the way. Deal?" Cassidy suggested.

"Cassidy?"

"Yeah?"

"Thanks. For everything, I mean," Nick said sincerely.

Cassidy patted his hand and smiled. "Oh, don't thank me too soon," she said as she narrowed her gaze playfully. "You'll get to return the favor at some point."

Nick laughed. "Looking forward to *that,*" he said. Cassidy raised her brow in question. "She nearly passed out seeing Barb in labor. Big, tough FBI agent," he mocked his sister. "Imagine if that was you? We'll need a stretcher at the ready for sure." Cassidy laughed at Nick's assessment. "I should go," Nick said. "Barb and Jake were both sleeping when I left. That won't last long," he chuckled.

Cassidy led her brother-in-law to the doorway. He called out his goodbye to the boys and turned back to her. "Thanks, Cassidy."

Cassidy rubbed his back gently. "Stop thanking me. I will see you Sunday." She started opening the door for Nick and found herself staring up into a pair of steel blue eyes. "Pip?"

"I promised I would come see the tree," he said. Cassidy was stunned.

"I gotta get going," Nick broke through the momentary silence.

"Oh, sorry...Alex tells me congratulations are in order," Krause said.

"Yeah. Thanks," Nick responded sincerely. "Thanks again, Cass." Cassidy just nodded.

"Bad time?" Krause asked.

Cassidy shook her head and gestured for him to come inside. "What's with the bags?" she asked.

Krause held up the two shopping bags in his hands. "These?" Cassidy raised her brow. "Oh...well, you can't have a tree without presents under it," Krause explained. "It's against the law."

Cassidy rolled her eyes and laughed. "Did you find that in the *Toles Code*?"

The comment startled Krause. "What?" he asked. Cassidy pointed to the Christmas tree in the corner of the room which was already brimming with brightly colored boxes.

"Oh," he muttered.

"All right Santa Krause; what gives?" Cassidy asked.

"What do you mean? You made me promise to come see the tree."

"Mm-hm. I suppose I did. So, then Alex didn't ask you to check in on us while she was away?" Cassidy asked suspiciously.

"No....I just..."

"What is it with you two anyway?" she joked. "Just admit you like each other and be done with it," she laughed. She looked at her friend and noted an unfamiliar expression. "Pip?" Krause looked to Cassidy and sighed. "What's going on? Alex..."

"Alex is fine," he said. "Cassidy," he stopped himself and offered her a shrug and a smile.

Cassidy shook her head. "Come on, I'll get you some coffee before those boys come down and torment you."

"I hope it's okay. She just worries, Cassie. I wanted to stop and drop off the presents anyway."

"I know she does, and of course it's okay. You don't need an invitation or an excuse. That's how family works," Cassidy said.

Jonathan Krause sat at the counter and watched his friend putter around the kitchen and place a cup of coffee in front of him before taking her seat. He gazed at her affectionately and realized that as much as he loved her, she had first and foremost been a friend he could trust. There were so few of those in the life he had chosen. "Cassie?"

"Yeah?"

Krause took a deep breath. "It's up to you. You and Alex." He handed her the letter he had retrieved in Stockholm. "I think maybe you should give it to her. Whatever you decide... even if you decide not to...well, I will always make sure Dylan is safe. I promise you."

Cassidy tugged gently at her bottom lip and nodded. Her lips gradually turned up into a genuine smile, and she covered his hand with her own. "He's a lucky kid," she said.

"Yeah, he is," Krause agreed looking at her. Cassidy understood. She could never deny that Jonathan Krause loved her. It was evident in every glance and every interaction. He stood in stark contrast to her ex-husband; he respected her. And, as she sat looking at him, she was reminded that she loved him too, albeit differently than he would have liked. Krause held her gaze for a moment and squeezed her hand. "He couldn't do any better than you and Alex," he said with more sincerity than Cassidy could immediately fathom.

Cassidy patted her friend's cheek and winked at him. "Don't sell yourself short, Pip," she said. "Stay for dinner?" she asked hopefully. Krause gave her an uncomfortable grin. "Get used to it," Cassidy laughed. "It comes with the package. Helen would disown me if I didn't feed you."

Krause continued to watch Cassidy and enjoy the effortless nature of their discussion until the boisterous entrance of two small boys interrupted them. "Uncle Pip!" Dylan squealed.

Cassidy laughed. "Slow it down, Dylan," she cautioned.

"You know what?" Dylan asked his Uncle Pip. Krause shook his head and pulled Dylan into his lap. "Cat got a brother."

"I heard that. That's exciting Cat," Krause said.

"Nah…all he does is poop," Cat shrugged. Cassidy had to turn away to keep herself from launching into a fit of laughter.

"It's still cool," Dylan said.

"I guess," Cat answered with a noncommittal shrug. Krause couldn't help but laugh. He remembered his younger brothers being born and how his initial excitement quickly turned to annoyance; annoyance that lasted on and off for the rest of his life. "That's just the way brothers are," he thought silently.

"Well, I think it's cool," Dylan said. "I asked Santa for one."

Cassidy spun around with her jaw slack. "You asked Santa for what?"

"A brother," Dylan said.

Krause looked at Cassidy with wide eyes. Seeing his friend uncharacteristically fumble, he intervened. "That's not exactly something Santa makes in his workshop, Dylan," Krause explained.

Dylan shrugged. "Alex says Santa is magic."

Cassidy shook her head in disbelief. "All right. On that note," she changed the course of the conversation. "You two need to go pick up Dylan's room before dinner."

"You staying, Uncle Pip?"

"If that's okay with you," he said.

"Yep. Come on, Cat," Dylan directed as he hopped off of his Uncle Pip's lap.

Cassidy continued shaking her head absently as she watched the two friends run off. "You know, he is magic," Krause said.

"Mm-hm," was Cassidy's only response.

"Never know what Santa might deliver, Cassie. He's surprised me a few times," he joked.

"I don't think Santa owns the sperm bank," she quipped.

Krause laughed. "Might have an 'in' though."

Cassidy threw a towel that had been laying on the counter at her friend. "You are worse than Alex," she laughed. "Do me a favor and go make sure those two are actually cleaning that room."

Domesticity was not Krause's strong suit, but he enjoyed spending time at Alex and Cassidy's. Both his parents had been gone for years. It didn't take long after his mother's sudden death four years before, for the rest of the family to grow farther apart. He had a nephew and a niece, but he rarely saw them. His father had been rigid, but his mother was warm, and he held fond memories of his childhood. Dylan seemed to rekindle that. He gladly obliged his friend's request.

Cassidy set about her tasks and paused to put her face in her hands momentarily. She felt for the chain around her neck and smiled. "Santa Claus, huh?" she giggled.

***

Monday, December 22nd

"Happy to be back, Ms. Toles?" Marta greeted her boss.

"Marta, for the love of God! Alex. Just call me Alex."

"Whatever you want. So, the big move starts today?" she asked.

"Yes, it does. You know, you don't have to make such a big move. I can certainly find a comparable spot for you here," Alex offered.

"No. Change is good. I worked for your father for the last fifteen years. He'd never forgive me if I left you high and dry. You were the apple of his eye, you know."

"No, I didn't," Alex tried to smile at the woman's earnest compliment. "He was fortunate to have you," Alex said honestly.

"I'm not sure he always felt that way, but thank you," Marta said.

"I know exactly what you mean," Alex mumbled as she entered her office. Alex sat down at her desk and began booting up the computer. She looked at the pictures carefully placed just inches away and then at a small, carefully wrapped box nearby. A gradual smile played across her lips as she thought about her family's first Christmas together. She closed her eyes attempting to imagine Dylan on Christmas morning.

"You look cheerful," she heard in the distance. Alex opened her eyes and was startled by the presence of her mother in the doorway. "Good thing you are inside and it's December, or you would be catching flies," Helen laughed.

"What are you doing here?" Alex asked.

"Happy Holidays to you too, Alexis."

"I'm sorry. I just didn't expect to see you," Alex explained.

"Well, I wanted to check up on my investments," Helen joked. Alex shook her head at her mother's playful nature. It was true, technically Helen Toles now owned fifty-one percent of Carecom. She had never displayed any interest in the actual workings of the company. Alex was more than aware that the only investments her mother truly had an interest in regarded family.

"Did Cassidy send you to make certain I finished my Christmas shopping?" Alex asked.

"No. She doesn't need my help keeping you in line, Alexis. I, however, am eternally grateful for her." Helen's reply was cheerful in its delivery, but Alex immediately sensed the underlying sincerity of the statement and she couldn't help but smile. "Actually, I was hoping I could convince you to have lunch with me."

"Mom, it's nine in the morning."

"Thank you. I have been able to tell time since before what they call the digital era. I meant later."

Alex laughed. "You really are spending too much time with Rose. I don't ever remember you having a sense of humor," Alex said as seriously as she could manage. Helen just smiled at her daughter and awaited a response to the invitation. "Why do I think there is an ulterior motive in this lunch?"

"Alexis, not everything is a case to solve," Helen sighed.

"What time were you thinking?"

"One-ish? I have a doctor's appointment this morning," her mother replied.

Alex's expression grew pensive. "Is everything all right?"

"I'm fine. Routine. How about Fazzini's? I have a few errands to run this afternoon in that area. I want to get them all put to rest so that I can leave for Nick's early tomorrow," her mother explained.

"That should work. I have a meeting at noon, so if I am a little..."

"I will get us a table," Helen said.

"All right. Mom?" Alex asked. "Everything is all right, isn't it?"

Helen walked to her daughter and looked at her lovingly. Alex's eyes glistened slightly, and Helen smiled. It had taken time for the two to reach this point in their relationship. Trust had to be rebuilt, and Alex did not trust easily. Helen was not certain what Alex had learned about her father since agreeing to take his place at Carecom. It was clear that her husband's actions toward Alex and Cassidy's relationship had wounded her daughter deeply. It remained a subject she did not approach with Alex. Looking into her daughter's eyes now she witnessed the naked fears of a little girl she once comforted after a nightmare. No matter what had come to pass, it was evident that Alex still felt the loss of her father profoundly and Helen could see the question in her daughter's eyes.

"I'm all right, Alexis. It's just a physical. I promise," she reassured her daughter. Alex just nodded. "We've just been spending so much time together. Well, to be honest, I would have loved to spend Christmas Eve with you and Cassidy. I've spent so many with your brother." Alex's surprise was evident. "But, Barb could use my help this year," she winked. "So? Lunch?" Helen asked. Alex nodded again. "Good. I will see you at one."

***

"Director Taylor?" Brian Fallon called through the door.

"Agent Fallon," Michael Taylor answered. "Happy Holidays to you," the NSA Director said cheerfully. "I didn't expect to see you in here this week."

Fallon nodded. "I hadn't planned on it. Something's come up. I didn't want to hold it until after the holidays."

Taylor rose and shut the door quietly. "All right."

Fallon placed a large manila envelope on the NSA Director's desk and watched as Michael Taylor slid the contents out and examined them. Fallon waited patiently, watching as his superior's face became tauter. Taylor set the contents down, placed his hands deliberately on them, and slowly leveled his gaze at the agent before him.

"I can't say for certain what it means," Fallon said. "It could definitely explain Christopher O'Brien's convenient accident."

"Maybe," Taylor conceded. "Skimming money off of a campaign is not really NSA material. Why not take this to the FBI?" Taylor asked with the quirk of his brow.

"Assistant Director Tate shut down any formal investigation into O'Brien's accident last April," Fallon reminded his boss.

"Yes. But, this is a federal crime; if it's true."

"I understand that," Fallon said. "You don't seriously think it's unrelated? It's not thousands of dollars…it's…."

"I can see what it appears to be, Agent Fallon. Why do you think the FBI refused to pursue that investigation?" Taylor asked.

"I can't say that, Sir. There were many inconsistencies as you know," Fallon responded.

"I am aware."

Fallon pointed to the documents on the desk. "Sir, if Assistant Director Tate had decided to pursue the investigation he would have had to involve the Attorney General. We both know that politics effect the decision-making process at the bureau more than they do here," he said.

"That they do," Taylor agreed. "So, what is it that you want, Agent Fallon?"

"A closer ear to the congressman," Fallon replied.

"You know that the NSA carefully watches transcripts from all campaigns," Taylor answered.

"I do. But those are limited to key phrases. As they are for candidates," Fallon reminded him.

Taylor took a deep breath and let it out slowly, considering the request. "Has Alex seen this?"

"No." Fallon watched the doubtful expression cross Taylor's face. "Director Taylor, I came to you first. If Alex saw this now…

well, let's say O'Brien can fire her up like nothing I have ever seen."

Taylor laughed at the observation. "All right. It will take a few days. Believe it or not I have channels I need to navigate as well."

"I know," Fallon said.

"Give me until Monday," the director offered. Fallon started to speak, and Taylor stopped him. "Don't thank me. This is your op, Fallon. Yours and yours alone."

"I understand," Fallon replied.

"Good. Have a nice holiday, agent," Taylor said with a smile.

"I will. You as well."

Michael Taylor watched as Fallon took his leave. He ran his hand over the top of his head in frustration. Returning his focus to the papers on his desk, he glanced over them again before crumpling one is his hands and tossing it violently across his office. "Shit." Shaking his head, the director picked up his phone, punched in several numbers and waited. His voice dropped an octave as he spoke. "We have a situation."

***

Claire Brackett stretched her long frame across the king size bed and closed her eyes. Belarus was not exactly her first choice for holiday vacations, but if she had to be here, she intended to make the most of every moment. She turned over and moaned slightly at the strength in the hands now kneading her tired muscles. "What makes you think anyone from the ambassador's staff is going to tell you anything?" a deep voice questioned.

"Oh, I have my ways," she replied.

"I'm sure that you do, Claire," he said. "I've heard you can be very charming," he chuckled wryly. "Not that I have ever seen any evidence of that."

"You find me perfectly charming," she replied.

Agent Marcus Anderson smacked his partner's bottom and laughed. "There is a difference between being charming and being salacious," he reminded her.

"Are you implying that I am a slut?" she asked. There was no malice in her tone. It was tinged with a hint of both curiosity and amusement.

"No, but I think you need to broaden your methods of *influence*," Anderson said.

"Agent Anderson, if you wanted to be Captain of the Morality Squad, I am afraid you picked the wrong agency."

"It has nothing to do with morality. It's about practicality," he explained. Brackett rolled over and opened one eye, squinting to bring her partner into focus. "You need more than one weapon in your arsenal," he told her.

She pursed her lips. "I'll get the information with whatever weapon I need to deploy," Claire said. "Some are less....well, let's say I prefer less clean up. Don't fool yourself, Marcus. I have a few techniques you have not seen."

"I'm sure," he said with a smirk.

"Are you complaining? You should be grateful. You get to listen." Her lips turned up slightly into a cocky grin. "I suppose either way there will be screaming," she said, licking her lips as her smile widened. Claire sighed and closed her eyes in contentment. Anderson shook his head. "Oh, Marcus. Why don't you keep me company? Don't tell me you aren't curious?" she baited him.

"I'm very curious, Claire."

"I'm sure," she said softly without any movement.

"Just get the information," he said. "I'll be next door.... waiting."

***

Alex walked into Fazzini's Restaurant fifteen minutes late and looking slightly frazzled. "Sorry, Mom," she said.

"Are you okay?" Helen asked in concern.

"Huh? Oh yeah. Just trying to get things squared away with moving the office. I wish that's all I had to deal with this week."

Helen studied Alex intently. "Alexis?"

"Hmm?"

"Are you happy working at Carecom?" Helen asked pointedly.

Alex looked up from the menu in front her with a puzzled expression. "What do you mean?"

Helen took a sip from her water. "I mean, are you happy there?"

"I'll be happier when the office is moved. Is that why you wanted to have lunch? Are you concerned about me running Carecom?" Alex asked.

"No. I wanted to have lunch with my daughter; who arrived looking a great deal more stressed than she was this morning," Helen responded firmly.

Alex released a heavy sigh. "I'm not unhappy there. It's been a big transition."

"I'm sure it has," Helen agreed. Alex narrowed her gaze as her mother opened the menu before her.

"Mom? Seriously; what is it?"

"Let's order lunch first, Alexis." The two women sat quietly, both pretending to peruse a menu of items they could have easily recited from memory until the waiter arrived to take their orders. They continued their silent companionship until he was far from sight.

"Alexis, don't let your father's life become yours."

"What is that supposed to mean?" Alex asked somewhat defensively.

"It means that a great deal of what you saw in your father came from running that company for so many years. It changed him. That's what it means. You have a beautiful family. I just...."

Alex closed her eyes and nodded. Cassidy often pressed Alex to be more open with her mother. For a while, Alex resisted, afraid of being rejected again. She opened her eyes and looked at the older woman. Her mother had changed dramatically over the last year. It started in earnest the day that Alex walked into her parents' home and confronted her father about his dealings with Christopher O'Brien. There were still moments that Alex still felt her world reeling from the memory of that day. How could a father knowingly do anything to hurt his own child; worse something that would hurt Cassidy or Dylan? Giving Cassidy's ex-husband ammunition about Alex's personal relationships for the press was something that Alex could not easily forgive. She could not fathom any parent betraying the trust of a child. Alex shuddered slightly at the memory of her father working with Christopher O'Brien at all. Two fathers who had seemingly dismissed all care for their children; for her son. It sickened her as a daughter and even more so as a parent.

There was one evolution from that day that Alex had become grateful for. That was a renewed relationship with her mother. It was not a storybook reunion in which Alex forgave every transgression and confided her deepest fears to the mother she had missed. It was more akin to strengthening a bridge that had buckled to the point of total failure. It was strengthened piece by piece and tested one step, one weight at a time. Now, as Alex looked at her mother, she felt the last remaining vestiges of doubt fade. Helen Toles loved her. She loved Alex's family. It was worry that creased the older woman's brow at this moment. It was the protectiveness of a parent that sat in the driver's seat of this conversation. That was an emotion Alex had come to understand all too well.

Alex smiled at her mother and reached for her hand. "I'm not Dad."

"I know that, but whether you like it or not....well, you are very much like him in some ways," Helen reminded her. She could see Alex mounting her protest, and she squeezed her daughter's hand. "Alexis, you need the challenge, any challenge. That's what I mean. It can consume you...and then..."

For the first time in her life, Alex noticed a distant pain evident in her mother's eyes. She suspected the older woman had held it at bay deliberately for many years. Alex squeezed her mother's hand gently in understanding. "If I ever start to feel that my job, no matter what it is, compromises my family....I promise you that will be the end of it. Nothing means more to me than my family."

Helen smiled. "I know how much you love them..."

"In case you forgot, you are part of *them*," Alex reminded her.

"I know," Helen smiled. "But it is nice to hear you say that."

Helen got up from her seat and went to hug her daughter. The public affection startled Alex momentarily. It was another change that Alex was still adjusting to. The once reserved matriarch of the Toles family had become far more demonstrative since the death of Alex's father. Alex surprised herself by welcoming her mother's embrace enthusiastically. She watched as Helen pulled back slightly and reached for the chain that hung around Alex's neck. Alex had not removed it since her wedding day. It was the second most precious gift she had ever received. The first was Cassidy's love and commitment, the other a promise from their son, her son. Dylan made a vow to them both, embodied in a simple heart adorned by two stones. One stone; a diamond represented Dylan's birth, and a sapphire represented Cassidy's. She watched her mother finger the delicate charm and recalled Dylan's words. *This is for you, Alex. This is the half of my heart I give to Mom, so you can always keep us close.* Alex noticed her mother studying the charm carefully.

"Mom? What is it?"

"Alex, this is loose," Helen said.

"What are you talking about?" Alex asked in confusion.

"This stone on the pendant Dylan gave you," she pointed to the diamond. "It's loose." Alex moved to grab hold of it, and

Helen stopped her. Her daughter's eyes were quickly filling with tears. "Alexis," she soothed. "It's all right. Don't play with it. It will make it worse."

"I can't lose it. Dylan...:"

"Here," Helen said as she moved behind Alex. "Let me unfasten it."

"But..."

"Alexis....I will take it to Marv this afternoon. He'll fix it as good as new."

Alex nodded sadly. "I haven't taken it off since...:

Helen's eyes danced as she watched her daughter close her eyes to still her emotions. No matter how close they had become, Helen continued to marvel at Alex's devotion to Cassidy and Dylan. "I'll bet he can have it done before I leave. I'll drop it off with Cassidy on my way to Nick's. Okay?"

Alex just nodded. When she finally looked back at her mother, she noted that a smile had replaced the lines of concern from a few moments ago. "You look like you are relieved about something," Alex noted.

"I am."

"What?" Alex asked.

"Well, let's just say that I believe you. The look on your face when I unfastened this," Helen reached out and touched her daughter's cheek. "I just want you to be happy. Your father never felt he could make that choice for some reason. Even when I knew he wanted to. He wouldn't leave the company, not even...."

"I'm sorry, Mom."

Helen sighed. "No, I'm sorry. I should have said that a long time ago."

"You don't owe me..."

"I do," Helen said as she reclaimed her seat. "Don't feel sorry for me. I do miss him," she said softly. "But, you and Nicky have given me more than you know; wonderful grandchildren and two remarkable daughters I never expected." Before Alex could respond the waiter returned with their food. Helen saw the silent tear traveling down her daughter's cheek and smiled proudly. "Now eat your lunch," she ordered.

Alex quirked a slight grin and toyed with the pasta on her plate. She kept watch on her fork intently. "I love you, Mom," she barely whispered.

Helen closed her eyes to suppress her tears. "I love you too, Alex." Alex's head jerked up at the use of her preferred name. Helen felt her gaze but remained focused on her salad. "Eat that before it gets cold," she said.

***

Chapter Nine

Tuesday, December 23rd

Joshua Tate walked into the small observation room and peered through the mirrored glass at the fidgety blonde woman on the other side. "When did she get here?" he asked.

"About fifteen minutes ago. She's very agitated."

Tate stroked his hand over his chin repeatedly. "Who knows?"

"I'm sorry?" the agent in the room questioned the assistant FBI director.

"Who else knows she's here?" Tate asked forcefully.

"Myself, Agent Briggs and Agent Stuart at the desk," he replied. "She asked for…"

"I know who she wanted to see. That's not an option. Is Agent Fallon here?" Tate asked.

"I'm not certain. Sir, this isn't his division….he…"

"I think I know who is assigned where, Agent Rolands. Find out. If he's not, call him in."

"Sir?"

Tate turned briskly. "It's not a request, agent. Get Briggs to bring her something to drink and sit with her and send Stuart to me," Tate directed.

The young FBI agent began making his way from the room. He had never seen his boss issue such succinct and firm demands. He couldn't imagine what the attractive woman in the other room could possibly have spurred in his mentor that would evoke such a pointed response. Tate waited until the door closed and made his way to the phone that sat on a small table. "You won't believe who just walked in," he said.

***

"Eleana," Claire Brackett extended her hand.

"Claire," the woman accepted the hand before her, taking a moment to stroke it gently. "It's been a long time."

"Too long?" Claire asked.

"Perhaps," the woman answered softly.

Eleana Baros stood exactly even with Claire Brackett. She remained one of the few people in the world that Claire Brackett respected. Claire enjoyed what she had always perceived as the equality between them in every way. That included the reaction that they often sparked in others. Claire had few occasions to travel in Eleana's company in recent years. Regardless of how much time passed, their mutual presence always solicited interest and attention. It was an appealing benefit to their friendship for the young Claire Brackett. They were opposites that somehow suited one another almost perfectly.

To describe either woman as attractive would have been an understatement. Eleana was an elegant beauty. Claire looked a great deal like a runway model; fair skinned, enviable red hair, tall, and slender with legs that seemed to go on forever. Eleana was athletic; blessed with undeniably feminine curves and olive skin. Her hazel eyes complimented dark hair that often reflected subtle hints of red and gold. Eleana was brilliant, clever, and intuitive; just like Claire; all qualities that the young Brackett admired. The two had known each other since childhood, attended private school together, and created a fair amount of chaos for their parents over the years.

Claire had always been adventurous with an insatiable desire to experience everything in life. She possessed a competitiveness that sometimes drove her to act impulsively. It was something that Eleana had always found both intriguing and disconcerting about her friend. Eleana, on the other hand, carried herself with a quiet confidence. Where Claire's demeanor radiated a blatant cockiness; Eleana's stride did not exude arrogance, but rather assuredness. Claire strived to impress everyone. Eleana cared little how others perceived her, preferring to work with others rather than compete with them. In school, Claire was determined to best everyone whether on the basketball court or the debate team. Eleana was content to guide. And yet, somehow they seemed to accept each other without any judgment.

"What brings you to Minsk?" Eleana asked.

"I could ask you the same thing."

"Yes, but I live here," Eleana winked.

"I was in the neighborhood," Claire said.

"And whose neighborhood would that be?" Eleana inquired.

"Does it matter?"

"That depends," the tall brunette said.

"On?"

"On whether you wanted to see me for personal reasons or professional ones," Eleana said honestly.

Brackett stopped their movement and leaned heavily into her friend. "Eleana, it is always personal when I see you."

Eleana raised her brow. "Well, I guess I won't have to be so careful about my pillow talk then."

Brackett smiled. "You'll give it all up long before anyone's head hits the pillow," she promised.

"Oh, Claire. I do miss you," Eleana admitted as they entered the doors of Claire's hotel.

***

"Mom!!"

"Dylan, where is the fire?" Cassidy laughed as she entered the living room. She looked at the display in front of her and felt her heart swell. Dylan had a large roll of wrapping paper sprawled across the floor. There was some strangely shaped object covered in bright Santa Claus paper sitting in a heap, adorned by wads of tape in the middle of the room. Another smaller object poked out through a colorful lump that sat nearby. She bit the inside of her cheek gently to prevent her laughter from surfacing. It was a sight that she knew she would always remember. "What's going on here?" she asked gently.

Dylan huffed in frustration. "They don't look like yours," he moaned.

"Mm." Cassidy sat down on the floor beside her son. "Would you like me to help you?" Dylan nodded a bit sadly. "Dylan, it took me a very long time to learn how to wrap presents like that," she said, gesturing to the Christmas tree in the corner of the room. He just shrugged. She studied him for a moment. His pout was adorable. She felt a sense of pride at the determination she witnessed in his eyes. Cassidy pointed to the smaller object first. "Do you want to start with that one?" Dylan sighed. "What's wrong, sweetheart?"

"That one's for you and Alex," he mumbled in disappointment.

"Oh," Cassidy replied. "I understand. How about this?" He looked to her hopefully. "YaYa will be here in a little while. I will just bet she would love to help you with that one."

"Really?" he asked. Cassidy rubbed his back and smiled at him. "Okay."

"So, what about this one here?" she looked at the awkward object. "Who is this one for?" Cassidy asked curiously. Dylan blushed slightly and shrugged again. "Dylan?"

"You'll laugh at me."

Cassidy jostled herself around and faced her son. "Dylan, I would never laugh *at* you. Only when you are trying to be silly."

"It's for my brother," he whispered.

Cassidy nodded. She pulled him into her lap and kissed his head. "Oh, Dylan. Santa can't really bring you a little brother; you know that?"

"I know. Not like on Christmas. I have to wait like Cat did." Cassidy listened carefully to her son as he explained his seven-year-old logic. "But, he should still have a Christmas present. I forgot to ask Santa to bring him something," Dylan said a bit sadly.

"Dylan…Santa doesn't actually bring babies."

"I know, but he's magic," he reminded his mother. Cassidy sighed. "And, I heard you."

"Heard me?" she questioned.

"Yeah," he looked up to his mother. "You told YaYa if you could ask Santa for anything it would be a baby."

A new understanding swept over Cassidy. "You heard that, huh?" Dylan nodded. "Well, that's true, Dylan."

"Did you write him a letter?" he asked. Cassidy's eyes twinkled as she shook her head. "You should," he told her.

"I should, huh?"

"Yep. And then, if you get your present, he won't feel left out." Cassidy raised her brow in question. "He has to have a present too. I mean if he's our present."

Cassidy nodded. Part of her was tempted to sit her son down and try and explain why Santa couldn't bequeath them with a baby, but the sincerity and the wonderment in Dylan's expression stopped her. She was reasonably sure that Dylan understood Santa would not fly in with an actual baby. Ever since his cousin was born, Dylan had been adamant that he wanted a little brother. Alex and Cassidy had both explained that babies take time and that someday they were sure he would have a sibling, but they couldn't promise when, and they certainly couldn't promise a brother. Dylan was seven. He saw the world through innocent eyes, and Cassidy had no intention of breaking that spell today.

"Dylan, you know it could be quite a while before you have a brother or a sister," she said softly.

"Yeah. It takes time. He still should have a present, though," Dylan said decidedly. "I don't want him to be left out," he explained.

"Always a him," she chuckled. Dylan shrugged again. "So, can I see what you have here for this magical baby?" Cassidy asked.

Dylan opened up the paper to reveal the Lego Batcave he had spent hours upon hours building by himself. Alex had been worried that Dylan's frustration would get the better of him when he announced he wanted to complete the project on his own. There were many nights that Cassidy would catch Alex watching him as he struggled to follow the diagram. It took him weeks, but he finished. Cassidy still remembered how he stood so proudly in front of his creation. He had covered it in a blanket and revealed it as if it were an engineering wonder. And, for Dylan, it was.

"Dylan, that's your Batcave," Cassidy said in amazement.

"I know."

"You worked so hard on that," Cassidy observed.

"Yeah."

"You want to give that away?" she questioned him carefully.

Dylan nodded. "That's what I am supposed to do," he said. "I am supposed to protect him. I mean, Alex is Nick's protector. He said so."

Cassidy kissed her son's head. "So, this will protect him, huh?"

"Sure," Dylan said. "It protected me from bad dreams and stuff."

"I didn't know that," Cassidy said holding Dylan to her. "Don't you want to keep it then?"

Dylan shook his head. "I'm seven. Besides, I still have Batman over my bed if I have a bad dream…and anyway," he continued his explanation thoughtfully. "I'm not a baby. I can walk into your room. Babies can't do that," he explained.

Cassidy looked at him thoughtfully. He had clearly given this a great deal of thought, and she found his reasoning and his sentiment unbelievably touching. "I suppose that is all very true," she agreed. She kissed his forehead and put her hands on his small shoulders. "All right, Dylan. I think I have a box in the garage we can use. Then we will wrap your present." Dylan smiled broadly and bounced a bit on his mother's lap. "Someone is going to be very lucky someday to have you be their big brother," she complimented him.

He basked in her praise and hugged her tightly. "I'll help you write to Santa," he whispered in her ear. "I'm really good at that."

Cassidy chuckled softly. "Okay. Let's get this done," she said as she hopped to her feet.

"And then we can write your letter?" he called after her.

She winked at him. "And then you can help me write a letter," she promised. Cassidy turned back and watched as Dylan ran his hands over his creation proudly. She was certain that Alex would be amazed by his gesture, and Cassidy wished that her wife had been there to hear her conversation with their son. "I can't wait to see Alex's face," she laughed.

***

Brian Fallon walked into the conference room and pulled out a chair. He set his coffee in front of him and smiled at the woman across the table. "How are you doing?" he asked.

The woman looked up to him and shook her head. "I wanted to see Agent Toles."

"Agent Toles hasn't been with the bureau in months. You know that," he said. She shook her head. "If you wanted to speak with Alex, why didn't you just go see her? You've done that before; haven't you?" he asked. She did not answer. "Cheryl? Look, I don't know what has happened. I certainly know you did not show up here without a reason. You know Alex is no longer an agent, and yet you still came here. I want to help you, but..."

Cheryl Stephens looked up at him, skepticism mingling with hope. "Who is listening?" she asked. Fallon looked at the mirror and nodded. "I do watch television," she said.

Fallon chuckled softly at her feeble attempt to make light of the situation. He sipped his coffee. "The only person listening is my boss." He gestured to the window.

"Do you trust him?" she asked.

Fallon looked back at the far wall knowing Joshua Tate was listening to every word and watching every expression that crossed both their faces. He considered his reply for a moment. Did he trust Joshua Tate? He scratched his cheek in consideration, nodded and answered truthfully. "Yes, Cheryl. I do."

Joshua Tate watched and listened with rapt fascination as the woman looked toward him. He had a decision to make, and he made it quickly. In less than a minute, the door to the conference room had opened, and Joshua Tate walked through. "Not here," he said in Fallon's ear.

Fallon looked up to the assistant director and nodded. He turned back to Cheryl to excuse himself. Before he could stop her, she spoke. "He tried to kill her," she said. "He doesn't think I know. I know. I heard him. He's…he," she took a paper out of her bag and handed it to Agent Fallon.

Fallon read it and handed it to the assistant director with the raise of his brow. "Cheryl, here is not the best place. Do you understand?" She looked at him fearfully, and he placed his hand over hers in quiet reassurance. "Alex is my friend," he said. "Trust me." She nodded. Tate motioned for Fallon to follow him outside.

"Make this solely about the accounts on that paper," Tate said. "Take a statement. Leave that comment out of it. I need to take care of the recording." Fallon understood. "I know you still have your doubts, Agent Fallon, but you need to trust me. She may be the link we need."

"I know," Fallon said. "Just…what she handed me puts her at risk; doesn't it?"

Tate nodded. "Take the statement and then take her here," Tate said, handing Agent Fallon a business card.

"Sir?"

"Fallon, you are going to have to trust me on this one," Tate said. Fallon nodded. "All right. I will meet you there at four o'clock. Don't let her out of your sight. Do it as discreetly as you can."

"Sir….should we place her in protection?"

Tate shook his head. "Agent Fallon, her decision to walk in here so boldly just guaranteed that is an impossibility. There isn't an agency that can provide that assurance."

Fallon swallowed hard. "I'll get her statement."

Tate watched Fallon as he re-entered the conference room. He made his way back to the observation area and retrieved his cell phone. "I know I am the last person you expected to call. We have a problem…..No. It's O'Brien…..His girlfriend walked in……Agent Fallon is with her now…..I know that…..I know that…..If we do this, it puts her….I know….I don't like it, but I agree…..Fine. Merry Christmas," he said in disgust.

***

Brian Fallon pulled into a deserted parking lot at four o'clock and waited. Cheryl jumped when the backdoor to the sedan opened and Joshua Tate slid in beside her. "Drive," he told Fallon.

"Where?" Fallon asked

"Anywhere. Just drive," he ordered. He turned to Cheryl and softened his gaze. "What made you walk into the FBI?" he asked.

"I can't. I can't live with knowing. I know he would do it. I believe it. He's capable," Cheryl rambled.

"Capable of what?" Tate asked.

"Killing someone," she said.

Tate nodded. "You think Congressman O'Brien tried to kill someone?"

"No. He did. I thought it was all talk. It's not. He was with her….that redhead. I don't know who she is," Cheryl seethed.

Fallon glanced in the rearview mirror and caught Tate's eye. "Well, he thinks I am stupid. I'm not stupid. He meets her at all hours; you know? This little dive on the corner of K Street. Didn't even notice me there."

Tate groaned. "Ms. Stephens, the information you gave Agent Fallon....when did you discover that the congressman opened accounts in your name?"

Cheryl looked at him directly. "I went in his office Sunday. He was out. I can't begin to imagine where," she rolled her eyes. "Probably at a *meeting*. Well, I wanted to know...who she was...who she is. Was it true? Or just more of his egotistical bragging. Killing Agent Toles, I mean." Tate listened quietly. "Well, I don't know who she is. But...I believe it. I saw my name on the top of a paper on his desk. At first...well...I thought maybe it was...I don't know what I thought. I certainly don't have five million dollars."

"She's an agent," Tate said plainly. Fallon looked in the mirror again, stunned. "Well, Agent Fallon? She put herself in this. There's no point in lying to her," he asserted. He turned back to Cheryl.

"She's an FBI agent?" Cheryl asked.

Tate laughed. "Not exactly." He glanced out the window and then returned his focus to the woman beside him. "What makes you think he's capable of killing someone?" Tate asked curiously.

Cheryl unzipped her coat, slid it down and slid her blouse off her shoulders, revealing a set of dark bruises on her collar bone. Fallon felt his stomach lurch in the front seat. He couldn't see clearly in the darkened car, but he didn't need to see anything to understand the awkward silence in the backseat. He had spent many years as a cop, both walking a beat and as a detective. Abuse was something he had seen one too many times for his taste. His thoughts immediately traveled to Cassidy.

"You don't think he could?" Cheryl asked Tate pointedly as she pulled her coat back on.

"No. I believe you because he did try," Tate answered. He looked to the front seat and saw the tightening in Fallon's shoulders. "He shot Agent Toles last spring. What is it that you want us to do?" Tate asked her.

"Arrest him. Throw him away," she yelled.

"Not quite that simple," he said. "Are you willing to help?

Fallon could taste the bile in the back of his throat. Cheryl was not an agent. She was not a detective. She had no way to protect herself. "Sir..."

"Agent Fallon," Tate warned him sternly. He turned back to Cheryl.

"What would I have to do?" she asked.

He retrieved a card from his pocket. "Tell him you are leaving. Go to this hotel. Your room will be waiting."

"When?" she asked.

"I understand he is away until tomorrow?" She nodded. "Tell him when he comes home."

"On Christmas Eve?" she questioned.

"Were you looking forward to the holiday with the congressman?" he asked with as much sincerity as he could muster.

"No."

"Good. Then tomorrow."

"When he asks why?" she looked to Tate for guidance.

"Hand him this," he said retrieving a photo.

"What is this? This isn't her," Cheryl said as she studied the photo of her lover and a tall brunette engaged in a fiery kiss. Tate just nodded. "Jesus Christ," she yelled.

"He is quite the catch," Tate's revulsion seeped through his words.

"What will that do?" she asked.

"Remove you," he answered.

"How is that?"

"Ms. Stephens. The less you know, the better. Tomorrow, I want you to file a domestic violence complaint."

"What? I don't..."

"Go to the hotel first. I will have someone keeping an eye on you," he promised. "Do it."

"I don't understand..."

"I know you don't. It's better if you don't. Now, where can Agent Fallon drop you?"

Cheryl covered her face in her hands and mumbled an address. The threesome drove without further comment to the destination the woman had provided, and Tate grabbed her knee gently before she could exit. "You are in the middle of something, Ms. Stephens. Showing up at the bureau took guts, but it put you on the radar. Do you understand?" She nodded mutely. "All right. Agent Fallon and I will do what we can." She offered him a weak smile and made her way out of the vehicle.

"What the hell?" Fallon asked when she closed the door.

"Drive, Fallon."

"Where now?"

"Baltimore," he answered. Fallon shook his head.

"What about her?" Fallon asked in concern. "You're going to have the money withdrawn from the account; aren't you?" There was no answer. "Jesus. He'll be a sitting duck." Tate still made no reply. "Tate!" Fallon snapped.

Joshua Tate just looked out his window. "Just drive, Agent Fallon."

***

Alex stretched her feet out along her mother's sofa and sipped on her Diet Coke. She smiled when she felt her phone buzz next to her, not bothering to look at the number. "I miss you," she answered.

"That certainly improves my day," Fallon answered.

"Fallon?"

"Yeah. Are you at your mom's?"

"Yeah. Got a few last minute things to do in the morning before I head home."

"Christ, Alex, tomorrow is Christmas Eve," Fallon said.

"What are you the Elf Squad or something?" she joked.

"Sounds better than my current job," he said warily.

"What's going on?"

"Oh, nothing much. Had a walk in today is all," he said.

"Anyone interesting?" she asked.

"You could say that."

"Well, for Christ's sake, Fallon; who was it?"

"Cheryl Stephens."

"What?"

Fallon flinched at the volume of Alex's voice in his ear. "Tell me about it. Seems the congressman opened some accounts in her name. She's suddenly a wealthy woman."

Alex chuckled. "I'm not surprised she turned on him," Alex told him. She remembered the woman's arrival at her home months ago. Cheryl was distraught over O'Brien's affairs, and Alex knew she wanted to even the score in some way. She could also see the genuine compassion in the woman that underlined her reasoning, even if anger was the primary motivator in the visit. "I'm surprised it took her this long."

"Listen, I just wanted you to know. Tate's going to drain that account. Try and tip the scale on O'Brien," Fallon explained.

Alex pressed on her temples lightly. She could detect her friend's trust in Joshua Tate. "All right....let me know how everything goes."

"Sorry, not the best holiday news, huh?" he said.

"Could be worse," she said. "No one shot me."

Fallon laughed. "All right. Alex, enjoy your Christmas, okay? I'm on this."

"I know. I will. You do the same." Alex had barely disconnected the call when the phone buzzed in her hand. "What did you forget to tell me you loved me or something?" she said lightly.

"I hope not," Cassidy's voice answered.

"Cass?"

"Yes? Someone else calling to profess her undying love that I should know about?" Cassidy asked teasingly.

"Yeah. His name is Fallon."

"Should I worry?" Cassidy tried to sound wounded.

Alex burst out laughing. "I have to go to sleep soon. No disturbing images, please," she countered. Hearing Cassidy's soft laughter made Alex close her eyes. "How was your day? Did you finish everything you wanted?"

"If you mean wrapping your presents; yes I did," Cassidy answered. "Although, you have to put together that racetrack you bought Dylan after he goes to bed tomorrow."

"Yeah, yeah. What else did you do?"

Cassidy had grown to cherish these conversations. When Alex was away, even for a day, she wanted to know all the details of what she had missed. "I spent some time helping Dylan wrap his presents."

"Really?" Alex prodded.

"Mm-hm. Seems he has been busy making Lego creations for everyone in the family. It thought it was just a couple. He kept bringing them down. One for YaYa. One for Grandma. One for Uncle Nick and Aunt Barb. One for Cat. Of course, one for Jake," Cassidy's voice trailed off slightly.

"He's so sweet," Alex said proudly.

"Yeah. They were all small ornaments. I'm not sure where he got the idea, but he was very pleased with all of it," Cassidy said. "He had another one he wanted me to wrap."

"For who? Does he have some girlfriend already?" Alex laughed.

"No," Cassidy giggled. "Alex, he wanted me to wrap his Batcave up."

"What?" Alex's eyes flew open. "He wants to give away his Batcave? He worked on that for weeks! What did you do?"

"I helped him wrap it."

"Cass…"

"Alex, he wanted it to be a present for his little brother."

Alex couldn't help the smile that overtook her. Dylan was determined he was going to have a brother. "Oh boy. You wrapped it? What did you tell him?" Alex asked.

"I wasn't going to, but I couldn't resist him," Cassidy admitted. "You should have heard him, honey. He overheard me tell your mom that if I could write to Santa, I'd ask for a baby."

Alex felt her heart sink slightly. She knew that Cassidy was disappointed they hadn't conceived yet. "Cass...I know…"

"It's all right. I was so touched. He told me that he would help me write a letter to Santa."

"I'll bet he did," Alex laughed. "He certainly is determined."

"Apparently someone told him that Santa is magic," Cassidy laughed.

"Well, he is!" Alex declared. "So, did you write it?" she asked her wife.

"Yes, I did, in fact," Cassidy told her.

"You asked Santa for a baby?" Alex chuckled. "Did you mail it?"

"No. Dylan was very clear it was too late for that. He showed me Santa's email. I wonder where he learned that?" Cassidy mused knowingly.

"Can't imagine," Alex countered. "He's smart like his mom."

"Nice recovery, Agent Toles."

"I hope he's not going to be crushed," Alex said thoughtfully.

"Well, he knows it takes time," Cassidy assured her.

"I know, but…."

"Alex, no one ever gets everything on their list. It will be okay," Cassidy said.

"So, what else is on your list, Mrs. Toles?" Alex asked.

"Hmm. I suppose a nice Caribbean cruise would work."

"I'll bet it would," Alex said.

"I'll just settle for a beautiful woman to wake up with me on Christmas morning."

"A beautiful woman, huh? Anyone particular in mind?" Alex flirted.

"No, not really. Any beautiful woman will do," Cassidy quipped.

"Is that right?"

"Well, to be honest, I'm not sure how my wife would feel about that," Cassidy giggled. "I miss you, Alex," Cassidy admitted.

"I know. Me too. I'll be home tomorrow afternoon," Alex promised.

"I can't wait."

Alex closed her eyes. "You know, Santa might need a little encouragement to fill that request."

"Oh?" Cassidy responded playfully.

"Better get some rest," Alex suggested.

"I love you, Alex."

"I love you too, Cass. I'll see you tomorrow."

***

Wednesday, December 24th

Claire Brackett rolled over and slowly ran her hands down the form beside her. She had taken Eleana as a lover many times since high school, and she never tired of the woman. Eleana seemed to be able to anticipate Claire's needs and Claire was always willing to submit to her friend's touch. She kissed Eleana's neck gently and whispered in her ear, "Merry Christmas."

"It's not Christmas yet, fool," Eleana answered.

"Are you sure?" Claire asked, unwrapping the woman next to her from her silky confines. "I could swear I am unwrapping something."

Eleana rolled to her side and pulled Claire to her. "Tell me why you're here," she said.

"I thought that would be clear," Claire responded, dropping her hand to the swell of Eleana's breasts.

Eleana grasped the redhead's wandering hand and held it firmly. "Tell me, Claire." Claire Brackett looked into her friend's hazel eyes intently. Eleana sighed softly. "I thought we agreed we would always tell each other..."

"We did," Claire said. She threw her head back on the pillow. "Strickland is sending some help to Moscow."

"I know," Eleana said.

"Yes, but...no one knows when."

Eleana brushed a falling curl from the side of Claire's face and hovered over her. "You think I know?"

"Your father..."

"I see," Eleana said. "He doesn't even know my involvement. You know that. He doesn't talk shop with me. What about your father?" she asked. Claire shook her head. "That bad?" Eleana inquired. Claire remained silent. "All I know is they are set to arrive January 3rd. That's all I know."

Claire nodded and opened her eyes. She reached up and pulled Eleana to her, kissing her deeply. "I should visit more often."

"Something tells me you don't have much cause these days," Eleana smiled. Claire looked at her longingly. "Oh, Claire," Eleana bent down into her ear. "When will you learn, love?" she whispered.

Claire smiled and gave over to her lover's kiss. "Why don't you teach me?" she breathed in an attempt to shift the mood and the power back in her favor.

"Another lesson in futility it is," Eleana answered. "Be careful," she pleaded. Claire suddenly looked vulnerable. It was an expression reserved only for the woman above her and Eleana smiled. "I can't always protect you like when we were kids," she wiped a single tear from the corner of her friend's eye. "I can love you, Claire. But, I can't protect you."

***

Chapter Ten

Dylan walked in the back door, took off his coat and sneakers and slid across the floor toward his mother. "Are they almost done?" he asked.

Cassidy wiped her hands on her apron and gave him a little pout. "I thought you were going to help me," she questioned him.

"I got busy," he said.

"Is that so? I thought these cookies for Santa were important," she said.

"Yep."

"So, then…where did you disappear to?"

"Santa might be able to find me, but I had to make sure that the reindeer would be all right," he explained.

Cassidy narrowed her gaze. "Do I want to know what that means?" Dylan shrugged and grabbed his mother's hand. He led her to the sliding door and pointed out toward the stone patio. Cassidy shook her head in amusement. "That's very creative, Dylan," she said sincerely.

"It's my name," he pointed.

"Yes, I see that. You spelled your name with my bag of carrots. I'm sure the reindeer will remember you now."

He gave her a toothy grin. "Yep!"

Cassidy brushed her hand over his head. "You thought of that all by yourself, huh?

"Yeah. I figured they might get hungry. Uncle Pip said he always fed the reindeer just to be sure they put in a good word with Santa. He said they had…ummm…" Cassidy raised her brow at him. He scrunched his face up for a minute in thought. "Sway," he said. "What does that mean?" he asked her.

"Who has sway?" Alex asked from a few feet away.

"Reindeer," Cassidy explained. Alex nodded.

"Yeah, come here, Alex. Look!" Dylan called to her.

Alex made her way across the room. She looked out over Dylan's head and pulled Cassidy to her. "Hi," she whispered in her wife's ear.

"Hi," Cassidy said softly, accepting a kiss to her cheek.

"So, what do we have here?" Alex asked.

"Uncle Pip told Dylan the reindeer have *sway* over Santa," Cassidy nudged Alex.

"Yeah? That's probably true, Speed," Alex agreed as if it were an important piece of evidence she had just discovered. Cassidy rolled her eyes, kissed her wife gently and headed back toward the oven.

"Mom made cookies for Santa," he tilted his head back toward Alex.

"Just for Santa?" she asked.

"No!" he giggled. "You can have some too, but Santa gets the biggest one."

"Guess that's only fair," she agreed. "Mom's got Santa covered, and you took care of the reindeer. What's my job?"

Dylan looked up to Alex and tapped his cheek. He beckoned her to him and whispered in her ear. "Oh….I hadn't thought of that, Speed. Good thinking," she said. "Why don't you go wait for me in the living room? I'll be right there, and we'll make sure that the fireplace is free and clear for Jolly Ole' Saint Nick," she promised.

"Hey!" he stopped. "Santa's name is Nick!" Alex nodded. Cassidy giggled as she listened. "Maybe he's really Uncle Nick!"

"Santa is a lot older than Uncle Nick," Alex reminded him. "He used to bring Uncle Nick his presents too."

"Oh yeah," Dylan said. He just shrugged and slid across the floor toward the counter where Cassidy was laying out the cookies to cool. "Can I have one?" he asked his mother hopefully.

Cassidy placed one on a napkin and handed it to him. "One, Dylan." He accepted it happily only to slide off again. Cassidy watched him, reveling in his youthful exuberance. The feel of Alex's hands around her waist caused her to sigh deeply and lean into her wife's arms.

"What about me?" Alex asked lightly.

Cassidy caressed Alex's hands for a moment, opened her eyes, grabbed a cookie, and then spun around to place it directly in Alex's mouth. "A mom's work is never done, I guess," she sighed, returning to the task at hand.

"It's good," Alex choked out through a mouthful.

"I'm glad you are happy," Cassidy began when she felt herself spun around.

Alex put the cookie on the counter and kissed her wife passionately. She heard a soft moan escape Cassidy and pulled back with a playful wiggle of her eyebrow. "See? Good."

Cassidy wiped a smudge of chocolate chip from the side of Alex's lips and kissed her sweetly. "I'm glad you are home."

"Me too," Alex said.

"Alex!" Dylan called from the other room.

Cassidy laughed a bit harder. Dylan was beyond wired. "Duty calls," Alex said. "We wouldn't want Santa to miss us!" she exclaimed in excitement that mirrored Dylan's. Cassidy watched her wife sprint off, grabbing two more cookies on the way. "I said one, Alex," she called after her wife. "You are worse than Dylan," she chuckled. "Well, if Santa misses this house, it won't be for lack of trying," she mused.

***

Alex and Cassidy tucked Dylan in and kissed him goodnight. His overexcitement had led directly to exhaustion. Before Alex had him fully covered, he was already asleep. She felt Cassidy's hand slip around her waist and the weight of her wife press against her. "Well, now that Santa's got his cookies, and the reindeer are properly fed, I think someone has a project to tackle," Cassidy reminded her wife.

Cassidy led Alex from the room, and they made their way back down the stairs. Alex headed off to the garage to retrieve the race track they had purchased for Dylan from Santa. "I haven't built one of these in years," Alex said with wide eyes.

Cassidy loved the playfulness of her wife. She could see the way Alex's eyes lit up as she carried the box toward the living room. She started toward the coat rack and retrieved her jacket when Alex captured her attention with a quizzical expression. "I have to make sure the reindeer eat their carrots, Alex," Cassidy explained. Alex nodded her understanding. "I figured I would make some hot chocolate when I'm done, and then you can help me with Santa's cookies," Cassidy said.

Alex beamed. "Okay!"

Cassidy headed off to the patio and began removing a few carrots here and there. She took a bite out of several that were left. "I cannot believe the things I do." She snickered at the slight absurdities that accompanied parenthood. Once Cassidy finished throwing the extra carrots off into the woods, she headed back to the house. Closing the door, she heard Alex singing Santa Claus in Coming to Town and allowed the sound to wash over her. She continued to listen, occasionally catching herself humming along as she prepared their cocoa.

"How's it coming?" Cassidy asked.

"Just about done, actually," Alex said.

"That was quick."

"Eh, it was easy. Let me get his other Santa presents and put them under the tree," Alex said. "Be right back."

Cassidy set the cocoa on the small table next to the couch, put one of her favorite CDs on and turned off the remaining lights, leaving only the tree to illuminate the room. She watched Alex place the rest of the toys Santa would deliver strategically under the tree. Alex placed the last box where it was only slightly obscured by a few branches and then turned to Cassidy. "All done," she announced proudly.

Cassidy's nose wrinkled into a devious smile, and Alex's brows raised in silent questioning. "Well, actually there is one more," Cassidy said.

"No. I don't think so. I got them all."

"No, there is," Cassidy said definitively. "But, before I show that to you, I have something for you." Cassidy patted the couch and handed Alex a small box as the agent took her seat.

"You're giving me a present tonight?" Alex asked. Cassidy just shrugged. "Well, then I should..."

Cassidy grabbed Alex's wrist. "Just open it," she said.

Alex slid the bow off and tore the paper to reveal a jewelry box. She stopped and looked at Cassidy, receiving a raised brow in encouragement. Alex opened the lid slowly. "You got it back! It's my necklace from the..." A crease crept across Alex's forehead. She shook her head a bit sadly. "Cass, this isn't mine."

"I think it is," Cassidy said.

"No...look," Alex said as she lifted the necklace from the box and looked at her wife. The sparkling smile that greeted her caused Alex to search Cassidy's eyes deeply. She explored the familiar twinkle of green and blue that tonight seemed to reveal a hint of mischief and mirth. Alex continued to study her wife intently. As Cassidy moved to look at the box in Alex's hand, her blouse drifted open, reflecting the light from the Christmas tree off of the stones in Cassidy's necklace. Alex thought she might have stopped breathing. She reached out and took a gentle hold of Cassidy's charm, noting the extra stone sitting next to the diamond marking Dylan's birth. She slowly allowed her gaze to meet her wife's eyes again, trying to process what Cassidy was telling her.

"I guess, maybe Santa got my letter, huh?" Cassidy said with a caress of Alex's cheek.

Alex froze. "Cass?"

Cassidy continued to caress Alex's cheeks softly, ensuring Alex could see the truth in her eyes. "Yes, Alex. We're having a baby." Tears immediately escaped Alex's eyes as she looked at Cassidy, awestruck. She had instantly become immersed in a sea of emotions that pounded over and through her in waves. "Alex?" Cassidy called gently as Alex leaned forward and kissed her. Cassidy felt Alex's hands raise to take hold of her own, both of which were still gently placed on Alex's cheeks.

Alex tenderly placed her forehead against Cassidy's. "Cass," Alex whispered as she pulled back. "Are you sure?"

Cassidy smiled. "Yeah, I'm positive, honey. Though, it's possible we might have to change that stone if this little one decides to wait a bit longer. If not, it looks like we'll have two July birthdays to celebrate this year," she said. "I hope you don't mind sharing," she winked.

"You're gonna be a mom!" Alex exclaimed as the emotional reality shifted suddenly to elation. "Cass! You're gonna have a baby."

"I know," Cassidy replied trying not to fall into a fit of laughter at Alex's sudden outburst. "I think you might be forgetting something," Cassidy smirked.

"What do you mean?" Alex asked.

"You're going to be a mom too," Cassidy raised her brow.

"We're having a baby," Alex looked at her wife. All Cassidy could do was smile back. "Oh my God, Cass...Dylan's gonna freak! He'll believe in Santa til he's twenty for sure! Hell, I think I believe in him."

"I think I just might agree with you," Cassidy said. "On that subject," she handed Alex another box and directed her to open it. "I thought that could be a present Santa drops off at Nick's for Dylan."

Alex explored the contents of the box. She looked back to Cassidy, beaming with excitement. "You are such a terrific mom," Alex complimented.

"You think so?" Cassidy asked genuinely.

"Yeah, I do," Alex said, sealing her words with a kiss. She dropped her hand to Cassidy's stomach and closed her eyes. "There's a little Cassidy in there."

Cassidy watched the emotions cross Alex's features like ripples across the water. Each one seemed to travel directly through to her heart. "Merry Christmas, Alex."

"Merry Christmas." Alex kissed her wife's forehead. "I love you, Cassidy. Thanks for giving me the best Christmas I've ever had."

"It's not even Christmas yet," Cassidy noted.

"Well let's see if we can't give you something to unwrap slowly until it is," Alex countered.

"Are you propositioning me?" Cassidy asked. "I'm a married woman, you know. A married, pregnant woman."

"I'll take my chances. I have an 'in' with the big man in red," Alex answered, offering Cassidy her hand and pulling her up.

"Think he'll let me ride in his sleigh?" Cassidy sniggered. Alex picked Cassidy up into her arms. "What are you doing?" Cassidy squealed.

"I don't have a sleigh, but I'm more than happy to give you a ride, Mrs. Toles."

"Well, then…on Dasher…"

***

Christopher O'Brien walked into the townhouse and began searching out his girlfriend. "Cheryl?" he called out. There was no answer. "Cheryl! Where are you?"

O'Brien weaved his way down a narrow hallway toward the kitchen. It was empty. He continued his exploration of his home, stopping in his office, the living room, and even checking the bathroom. He climbed the stairs to the second level and called out again. "Cheryl?" He shook his head in frustration.

"It's Christmas Eve. We have dinner plans at seven. What are you doing? Sleeping?" he continued to ask questions and speak as if his girlfriend was beside him. Reaching the master bedroom, he was surprised he still had not found the woman. He began removing his tie when a neatly folded paper in the middle of the pillows captured his attention. He began opening it and watched as a small black and white photo slowly cascaded down toward the bed. He picked it up and groaned. Returning his attention to the paper in his hand; he felt his frustration and anger building quickly.

Chris,

I hope you have a lovely Christmas. Mine has consisted of discovering that you have been sleeping with half of D.C. I wonder if they all have as much to show for their efforts as I do. You were right. I am an idiot. I truly hope you get everything that you deserve and more.

The movers will be there Saturday. Merry Christmas. Maybe the redhead will be able to fit you in.

Cheryl

"Fabulous," O'Brien muttered.

***

Thursday, December 25th

Alex shifted slightly in the bed and pulled Cassidy into her arms. "Merry Christmas," she whispered with a kiss.

"Ummm," Cassidy grumbled.

"Dylan's going to be in here any minute, you know?" Alex chuckled. Cassidy just snuggled closer, and Alex closed her eyes. "Why don't I go down and get some coffee started? Your mom will be here in an hour or so," Alex offered.

Cassidy pried her eyes open and smiled. "Just stay here until he wakes up," Cassidy whined.

Alex raised her eyebrow slightly. "Tired?" she inquired.

"Can't imagine why. Someone had me up half the night under the pretense of hearing Santa Claus," Cassidy teased.

"Well, it's good practice," Alex offered her explanation.

"For?" Cassidy asked.

"I imagine we will be up half the night a lot. Might as well do it on our terms while we can," Alex explained her reasoning.

Cassidy propped herself up and looked at her wife. She felt an incredible sense of love and completion wash over her. They had spent most of the night awake, talking, laughing, and making love. She was amazed at the range of emotions Alex had displayed throughout the night. At times Alex was playful, almost giddy with excitement. Cassidy loved that part of her wife's personality. It often surfaced when Alex interacted with those she loved, particularly Dylan. Cassidy had expected Alex to display her playful nature when she heard the news that Cassidy was pregnant. The incredible emotional shifts that they both seemed to experience over the course of the night had taken Cassidy by surprise.

At times, Alex would stop their bantering and gaze longingly into Cassidy's eyes, searching in silent contemplation. Those moments inevitably ended with a languid kiss. Their lovemaking had been slow and sensual, an achingly complete exploration of the other. Their needs had little to do with desire or release. The touches they had shared had been reverent and compassionate. To Cassidy, it felt as if they could both sense new life between them. Somehow, that seemed to spur the ghosts of their pasts, creating a yearning to seek forgiveness and acceptance in one another for all that they had been and all that was to come. It was an intimate promise; a commitment reaffirmed.

Intimacy existed in every moment that passed between Alex and Cassidy. For Cassidy, it mattered little whether they shared a kiss, a laugh, a conversation or even an argument; she felt Alex's presence within her constantly. She would not have believed that anything could bring them closer, but waking now, looking at Alex after the night that they had shared; she could not deny their connection had grown even stronger.

She smiled and cupped Alex's cheek, bringing her lips slowly to her wife's in an effort to convey the depth of her emotion.

"What was that for?" Alex asked.

"You."

"Me?" Alex asked.

Cassidy nodded. "Thank you," she said softly.

"Thank me? What are you thanking me for?" Alex wondered aloud.

Cassidy kissed Alex again. "I think you *are* Santa Claus," she giggled.

Alex felt Cassidy's head as if she were checking for a fever. "You feeling all right?" Alex asked in mock concern.

Cassidy swatted her hand away. "Knock it off," she giggled. "I'm serious."

"Last time I checked I don't own a red suit or any reindeer. I do like cookies," Alex's diatribe was again halted by a kiss.

"There's only one thing I've ever really wanted, Alex," Cassidy said seriously. Alex's expression softened; listening to her wife as she reached out to tuck Cassidy's hair behind her ear. "All I ever wanted was to have a family with the person I loved. That's all. I'd given up on that, you know...until I met you. It would have been enough for me to share the rest of my life with you and Dylan...but, Alex...this....having a baby with you..."

"I know," Alex said with a kiss to Cassidy's cheek.

"I wouldn't care if I never got a Christmas present again," Cassidy chuckled through a sudden emotional sob.

Alex nodded with a smile and pulled Cassidy close. Cassidy's eyes revealed everything that passed through her mind and her heart. Alex had discovered that the moment she met the school teacher. Cassidy's eyes were more than expressive; they were a window. Alex had often mused that the adage 'the eyes are the window to the soul' must have been written about Cassidy. She had watched her wife's eyes mist over repeatedly throughout the night as the gravity of their new reality took hold of them both. She had witnessed the unbridled passion in Cassidy's darkening eyes. Alex understood her wife's longings. Cassidy was meant to be a mother; to nurture. It was one of the many parts of Cassidy that Alex marveled at; her capacity to love so generously. She kissed Cassidy's forehead as her wife's tears subsided and were replaced with soft laughter just as Dylan's door creaked open across the hallway. A new day, full of surprises was about to begin. Alex painted a mischievous grin on her face and shifted the mood. "Guess I'll just take those presents I bought you back then; since you won't be needing them anymore."

"You will not!" Cassidy poked her wife as the door flew open.

"Come on!" Dylan urged. "Alex, come on," he made his way to the bed.

Alex laughed. "We're coming, Speed."

"Mom! Come on…we have to see if the reindeer ate their carrots!" he grabbed for his mother's hand.

Alex hopped off the bed and pulled Cassidy with her to follow their son down the stairs. "Well, come on Vixen," Alex implored.

Cassidy put her hands on her hips. "Excuse me?"

"Hey," Alex whispered. "Don't look at me. You're the one who nibbled the carrots."

"Mm-hm," Cassidy groaned playfully as they watched Dylan bound down the stairs. She patted Alex's tummy. "Vixen, huh? Guess you really are Santa then."

"Told you; I like my cookies," Alex answered. Cassidy felt Alex's lips brush the top of her head as they reached the bottom of the stairs.

"He was here!" Dylan exclaimed, noting the presents under the tree. Alex and Cassidy watched as he sprinted to the small table that had held Santa's cookies and milk. "Santa ate your cookies, Mom!"

"Did he?" Cassidy asked, smirking at Alex. Alex just shrugged.

Dylan sprinted off to the back door in the kitchen and pumped his fist in the air. "See? It worked, Mom. It did, Alex! The reindeer ate my carrots!"

"That's great, Speed," Alex told him as he ran full tilt back toward the living room. She nudged Cassidy gently. "I'll bet they were hungry from keeping all of Santa's *secrets,*" Alex mumbled in amusement, receiving a gentle whack in return.

Alex and Cassidy settled in for the rest of their morning, watching as Dylan explored the gifts Santa had left. Dylan excitedly showed his parents all of his haul. He handed Alex his new video games and jumped up and down at the toy Batman figures and Iron Man mask Santa had left under the tree. He continued to explore while they waited for his grandmother to arrive so they could move on to the colorful boxes that remained wrapped under the tree.

"Are you going to tell your mom when she gets here?" Alex whispered.

"No," Cassidy answered. "Only your mom knows and that's only because I needed her help to execute my plan."

Alex watched as Dylan scurried around the tree, looking intently. "What are you looking for, Speed?" she asked. Dylan just shrugged, looking slightly defeated and then settled back at his racetrack. "Oh boy," she whispered to Cassidy.

Cassidy heard her mother's car pull in and patted her wife's shoulder. "He'll be fine, honey," Cassidy assured her wife as she headed toward the door.

Alex smiled down at Dylan, who was back playing with his racetrack and started to follow. "Maybe we should...."

"Ohhh no, you don't," Cassidy warned. "You remember your plan to announce our engagement?" she reminded her wife. Cassidy pointed to Dylan. "CNN is not breaking the news for us this time." Alex pouted slightly. Cassidy patted her cheek. "You know what the song says, Alex...you'd better not pout."

"I already got my present," Alex declared.

Cassidy stopped with her hand on the doorknob and kissed Alex's cheek. "Come on, Santa, we'd better help Grandma before she gets run over by one of those reindeer."

***

"This had better be good," the president said as he moved through the White House.

"Sir," his chief of staff began, "I don't know what this is about, but whatever it is, he said it could not wait."

President Strickland was irate as he entered the small office that adjoined the Situation Room. "Leave us," he ordered. He pressed a button on a small console, instantly concealing the glass enclosure. "What the hell is so important that you had to disturb me today?"

"I wasn't aware that the president was ever off duty," the man answered.

"Admiral," Strickland cautioned.

"What the hell were you thinking, Lawrence? Where the hell did you get the idea to bug Alex Toles' home?" Admiral William Brackett bellowed.

"That warrants you barging in here under the pretense of national security on Christmas?" the president answered in kind.

"It does when we are ready to deploy assets to Moscow. Not to mention Dimitri has his hands on nuclear material. My daughter is off in Belarus with her oldest friend, who happens to be Edmond Callier's daughter, and who works for Russ Matthews, and Christopher O'Brien's girlfriend walked into the FBI two days ago," Admiral Brackett answered.

"While fascinating, I don't see any correlation to national security," Strickland replied harshly.

"No? Really? Then you are either blind or utterly stupid.... or there is something you have not told me. Perhaps that is it," the admiral guessed.

"Bill," the president cautioned. "What do you want?"

"This needs to be addressed now. Not tomorrow."

"Admiral, I think you are overreacting. O'Brien is..."

The admiral slammed his fist on the desk. "O'Brien knows more than you give him credit for. And he has information he should never have had, thanks to you."

"I should think this would be a conversation for your daughter. Where is she this holiday, Bill? No family Christmas this year?" Strickland struck at the admiral.

"Listen to me. O'Brien is a bigger liability than you think. No moves until he is taken care of," the admiral said. "No moves."

"And just how do you propose to do that, Admiral Brackett? Another car accident? I doubt your daughter will be so willing this time," the president responded.

"No. No car accident. Claire didn't create this. You did. So you are going to help me solve it," the admiral said. He picked up the secure phone line and handed it to the president. "You have some calls to make."

"And just what are you suggesting? I have made commitments, Bill," Strickland said.

Admiral Brackett handed the president a paper. "Read it. You think this is a joke? You just stirred the hornet nest, *Larry*. You have no idea who you are dealing with. You're worse than Claire. She once told me she was like a cobra," the admiral shook his head. "You think that a title, an office somehow puts you in control? Who do you think Viktor Ivanov is? What about Jon Krause? Alex Toles? Edmond Callier? Commitments? You don't know the meaning of the word. You treat these people as if they are simpletons. Like they are insects that you can swat at will. That might be true if it were only one. Ever seen hornets protect their nest, Larry? Protect their young? Their home? They're workers by nature. They build a formidable fortress to protect their family. Threaten their nest, they swarm violently, and when they attack...well, let's just say you don't want to disturb a hornet nest."

Strickland attempted to swallow the sudden dryness in his throat. "You work for this office, Admiral. This is your department to deal with."

Admiral Brackett laughed. "Not today, it's not. Merry Christmas, Mr. President."

***

Dylan and Cat had run off to play with one of Cat's new video games while the adults continued talking in the dining room. Christmas at Nick's began as it always did; with a family dinner that was more akin to a festival brunch. Between Alex's brother and mother, there was always enough food to feed a family three times their size. Alex chuckled slightly as the thought passed through her mind that in a few years they might actually need this much food. The boys were content for the moment, although Alex had spied them shaking some of the boxes under the tree when they thought no one was looking. She laughed quietly at the sound of Dylan's voice in the distance and then returned her attention to Cassidy, who was seated beside her.

"Do you mind?" Barb asked Cassidy, placing the baby in her arms. Cassidy just looked up and smiled, accepting the small package gratefully. Little Jacob was quite wide-eyed at the moment; doing his best to focus on and explore the face looking down on him. Alex looked on, watching how Cassidy's eyes softened when the baby grasped her finger. She heard Cassidy whisper endearments to their nephew and felt her heart rise dramatically into her throat.

Helen watched from across the table, a smile tugging at her lips. She noticed that both Alex and Cassidy wore their charms from Dylan underneath their sweaters. She was curious how Cassidy's news was received. At the moment, she was deriving great pleasure from the expression on her daughter's face as she watched Cassidy with the baby. She cleared her throat slightly and reached her feet. "Those boys will be restless soon enough," she said. Helen made her way behind Alex and squeezed her daughter's shoulder. "Alexis, help me clear this; will you?"

"Mom, I can do that," Nick piped up.

"No. No. You and Barb go with Cassidy and Rose and wrangle the kids into the other room. Alexis and I have a system," she smiled.

"Geez. Mom finally got you trained, huh?" Nick laughed. Alex rolled her eyes at him.

"Come on, Cassidy. We get a free pass today," Nick said as he left the room.

Alex leaned over and touched Jake's tiny hand. Cassidy looked up and sighed, receiving a tender kiss on her cheek from her wife. "Looks good on you," Alex whispered. Cassidy winked and followed Nick into the other room. "So," Alex said as she picked up plates and brought them to the sink. "Let's get this mess cleaned up so we can get to the presents!"

Helen grasped her daughter's forearm and pulled her back. When Alex turned, she could see her mother's eyes had grown misty. "I'm so happy for you, Alexis," she said as she enveloped Alex in her arms.

"You're sneaky," Alex whispered.

"You'll learn," Helen chuckled. "Comes with the parental territory."

"Mom?" Alex began to grow serious.

Helen looked curiously at her daughter. "What is it?"

"I don't even know how to tell her," Alex said softly.

"Tell her what?" Helen asked.

Alex looked up with pleading eyes. "How much I love her. How much I love them."

Helen smiled and kissed her daughter's forehead. "She knows. Dylan knows. That baby will now, Alexis. It's written all over your face. You couldn't hide it if you tried."

"That reminds me," Alex said, holding up a finger. She ran to the far side of the room and retrieved a box wrapped in special paper. Cassidy had wrapped the box in bright red foil with a metallic green bow. She had Alex scrawl out a card for Dylan in an unfamiliar hand.

Alex handed her mother the box and winked. "That has to be last. Like you found it here; okay?" Alex explained.

Helen read the inscription and shook her head. A warm smile painted her lips and she patted her daughter's cheek affectionately. "You two are too much," she said.

"It was Cassidy's idea," Alex shrugged.

"I'm sure it was. I'll take care of it," Helen promised. She watched as Alex hurriedly set about cleaning up the kitchen. "Let's go," Helen held out her hand.

"We're not done," Alex observed.

"We are for now. I can't take this suspense. Besides, Rose is going to kill me when she finds out I've known for over a week," the older woman chuckled.

"Yeah, aren't you the little conspirator," Alex poked.

"You'll forgive me when you need a babysitter," Helen said.

Alex kissed her mother's cheek. "I don't think she'll ever know how much it meant to me that she chose to confide in you, and wanted you to be the one to help."

"She knows, Alexis. That's why she did it," Helen said with a wink, heading off into the other room.

Alex sighed. "You really are something, Cass."

***

Alex watched as the boys opened their last presents. Cat was doing his version of a happy jig over the authentic Boston Red Sox Jersey Rose had purchased for him. It had his favorite player's number emblazoned on the back, and it was topped off with a new team hat. Cat loved all things baseball, and Rose loved to hear him rattle off statistics about his favorite team. Being the best of friends, Dylan had begun to follow suit, and his grandmother had bought him an identical jersey with the number '15'. The gifts came complete with a promise to take the boys to Boston for a day in the city and a game at Fenway Park when the new season began.

Dylan had followed his cousin's lead and donned his jersey, but rather than dancing about, he sat quietly fiddling with a toy. "Dylan! It's so cool! We're gonna go see a game with Grandma Rose!" Cat prodded his cousin. Cassidy nudged Alex knowingly, and Alex looked over to her mother with a raise of her brow.

On cue, Helen disappeared, returning with a colorful box in her hands. "Umm? This was in the foyer," she said. "It has a note addressed to you, Dylan."

Dylan accepted the box and looked at the card that was taped to its front. He began trying to sound out all of the words. Seeing his forehead wrinkle in concentration, his grandmother stepped in from behind to help him. Rose looked at the card and read it out loud. "It says: *Rudolph found this in my bag after we left your house. He says thanks for the carrots. Tell your mom she makes great cookies. Merry Christmas, Dylan. Santa.*" Rose looked at Cassidy suspiciously. Cassidy grinned and shrugged innocently.

"Well, open it!" Cat urged.

Dylan ripped off the paper and held his breath. He peeled back the tissue and traced the item with his fingers. "Big…"

"Brother!" Cat yelled. "It says Big Brother!"

Dylan looked puzzled for a moment. He pulled out the T-shirt and studied it. Rose closed her eyes momentarily as the message suddenly hit her. She bent over and whispered in his ear and pointed to the Batman symbol in the middle. "It says *Big Brother, Sidekick Coming in July*. It means, you're going to be a brother, Dylan," she explained.

Cassidy had placed her head on Alex's shoulder and was smiling broadly, waiting for the outburst she knew was due any minute. She hadn't expected it to come the way it did.

"Mom!" Dylan screamed in excitement. Cassidy and Alex both jumped slightly as Dylan darted toward them, dropping the box. "Santa got your letter, Mom! I told you. You're gonna have a baby!" he exclaimed as if he were delivering her the news. He jumped up in between his parents. Helen and Rose fell into a fit of laughter as they looked on. Nick looked at

Barb, still somewhat confused and Barb pulled him close to whisper in his ear, "Cassidy's pregnant."

"Yes, I am, Dylan," Cassidy said.

"Santa *is* magic. I told you," he said earnestly. "Alex, I'm gonna have a brother!"

Alex laughed. "Well, you might have a sister, and that would be just as cool."

"Yes, it would," Nick agreed.

Dylan flashed Alex a toothy grin and gave her a high five. Cassidy shook her head. "Have you two been talking behind my back?" she joked.

"Us?" Alex feigned innocence.

"Mom, is there a baby in your tummy like Jake was in Aunt Barb's?" he asked.

Cassidy adored her son and cherished his innocence. "Yes, Dylan, there is."

"That's so cool!" He hopped off the couch, grabbed his box and ran off.

"Where are you going?" Alex called after him.

"I gotta put on my shirt!" he yelled back.

Alex noticed Rose making her way toward them and immediately reached her feet. She was taken slightly off guard when Rose took her into a tearful embrace. "Thank you, Alex."

"I didn't do anything....honest," Alex joked. "Ouch," she winced as Cassidy pinched her backside.

"You are fifty percent responsible, Alex Toles," Cassidy said flatly.

"And happily so," Alex agreed.

Rose sat down beside Cassidy and hugged her. "I'm so happy for you, Cassie."

"So?" Barb asked from across the room. "Come on, I want the skinny! When did you find out?" she asked Alex.

The moment was interrupted when an exuberant seven-year-old danced back in the room. "Big brother, Batman!" he danced in, singing a tune of his own creation.

"All right, the inquisition will begin in the dining room with desert," Helen announced.

Alex grasped Cassidy's hand. "See you in a minute," she said, leaving her wife and mother-in-law on the couch.

Nick grabbed his sister's arm. "Alex, you're going to be somebody's mom," he said. Alex looked back at where Dylan was dancing around in his 'big brother' T-shirt, making up some song and putting on a show for his mother and grandmother. "Alex?" Nick called for his sister's attention.

Alex took a deep breath, enjoying Dylan's antics and delighting in his excitement, thinking how much she loved him. "I already am, Nick," she said proudly. "I already am."

***

Chapter Eleven

Wednesday, December 31st

"And? Is it done?" Admiral William Brackett asked through his secure line.

"It will be," the replay came.

"Will be is not good enough. The sooner, the better," Admiral Brackett responded heatedly.

"Daddy, calm down," Claire Brackett answered. "I'm surprised you would call me."

"Claire, I don't have any illusions about you; daughter or not. Believe me, I don't. You do know as well as anyone that this has to be contained. And, you do know that if it isn't, Dimitri will hold you responsible. It compromises everyone's work. I have Edmond and Strickland to deal with now. You need to..."

"Well, it's nice to know you have such confidence in me," Claire answered sardonically.

"Your abilities were never what I have questioned, Claire. Just take care of it."

"All right. We'll start the new year off with a bang," she chuckled.

"I'm glad you find it so amusing," her father sighed. "You do realize that innocent...."

Claire Brackett rolled her eyes on the other end of the call. "There is no such thing as an innocent person, Daddy. You taught me that a long time ago. Now, I have to go. It appears my father found me a date to ring in the New Year," she said as she hung up the call.

Admiral William Brackett stared at the phone in his hands. He struggled against the sudden wave of nausea that swept through his organs. "Jesus, Claire," he whispered.

***

Alex had been up for a few hours, eagerly awaiting Cassidy's appearance. She wondered how a short week could have felt so long. Alex had enjoyed the Christmas holiday immensely. She hated having to pull herself away and back to Massachusetts for the week. The news of Cassidy's pregnancy had motivated Alex to finish moving the executive offices at Carecom as soon as possible. There were T's to cross, I's to dot, and loose ends to tie up. While Carecom was, at its heart, a CIA sanctioned business; in order to operate efficiently it functioned as a legitimate corporation that employed nearly a thousand people. Alex understood that the vast majority of people within her father's company remained completely unaware of the true nature of the business. They depended on Carecom for their livelihood and the well-being of their families. It was a responsibility that Alex had not considered when she agreed to take her father's place. Her intention was to achieve greater access for her investigation, not provide for the workers. It weighed on her at times; the deception that was her life. She pinched the bridge of her nose and sighed. She was startled from her thoughts by the sudden feeling of two arms encircling her waist.

"Hey there," Alex said. Cassidy just grumbled. Alex turned and kissed her wife's forehead. "You want some breakfast?" Alex asked. "Speed had his usual delicacy. You know….cereal," she laughed. "I can make you an omelet." Cassidy shook her head. Alex noted that the color had drained from her wife's cheeks. "Cass?" she asked with concern.

"No food," Cassidy answered and rested her head against Alex's chest.

"You all right?" Alex asked as she stroked Cassidy's back.

"I'm not puking," Cassidy said bluntly. "I can't even look at food right now."

"Are you sick?"

"Mm," Cassidy groaned. "I'll be all right," she mumbled.

"Cass, maybe we should cancel having people over tonight."

Cassidy pulled back and narrowed her gaze at Alex. She patted her wife's cheek and smiled. "Honey, I'm fine. Believe me, if this is as bad as it gets I will be grateful."

"As bad as what gets?" Alex asked in concern.

Cassidy chuckled. "Let's just say that I would prefer not to test my driving skills from the couch for the next couple of weeks."

Realization dawned on Alex. She kissed the top of the smaller woman's head and recalled one of the first stories Cassidy told her about herself. Cassidy had just handily beaten Alex and Dylan at a driving game, and Alex couldn't help but be curious where the teacher had learned the skill. Cassidy laughed and explained that she had spent several weeks on the couch keeping close company with a bucket and a PlayStation when she was pregnant with Dylan. "Oh," Alex said softly. "Let's just cancel, Cass."

Cassidy smiled. She was looking forward to their New Year's Eve. She hadn't seen Jane Merrow and her daughters since the early fall. Life had been insane for everyone. Stephanie and Alexandra Merrow were both away at school. Jane was still adjusting to life without her husband, and the press had been relentless is pursuing all things Jane Merrow. Cassidy spoke with Jane quite frequently, and it infuriated her that the public could not seem to respect the former first lady's time for grieving. Cassidy had distanced herself from most of the friends in her life. They had been part of the social scene she traveled in as a congressman's wife. When she left that life, her social calendar diminished considerably. She had come to cherish Jane's friendship, and she was anxious to see her.

"No. I promise, I am all right. At least for now, okay? Besides, I want to tell Jane and the girls about the baby," Cassidy explained.

Alex nodded. "I know. Me too. But there will be quite a few people here and Cat for the rest of the week. They'll understand if you're...."

"Alex, I'm fine," Cassidy promised. She kissed Alex on the cheek and made her way toward the family room to see Dylan.

Alex paced the floor a bit and sighed, sipping her coffee thoughtfully. She could hear the determination in Cassidy's voice and she was certain that any effort to dissuade her wife would be futile. Ten minutes later she walked into the family room with a bowl of cereal and a glass of juice.

"What's this?" Cassidy asked.

Alex shrugged. "You have to eat. Better to have something on your stomach even if you do get sick," Alex said as she placed the items in front of Cassidy. "Just try; okay?" Alex asked hopefully. Cassidy nodded. "Take it easy today; all right? I'll take Dylan with me to get Cat this afternoon. I called Rose, she'll be here early. No one will be here until at least five. Just relax."

"Alex..."

"You won't win the argument," Alex chuckled. "You can play hostess tonight." Alex smiled and placed a kiss on Cassidy's forehead before leaving the room. "She'll be fine. It's all worth it, right?" she mused to herself quietly as she left the room.

Cassidy giggled and called out to her wife. "I am fine and yes it is. Every single second."

Alex chuckled in amazement. "I hope our kids don't inherit that skill."

***

"Cassie?" Rose called out.

"In here!" Cassidy called back from the kitchen.

"I thought you were supposed to be resting?" Rose questioned her daughter.

"Alex give you orders for me?" Cassidy laughed watching her mother nod. "I wasn't aware I married a doctor," she joked.

Rose watched as Cassidy moved about the kitchen. "She just said you weren't feeling well."

"I'm fine, Mom."

Rose pulled up a stool and watched her daughter work steadily preparing platters for the evening. "You started the minute she left; didn't you?" she asked her daughter. Cassidy just shrugged causing her mother to roll her eyes. "Well?" Rose asked.

"Well what?"

"You know perfectly well what, Cassie. How sick are you?"

"Jesus!" Cassidy threw her hands up in exasperation. "I'm not dying for God's sake. I'm pregnant. Don't you go siding with Alex on me," she warned her mother. "She'll have me in lockdown the moment she sees me running for the bathroom."

"She's just nervous, Cassie."

"I know. She's been wonderful," Cassidy said. "I just don't want to be put on house arrest."

"Well, there's a first," Rose laughed.

"Excuse me?" Cassidy asked.

"And here I thought you married Alex for her handcuffs."

Cassidy plopped onto a stool and shook her head. "You are sick," she said.

"Nah, just jealous."

Cassidy raised her brow. "You want to share my bucket?"

"No, but I wouldn't mind the handcuffs," Rose quipped. Cassidy swatted her mother. "And, thank you for the confirmation," Rose added. She saw her daughter pout slightly. "How long have you been getting sick?"

"A few days," Cassidy admitted. "But honestly, nothing all that horrible. Certain smells trigger it. It's nothing like it was with Dylan."

Rose understood. "Are you sure you are up to this tonight?"

Cassidy sighed. "Mom?" she began, watching her mother's eyebrows raise in question. "It really won't be very long, and I will have Dylan, a newborn, and Alex to contend with," she said. "If I can't navigate a little queasiness now, I am in *big* trouble."

Rose let out a hearty laugh. "Point taken. So, what can I help with?"

Cassidy started to give her mother directions when the doorbell rang. She looked up at the clock, puzzled. It was still early for guests. "I'll be right back," she assured her mother before heading for the door. She blinked in surprise at the sight that greeted her. "Pip?" Jon Krause just smiled. "Well, get in here," Cassidy directed him. "I thought you were away? Alex said..."

"Yeah, I was. I got this," he reached in his coat pocket and retrieved a small Lego keychain that spelled the word 'uncle'.

Cassidy smiled and rubbed his arm. "He will be thrilled that you made it," she said. Krause shrugged, somewhat embarrassed by the way in which Cassidy and Dylan could affect him.

Cassidy, sensing his discomfort intervened. "Well, come on. Since you're early, you get the wonderful prize of contending with Mom and me for the next hour. And, you get to help!"

Krause followed his friend back into the kitchen and waved to her mother. "Jonathan!" Rose greeted the man. "Happy New Year. Sorry, we didn't see you over the holiday."

"It's good to see you, Rose," he said genuinely.

"What the?" Cassidy was startled by the sound of the front door opening.

"Hello!" Helen's voice called out.

"I'll go help her," Rose said.

Krause couldn't help but chuckle at the constant bustle of the Toles' homestead. "What?" Cassidy asked. The smell of Helen's homemade lasagna began to permeate the house, and Cassidy felt her stomach rebel. "Shit," she grumbled and ran down the short hallway toward the bathroom.

"Cassie?" Krause called, following close behind.

Helen glanced down the hallway at the sounds echoing from the bathroom. "Oh boy," she looked at Rose.

"Think we should rescue him?" Rose asked.

"Nope," Helen replied. "That's one way to hear the news," Helen pursed her lips in amusement. Rose giggled conspiratorially.

"Cassie?" Krause called through the bathroom door.

Cassidy regained her bearings and splashed some cold water on her face. She opened the door slowly and offered her waiting friend a sheepish grin. "Sorry about that," she apologized.

"Are you okay?" he asked.

"Mm." Cassidy leaned against the sink and sighed. "I wanted Alex to tell you."

"Tell me what?" Krause asked.

Cassidy faltered slightly. "Alex and I," she uncharacteristically stumbled, "we're expecting in July." It took a moment for the statement to register in Krause's head. Cassidy watched as his expression moved from confusion to what looked like sincere happiness. "Pip?"

"That's great, Cassie," he said, taking her into a hug. "I'm happy for you. Both of you," he said.

"Thanks."

Krause pulled back and brushed Cassidy's hair aside. "So this is what? Morning sickness? It's not exactly morning," he observed.

"It doesn't always work that way," she winked.

"You're okay though?"

"I'm fine. Apparently the smell of garlic and I are not the best of companions these days. Guess Helen's home cooking is off the table for me," Cassidy joked. She saw Krause shift his stance uncomfortably.

"I'm sorry," he said tacitly.

Cassidy laughed. "It's not your fault," she said. "Believe me it was much worse with Dylan," she told him. "It will pass in a couple of weeks." Krause just nodded. "Pip? What's wrong?" Krause looked up at Cassidy and shook his head. Cassidy wasn't certain, but she thought she might see a tear forming in his eye.

"What's going on? Something is bothering you," she observed. "Is it this...I mean, I don't want..."

Krause took her hand and gave it a gentle squeeze. "No. Nothing is wrong at all. I just am not used to this uncle thing," he said.

Cassidy watched him closely. "Mm-hm. Okay. I'll let it go for now, but there is something you are not telling me."

"Cassie...honestly..."

"Nice try. Sometimes you remind me so much of Alex," she said pulling him from the bathroom. "How you two ended up as spies is beyond me. You can't lie to save your lives. Now let's go get this place ready. And do me a favor?" she asked. He nodded. "Keep me free and clear of the kitchen when Helen puts out that lasagna. Thrilling as this has been, I'd like to avoid a repeat performance."

***

Brian Fallon approached the flurry of activity in the park with a deep sense of foreboding. The sight of yellow tape erected in straight lines spanning from one tree to another made him shiver. He had seen the handiwork of mafia hit men, drug dealers, and serial killers, but he could never get accustomed to the smell and the feel of death. He'd heard investigators talk about crime scenes over the years as if they were playing a part in a movie; for Brian Fallon the stench was all too real. He flipped open his identification and slid under the tape.

"Can I help you?" a large man in a plastic suit asked.

Fallon released a sigh and flipped open his identification again. "Agent Brian Fallon, FBI," he identified himself.

"Well, Agent Fallon. I don't recall calling any Feds in on this. What peaks the interest of the FBI on a casual Jane Doe?"

"And you are?" Fallon asked the officer.

"Detective James Beers. So?" the detective asked again.

"The description sent up a red flag on a case we just opened," Fallon explained. He looked at the body a few feet away. He could see that the victim was on her side and that the body still had not been moved from its original position. "May I?" he pointed to the body.

"Be my guest," the detective answered.

"So, what do you have so far?" Fallon asked as he approached the victim slowly.

"Not much. Looks like she was walking through the park. Can't say for sure if there was any rape. Have to wait for them to process her. Strangled. Son of a bitch had quite the choke hold on her based on the marks around her throat. Looks like she took a hell of a beating. No I.D. She's so bruised up about all I can tell you is what you see for yourself; gender, height, and hair color."

Fallon crouched down over the body and moved closer to the woman lying in the leaves. He pulled out his flashlight and pointed it toward the swollen face. "Shit," he groaned.

"Friend of yours?" the detective asked.

Fallon let out a heavy sigh and closed his eyes. "Not exactly," he said. Standing back to his full height, he looked the detective in the eye. "I think this is officially in my court now, detective."

"Oh yeah? Feel like telling me how some poor woman walking through the park warrants the bureau?"

"No, I don't, actually," Fallon said pointedly. "Excuse me, for a minute. I need to make a few calls."

Fallon distanced himself from the scene, still remaining close enough to monitor the movement of those around him. He picked up his cell and waited. "Bad news," he said. "It's her. I'm certain.....No.....No, I think she'll want to hear in person.....I know I can't. Just get me some bodies down here. I'll make certain she finds out." Fallon placed his palms over his eyes and rubbed vigorously. "Shit."

***

"Edmond," the voice greeted. "I am surprised to see you here in Washington and on a holiday no less."

"I have business here, Bill," Callier replied.

"You know our daughters were together last week, for several days I am told," Admiral Brackett gauged the knowledge of his friend.

"I'm aware," Callier responded bluntly.

"I see. You don't seem overly concerned," the admiral observed.

"About Claire seeking Eleana? I should think we have more important things to worry about now. Eleana is not in our business. You know that," Callier offered.

Admiral Brackett poured two glasses of scotch and released a groan of frustration. "Perhaps not, but her affiliation with Matthews does give her access to certain information."

"She's a freelance translator, Bill and an expert on Russian culture. She's not a spy, not a broker, not in this game. I am grateful for that," Callier said as he sipped his scotch.

"Did she contact you?" the admiral asked.

"Claire was interested in when the diplomatic envoy to Moscow would be arriving," Callier said.

"Did she give Claire the information?" Brackett asked.

"She gave her confirmation of the date," Callier responded.

"Good. That should buy us some time," the admiral said with a hint of relief.

Callier chuckled. "Time is up, Bill. Jonathan knows. It's only a matter of time before Alexis discovers the truth as well. We both know where that will lead them."

"You told him?" the admiral asked in disbelief.

"It was time. You and I both know that Ivanov is pulling the strings in Moscow. Neither Kabinov nor Markov will make a move without him. Nicolaus cut off funding to ASA in April. Alexis wants to know why. We both know that Ivanov needs to generate capital quickly. There is no other way except to create a new enemy. Dates don't matter. The Russians will act, with or without our intervention. It is inevitable. Jonathan and Alexis are the best chance to reset this course," Callier said.

"You're waging a game just as dangerous," Brackett warned.

"No, Bill. I am following the only course that is reasonable or justifiable," Callier answered.

"Edmond, you put them at greater risk by doing this than I ever have," Admiral Brackett sighed. "My God, what good do you expect to come from revealing that truth? It is a slippery slope. We agreed, all of us..."

"*Combien de générations vont souffrir de nos offenses, comme nous avons souffert de celles de nos pères?* (How many generations will suffer our sins, as we have our father's)?" Callier said regretfully. "I have already lost my son. I will not lose any more children to this. If I am to lose them it will be to the truth and not to this madness we have created."

"The truth is not always the safest course. You and I both know that. We have done what we needed to do to protect..."

Callier swiftly reached his feet and grabbed the admiral by the collar. "Stop fooling yourself! We protected nothing but our vanity," he bellowed. Edmond released his grip on his friend and paced the small room. "You know, my friend; my Elliot and your Claire; they are not so different. They are both intelligent and capable, both ambitious with an insatiable appetite for everything pleasurable, and both naïve enough to think they're invincible. Where do you think they learned that?" Callier asked. "Ironic that it was Claire who took my son's life, don't you think? An oath we swore to each other, the five of us in this very room, all those years ago. We would pay with our lives to keep our children safe. It was our duty to each other; to them. Stronger even than the commitment to our mission. We failed. We failed them."

"We did what had to do," the admiral maintained, his voice betraying the confidence of his words.

"We can no longer shield them. They are far more astute than we ever were. We can only steer them so far," Callier said with a sad smile. "It's time."

"If you are suggesting what I think…it is much too soon…."

"No, it is much too late. It is time to bring in Sphinx," Callier said.

"Even Sphinx does not have the power to stop what is already in motion," Brackett reminded his friend.

"I know."

"Then why?" Brackett asked.

"Because. *Nous ne pouvons pas changer l'avenir si nous ne faisons pas face a notre passé, mon ami.* (We cannot change the future if we do not face our past, my friend)."

Admiral Brackett closed his eyes in silent resignation. He set his scotch on the oak table beside him and shook his head. "Are you certain?" he finally spoke. Seeing the solemn grin Callier forced, Brackett nodded. "They will never forgive us."

"I do not expect that kindness," Callier said.

***

The Toles house was filled with the sound of laughter and music. By anyone's account, the party had been successful. Alex was enjoying herself but keeping a close eye on her wife. It had not escaped her notice that Cassidy had steered clear of the kitchen all evening. "How are you doing?" Alex whispered in her wife's ear.

"I'm good," Cassidy answered with a smile, pressing the weight of her body against Alex.

"You haven't eaten," Alex observed.

"No."

"Cass, how awful are you feeling?" Alex softened her gaze in concern.

The look in Alex's eyes melted Cassidy's heart instantly. She reached up and cupped Alex's cheeks. "You worry too much, love."

"No. I don't. I worry when I need to worry," Alex whispered.

"Garlic," Cassidy said.

"I'm sorry?" Alex responded in confusion.

"The smell of garlic, it makes me nauseous," Cassidy explained.

"That's why you are avoiding the kitchen?" Alex asked. Cassidy nodded. "Why didn't you say something?" Cassidy just shrugged. "If I go get you something garlic free, will you eat it?" Alex asked hopefully. Cassidy nodded. "Cass, you have to let me help."

"I know. You won't always be here, honey," Cassidy reminded her. "And besides, you don't need to wait on me. I was alone the whole time I was sick when I was pregnant with Dylan." Alex bristled slightly and reached for the bridge of her nose. "Alex?" Cassidy called to her.

"I know I won't always be here, but you won't always be alone. I need to..."

Cassidy halted Alex's words by pressing two fingers to her wife's lips. "I'm sorry," she said. She felt Alex start to speak and cautioned her with a glance. "Let me finish," she said. "I know you need to be a part of things. I do know. I just...you've been away so much..."

"I'm sorry about the last few months, Cass. There will be times I will have to be away, but I promise it will never be for long."

"Aunt Jane!" Dylan yelled from the top of the stairs.

"Uh oh," Alex said. "I think CNN might be on the story again."

Cassidy laughed. She and Alex had been waiting for Stephanie Merrow's arrival to deliver their news. The eldest of the Merrow children was living in New Haven and was expected to arrive a bit later in the evening. Barely twenty minutes had passed since Stephanie had made her appearance. Cassidy was sure that Alex had hit the nail on the head. "Let him have his moment," Cassidy smiled.

Alex wrapped her arms around Cassidy and Cassidy collapsed back into her, holding Alex's hands gently in place on her stomach. "This should be interesting," Alex whispered.

"What is it Dylan?" Jane Merrow called back.

"Cat, you go down and make sure they are all there," Dylan's voice not too softly dictated orders to his cousin. Cat made his way down the stairs and surveyed the room. He looked back up to Dylan and gave the thumbs up.

Dylan made his way dramatically down the stairs. He had on his Batman mask, and he held his black Batman cape round him. "Santa came to the Batcave," he announced. "Dun Dah… Dun Dah!" He moved to the center of the room as the adults surrounding him watched his display with amused and affectionate eyes.

"What is he doing?" Krause sidled up to Alex and whispered.

"Oh, just watch," Alex told him.

Dylan stood in the middle of the room, ensuring that everyone could see him. "I already have Alfred. But, every superhero needs a sidekick," he said in the lowest voice he could muster. Alex could feel Cassidy lightly shaking with laughter. Dylan spun around and then opened his cape. "Dun Dah! Big Brother, BATMAN! I get my own sidekick!" he said with excitement.

Alex shook her head and erupted in an unusual animated guffaw when she felt Cassidy give over entirely to her laughter. "I don't care what anyone says," Cassidy continued to laugh. "He is *your* son."

Jane approached Dylan and gave him a hug. "So, you are going to have a little brother or sister, huh?"

"A sidekick!" he exclaimed happily.

"Of course, a sidekick," she agreed.

Stephanie Merrow pointed to her younger sister and whispered in Dylan's ear. "Welcome to the club, little man!"

"So?" Jane said as she made her way to Alex and Cassidy. "Holding out on me, huh?"

"Never," Alex said as Cassidy continued to laugh.

Jane pried Cassidy away from Alex and took her into an embrace. "Oh, Cassidy. You must be on cloud nine."

"More like on the bathroom floor," Cassidy whispered with a chuckle.

"Oh boy," Jane giggled. "Alex driving you crazy yet?"

"No, but you know..."

"Hey," Alex interrupted. "What are you two whispering about over here?"

"Oh, Alex....please," Jane dismissed her. "This is girl talk."

"Umm...last time I checked," Alex began.

"Go on," Jane waved her hand. "Go play with Jonathan for a while," she ordered.

Alex stood with her mouth agape as she watched Cassidy happily allow Jane to lead her away. "I give up," she chuckled. She returned her focus to the center of the room where Dylan was engaged in telling an animated story to the captive audience of the Merrow sisters. Rose and Helen were sitting on the sofa; both sipping wine and talking quietly. She smiled at the display. "Who said things never change?" she said to herself.

"Alex?" Krause made his way quietly toward his friend.

"Hey," she said. "Listen, I'm really sorry I didn't tell you sooner, I mean...I just wanted to tell you in person."

"Alex, don't worry about it," he said.

Alex looked at him and immediately noticed the worry that was creasing Krause's forehead and how his thumb was absently scratching his chin. "What is it?" she asked.

"Fallon just left me a message. Can we...."

Alex nodded. "Follow me," she said, leading him toward the kitchen. "All right. What is it?"

Krause sighed heavily. "You know that Cheryl Stephens walked into the FBI right before Christmas."

"Yeah?" she prodded him.

"Tate assigned an agent to follow her. Last night they found that agent in his car. He was shot at point blank range," Krause told her. He watched Alex's eyes harden and her jaw tighten.

"Who was the agent?" Alex asked. Krause hesitated. "Krause...who was the agent assigned?"

"Rolands," Krause answered.

"Shit," Alex exhaled forcefully. "Shit. Rolands has two kids. Jesus."

"Alex, there's more. It sent up red flags…this morning they…."

"Oh for Christ's sake, Krause! You've engineered assassinations. Just tell me," Alex finally exploded.

"She's dead, Alex. They found Cheryl in Douglas Park," Krause finally told her.

Alex lifted her hands to her temples and began to knead forcefully. Cassidy and Jane who were making their way back down the hallway heard Alex's voice rising steadily and had made their way to the room. Immediately, Cassidy noticed the tell-tale signs of stress in her wife. She took a deep breath, praying that her stomach would not revolt. "Alex?" Cassidy called. "What is going on?"

Alex looked up and across the room to her wife and friend. "Not here," Alex said. "Let's go into the family room."

"Alex, I am okay," Cassidy began.

"I know. It's not that," Alex said as she wrapped her arm around Cassidy's waist. "Please, trust me. Come on, Jane. You might as well hear it now too," she said, leading the group down the hall. Alex directed Cassidy and Jane to sit and took a seat beside her wife.

"All right, what is going on?" Cassidy repeated her earlier question.

"Cass…remember I told you that Cheryl walked into the FBI?" Alex asked. "She…Cassidy, they found her body this morning…"

"What are you saying?" Cassidy questioned. "Someone killed Cheryl? Why? Who?"

"I don't know," Alex said softly. "We were just getting to that when…"

Cassidy immediately looked to Krause. "Pip?" she implored him.

Krause glanced at Alex to ensure he wanted her to proceed. Her assent was clear, and he took a deep breath to continue. "I don't have all of the details. Only what Fallon left on my voicemail," he told them. "They found her in the park without any identification. Fallon identified her. She," Krause struggled under Cassidy's gaze. "She was brutally beaten and strangled." He heard Cassidy's gasp and watched as Alex pulled her closer. He looked at Jane, who had covered her face with her hands in disbelief. "There's more," he said cautiously. Alex looked at him fearfully.

"Go on," Cassidy said quietly, still holding onto Alex.

"Cassie....she left Chris on Christmas Eve...she filed a complaint....they're bringing him in for questioning," he said as gently as he could.

Cassidy covered her mouth with her hand. "Excuse me," she said, fleeing the room.

"Shit," Alex groaned. "I'll be back," she said.

"Jonathan," Jane looked to her friend. "You don't think he really did this; do you? I mean I have no use for the man, but..."

Krause took a deep breath. "No, but I wouldn't shed any tears if he went down for it," he said flatly. Jane looked at him suspiciously. "That son of a bitch threatened Cassidy. Raised a hand to her...once."

"How do you know that?" Jane asked.

"It's why she went to France," he said.

"She told you?" Jane gasped slightly. "You don't think he ever hit her again...I mean..."

"No. She got away from him the first time. I promise you he never did it again."

"You threatened him, didn't you?" Jane asked. His lack of response was the only answer she required. "Is it possible?" she wondered aloud.

Krause considered his response for a moment. "I think someone leveraged the situation. O'Brien's been moving money, outside of Collaborative directives. He opened accounts in her name. That's what finally drove her into the FBI. That and his continued philandering...but, from what Fallon told me...well, he'd left his mark on her more than once. He might not have been the one to strangle her Jane, but he certainly killed her."

Cassidy entered the room with Alex close behind just as Krause finished his explanation. She closed her eyes to steady herself. "All right. What do you and Alex need to do?" she asked Krause. He looked at her in confusion. "Do you need to leave?" Cassidy asked pointedly.

"No," he answered. "I didn't want you to turn on the television expecting a New Year's celebration or cartoons and see the congressman in handcuffs, or details about Cheryl," he explained.

Cassidy nodded and squeezed Alex's hand. "Then let's put this aside for the rest of the evening," she said firmly. Krause nodded and took Jane's hand to lead her from the room. Alex felt Cassidy's sharp intake of breath as they left.

"Cass, I know that you are upset...."

Cassidy turned to face Alex. She looked steadily into her wife's eyes and nodded her agreement. "I am upset. Not for him," she said pointedly. "Too many people have paid the price for his mistakes. This...this is the happiest New Year of my life, Alex. We are in our home with our family and friends. Our son is happier than I have ever seen him, and I am having a baby with the person I love more than anyone in this world. I will be damned if that asshole is going to spoil anything else for me. I may not be able to withstand or avoid garlic, but Christopher O'Brien is not getting one ounce of my time or energy for the rest of this evening." Alex quirked a playful smile at Cassidy's candid diatribe. "What?" Cassidy asked, unable to hide the growing smirk on her face.

"*Tu es belle* (You are beautiful)," Alex complimented.

"French?" Cassidy asked. She offered her wife a cockeyed grin. It had been a while since Alex had spoken French to her unprompted. "*Êtes-vous en état d'ébriété* (Are you drunk)?" Cassidy arched her brow.

"No," Alex chuckled. "Are you sure you are okay?"

Cassidy patted Alex's chest in reassurance. "Yes. No more work talk. No more ex-husband talk. No more garlic," she said as seriously as she could manage. "You, me...kissing at midnight..." Before she could finish, Alex had captured her lips in a gentle but passionate kiss. "Mmm...Not midnight yet, Agent Toles."

"It's midnight somewhere," Alex answered. She offered Cassidy her hand and turned off the light in the family room.

"You know, there are a lot of time zones, Alex," Cassidy observed.

"I thought you taught English, not geography," Alex poked.

"I am well-traveled," Cassidy replied evenly.

"Well then, Mrs. Toles, I eagerly await my geography lesson," Alex countered.

"Don't expect to get much rest. It will be a long lesson. It's a *big* world," Cassidy whispered as they re-entered the room filled with their guests.

"No worries," Alex whispered back. "I was always an attentive student," she mumbled under her breath.

"Oh, I'm counting on it," Cassidy winked.

***

Chapter Twelve

Saturday, January 3rd

"What are you talking about?" Claire Brackett seethed.

"There's no movement," Agent Anderson answered. "There is absolutely no record of any departure to or near Moscow, Claire. You've been duped."

"Eleana would never betray me," Claire defended her lover.

"Maybe you are too close to see things for what they are," her partner suggested.

"No. You should keep your mouth shut about things you have no knowledge of."

Anderson studied his partner's expression carefully. "Fine. You are that certain you can trust this woman? I've never seen you like this, Claire. Are you certain your feelings for this woman aren't clouding your judgment?"

"My what?" Brackett turned on her heel. "What the hell are you talking about?"

"You're quick to defend," he said.

Brackett painted an insincere smile on her face and began to circle her partner slowly, reaching out to graze his shirt seductively with her hand. "You are so perceptive, Marcus. That must be why he chose you. What? To find my weakness?" she cooed in his ear. "You think that Eleana is my weakness," she continued. "No. No. Marcus," she pressed herself up against him and nipped his ear. He stood resolute, his posture straight and unwavering. "Ohhhh....so strong," she teased him. She moved to turn and swiftly pivoted, lifting her knee to his chest and driving him backward forcefully into the wall. She heard the sound of the breath involuntarily escaping his lungs and smiled with satisfaction at her small victory. "You listen. Listen now, no speaking," she laughed, knowing he could not muster speech at the moment. "Eleana is not my weakness. She, she is my strength. You think…everyone thinks they know who Eleana is, who I am; who we are not. They think they know where we will move, how we will move," she shook her head and leaned back into him. "Someone is playing a game, Marcus, and you just got moved across the board….so did I. Time to turn the table," she asserted. She pounded his chest with the palms of her hands and turned away. "No more waiting for someone else's move," she said. "Checkmate…time is up."

***

Tuesday, January 6th

"I thought this was taken care of!"

Assistant FBI Director Joshua Tate flinched at the thunderous echo in his ear. He had taken great caution and accepted even greater risk in entering this building while the men in the room below him were here. This obscure warehouse served as inter-agency headquarters. It served as a window into a world that he had grown to view as soulless in its motivations. Loyalty, dedication, service, duty, a calling; these were the catch phrases of those appointed to recruit men and women into this 'noble' life. They were no better than two-bit, used car salesmen in his opinion. He had left a life protecting his community for the opportunity to serve an even greater purpose. Now, he understood. Purpose was questionable. Loyalty was flexible. Duty was mainly evident in the service to one's ascent up the ladder; a ladder that had little to do with any noble cause and everything to do with power. He sighed in disappointment as he listened to the continuing conversation.

"It's only a temporary setback. Relax," another man's voice responded.

"Of course, it is," the older man answered. "Like what? First you screw up O'Brien's accident...he should have been removed from this long ago!"

"I did not arrange that. Claire...."

"I know who arranged it. Claire did what she was told. I want to know why he survived. That's what I want to know, Agent Brady. Why did he survive? You have a record of failure. A serious record of failure. Jesus Christ! Thank God Agent Krause found his way to Mrs. O'Brien's that day. Otherwise, we'd probably still be dealing with Carl Fisher and one mightily pissed off Agent Toles. I want to know....How the hell did John survive that shot as long as he did? Were my instructions not clear enough for you?"

Agent Brady felt his blood pressure rising steadily. "He moved."

"He moved? Fabulous. That movement bought him time. If I hadn't intervened afterward it might have bought him a second chance. Now we have O'Brien shifting funds. I want him gone. Gone; out of the picture. I don't need him firing up Alex and Krause. Christ only knows where Callier and the admiral fall in all of this. I want O'Brien out of the way; permanently."

"He'll go down. Investigations take time," Brady said flatly. "You know that."

"Fix it. I don't care how you fix it. Just fix it now. Dimitri has made new plans. I want him out of commission before that. No more mistakes, Stephen," the voice warned.

Tate turned off the recorder and threw his head back in disbelief. "Christ, John. You were right. All along, you were right. He was at every turn," Tate sighed. He swallowed hard and placed what he knew would be the most difficult call of his life. "We need to meet," he said. "No. I will come to you.....No, this is something you both need to hear.....Fine....No. We keep Agent Fallon on Claire. She's still the wildcard.....I'll see you soon," he said. Tate ran his hand over his head repeatedly. He would need to wait and ensure his targets had left the premises before making his presence known. "Now what?" he muttered.

***

Thursday, January 8th

"Dylan?" Cassidy called out. Dylan had been begging to go outside since he woke up. It was the first heavy snowfall of the winter, and that meant no school. Cassidy had cajoled her son into a quiet morning with the promise that they would get outside before lunchtime. "Hey…I thought you wanted to go outside in the snow?" Cassidy asked as she entered the family room.

Dylan was sitting completely still, staring at the television. Cassidy followed her son's gaze and her heart stopped. She grabbed the remote, clicked the off button and placed herself squarely in front of her son. "Dylan," she called to him softly. Dylan's eyes moved in a painfully slow motion to meet his mother's gaze. The fear behind his expression was unmistakable, and Cassidy immediately grasped both his arms in comforting reassurance. "Dylan, sweetheart…look at me; okay?" He complied, his lip noticeably quivering. "I'm sorry you had to see that, sweetheart."

"He hurt her," was Dylan's hushed response.

Cassidy bit her bottom lip and closed her eyes momentarily before placing her hands on either side of Dylan's small face and looking directly into his eyes. "I don't know, sweetheart."

"He did," Dylan repeated. "Why did he?" he asked as his tears began to surface.

Cassidy moved beside him and pulled him into her lap. "Oh, Dylan. I don't know why people hurt one another. I wish I could tell you. I don't have that answer."

"She died," Dylan whispered.

Cassidy fought the urge to be sick. She could feel the pain pouring off of Dylan in waves. She and Alex had tried to prepare

Dylan for the news he might see. As she sat holding him now, she realized there was no way to prepare him for the images he would inevitably confront. No matter what had come to pass, he had spent seven years calling the man he just saw in handcuffs 'Daddy'. How could anyone explain to a seven-year-old the depths of ugliness that a human heart can hold? She rocked him gently for a moment, occasionally kissing his head and stroking his hair. "I'm sorry, baby," she said. "I love you so much, Dylan."

"Mom?" he asked.

"Yes, sweetie?"

"I hate him," Dylan said harshly.

Cassidy sighed. "Dylan...."

"I do!" Dylan yelled as his tears erupted. "He's bad....he's a bad," Dylan's outburst turned rapidly to hysterical crying and Cassidy was helpless to do anything but hold him and rock him.

"Goddamn you," she silently thought. "How could you put him through this?" She felt Dylan shaking and held him tight. "Alex," was the only word that Cassidy could make out through Dylan's tears.

Cassidy kissed his forehead. "All right, sweetheart. Try and calm down; okay? I promise you are safe. It's all right, Dylan. Alex and I will never let anyone hurt you," she gently assured him. She scolded herself for the words as they escaped her. There were many ways to cause someone pain. Christopher O'Brien had caused more than his fair share of pain in their family. "Listen," she pulled away slightly and directed him to look at her. "Everything will be okay. When Alex comes home tonight, we will all sit down and talk about this." Dylan nodded and wiped his eyes with the back of his hand. "Let's get you washed up and then we'll try to call Alex; all right?" He nodded again. "Okay. Do you want me to come with you to the bathroom?" Dylan shook his head 'no' and Cassidy offered him a sad smile. "Still want to play in the snow with me?" she asked hopefully. She smiled when he wrapped his arms around her neck. "Good. Now, come on. You go on ahead, and I will call

Alex. After some time in the snow I'll make us some cocoa and we'll warm up with some Batman," she winked.

Dylan managed a slight smile at her offer and turned to head for the bathroom. "Mom?" he called back.

"Yes, sweetie?"

"You are way cooler than Batman," he said lovingly.

Cassidy felt his compliment in every fiber of her being. She winked at him and smiled. "And, you will always be my hero," she promised her son. He finally managed what she knew was a genuine smile, albeit a small one. She was relieved to see a slight bounce to his step return. "God forgive me," she said once Dylan had left the room. "I hope they lock him up and throw away the key for putting him through this."

***

Alex sat on a bench in the back of the van with her face in her hands. She could feel the heat of both Krause and Tate's gaze settling on her. She needed time; just a moment. In an instant, her world had once again been turned upside down. The sting of deceit left her feeling hollow. So much she had entrusted in him. She found herself wondering again if there was anyone she could trust at all. She pressed the heels of her hands into her temples and took a deep breath. "I don't understand what Taylor gains in all of this." Disappointment and distress were evident as she spoke the words.

"I can't say that," Joshua Tate answered. "John suspected for some time that Director Taylor might have a different agenda. For a long while, actually."

"That's why he wanted me back at the NSA; isn't it?" she asked him. Tate's nod was her confirmation. "And, Brady? Jesus. How did Stephen Brady get mixed up in this? Krause, he was working with Ian. I don't…."

Jonathan Krause looked across to his partner and friend with sympathetic eyes. It was not only Alex's betrayal to feel.

He had placed the chatter surrounding the assassination attempt on President John Merrow squarely in the NSA's backyard for Stephen Brady and Michael Taylor to uncover. Krause felt a sickening familiarity in this new information. John Merrow never shared his suspicions about the NSA Director with his best friend. The president's death was a foregone conclusion. It made sense now to Krause. Merrow knew there would be no escape. He was backed into a corner, surrounded with no chance of escape. Krause had trusted Stephen Brady. He had trusted Michael Taylor. It was a lapse in judgment he was not certain he could ever forgive himself for making.

"How far back?" Alex asked her former boss. "Tate? How far back did John suspect Taylor had a different agenda?" She watched the assistant FBI director's temple twitch under the stress. "Jesus," she sighed, shaking her head. She looked back at Tate and asked him pointedly, "Iraq?" His expression remained remarkably unchanged, only his eyes closing in confirmation. Alex covered her face again, grasping the bridge of her nose in frustration and disbelief. "Oh my God. That's what he meant," she looked across to Krause. "John told me the attack in Iraq was his fault...he meant Taylor."

Krause released a heavy sigh. "Alex," he stopped and gathered his thoughts. "Taylor is not working with The Collaborative. Whatever he is doing, it isn't with the admiral or Edmond."

"I know," Alex said. "So, now what? This isn't something that developed as recently as we suspected," she said frankly.

"No," Tate interrupted. "It isn't. I suspect you will find that Taylor has friends at ASA," he concluded.

Some of the pieces were coming together for Alex. "So, we play him?" she surmised. Krause and Tate both offered her a weak smile. "Great. We see how many other lives he can manage to trample in the process. Jesus."

"Alex, at least we know whose trail to follow," Krause said.

"I want the son of a bitch," she responded with conviction.

Alex felt the buzz of her cell phone. “I need to listen to this,” she told the men, lifting the phone to her ear.

Tate looked at Krause, concern painting his irises like the color of a stormy night sky. Krause shook his head in agreed disgust. He turned back toward Alex and watched as her face flushed in anger, and her thumb began to dig into her temple. “Alex?” Krause called for her attention.

Alex rolled her tongue across the inside of her cheek in a desperate attempt to quell her growing rage. She looked at the two men seated across from her and channeled her fury into a steely resolve. “I don’t care what we have to do. Taylor, Brady, O’Brien, Brackett…whoever had a hand in this….I want them. I don’t care where it leads,” she stated, leaving no room for any questions.

“Tate?” Krause looked to the older man. “Are you in? You know if you stay this course, well….Taylor, Brady….Claire… they’ve proven they will sacrifice anyone.”

“I’m in,” Tate agreed.

“Krause?” Alex called to her partner. “If we commit to this….”

“John was like my brother, Alex. You know that. Dylan…. this is…It’s family, Alex,” Krause choked slightly on the words. “There is nothing else left to commit to.”

Alex offered him a cockeyed grin. Krause was emphatic. “All right. We play their game. Let them think they are still controlling the board. Nothing to Jane or Matt for now,” Alex ordered. “Pip, you know Callier best. Your call if and when we bring him in,” Alex said. “For now, it’s us and Fallon. Agreed?” The consensus was clear. “Tate you bring Fallon up to speed and watch yourself. They won’t hesitate…”

Tate smiled and grasped Alex’s shoulder. “I can take care of myself, Agent Toles,” he said as he moved to open the van’s door.

“Tate?” Alex stopped him. “One last thing…..Why did you tell Fallon that Krause and I were never supposed to meet?”

Tate jumped slightly at the question. He looked at Jonathan Krause and quickly returned his gaze to Alex. "Agent Toles, I am not the person to answer that question. I suspect you already have some ideas."

"Trust is," she began.

"Trust is both earned and broken," Tate said as he leaned in her ear. "It is not only you I have made commitments to," he said. "Be careful."

***

"Get your hands off of me!" Christopher O'Brien demanded. "What the hell is this?"

Brian Fallon entered the small interrogation room and directed the detective to leave with a brief glance. He looked at the congressman sitting handcuffed in a chair and shook his head, a smile creasing the edges of his lips. "Took a little longer than I had hoped," Fallon said as he flopped into a chair in the corner.

"What the hell are you doing here?" O'Brien asked.

Fallon stretched his legs out in front of him and laced his fingers behind his head as if he were lazing about his home. "Just getting comfortable," he mocked the congressman.

"I'll be out of here before you can even fire off a question," O'Brien asserted.

Fallon shrugged. "You might be safer in here," he responded. The congressman shot him a look of disdain. "Not really a great idea to syphon funds from the people you work for. Putting those funds in an account in your girlfriend's name… well, if it had worked, maybe a stroke of brilliance," he said. "But then, you have never been that lucky; have you?" Fallon watched as O'Brien grimaced. "I hope Claire knows what she's gotten herself into," Fallon chuckled. The unexpected comment prompted O'Brien to flinch. "Oh? Was that supposed to be a secret? You aren't so great at keeping those either,"

Fallon shook his head as if he were disappointed. "So? This is a pattern, then. The women in your life end up the victim of some maniac. That's coincidence?" Fallon asked. "So, you didn't murder Cheryl? Just like you didn't know Carl Fisher? You almost got Cassidy killed."

"I'm not saying anything to you, Agent Fallon. You are wasting my time and your breath. I'm not a murderer," O'Brien said.

Fallon swiftly pulled his chair in front of the congressman. He placed his forehead squarely against O'Brien's and whispered hoarsely. "Just an attempted murderer, then?" O'Brien did not answer. Fallon leaned over, his breath filling the congressman's ear. "You tried to kill Alex. Women should stay away from you.....Tough man hits a lady." Fallon pulled the chair back and stood. "So? Why did Cheryl leave you, Mr. O'Brien?" No response. "Where is Claire these days? Not here to rescue you, huh?" Fallon chuckled.

"I want my lawyer."

"I'm sure. We all want something," Fallon shrugged.

O'Brien's frustration was growing by the second. "I have the right to my attorney."

Fallon pursed his lips in consideration. He tipped his head and winked at the man in the chair. "Well, I will have him brought right in, Congressman O'Brien," Fallon said sweetly. O'Brien narrowed his gaze at the unexpected agreement to his demand. "Talk with your attorney all you like. I can assure you, Congressman; you are not getting out of this. In addition to conspiracy to commit wire fraud and making false statements, you have door number three: felony murder, which, by the way, well...you are a lawyer...Stanford, right? So you know you can be tried by both the State of Virginia and in Federal Court," Fallon gleamed as he listed off the charges. "You look confused? Let's just say the money trail is enough to make a case for a threat to national security; at least to my superiors.

And, since the motive for murder appears to be that Cheryl discovered your little game…well, you understand."

"They already told me the charges," O'Brien answered. "Just get my attorney."

"Certainly, Congressman," Fallon agreed. Before leaving he bent over into the congressman's ear again. "Personally, I hope he does get you out." O'Brien looked up at the FBI agent, baffled. Fallon chuckled as he leaned back into O'Brien. "They just wanted you removed," Fallon said. "Out there? They'll want you dead. Frankly, I hope you get your wish you son of a bitch."

O'Brien watched Brian Fallon calmly leave the room. He closed his eyes and struggled to swallow the dryness in his throat. The bitterness in Fallon's statement did not change its truth. He wondered as he waited, if anyone would come to his rescue or if he had finally become a sheep awaiting its slaughter. He shook off his questions. There was always a bargaining chip. He could manufacture one. The only question in his mind now was who he could convince to negotiate with him.

***

Cassidy quietly made her way toward the bathroom, observing Alex as she massaged her temple with one hand while leaning heavily on the sink with the other. She gently caressed Alex's back and spoke softly. "I'm sorry, Alex."

Alex sighed and turned to face her wife. "You have nothing to be sorry for."

Cassidy fell into Alex's embrace. "I know it's not right. It's terrible. I know it…but I hope Chris rots in there," Cassidy said.

"It's not terrible," Alex said. "When I got your message…. Cassidy, if O'Brien had been anywhere near me I swear I could have killed him myself."

Cassidy pulled back at the severity in Alex's voice. "You wouldn't do that," she said.

"No. I wouldn't because of you and Dylan, which ironically is the same reason I could do it and feel no remorse."

"I don't believe that," Cassidy said. "You would never. It's not who you are. I do understand how that feels. I won't shed any tears watching this, Alex. I don't have any left for him. Not after seeing Dylan…"

"I know. There is one bright side," Alex offered.

"I'm all ears," Cassidy forced a smile.

"Custody won't be an issue. He's going down, Cass. One way or another he will be out of the picture. That's a guarantee."

Cassidy licked her lips and sighed in contemplation. The implication of Alex's words was not lost on her. "Alex, what aren't you telling me?" Alex turned on the shower and the fan in the bathroom, signaling Cassidy that what she was about to say required some safeguards. Cassidy felt a chill travel swiftly up her spine.

"Cass, he's into something. I knew that when we were dealing with Fisher, but it's deeper than I thought and now he's marked. I just couldn't piece together who he was working with until…I still can hardly believe…"

"Alex," Cassidy took hold of her wife's hand. "Just tell me, please."

Alex closed her eyes and steadied her breathing. The wound that was Michael Taylor's betrayal was raw. "It was Taylor, Cass. It was him all along; at least he pulled most of the strings. I said O'Brien was a puppet? Claire? I guess you can count me in that show. Michael Taylor is a master puppeteer."

Cassidy searched Alex's eyes, attempting to convey her understanding and love. "Oh, Alex; are you sure?" Alex nodded sadly. "I don't understand," Cassidy sighed helplessly.

"It's complicated and it's not. At the end of the day, I expect we'll find money is at the root. Isn't is always?" Alex chuckled in disgust. "Taylor arranged O'Brien's accident, Cass. He and Brady. He's probably been moving money for a long time. I can't believe Taylor…I mean, how could he? God…Cass?" Alex strained to make the words come.

Cassidy tightened her grip on Alex's hand in encouragement. "Tell me."

"He killed John, Cass. The assassination, it was Taylor…. he," Alex took a deep breath. "That book shop on Mutanabbi Street….I thought John was responsible that day. When he told me it was his fault, he meant Taylor…he should have been watching Taylor," Alex finished and let her head fall onto Cassidy's shoulder.

Cassidy held Alex close, tenderly rubbing circles on her back. Their relationship had been plagued for many months by nightmares. Alex struggled with memories of a horrific IED attack when she was in Baghdad. She would awaken in a panic, reliving the day. Alex had been working with the locals and befriended a bookshop owner and his daughter. She told Cassidy she never suspected anything about the man who owned the bookshop. It was her job to assess threat risks; to reduce them. She walked headlong into a trap with five other officers, losing three of her best friends in the process and suffering severe injuries herself. Both her Colonel, John Merrow, and her Captain, Michael Taylor, were also injured. It had formed a bond between the three. Alex spent years shouldering the blame for the attack. She should have seen the warning signs. Alex had come to believe in recent months that John Merrow had knowledge of the attack. Now, it appeared it was her Captain. Either way it was an unthinkable betrayal.

Cassidy pulled back and stroked Alex's cheek. "I'm sorry, love. Let me clean up in here. Go lie down. I'll be right there," she directed Alex. Cassidy turned off the water and the fan, shut off the light and made her way to the bed. "Come here," she said, pulling Alex to her.

"I'm tired, Cass," Alex barely whispered.

Cassidy ran her hands through Alex's hair to calm her. "I know."

"Cass?"

"Yeah?"

Alex's voice trembled slightly as she began to speak, "I know I said it solved the immediate problem with Dylan..."

"But...you want to declare Jonathan as his father," Cassidy guessed.

"I know. It doesn't make sense. How can I even trust Krause? Look at what..."

Cassidy stopped Alex's rambling with a kiss. "You do trust him," Cassidy said.

"Yes," Alex answered. "But I have no reason to."

"I think you do," Cassidy said flatly. "Alex, what does your heart tell you?"

"Cassidy, this is no business for emotions."

"I disagree. Then why do you do it?" Cassidy asked.

"What do you mean?" Alex was perplexed. "It's my job."

"No. You could do anything. It's not just the challenge, Alex. I know you love that. You find a challenge in everything," Cassidy observed. "You moved heaven and earth to get to me when Carl Fisher was alive. Why?"

"I love you," Alex's reply came swiftly.

"Mm-hm. I know. You care. Alex, you care what happens to people. You might not like to admit that, but you do."

"Maybe. That doesn't mean I can afford to trust them," Alex said.

"How do you know you can trust me?" Cassidy asked.

"Cass, I trust you with my life."

"I know. I trust you with my life. That's not what I asked you. What made you believe you could trust me with your life?" Cassidy asked again.

"I don't know. I felt it. I feel it. I just know," Alex said honestly.

Cassidy smiled and kissed Alex's head. "But, I kept something from you. I didn't tell you that John was Dylan's father right away."

"Yes, but you didn't do that to deceive me. That was to protect Dylan," Alex said.

"Partly…and to protect me. I was afraid of losing you," Cassidy admitted.

"Not the same," Alex assured her wife.

"Maybe not. The point is, no one will ever be perfect. You only hurt yourself if you keep score. You know that. Pip cares for you," Cassidy said. "I feel it. So do you. I understand why you are afraid to trust. I honestly do. I felt that way after Chris. So many lies. So many affairs. The truth is, Alex, I felt that way after my father died too."

"You were just a kid," Alex reminded her wife.

"That's true. I still felt deceived; lied to," Cassidy explained. Alex propped herself up and listened intently as Cassidy continued. "I trusted him to be there for me. He said he would be. One day he wasn't. When my mother told me the truth; that he was drunk…even after all those years; I felt so betrayed. Strangely not as much by her. She wanted to protect me. My father? The man I worshiped all those years? He left. He cared more about that bottle than he did about either me or Mom."

"Cass, that's not true and you know that is not the same…"

"Yes, Alex, it is," Cassidy said. "It might be a play that is happening on a different stage, but it is the same plot. Something was more important than you to a person who you thought was your friend. Just like something was always more important to Chris than Dylan and me. Something is more important to you now than the cases you solve. You can't lock away your heart because people will disappoint you. If you feel you can trust Pip; trust him. You trusted him enough to bring him into this family. He trusted you enough to follow." Alex sighed. "Your mother told me that you often remind her of your father," Cassidy said cautiously.

"I'm not my father," Alex responded a bit more aggressively than she intended.

Cassidy took it in stride, undaunted in her mission to reach her wife. "No, I'm sure in many ways you are not. She was talking about commitment. He had obligations to many things,

Alex; just like you. There is no excuse for what you told me tonight. I'm not saying there is. But, what would you tell our children? If they were afraid to trust? If they were hurting?"

Alex laid her head back on Cassidy's chest and smiled. "That's why you are the mom," Alex said lovingly.

"Alex, you are a mom too."

"I know. But, you are like everyone's mom," Alex said proudly.

"What does that mean?" Cassidy asked.

"Like just now. I wouldn't know what to say; not like you just did."

Cassidy took a deep breath and looked down at Alex. "That's not true."

"Sure it is," Alex said, snuggling closer.

"No. It isn't. I heard you in there with Dylan. What did you say to him?" Cassidy asked. Alex shifted uncomfortably. "You told him that sometimes people hurt us, not even knowing they are doing it. It's not okay. It is okay that he is hurt and angry, but deep down that's because he trusted his father," Cassidy repeated the gist of Alex's conversation with Dylan. "And then, you told him that somewhere deep down his father loves him and to remember the times that they went to the beach, or played catch in the yard and to hold onto that." Cassidy smiled and pulled Alex closer. "You should take your own advice, Alex. Whatever happens, hang onto the good stuff. It always gets you through."

"How did you get so insightful?" Alex asked.

"I didn't tell you anything you didn't already know. You just needed to hear someone else say it," Cassidy said with a kiss.

"Is that what you do?" Alex asked curiously, pulling herself up to look in Cassidy's eyes.

"What do you do? When you are upset, off course; how do you get through it? What did you think about today on your way home?" Cassidy turned the question back on Alex.

Alex smiled. "I thought about Dylan dancing around on New Year's Eve telling everyone about his sidekick," Alex chuckled.

"See? Good stuff," Cassidy winked at her wife.

"Yeah, I guess there is," Alex admitted. "Thanks," she said. Cassidy tipped her head in confusion. "You know for what," Alex laughed, answering her wife's unspoken question. "Sometimes I don't know what I did without you."

"You ate a lot of junk food for one thing," Cassidy recalled.

"I took a lot of risks," Alex admitted honestly. "I won't make those mistakes now."

"Yes, love; you will. It's part of who you are," Cassidy said.

"Cass, I promise you, I would never run into..."

"I've told you before, don't make promises you can't keep, Alex. I fell in love with Alexis Toles. That's who I want to grow old with, but I accepted the risks that come with that when I married you. Just remember there is good stuff waiting for you here. That's all I ask," Cassidy said honestly.

Alex nodded and kissed Cassidy tenderly. "You'll never know how much you mean to me," Alex whispered, her eyes growing heavy.

"I do know. It's been a long day," Cassidy said as she felt Alex's body wrap around her. "Enjoy this while it lasts," she laughed. "A few months and you'll be lucky to fit beside me."

"Good stuff," Alex mumbled.

"Yes, it is."

***

Chapter Thirteen

Friday, January 16th

"Eleana," Ambassador Russ Matthews greeted his friend.

"Ambassador," Eleana returned his pleasantries.

"I confess I am surprised to see you in Moscow now. I thought you were traveling," he said.

"I was," she replied.

"Still residing in Belarus?" he asked.

"It serves my purposes," Eleana explained.

"Ah, and what is the purpose of today's visit?" the ambassador wondered.

"I had company for Christmas," she began. The ambassador looked at her curiously. "It was Claire," Eleana told him.

"I see. Fishing for information I assume?" the ambassador guessed.

"Yes. I gave her the original dates for the diplomatic team to arrive," she said.

"Eleana, I appreciate your loyalty, but compromising yourself with Claire Brackett....we both know that I'm a target. You can't change that now," he told her.

Eleana Baros regarded Russ Matthews as more than a colleague; he was a friend. "Russ," she took his hand. "Claire will never suspect me of disloyalty."

"Did she say anything else?" Matthews asked.

"Specifically, no. Claire says a great deal without needing many words," Eleana sighed.

"You care for her," the ambassador surmised.

"Yes," she admitted.

"And yet you are here," Russ Matthews shook his head. "Eleana, don't put yourself on the fence. Believe me they will discover you far more quickly."

Eleana moved to sit beside her friend. "I am not on any fence. I made my choice. I will not be a traitor to it," she assured him.

"You realize that when those cars arrive here, we will become a sitting target," the ambassador said assuredly. He pulled himself up and paced around the room slowly. "It is an inevitability, Eleana. I sat on that fence too long before I made my choice. I should have listened to John much sooner. If your father finds out that you..."

"He will. Sooner or later; he will," she said.

"He will never forgive us for allowing you to become involved," Ambassador Matthews said.

"I don't need my father's permission, so you need no absolution. You and I both know that if Viktor Ivanov gets his way ASA will slowly run the table on an oil monopoly among other things. He's already embedded ASA in Libya, Syria, Yemen, and Pakistan, not to mention his interests in Asia and Central America. He is greedy and ruthless. John saw that. I see it. My father knows it. I cannot turn away from that," she told her friend.

"You do know Claire is in their fold?" he asked her.

Eleana nodded. "I love Claire, Russ. God help me; I do. I have since we were in grade school. She broke her commitment to that long ago. It forced me to live my life, away from Claire. I may love her, but she has never loved me. She is too preoccupied with proving herself to love anyone. I spent years trying to change her. In the end, I only could change myself. Claire made her choice," she said softly.

"Are you prepared to," Matthews began to ask his friend the ultimate question. Could Eleana take Claire Brackett's life if it became necessary? He stopped when he saw the anguish in her eyes.

"I lost her a long time ago, if I ever even had her," Eleana admitted. "But, the answer is I don't know. If it were between you and Claire; if it were between anyone and Claire; could I pull the trigger? I've asked myself that question a million times these last few weeks. I don't know."

Ambassador Matthews nodded. "You are far too honest for this life, Eleana," he complimented her. "Your father was wise to keep you at bay for so long. I understand." The ambassador made his way to a small window and watched for the approaching vehicles. "Any word on that Cesium?" he asked her.

"It crossed the border yesterday, traveling north."

"Toward us," he concluded.

"In all probability; yes," she confirmed.

"God help us," Matthews' voice dropped an octave.

Eleana crossed to the window. "Perhaps we have more time than you think," she suggested.

He turned to face her when a whirling sound distracted him. "Eleana!"

***

"Do you want to know?" Alex turned to her wife from the driver's seat.

Cassidy stroked the back of Alex's hand absently with her thumb. "I don't know. Part of me does. Part of me would rather it be a surprise. What about you?"

Alex had been thinking a great deal about Cassidy's pregnancy and the arrival of a new person into their lives. Before Cassidy, the idea of parenthood seemed preposterous at best to Alex. Babies were not something that she spent much time daydreaming about over the years. The majority of her close friends had been men, and they rarely discussed their wives' pregnancies in any detail. Alex had been so surprised to hear the baby's heartbeat that when Cassidy's doctor asked if they had discussed the question of determining the baby's gender;

Alex deferred immediately to Cassidy to answer. "I think whatever you want is fine," Alex finally responded.

"I think we should make this decision together," Cassidy corrected her wife.

"I wonder why she asked that today," Alex inquired.

"Just making conversation I would suspect," Cassidy said. "Getting to know us. That's all. We have time, Alex. She didn't expect an answer today."

"Just out of curiosity; why wouldn't you want to know?" Alex asked.

Cassidy chuckled. "Oh, well…I don't know. I suppose an element of surprise gives me something to look forward to during those few hours that come before."

Alex was slightly puzzled. "But, wouldn't you still be curious? I mean, about what he will look like and all that?"

"Wrinkly," Cassidy laughed. "Honestly, I always laugh when babies are first born; how people say they look just like someone in the family. They look like babies." Cassidy looked across to Alex and had to bite down on her lip at the look of consternation on her wife's face. She squeezed Alex's hand gently. "I'm kidding. Of course, I would still be curious."

Alex sighed in relief as she pulled into the garage. "Do you think you can make your appointments for Fridays?" she asked Cassidy. "I don't want to miss any," Alex said. "What if I miss something important like your ultrasound? I don't want to just see his picture."

"His?" Cassidy asked. "What is it with you and Dylan anyway? What makes you so sure it's a him?"

"I don't know. Just seems like I should say him," Alex explained.

"I see," Cassidy grinned. "Well, I'll see what I can do about Fridays. You need to stop worrying, though. You are not going to miss anything important; I promise. There will be lots of appointments," Cassidy said as they made their way toward the house.

"Yeah, and I intend to be at all of them," Alex said pointedly as she opened the door for Cassidy.

"Will you take stirrup duty for me too?" Cassidy turned back to her wife.

"Only if…" Alex immediately stopped their banter at the sight of Rose in front of the door. The older woman's jaw was set firmly, and the dismay in her eyes startled Alex.

Cassidy watched Alex's playful expression fade rapidly from view. "Alex?"

Rose swallowed her apprehension. "Dylan is upstairs in his room," she said as Cassidy turned to face her. "I….Alex…"

"Mom?" Cassidy implored.

Rose shook her head. "Maybe you should just see for yourself."

***

"Mr. President, we need to move to the Situation Room."

President Lawrence Strickland followed his entourage through the halls of the White House on a familiar course. "What do we know?" he asked.

"Not much," General Michael Snyder responded. "One of our people called in about ten minutes ago. The message was interrupted, but it appears that the embassy in Moscow has been attacked."

The president calmly took his seat in the large room and waited for his aides to assume their positions. There was a definite advantage in having foreknowledge of such events. The president was able to react in a controlled and deliberate manner. Everyone expected the presence of a confident and secure leader and Lawrence Strickland intended to personify that now. "Everything we know; now," he directed.

"Sir," the general stood and directed everyone's attention to the large screen at the front of the room. Images of a smoking building immediately came into focus. "This is what we have so far."

"Where are our satellite images, General Snyder?" the president asked. Within seconds, the screens hanging at either side of the room depicted satellite imagery. "So?" the president asked pointedly. "Are we confirmed? Is it the embassy?"

"Yes, sir. Unfortunately, it is," a voice responded.

The president leaned forward on his elbows, studying the faces that surrounded him. "Responsible party?" he asked.

"Still undetermined, Mr. President. No one has claimed responsibility. It does appear that the building was hit from an exterior force," General Snyder offered.

"Meaning?" Strickland asked.

"Meaning there was no bomb in the building itself. We are pulling up satellite data and telemetry now. There were no planes in the area. It's a no-fly zone. So, we are looking at some type of short-range missile in all likelihood, or some combination of…"

"I don't want speculation, people!" President Strickland bellowed. "I want answers. Get Secretary Johnson and Mr. Mansfield here now."

"Already on their way," a voice answered.

"Jason, get President Markov on the line," Strickland ordered. "Now!" The president stroked his chin in thought. He watched as his advisers ran about, carrying out his demands in a flurry. Inwardly, he began to gloat. This tragedy would be a small price to pay for the ultimate reward; to lead the nation through crisis. "What about the news?"

The large screen changed abruptly to several inset images of national newscasts. "Bob!" President Strickland called to his press secretary. "Start preparing a statement. I want it ready for my review when I am done with President Markov," he said. "Do we know?" Strickland turned back to the full table. "Do we know who was in the embassy at the time?"

"Sir," the president's chief of staff began softly. "Yes, sir. As of now, it appears fifteen Americans, six Russian workers, and a Spanish national."

"What about the envoy?" the president asked. A team of ten men and women with expertise ranging from Russian culture to economics had been scheduled to arrive at the embassy in Moscow that afternoon.

"We don't know," General Snyder answered.

"We can see someone picking watermelon seeds from their teeth, General! What do you mean you don't know? Did they arrive or didn't they?" the president's voice reverberated off the walls.

"They left the airstrip. If they arrived at the embassy, they had not signed in..."

"Jesus Christ!" President Strickland slammed a hand on the table. "Find out. We can't wait to issue this statement. I don't want this screwed up!"

"Mr. President," a youthful voice called. "President Markov is on the line."

"Thank you, Dan," President Strickland said calmly as she headed for the small office set aside for his use. "When I am done I want that statement in my hands, and I want some damn answers. I don't want to rely on Yegor Markov's word. Understood?" he asked. The room remained silent, all eyes on the president. "Good," Strickland said as he entered the small room.

***

"Successful?" Viktor Ivanov asked, looking at the screen.

"It appears so," Dimitri Kargen answered.

"Excellent. What of Kabinov and Markov?" Ivanov asked. "Are they prepared to make the accusation?"

"The statement will be issued shortly," Kargen said.

"Viktor," a man's voice broke through the speaker. "Be cautious. You move too quickly with these assertions, and you will become cannon fodder yourself."

"Calm down, Michael," Ivanov responded. "Things are in line as we predicted and planned."

"There is one unforeseen complication," Dimitri Kargen interrupted the conversation.

"What complication?" Ivanov asked hesitantly.

Dimitri Kargen scratched his brow with his thumb and winced slightly as he delivered the news. "Eleana Baros was visiting the embassy." Viktor Ivanov's face flushed a deep crimson. Dimitri could see the quivering in his uncle's temples as Viktor Ivanov's rage mounted.

Ivanov took a step closer to his nephew. "Are you telling me that Edmond Callier's daughter was in that building when it blew?"

"Jesus!" Michael Taylor's voice called through the open line.

"*Zamolchi, Teylor! Eto nepriyemlemo! Nepriyemlemo, Dmitriy*! (Be quiet, Taylor! Unacceptable! Unacceptable, Dimitri)!" Ivanov scolded both men. "Callier is already problematic thanks to Sparrow!"

"Uncle Viktor," Dimitri began. "There was no way to prevent that..."

"*Menia ne interesujut tvoi opravdanija*! (I am not interested in your excuses)!" Ivanov blared. "Michael, you will see that this story is weaved correctly through that imbecile you call your president."

Michael Taylor could not help but snicker slightly at the statement. He had no use for President Strickland. Taylor saw Strickland as a marionette whose strings were being pulled by anyone and everyone who offered the slightest praise, threat, or perceived opportunity. He knew that Strickland was intelligent and well connected, but Taylor also understood that Lawrence Strickland epitomized weakness. The president had no principles, no larger goal than his continually polishing his image. He was a politician, not a leader. For men like Michael Taylor, President Lawrence Strickland was little more than a fly that needed to be swatted. "I will ensure Strickland's compliance," he said. "But, Viktor," Taylor cautioned his friend. "I can do little about Edmond Callier."

"We will deal with that as we always have. It is an unfortunate inconvenience. We can navigate Mr. Callier. We have for years. The story will create enough diversion on its own," Ivanov said. "A member of your diplomatic envoy was carrying nuclear material into Moscow with the intention of selling it to anti-Markov terrorists. He made the mistake of one too many bidders and one too many commitments."

"Creative," Taylor mock complimented Ivanov's fabrication.

"They will believe whatever we tell them," Ivanov said. "That never changes."

***

Alex and Cassidy sat glued to the images rolling across the television screen. Cassidy could feel the tension in her wife. It seemed to rise off of Alex much like heat off pavement in the dead of summer. The news was still sketchy. There were reports of casualties, but no names or numbers had been released officially. Alex began methodically massaging her temples. Cassidy looked to her mother helplessly. She was as certain as she could be that when confirmation came, Russ Matthews' name would be added to a long list of lives lost to senseless violence. That didn't stop her from trying to offer some degree of hope to the woman she loved. "Alex, maybe Russ wasn't…"

"No. He was. There's no question about it," Alex said definitively. "The only question is who will be blamed."

Cassidy couldn't seem to find any words. Words simply felt empty. She watched as Alex's hand reflexively moved to pinch the bridge of her nose. "What can I do?" Cassidy asked gently.

Alex turned to her wife and offered her an appreciative smile. "I have to make some calls," Alex said. She leaned in and kissed Cassidy's cheek as she made her way off the sofa. "Just keep holding onto the good stuff," Alex whispered.

"Cassie?" Rose looked across to her daughter. "They were friends; weren't they?"

Cassidy let a nervous chuckle pass. "Yes. They were," she said. The ache in Cassidy's heart mingled with a deep sense of resentment for all the loss and upheaval her family had faced in recent months. She covered her face with her hands in frustration. "When will it be enough?" she asked in exasperation.

"Cassie," Rose called gently.

"No. I want to know," Cassidy dropped her hands dramatically. "When, Mom? When is it enough? Hasn't she lost enough? Dear God! John, her father....all these," Cassidy's emotions were a rising tide, threatening to completely overflow at any moment. She struggled to press down the advancing tirade she knew was about to break through her normally composed surface.

Rose moved beside her daughter and pulled her close. "I don't know, Cassie. I don't know when it's enough. All you can do is love her."

"What if that isn't enough?" Cassidy asked uneasily.

"For Alex?" Rose asked. "Cassidy Rose, Alex loves you more than anything. You know that."

"I do. I do know that. But, Mom....it just keeps coming. Lies, death...."

Rose took her daughter's face in her hands. "Love, life," she reminded Cassidy with a smile. "There will always be pain. I don't know why. What I do know is....the only way you survive it is by loving."

"How did you? I mean, after Dad died...you had to feel..."

Rose smiled and brushed Cassidy's hair aside as if she were still a little girl. "I had you," she said affectionately. "That was enough for me. When the sadness started to settle in; I had you." Cassidy drifted into her mother's embrace and sighed. "When the bad things happened, I always tried to think of something I was looking forward to," Rose explained. "Your next birthday party, your concert, just seeing you come home from school. Somehow that always seemed to relieve the sadness. It still does."

"It scares me," Cassidy confessed.

"What scares you?" her mother asked.

"Alex needs to understand these things. Not in the way that you or I would. She needs to try and change things, literally. It's...."

"It's who she is," Rose finished Cassidy's statement. "Yes, I know. There is a lot I don't know, Cassie. I am confident of that fact. I do know Alex. You need to trust her."

"I do trust her," Cassidy said confidently. "I just don't want to lose her."

Rose held her daughter close. Alex and Cassidy had almost lost each other more than once in a short period. She vividly remembered seeing the haunted look in her daughter's eyes after Alex had been shot. It mattered little that Alex was home and safe in abating Cassidy's fears. Cassidy was a master at self-control outwardly, but Rose could often see the evidence of the inner turmoil her daughter struggled with. Loss was something Cassidy had faced early in life. The sudden loss of her father embedded a deep-rooted fear in Cassidy's heart. She hid it well from nearly everyone, but it was no secret to her mother.

"Cassie, listen to me. I know how much losing Alex frightens you," Rose said. She felt Cassidy stiffen in her arms. "No, now listen. You forget sometimes how much Alex needs you. When you came home that night after your abduction; you were upstairs in bed, and Alex came down to talk with Nick and Barb and me. You didn't see her. I knew well before that moment that she loved you; that you loved her. But, Cassie...I have never seen that expression on her face, not once since. It was as if her world would end without you. All that mattered was that you were safe, that you felt safe and that she took care of you and Dylan. She knows that fear too. One day it will happen, my love. That's part of life too. Unfortunately, you had to learn that very young....much too soon. Don't let that fear taint all the wonderful things you have now," Rose implored her daughter.

"I know. I do know," Cassidy answered. "I just wish I could make it all go away."

Rose chuckled knowingly. "It will be all right Cassie. Alex has a great deal to look forward to."

Cassidy took a deep breath and tightened her hold on her mother. "We both do. I love you, Mom."

Rose closed her eyes. She felt transported to a different time. Somehow Cassidy felt so small in her arms at this moment. It was almost impossible to believe that the daughter she held now was carrying her next grandchild. No matter how many ticks of the clock passed, Cassidy remained the most precious gift in Rose's life. "I love you, Cassie. You are the best thing that ever happened to me. Makes all the bad stuff you keep worrying about seem so small," Rose said as a tear fell down her cheek.

Cassidy closed her eyes in contentment. She could faintly hear Dylan above their heads playing in his room and her hand instinctively drifted to her midsection. Her mother's words and the gentle arms that held her gave her permission to be a small child for a moment. She felt safe and loved, just as she did when Alex held her. Cassidy gave into the emotional fatigue and slowly drifted off enjoying the closeness of the woman who had protected her for so many years.

Alex slipped silently into the room and caught sight of the two women dozing on the couch. She marveled at them. It was no secret to anyone in Alex Toles' life that Cassidy meant everything to the agent. Cassidy had come into her life like a tornado. She uprooted the wobbly structure that had been Alex's life and replaced it with a much stronger foundation. Rose McCollum was a force of nature, and Alex adored her mother-in-law. She understood that Cassidy's strength and compassion was rooted in her mother's love and support. It was a relationship that Alex envied on many levels.

Rose opened her eyes slowly. Alex smiled and nodded toward Cassidy. "She all right?" Alex whispered.

Rose nodded and looked down at her daughter, still sleeping in her arms. "She's worried about you," Rose said.

Alex shook her head. "I'm okay," she winked. Cassidy began to stir, and Rose beckoned Alex to them. "What?" Alex asked Rose.

"This is your place now," Rose gently extricated herself from her daughter's grip, allowing Alex to slide into her place. Alex nodded gratefully as Rose left the room. "I'll have Dylan spend the evening with me," Rose offered.

Alex only nodded again, feeling Cassidy snuggle closer. She wasn't certain how long had passed before Cassidy spoke. "Is he gone?" Cassidy asked softly. She knew what the answer would be, but she still felt the need to broach the subject.

"Yes," the simple response came.

"How bad?" Cassidy asked.

Alex nestled against her wife and sighed. "Bad. Twenty-two dead including Russ. At least that's what Pip was able to confirm. The only good news is the diplomatic team never arrived."

"Are you leaving?" Cassidy's voice quivered.

"Tomorrow night," Alex replied honestly. She felt Cassidy shudder against her. "I'll be fine, Cass. I'm not missing any appointments. I already told you that."

Cassidy giggled as her tears began to flow. "I'll make the appointment for a Friday," she promised.

Alex laid back on the sofa, pulling Cassidy on top of her. She still couldn't rectify in her rational mind how feeling Cassidy beside her could eclipse all of the confusion and pain that surrounded them. Tomorrow would come much too quickly for them both. "Tacos would be good," Alex whispered.

"What?" Cassidy asked.

"We haven't had them in a while. When I get back," Alex answered.

"I'll see what I can manage," Cassidy promised before allowing sleep to reclaim her.

"Yeah," Alex said as she held Cassidy close. "You, me, Dylan and tacos. Good stuff."

***

"Get out!"

"Claire..."

"Marcus, get out of here!" Claire Brackett screamed.

Agent Marcus Anderson looked on as his partner's cool façade crumbled in front of him. Gone was any evidence of the brazen siren he had come to know as Claire Brackett. In her place stood a woman shattered. Anderson had never seen his partner show compassion for another human being, and he wondered what compelled him to make such an overture to her now. Perhaps it was the transformation of her features that seemed to soften her. He puzzled over the form in front of him. It seemed as if within seconds, her manufactured bravado had been stripped away revealing a vulnerable child cowering beneath the surface. He stepped cautiously forward and called to her again. "Claire, it's all right."

Claire Brackett collapsed onto the end of the bed and hung her head. Her mind was clouded by a dense emotional fog that her thoughts could not penetrate. "No," she said so quietly that he strained to hear her. "Nothing will ever be all right again."

***

"Where are you?" a man's voice asked in desperation.

"Still in Moscow," was the rattled response.

"Can you get to the border?"

"I don't know. My contacts here....they're gone," the voice trailed off.

"Sit tight. I will get you out."

"*Non! père, vous ne pouvez pas risquer une autre personne. Je vais trouver un* (No! Father, you cannot risk anyone else. I will find a way)," she scolded.

"*Eleana, il y as beaucoup de chose pour nous a discuter. Ce n'est pas l'un de ces points. Tenez-moi au courant. Ils vont vous rejoindre.* (Eleana, there may be much for us to discuss. This is not one of those points. Keep me apprised. They will reach you," Edmond Callier answered. "*Rester en sécurité* (stay safe)," his voice softened.

"*Je suis désolé* (I am sorry)," she said as the call disconnected.

Edmond Callier collapsed back into his chair and placed his face in his hands. He had managed to keep his nightmares at bay for many years. Now, they seemed to manifest in his waking life. He retrieved the phone at the center of his desk and placed the call. "I need your help."

***

Chapter Fourteen

Tuesday, January 20th

"Are you sure about this?" Alex asked her partner as they disembarked the small plane. "I'm betting you didn't tell Edmond your plan."

"No, I didn't. Trust me when I tell you that Eleana will agree. With what you saw on Daniel's desk and her knowledge.... well, Eleana is our best chance to get into ASA headquarters," Krause answered.

"You have an affinity for her?" Alex observed.

Krause kept his movement steadily forward. "I do," he said.

"More than an affinity?" Alex questioned curiously. Krause continued to focus on their destination and remained silent. "Pip?" she grabbed his arm.

Jonathan Krause spun around and faced Alex. "She's a friend."

Alex narrowed her gaze. "Krause," she drew out the length of his name slowly.

"It's not what you're thinking, Alex. I've known Eleana for years. I was the one who convinced John to bring her in. He was reluctant. Edmond never wanted her in this. For years, he managed to keep her away from this life. She's persistent," he said affectionately.

Alex slid into the passenger seat of the car, considering the tone in Jonathan Krause's voice. It seemed evident to her that his feelings traveled deeper than mere respect for the young woman, and that piqued her curiosity. Although Alex was aware of her friend's history with Jane Merrow, she knew that Cassidy still held his heart. She couldn't pinpoint the exact mannerism that gave him away, but the change in his demeanor when he spoke of Eleana Baros was apparent. "You're concerned for her; aren't you?" Alex asked.

Krause set the car in motion and nodded. "She reminds me of someone else I know," he said. Alex watched him closely, waiting for him to continue. Krause glanced over to see the anticipation in Alex's eyes and chuckled. "She's honest, Alex. She has integrity. Somehow she's managed to keep that intact."

"Who does *that* remind you of?" Alex asked sarcastically and shifted her gaze outside the window.

Krause looked across to Alex and shook his head. He wondered if she would ever realize what a rare commodity she was in the life that they led. He returned his attention to the road as his thoughts turned to the mission they now faced. If they were lucky, they might gain greater insight into Viktor Ivanov's connections and agenda. Failure would equate to nothing less than their demise. Success, he determined, would be defined in all three returning safely home. Tensions between the United States and Russia were escalating by the minute. Krause was acutely aware that if anyone discovered Eleana was alive she would immediately become a liability.

Krause had arranged to cross the Estonian border into Russia. It was too risky to attempt a border crossing from Belarus or the Ukraine. Advanced Strategic Applications housed its headquarters in Novgorod. Utilizing assets in Estonia was both the safest and most logical plan for a means of exiting Russia once they completed their mission. The attack on the American embassy and Eleana's presence created complications for Ivanov and opportunities for Krause and Alex. Eleana had extensive knowledge of the inner workings of the Russian government. She was an expert in communications technology, spoke multiple languages, and as Krause had once learned firsthand, Eleana Baros was adept at navigating an unexpected crisis. He was convinced that he and Alex, with Eleana's assistance, were the best hope of ever infiltrating ASA on Ivanov's home turf.

"Alex," he began, "are you sure you want in on this? Getting in might not be as difficult as getting out."

Alex turned slowly to her partner. "We'll get out," she said assuredly. "I just hope your friend is as good as you seem to think."

"She is," he said definitively. "Trust me."

"I do," Alex admitted.

***

"What are you doing here?" Christopher O'Brien asked.

"Not a very friendly greeting," Claire Brackett responded.

"I'm not feeling all that friendly, Claire," O'Brien snapped. "What do you want, anyway? Come to gloat? Dimitri send you? You his exterminator; come to snuff out the pest?"

"Clever," she offered her phony compliment. "No. No one knows I'm here. I was careful."

"So? What is it then?" he repeated.

"You're screwed, Christopher," she chuckled.

"Thank you," he sniped back.

"No, really. You are. Trust me when I tell you, you are headed right back to the pokey," Claire laughed in earnest.

"I wouldn't be so certain," he responded.

"I would," she said.

"Are you suddenly a lawyer?" O'Brien asked.

"No. Not at all." Claire flopped onto his sofa. "Got any wine?" she asked.

"Excuse me?"

"You're not a very good host, Christopher. I mean, all those years hosting political functions and you haven't even offered me a drink. That must be what you kept those little blondes for, huh?" she chided.

"Fuck you, Claire."

"Ooo…not now. And not before wine," she responded with a wink. "You have two options as I see it."

"And what might those be?" O'Brien asked.

"Well, you can stay here, drowning your sorrows in that bottle over there…..just waiting for the hammer to fall or…. you can get out of here, someplace safe and comfortable and help me," she explained.

"What the hell are you talking about?" O'Brien asked skeptically. "Have you lost your mind?"

"Not at all. You see, you and I now have something in common."

"Enlighten me," he implored her.

"You are caught in the middle, Congressman. My father, Toles, Krause…they want you out of the picture. Dimitri and Viktor? Well, you have betrayed their trust now too. You are a liability to everyone. They enjoy the suffering, though. They'd rather watch you squirm in insignificance than kill you," she said as she kicked off her heels and heaved her legs onto the table in front of her.

"And how exactly does that make us alike?" he inquired.

"My father doesn't trust me. Can't say I blame him. Toles, Krause…well, they would be more than happy to watch my demise," Claire said.

"That's nothing new," O'Brien observed.

"No. But you see….none of them ever betrayed me. It's just a game we play. Oh, Agent Toles and my father can delude themselves with a belief in some honorable cause. It's a game. Pieces on a board, matching strength and wit; nothing more," she said plainly. "It isn't personal. Dimitri, that's….well, all you need to know is that it *is* personal. And, I have every intention of seeing Dimitri and his uncle fall. How much money did you move that they've yet to discover?" she asked the congressman. O'Brien offered her a hollow stare in response. "Oh, come on, Christopher. We both know you've been moving money for years."

"What is it you want, Claire?"

"You help me with some creative financing, and I will ensure your needs are met," she promised.

"My life is here," he said. "My career, my family…"

"Your career is over. If you are referring to the lovely school teacher, I think you've missed the memo. You're a bigger fool than I thought if you think that's your family. Your life here is over, Congressman. Your future is a little cell in a big box. Although, you might find new found popularity there," she laughed.

"You want me to run?" he asked.

Claire Brackett shrugged. "Everyone is running, Congressman. It's a matter of what they are running from and where they are running to."

Christopher O'Brien sat in the chair across from his unexpected guest and dropped his face into his hands. He had spent the last two days desperately seeking a bargaining chip. He had devised a multitude of stories and scenarios, but when he stopped to review them every one seemed fruitless. The fact was, his career was over. He would never be able to rebuild any trust with the electorate. Cassidy was gone. She had made that clear. Dylan wanted nothing to do with him. In his mind, he could trace the death spiral of the life he once knew to the day that Agent Alex Toles walked into their lives. He took a deep breath and released it audibly.

"One condition," he said to the woman before him.

Claire Brackett did nothing to conceal her amusement. "You are hardly in a position to make demands," she told him. "But, I'm listening."

"You take out Toles in the process," he said.

Claire laughed. "Take out Alex?" she shook her head. "You are pathetic. I'll see what I can do," she winked.

"When?" he asked.

"Not even curious where?" she questioned him. O'Brien remained silent. "Just be ready. The less you know, the better for us both," she told him. "Now…about that wine…"

***

Wednesday, January 21st

"I don't want to go," Dylan complained.

"Why don't you want to go to school?" Cassidy asked. Dylan scowled and shrugged. "Dylan?"

"Everybody knows," he said. "I'm Dylan the villain," he mumbled.

"What?" Cassidy asked gently as she made her way to him.

"I don't want to be an O'Brien. Everybody thinks I'm like him," Dylan said flatly.

Realization dawned on Cassidy. It was not surprising that Dylan was combatting teasing at school. The newspapers and television were smattered with stories about Congressman Christopher O'Brien's downfall. It was a hot story. Cassidy and Christopher O'Brien were once considered on the short list of couples that would likely claim the White House. While her ex-husband's popularity had been flung into the sewer, Cassidy's was soaring. She was becoming more and more America's darling with each moment that passed. The public had always had an affinity for the attractive, easy going school teacher, and she was being hailed now as the only reason Christopher O'Brien ever made it to the center stage. There was plenty of talk surrounding Cassidy's marriage to Alex, but the press still insisted on calling her Mrs. O'Brien. She understood Dylan's frustration. Try as she might, the name just seemed to stick.

"Dylan, honey, I'm sorry. You love school. Don't let anyone spoil that for you," she encouraged him.

"Mom, everybody knows! You don't understand!" he cried in frustration.

Cassidy sighed. "I do understand," she said as she squatted to meet his eyes. "You tell them you are not an O'Brien, you're a Toles."

"But, I'm not a Toles," he said sadly. "When they call attendance I am in the O's. Dylan O'Brien."

Cassidy considered his dilemma carefully. Moments like these she wished for Alex's presence. When it came to issues about Dylan's place in the family, a unified front always seemed the most effective. There was more to this than Dylan's last name; she could feel it. "No matter when they call your name, Dylan, I promise you are as much a Toles as I am."

Dylan shook his head. "No, I'm not," he whispered.

"All right," Cassidy sat Dylan in a chair and knelt beside him. "What is this about?" Dylan shrugged again. "Dylan?"

"You'll all have the same name," Dylan said. "I'll still be Dylan the villain. My brother will be like Alex. Alex is a hero and everybody thinks I'm a bad guy."

"I see," Cassidy answered. "Dylan, do you think because you don't have Alex's name that means you aren't a Toles?" When Dylan didn't answer, Cassidy continued. "You know, I remember when I was your age. I wanted to be a Mackenzie." Dylan looked up to his mother curiously. "Yeah...my Nana was my best friend in the whole world. She was a Mackenzie, just like Grandma. I didn't have any brothers or sisters, and all my cousins were Mackenzies. I hated it. I always felt left out." Cassidy watched as Dylan studied her. "One Sunday I came in the house crying. My cousins had been picking on me. Nana said that no matter what anyone called me I was still a Mackenzie just as much as anyone else. I didn't believe her though," Cassidy admitted.

"Because you were an O'Brien?" he asked.

"No Dylan, I was a McCollum. When I married your...well, when I got married I became an O'Brien. And, when I married Alex I decided to become a Toles."

"But, I can't be," he said.

"Dylan, most people still call me Cassidy O'Brien. That's just how they know me. And, that's just how they know you, but we are both part of Alex's family now," she tried to explain.

"I'll be the only one and then Alex will love him more."

Cassidy took hold of both of Dylan's shoulders and looked squarely in his eyes. "Dylan James, you listen...there could never be any baby or any person who Alex could love more than you. Never. If I could change your name today I would, and so would Alex. Don't you ever think because you were born an O'Brien that it means you are any less a part of this family." He shook his head. "Do you think I am less than your mom because my last name is now Toles?" she asked.

"No," he replied.

"Okay. Do you think Grandma is less a part of this family because she is a McCollum?" Cassidy asked. Dylan shook his head. "Um. I see. So your brother or sister will be a Toles. That's true. You have the same parents. You have the same YaYa and cousins and Grandma. Names change in families all the time, sweetheart. It doesn't change who we are to each other. You are Dylan. You are part of all of those people who love you, and even who loved me and Alex. So, you are a Toles, a Pappas, a McCollum, a Burns, and even a Mackenzie; just as much as you could ever be an O'Brien. And, when you get older you can change your name to anything you want. It won't change who you are, though. And, it won't change how much we love you."

Dylan considered his mother's words for a few minutes before looking back up to her. "They won't believe me. That I am a Toles," he said.

"Well, you let me handle that," Cassidy winked at him. "Now, come on, let's get your jacket on and get you ready, Mr. Toles."

Dylan gave a faint smile. "Sounds weird," he said. Cassidy chuckled as she zipped his jacket. "Mom?"

"Hmm?"

"Do you still wish you were a Mackenzie?" he asked.

"I am a Mackenzie. Ask Grandma," Cassidy laughed. "Every day I look in the mirror I see a little bit more of my Nana looking back," Cassidy giggled.

Dylan was a bit puzzled by his mother's response as they walked toward the door. Whenever his mother spoke of her grandmother, she always seemed to smile. Cassidy told him many stories about her adventures with her Nana and how she wished Dylan could have known her. Dylan loved to look at pictures with Cassidy and listen to her tales. He never thought about being anything but an O'Brien until he met Alex. It was just who he was. Now it just didn't fit. He didn't even look like his father. In fact, he had heard his Grandma say many times that he looked a lot like her mother, Nana Mackenzie. It gave him an idea. "Mom," he said as he tugged at her coat.

"Yeah?"

"You should call him Mackenzie," Dylan said. Cassidy titled her head in confusion. "My brother," he said a bit exasperated by her lack of understanding. "If he's Mackenzie he can be part of all of us."

Cassidy kissed Dylan's forehead. "That's an interesting idea, Dylan. We have a while to think about that," she reminded him.

Dylan walked ahead of his mother to the car and gave her his usual shrug. "I would," he said.

Cassidy buckled Dylan in and closed the car door. "Well, Alex," she muttered. "I wonder what you would think of a Scottish Greek," she giggled. "He certainly has a point."

***

Thursday, January 22nd

"You sure this is the place?" Alex asked doubtfully. Alex was curious about the surroundings. The last communication that Krause had received indicated that Eleana had found refuge with some friends in Tver. She and Krause were to pose as professors. It made sense as they came upon the campus. "I guess we're too old to pass for students, huh?" she asked her friend.

Jonathan Krause agreed. "You're younger than me," he observed.

"Yeah, by what, like ten months?" Alex laughed. "How's your Russian, professor?" she asked.

"Sprosite Ijana, ya dumaju chto moj Russkij bolee krasnorechivij chem moj Anglijskij (I think if you were to ask Ian, my Russian

is far more eloquent than my English)," Krause attempted to keep the mood light.

"*Vozmozno on prav. Ya noniatija ne imeu o chem ti govorish v bolshinstve sluchayev* (He might have a point. I don't know what you are talking about half the time)," Alex cracked back.

"Funny, professor," Krause said as he pulled the car along a row of buildings. "This is the easy part."

"Let's hope so," Alex said.

Krause led Alex along the cement walkway toward a building that housed computer labs. Alex was cautious of everyone, particularly someone she had never met. She made certain that her partner knew she intended to keep her eyes and ears open with Eleana Baros. Krause had spent hours on their drive reassuring her that Eleana could be trusted. Alex's constant reply was, "I hope so."

Krause looked up to the writing on the front of one of the brick buildings. "This is it. Look for room 402. All this Cyrillic is making me dizzy," he said.

The pair traversed a narrow hallway, displaying identification they hoped would pass muster. Krause, Alex had learned, had honed some unusual skills over the years. She was impressed with the credentials he had been able to create with modest resources. The real test would be their ability to act and speak with ease. That was a reality she understood, and the first test appeared to be about three feet in front of them.

"*Mogu li ya vam pomoch'?* (Can I help you)?" the security guard asked casually.

"*Dobroye utro. Da, u nas yest' vstrecha s doktorom Sokol* (Good morning. Yes, we have an appointment with Dr. Sokol)," Krause offered he guard a glimpse of his identification.

To both agents' great relief the man smiled and directed them to pass. Both Alex and Krause offered a nod of thanks and proceeded down the hallway. "Why do I not think it will be that easy at ASA?" Alex chuckled.

"One can hope," Krause whispered as he opened the door to a small office. Eleana was sitting behind a large maple desk studying a computer screen and did not hear them immediately. "Eleana?" Krause called to her.

Eleana snapped to attention at the sound of Krause's voice. A sigh of relief escaped her lips as she stood to greet him. "Jonathan," she accepted his embrace.

Krause felt the tension in her body and pulled her closer. Eleana had been in the field for several years, but he was certain that nothing she encountered could have prepared her for the carnage she witnessed a few days before. Krause had no misgivings about Eleana's abilities or loyalty. He feared that the harsh and violent realities she had been thrust into might break her spirit. "Eleana," he whispered in comfort.

Alex looked on in fascination. She could just barely distinguish the unsteadiness in the younger woman's stance. It was perceptible, however. Alex was aware that the young agent was mentally working to disguise her fatigue and fear. She was equally intrigued by her partner. Over the last few months, Alex had come to understand that Jonathan Krause was a complicated man whose professional demeanor suggested his emotions barely skimmed the surface. Alex had slowly determined that Jonathan Krause embodied the meaning of the phrase 'still waters run deep'. For a long while she had considered him an enigma. Watching him as he consoled the young woman in his embrace, Alex reflected that she had come to understand him.

"Eleana," he said as he pulled back slightly. "This is Alex," he made the introduction.

Alex stepped forward and offered the young woman her hand and a smile. "Agent Baros, how are you holding up?" she asked.

Eleana accepted the proffered hand gladly. "I'm all right, Agent Toles. It's a pleasure to meet the legend. I wish the circumstances were different."

"I realize I'm older, but I am hardly Arthurian," Alex winked. "So, not to cut this reunion short, but what are we looking at?" Alex cut to the chase.

"Well," Eleana began, moving back to the computer. "ASA has incredible security. They have been the leading developer of weapons technology in Eastern Europe since World War II. They deal with everything from aircraft engines to nuclear technology. The SVR refer to ASA as *Krasnyy molot*," she said.

"The red hammer," Alex winced. "That's comforting."

Eleana pointed to the computer screen. "If you talk to the older generation, KGB, they will tell you that Andrei Ivanov was the left hand to Joseph Stalin's right. Viktor Ivanov has carried on that legacy," she said. "Here," she pointed to a building schematic on her screen. "There are several possibilities for entrance. Codes will be easier to create in the lower level security areas; obviously. But, right here.....if we enter through their avionics wing we should be able to access Ivanov's office through these two labs and then into this corridor."

"You have a plan for that; I assume?" Krause asked.

Eleana's eyes brightened. "I managed to hack into one of their servers and create pass cards that should work, at least to get us through," she handed Krause one. "I was only able to create two, which means we cannot split up three ways. The other problem is the number of access points. Going back the same way...."

"Agreed," Krause cut her off. "An alternative exit is best."

"Yes, but the only other feasible exit is here," she showed them. "That means once we get into Ivanov's lair we will have to work quickly. The communications and security area is on the other side of his office. I'll need to update and change the codes for our exit there. It requires a separate security authorization. I can't access that here," Eleana explained.

Alex looked at Krause and pursed her lips. This was not going to be easy. "How much time do you think we have; total?" Alex asked.

Eleana attempted a smile. "Thirty minutes in and out."

"Shit," Alex groaned.

"Eleana, are you up for this?" Krause asked.

"I'm fine," Eleana assured him.

"I don't mean just physically. There can't be any second guessing. Thirty minutes will pass like…"

"I'm good," Eleana interrupted him.

"All right. So, who are we then?" he asked.

"You," Eleana began, "Are Dr. Gregory Weisz."

"German?" he asked. Eleana just smiled.

"And you, are Dr. Anna Karpenko," Eleana informed Alex. "Jonathan, do us all a favor and let Agent Toles and I speak the Russian," Eleana suggested.

"My Russian is impeccable," he defended himself.

"Your Russian is passable," Eleana said seriously. "You speak too perfectly."

Alex tried not to laugh. Eleana Baros was quickly proving to be at the very least an entertaining edition to their partnership. "How do you know my Russian is up to par?" Alex asked.

"Agent Toles, trust me, most of these men will not be worried about your Russian," she explained.

"What?" Alex asked.

Krause snickered. "Don't worry about it Alex. It's a compliment," he said. "You ready? We'll stop tonight in Cherepovets. I have a contact there. I think some food and a good night's rest is in order. Plus, it will give you two a little time to get acquainted before we move," Krause said.

"Fine by me," Alex agreed. She watched as Eleana retrieved a small bag. The younger agent's gait was slow and tired. "Someone you need to see before we leave?" Alex asked her.

"No," Eleana answered. "It's best for him if we go."

Eleana's voice gave away a hint of sadness. Alex sensed the need to relieve the tension. "Well, then…let's go so that Pip here can feed us and tuck us in," she joked. Eleana regarded the interaction between her two saviors. There was a natural ease in their communication that surprised her. She was aware of Alex's marriage to Cassidy, but the familiarity between Alex and Krause made Eleana curious.

Krause opened the door for his companions. "Beauty before age," he winked at Alex appreciatively. "Thanks," he whispered to his partner.

"For what?" Alex asked.

"For giving her a chance," Krause said.

Alex nodded. "My eyes are still open," she said.

"I'd expect nothing less."

***

Chapter Fifteen

Friday, January 23rd

"You ready?" Jonathan Krause asked his friends.

"As I'll ever be, Dr. Weisz," Alex answered.

"The entrance to the avionics center is about three hundred yards ahead on our right," Eleana told them. "Jonathan, remember....Gregory Weisz has never been to a facility in Russia. He consults from his home in Hamburg. His name will be familiar, but not his face. You reviewed what I gave you both last night?" Eleana asked.

Krause and Alex nodded. "Electronic counter-counter measures is a mouthful. You're lucky I have such an excellent memory," Alex winked. "This ECCM language is..."

"Heady?" Eleana laughed.

"You could say that," Alex answered. "Let's just hope neither of us is approached for any major demonstrations or details or else I fear we may need to employ some counter measures of our own," Alex winked.

Eleana pulled the car to the security gate, rolled down her window and handed the guard an identification badge. "*Dobroye utro. So monoj vrachi Vays i Karpenko* (Good morning. I have doctors Weisz and had Karpenko)," she greeted the guard.

"*Oni ne nakhodyatsya v spiske* (They are not on the list)," he replied stoically.

"*Ya ne udivlena. Ikh vizit byl tol'ko podtverzden vchera. Doktor Karpenko budet rabotat' na proyekte prodolzitelnoj volny radara. Doktor Weusz priletel proshloj nochju na consultatssiju. Prover'te komp'yuter.*

YA uverena, chto oni v sisteme. (I am not surprised. Their visit was only confirmed yesterday. Dr. Karpenko will be working on a continuous wave radar project. Dr. Weisz flew in last night to consult. Check your computer. I'm sure it has been updated)," Eleana assured him.

The three watched as the guard reentered his small building. They could see him looking at something intently. "You have a plan B if this doesn't work?" Krause asked from the backseat.

"Yeah. Drive like hell," Eleana responded.

A few more moments passed, and the man returned to the side of the vehicle. He leaned closer into the window, looked beyond Eleana and addressed Alex directly. "*Vy zhe doktor. Karpenko, kotoryy napisal pro impul'snoy modulyatsiu i kodirovaniye?* (You are the same Dr. Karpenko who has written on pulse modulation and coding)?" he asked.

Alex turned deliberately and offered the man a smile. "*Okhrannik, zainteresovannyj razvitiem transpondera?* (A security guard interested in transponder development)?" Alex questioned him a bit condescendingly.

The man brightened slightly. "*YA na trenirovkakh, chtoby stat' pilotom* (I am in training to be a pilot)," he explained. Alex nodded her understanding. He smiled at her acknowledgement. "*Vi svobodni projeszat* (You are fine to pass)," he told Eleana.

Eleana smiled and proceeded through the checkpoint. "That was fun," she rolled her eyes as she pulled into a lot adjacent to the building. "Here we go."

Alex and Krause followed Eleana's lead into ASA. Passing through the next checkpoint was simple. There would be no reason for anyone to question their presence until they attempted to breach the avionics labs and enter the executive offices. The trio was able to traverse the labs effortlessly, returning the simple greetings offered them and moving steadily forward with evident purpose. "All right, this is it," Eleana said as they reached a large steel door. "Now we find out if my computer skills are as good as I hope," she admitted. She lifted her identification badge for one final time and held her breath as she swiped it through a small pad on the door. It seemed like an eternity passed as they waited, but within several seconds the signature beep sounded accompanied by a welcomed green light. "We're in."

***

"This is crazy," Cassidy said to her mother. She shook her head in disbelief and turned down the volume slightly on the television. "I can't believe anyone from that team tried to sell nuclear technology to terrorists. They're almost all academics. It doesn't make sense."

"I know. I thought we moved past this....Have you talked to Alex?" Rose asked.

"No. Honestly, I'm not even sure where she is," Cassidy explained. "Carecom has major contracts in both Western and Eastern Europe. I do know that a good deal of them are military related. With all the posturing going on...."

"She hasn't called?" Rose asked with some concern.

Cassidy offered her mother a smile. "No, but I didn't expect to hear from her right away. I got an email message last night. She just said that she met a new contact and hopefully she would be able to call sometime over the weekend."

Rose watched her daughter's body language carefully. She knew better than to question Cassidy specifically about Alex's business trip. She suspected that the business Alex was away on had far less to do with medical supplies than it did with the current state of world affairs. When Cassidy was concerned, she would absently massage the back of her neck. It was a quirk that Rose noticed developed during her daughter's college years. Cassidy had been rubbing the back of her neck on and off all morning. "Cassie?"

"Hmm?"

"Do you want to talk about it?" Rose inquired.

"Talk about what?" Cassidy tried to ask lightly.

"Um-hm. Are you worried about Alex?"

Cassidy took her mother's hand and clicked off the television. "No more than I ever am," she said. "To tell you the truth, I am more concerned about Dylan right now. I just wish she was here to talk to him."

"Something happen?" Rose asked.

"School. Teasing. Being seven. Having the man you know as your father all over the news accused of murder. Finding out your parents are having a baby. Having a different name. Trying to figure out who you are in a new family. You know, the usual stuff kids face," Cassidy sighed her frustration.

"Oh, is that all?" Rose winked. "Is he upset about his father?"

Cassidy rubbed her brow and considered her reply. "Well, I guess the kids have been calling him Dylan the villain. That sparked him to start thinking about who he is. I think what has him the most worried is having a different last name than the rest of us," Cassidy said. "I tried reassuring him, telling him names aren't important, but you and I both know that isn't as true as we would like it to be."

Rose understood. She remembered Cassidy wrestling with being different from the rest of the family when she was a child. "He wants to be a Toles," Rose guessed. Cassidy nodded. "Well, that's normal, Cassie."

"Yes, I know and I think it would be easier to handle if he did not have to deal with all this craziness with Chris in the news..."

"And if Alex were here to help?" Rose asked gently.

Cassidy let out a heavy sigh. "Yeah."

"You don't have to tell me anything, but I can tell you are worried...and before you argue with me let me tell you not to bother. I changed your diapers, endured your crushes, attended your weddings, and watched you give birth. You're not fooling me, Cassie. Alex is not Chris," Rose said flatly.

"I know that," Cassidy barked back.

"Yes. You do, but I know you. You were alone most of your marriage to Chris and most of your pregnancy with Dylan. This is reminding you of everything you faced when you were with him," Rose began. When she saw Cassidy begin to protest, she raised her hand. "No. Don't bother denying it either. And, for the record, I don't blame you. You know that Alex would move heaven and earth for you both. I am sure that she would rather be here than anywhere. If she's away there has to be a good reason."

"There is," Cassidy admitted. "And, yes, I know she wants to be here for us. The truth is part of her needs the challenge of what she does too. She's not..."

Rose smirked. "Cassie, you didn't exactly marry Betty Crocker." Cassidy couldn't help but laugh at her mother's assessment. "Look, don't do this to yourself," Rose cautioned her daughter. "Alex is completely devoted to you, and Dylan will be all right. What about the adoption?" she asked. "You haven't told him?"

"No. I don't want to say anything until we are ready to proceed," Cassidy explained. "There are still too many loose ends. At least Chris is out of the picture for the foreseeable future."

"Do you think he did it?" Rose asked.

Cassidy closed her eyes and swallowed hard. "I don't know what I think where he is concerned, Mom. I just know I want him out of all of our lives."

"I can't believe they let him out," Rose muttered in disgust.

"I know. I just will feel better about everything when Alex gets home," Cassidy admitted.

Rose patted her daughter's knee. "You know what I think?" Rose asked.

"I'm afraid to ask," Cassidy joked.

"I think we should get Dylan from school, sit in front of the television and eat junk food all weekend. I'll buy," Rose offered. Cassidy quirked her brow in question. "What?" Rose asked.

"Do crackers constitute junk food?" Cassidy asked.

"Sure. New plan. Dylan and I will eat junk food, and you feast on your crackers. We'll even skip the Saltines. I'll buy you a designer box," Rose winked.

Cassidy rolled her eyes. "You always know how to make things better," she laughed. "Designer crackers it is."

***

"Mr. President, you have to make a response to these accusations," the president's chief of staff observed.

"So, you think I should hold a press conference and deny the Russians' accusation without any verification at all?" Strickland asked sarcastically. "That would be foolish; don't you think? Before I speak, I want to know everything there is to know about Dr. Devin Montgomery. Are we clear? I want to know what cereal he ate every morning. The man is being accused of brokering a deal for nuclear material to terrorists. Do I believe it? No. Do we need a statement? Yes. Do we need to know who we are defending?" Strickland leaned menacingly toward his chief of staff. "I would say that would be prudent. Understood?"

"Yes, sir."

"Twenty minutes or sooner. I want it in my hands. Have Bob ready with a statement," Strickland ordered. "And, Jeffrey?" he called to his chief of staff. "Don't presume to tell me what we need again."

***

Eleana sat at the large desk typing in combinations of words and numbers, hoping for the magic sequence that would unlock Viktor Ivanov's personal computer. Krause closed the door quietly and made his way next to Alex, watching each keystroke of Eleana's fingers. "Bingo!" Eleana proclaimed triumphantly as she maneuvered Ivanov's files expertly.

"Stop," Alex directed. "Right there. Pip, look."

"What is it?" Eleana asked as she scrolled through a long list of numbers. "Looks like a list of locations....God, they're all over the globe," she observed. "But for what?"

"Scroll back up. Right there," Alex pointed to an open field. "I want you to type this in...41 169412 80 51717," Alex rattled off a series of numbers.

"What is this? Latitude and longitude?" Eleana asked. Alex and Krause watched as Eleana entered the numbers, revealing a new screen full of data.

"Son of a bitch," Krause looked to Alex. "They're not coordinates at all."

Alex shook her head as she read the information that continued to populate.

William James Brackett
United States Navy
CEI date 1963
Spouse: Sandra Moran Brackett–no affiliation
Father: James Donald Brackett CEI date 1941
Mother: Eleanor Fitzgerald Brackett–no affiliation

Children:
Claire Eleanor Brackett CEI date 2012
Assigned:
United States Military Operations Southeast Asia 1965-1973
Senior Officer KGB/CIA internal operations Washington D.C. 1974-1985
Rear Admiral/ Defense Initiatives Operations Chief 1985-present

"What the hell is this?" Eleana asked.

"If I didn't know better, I would say we just stumbled on The Collaborative's roster, or at least part of it," Alex surmised. "Try this 41 67259 94 04100."

Eleana followed Alex's directions. Alex repeated the exercise several times with Eleana. Each time revealed information about an individual tied to The Collaborative and its dealings. Some names were expected; others were unfamiliar. It was clear that the network was both vast and diverse. "Where did you get this?" Eleana asked.

"It was in my father's office along with a list of codenames. I just assumed it corresponded to locations that had some significance for The Collaborative...safe houses, something. Pip and I have been researching the coordinates for months looking for some common thread; nothing. We were looking at the wrong language," Alex surmised.

"It's so subtle. How did you even figure out these were code?" Eleana asked.

Alex shrugged and began scribbling numbers frantically onto a piece of paper. "Language is language. Numbers aren't that different from letters, actually. You just have to see the sequences. When you pulled up that first file, there were too many numbers that repeated for it to be coordinates. It's like music. Like a rhythm," Alex explained.

"Eleana," Krause interrupted. "Download as much as you can of that. Somehow, I don't think it's complete."

"It's not," Alex offered. "My best guess is the database is broken up. Maybe the senior members can access it through different points, or maybe each only has access to a portion as a safeguard."

"Do you think Sphinx is in here?" Eleana asked.

Alex looked at Krause and shook her head. "I don't know," she admitted. She handed Eleana the paper she had just filled with the numerals she had committed to memory. "Keep working these. See what you get. Those were all on my father's list," Alex said. Eleana continued working as hurriedly as her need for detail and caution allowed.

"Alex," Krause began. "If your father had a portion and Viktor has a portion..."

"I know. It stands to reason both Edmond and the admiral do as well. You thinking what I am?" Alex asked.

"We make a stop to see Edmond," Krause answered. Alex agreed.

"What the hell was that?" Alex asked as a banging noise filtered in from somewhere outside the door.

"I don't know," Krause replied as he made his way to the door. "Stay here."

"Where are you going?" Elena asked.

"Just stay here. I'll be right back," he said.

"Is he insane?" Eleana asked Alex.

Alex chuckled. "Probably. How's it coming?"

"I'm going as quickly as I can. I doubt anyone has accessed this much all at once. I don't want to send up any red flags," Eleana explained.

Krause snuck back into the office and closed the door gently. "Wrap it up, Eleana. We have company," he said as he moved behind the desk to look over her shoulder.

"Just a couple more minutes," the young agent pleaded, desperately increasing her pace.

"Now, Eleana," Krause ordered. "Kargen and Ivanov are down the hall."

"Shit," Alex grumbled.

"What the..." Eleana stared at the screen in front of her for a moment and then looked over her should to Krause. Krause turned his attention to the computer screen in an effort to see what had startled Eleana. He closed his eyes for a split second and shook his head in frustration. "Jonathan?" Eleana asked.

Alex stood by the door listening intently to everything surrounding her. "Voices, moving closer....you'd better move it," Alex instructed.

"Jonathan?" Eleana whispered.

"Not now," he snapped at her. "Wrap it up. Alex, you take Eleana and get out of here."

"What the hell are you talking about?" Alex questioned her partner.

"You heard me," Krause said as he moved around the desk. "Now! You get Eleana out of here. Ian will be waiting at the south gate to take you to the safe house in Cherepovets. I'll meet you there," Krause assured his friends. He started to open the door slowly when Alex pushed it shut with force.

"Are you out of your mind?" Alex scolded her partner. "We came in here together. We leave together. Jesus Christ. I'm not leaving you in here."

"Jonathan, she's right," Eleana urged him.

Krause looked at Eleana. His eyes conveyed his warning. He lifted his sights back to Alex at the door. "No, you're not right this time, Alex. Dimitri and Viktor will not be shocked to see me sitting in this office. They expect nothing less of me. You two on the other hand....No one can know Eleana is alive," he reminded Alex. "Alex...."

Alex pinched the bridge of her nose with some force and exhaled a breath of frustration. "They probably already do know," she reminded him.

"Maybe. We don't have time to debate this," he said as he cracked the door open again. "Eleana, you take the lead. Go, before they make their way here," he instructed her. "Alex will be right behind you...three paces." Eleana reluctantly acquiesced and made her way past him.

"Pip...." Alex started.

"Alex, you know I'm right. At the very least, it will buy you both some time, maybe even keep the goon squad from harassing you in the computer lab. We can't risk losing what we just found. Go. If I'm not there by morning..."

Alex grabbed hold of Krause's arm. He watched her eyes narrow to pin holes as she spoke. "You will be there tonight. No other option. Do you understand me?" Alex demanded.

Krause's lips curled slightly. "I'll see you tonight," he promised.

Alex shook her head and grasped her friend's hand. "Make sure that you do," she said as she headed out the door.

***

Alex grabbed Eleana's arm and pulled her back into a small hallway. "Shh…I know that voice," Alex said.

"What?" Eleana asked.

"Listen," Alex directed the younger agent to listen to the sounds coming from the room they needed to enter. "Here that?" she asked. "That man talking?"

"Who is it?" Eleana asked.

"NSA and no good. He will know us the minute we walk through that door." Alex said.

"So, what do we do?" Eleana asked. "Go back the way we came?"

"Too risky. Are you sure there is no other place you can access what we need for that keycard?" Alex questioned Eleana.

"Positive," Eleana responded.

"All right. Then we need to get hold of someone who already has one," Alex determined.

"That might not be so easy," Eleana said.

"No. You are the one that no one will expect to be here. Krause is right about that," Alex said.

"What are you thinking?" Eleana asked apprehensively.

Alex offered the younger agent a cockeyed grin. Marcus Anderson was on the other side of that door. Alex wondered if that meant Claire Brackett might be nearby as well. She was certain that by now, more than a handful of people were made aware of Jonathan Krause's presence at the facility; by extension hers would not come as a shock to anyone. Eleana held the information that represented the tip of an iceberg; an iceberg Alex and Krause needed to find a way to melt. Krause had been right about one thing; getting Eleana safely out of ASA was the main priority now. Alex thought that facing Marcus might just give them the best chance of success. If she could disarm Marcus Anderson, they might be able to use his credentials to make their escape. If not, Alex hoped to gain enough time for Eleana to accomplish that task.

"The agent in that room," Alex began, "his name is Marcus Anderson. He's been working with Claire Brackett for the better part of the last year." Alex saw the blood drain from Eleana's face. "Do you know him?" Alex asked the younger agent.

"No. No, but I do know Claire," Eleana said. Alex detected the note of sadness in Eleana's inflection as she spoke of Claire Brackett and tipped her head in question. Eleana forced a solemn smile. "We grew up together," she told Alex. "We were best friends for many years."

The notion that Claire Brackett was even capable of friendship surprised Alex. She could see the genuine emotion that crossed Eleana's expression at the mere mention of Claire Brackett's name. "Eleana, I don't think she's here. Even if she is, you won't be coming face to face with her." Alex looked down the hallway at the numerous doors lining it. "How well do you remember those schematics?" Alex asked.

"Perfectly," Eleana answered.

"Good. Which of these doors leads somewhere benign; a supply closet, something like that?" Alex inquired.

Eleana scanned the hallway. "There; the third door on the right," she said.

"Will your keycard open that lock?" Alex wondered.

"It should."

"All right. Here's the plan. You swipe that card in this door," Alex pointed to their original destination a few paces away. "As soon as you hear that chime you make for that door on the right. Understood?" Alex directed.

"What about you?" Eleana asked skeptically.

"Last time I saw Claire she wanted to dance," Alex smirked. "I think I'll see if her partner's moves leave anything to be discovered."

"You're going to confront Agent Anderson?" Eleana looked at Alex skeptically. "Why don't we just wait?"

"No time. Guaranteed the word is out that Krause is here. They'll be more vigilant. The sooner we move, the better. You wait no more than five minutes. One way or another I will get Anderson out of your way. Five minutes you make your way back here. If you don't see or hear me…then you follow the plan and get to Ian. Krause and I will catch up with you," Alex told Eleana.

"What if you can't get him out of there? Alex, we don't even know how many people are in there right now, and you are unarmed," Eleana cautioned.

"I know. We also have no idea how long he will be in there if we don't act. The longer we are out here, the more exposed we become. This is the best chance," Alex said confidently. "Trust me." Eleana nodded her agreement. "All right. Let's get ready to dance."

***

"Jonathan, what the hell are you doing in my office?" Viktor Ivanov demanded. Jonathan Krause had taken up residence in a large leather chair that sat behind Viktor Ivanov's desk. He reclined casually in it, resting his feet upon the desktop.

"Always a pleasure, Viktor," Krause drawled.

"Edmond send you?" Ivanov guessed.

Krause stretched with his hands behind his head and sighed. "No. I just missed your company," he winked at the Russian.

"*Konchai svoi igri! Chto ti khochesh Jonathan* (Enough with your games! What do you want, Jonathan)?" Ivanov demanded sharply.

"Oh, calm down," Krause said evenly. "Why so cranky?" Krause chuckled. "You didn't expect a visit after your latest short-sighted stunt?"

"If you are referring to the attack on your embassy; that was hardly my doing," Ivanov asserted.

"Of course not. Terrorists then? Isn't it always," Krause belittled Ivanov's claim with mock sincerity.

"What do you want, Jonathan?" Ivanov repeated his earlier question

"Curious, Viktor. It is very curious how an attack would just happen to occur on the day Strickland's team is due to arrive. I wonder how those terrorists managed that; quite well equipped for an anti-Markov group. Markov must be concerned….to think such a group could possess missiles of any kind…."

Ivanov moved to the front of the desk and hovered over it. "You've been too busy to have heard the news," Ivanov said sweetly. "Not that surprising, my friend. After all, it was one of your experts selling the weapons to the terrorists."

Krause nodded. He had expected a ridiculous fabrication. "*Our* experts?" Krause chuckled. "Who exactly might that be? You can't mean Claire and Marcus Anderson. Are you part of that equation? How about my father? Was he?" Krause hardened his gaze and pushed out the chair he was sitting in.

"Your father has been dead for years," Ivanov responded.

"No. He hasn't; has he?" Krause moved within inches of Ivanov's face.

Ivanov responded with a laugh. "So is that what this is about? Personal issues? You have something you want to ask me, Jonathan? Ask me."

Jonathan Krause stared at the older man in front of him. He did have a question. It seemed that this plan might work to everyone's benefit. "Who is my father?" Krause asked directly.

"Are you certain you want that answer?" Ivanov asked. "I suspect you already know. You want confirmation? Who told you; William or Edmond?" he asked the younger man.

"Just answer the question," Krause said.

"How is your sister these days, Jonathan?" Ivanov asked. "I guess she hasn't been enlightened….I'd have expected to see you both…."

"Leave Alex out of this," Krause threatened.

Ivanov paced to his desk and took his rightful seat. "Protective. So you have your answer. Does it even matter?" Ivanov asked. Krause did not respond. "Yes, well," Ivanov continued, "What do you really want to know? You want to know who your father was; is that right? Not his name. Why don't you ask Edmond?" Ivanov chuckled. "You think I will give you a more accurate picture of the man. That's ironic, wouldn't you say?" Krause just listened silently. "Who was Nicolaus Toles? Damned if I know. Damned if any of us do. Where would he have fallen in all of this? Is that your question?" Ivanov asked. The Russian watched as Jonathan Krause's normally impassive expression gave just the faintest indication of distress. "He would fall as he always did, on whatever side suited him best," Ivanov explained.

"You're saying he stood for nothing," Krause determined.

"*Moshch eto soblaznitel'naja lyubovnitsa, Jonathan. Eto i yest' vash otvet.* (Power is a seductive mistress, Jonathan. That is your answer)," Ivanov said definitively. Jonathan Krause stood regarding the man and his words silently. Ivanov's words were confirmation of what he already knew was the truth. It did little to explain why it had been kept a secret for so long or who the man known as the broker truly was. "If that is all," Ivanov said with a wave of his hand.

Krause nodded as he turned and headed for the door. "Why such a secret?" he asked without turning to look at the man behind the desk.

"Secrets are power's ally," Ivanov answered evenly. Krause shook his head and stepped through the doorway. "She will discover the truth, Jonathan. How she discovers it might just determine where she will fall in all of this," Ivanov said.

Krause nodded. He had no use for the man behind him, but he could not deny that there was truth in the words he spoke. Alex would inevitably learn who he was; who they both were. It was in the files that Eleana held. It was time to decide. He poured over Ivanov's reasoning. It was a thought process he once embraced. Now he found it severely flawed. "Secrets are not power's ally," he muttered. "Trust is."

***

Alex glanced to see Eleana reach the door to the room they had chosen. Alex stepped through the large steel door in her hands. She immediately caught sight of the tall NSA agent standing roughly four feet in front of her. She had never worked with Agent Anderson. His reputation, however, was praiseworthy. It had been an unexpected development to see him in the company of Claire Brackett. Alex couldn't help but play through a number of scenarios as she approached him. Was he simply another agent acting at the direction of a superior; an unwitting conspirator in a larger game he had no knowledge of? She shook off her musings for a later time.

"Well, well…Agent Anderson. You certainly keep interesting company these days," Alex called to him.

Marcus Anderson pivoted slowly. "Agent Alex Toles," he greeted her cordially. A second man went to reach for his sidearm, but Anderson stopped him. "You are just full of surprises. What brings you to Russia?" Anderson asked. "Looking for something you misplaced, perhaps?" he winked.

Alex laughed. "You mean that lovely metal case you and Agent Brackett liberated from my company last year?" she asked. "No. Shopping isn't my thing. Ask my wife," Alex quipped.

Anderson raised a brow. "So, what can I do for you?" he asked.

Alex quickly surveyed her surroundings, committing to memory as many details as her brief assessment would allow. She smiled as she scanned the agent before her, noting the placement of his sidearm near his right hip. Steadily, she approached her adversary. The irony was not lost on her. He reported to the man she once considered a trusted friend and mentor. In her previous life, she would have considered Agent Anderson an ally just by his affiliation. This was a new life and a new time. Alex stepped up to the tall agent and raised her brow suggestively. "Agent Anderson, do you know who you work for?" she asked.

"Do you?" he returned the question.

"My eyes are open," Alex assured him. More swiftly than he could have anticipated Alex had spun him around, twisting his right arm behind his back. She looked forward and recognized Anderson's companion's efforts to draw his sidearm. "Bad idea," she chastised him. She brought her foot forcefully into the back of Anderson's knee instantly driving him downward. In one fluid motion, she took possession of the Glock pistol on Anderson's hip. "Put it down," she ordered, aiming it at the man in front of her as he raised his weapon. When he did not comply, she repeated her demand. "*Bros' yego, ili ya broshu tebia* (Drop it, or I drop you)," Alex warned him.

"Alex!" Eleana screamed as she entered the large room.

Alex moved toward the sound of the younger woman's voice and captured Anderson's move for a knife in his boot. She felt the blade graze her calf as he struggled to regain his bearings. Alex fought the pain traveling up her leg and spun to her left, landing a powerful kick to Anderson's temple. "Stay down!" Alex yelled. She pivoted to her right and kicked the second man's side arm away. "Get his weapon," she ordered Eleana.

Anderson shifted his weight and pulled himself to an upright position. He wiped the small trickle of blood running down his face and attempted to focus on Alex. He squinted repeatedly to remove the fog over his eyes that lingered. Alex grabbed the second man by his collar and threw him across the floor toward Anderson. "Jesus, Toles," Anderson complained. "That's how you treat your friends?"

"My friends?" Alex asked. She turned back toward Eleana. "How much time do you need to recode that badge?"

"Just a few seconds," Eleana answered.

Alex leaned over Anderson. "You have an interesting group of friends, Agent Anderson. How is Claire?" her voice dripped with disgust.

Anderson chuckled. "Torn up over your friend over there. What's her codename? Catwoman? Got nine lives or something?" he asked. Alex looked back briefly to Eleana, who raised her head for a split second at his revelation. Eleana struggled to breathe and returned to the task at hand.

"Huh. Never imagined Claire as having any compassion," Alex said flatly.

"Got it," Eleana called out.

Alex moved into Anderson's ear. "I don't know whose game you're playing, or on whose team, Anderson. If word gets back to your little friend the sparrow that Eleana is alive, then I will know it is not on mine. Watch yourself," she cautioned him. "Never a good thing to have mistrust between partners." Alex started to pull back when she felt his hand grab her wrist.

"I see. Better you think to work with family? No possibility for conflict there," Anderson inferred his doubt.

Alex shook her head in confusion. "I hope you know who you are working with," Alex told him.

"You too," he said. "I'll give you a head start," he whispered. "Two minutes. I'd give you five, but that kick was a bitch." Eleana beckoned to Alex to follow. Alex pulled away from Anderson's grasp and studied him for a brief second. His eyes were bright and his gaze steady. She made a mental note to add Marcus Anderson to the list of puzzles she needed to complete.

"Alex!" Eleana called again.

"Right behind you," Alex assured her and sprinted to follow.

"Two minutes, Toles. Two," Anderson called to her as she exited the room.

***

Chapter Sixteen

"I want to know where the hell she is!" Michael Taylor's voice blared through the small office.

"I don't know," Agent Stephen Brady answered calmly. "Claire is not exactly one to have a leash," he observed.

"You think I need a lesson on Agent Brackett, Agent Brady? Is that it?" the NSA Director asked heatedly.

Agent Brady tried not to chuckle at the tirade his superior was throwing. He had enjoyed witnessing Michael Taylor's unravelling upon receiving the news that Claire Brackett was missing in action. "Have you contacted her father?" Brady made a gentle suggestion.

"No and I have no intention of doing so," Taylor answered,

"Well, if you don't want to involve the admiral; what is your plan?" Brady asked his boss.

Michael Taylor mulled over the question for a few minutes. Claire was a wild card. That was a reality that Director Taylor continually wrestled with for the last two years. "She'll surface," Taylor assured Brady. "I just wonder what it is she is doing in the meantime."

"Maybe she is concerned about O'Brien," Brady offered.

Taylor released a raucous laugh. "Claire? Worried about that fool? I doubt it," Taylor said as he caught his breath. "The problem with Claire is that she is...."

"Reckless?" Stephen Brady guessed Taylor's thought.

"Yes. The only advantage is that she has no skin in the game. The only thing she fears losing is her position or at least what she perceives that to be," Taylor said.

"And you think that is a good thing?" Brady looked to the assistant director doubtfully.

"Reckless is never a good thing. A reckless person with passion is worse. A person who fears something, loves something, needs to protect or avenge....that recklessness becomes the most dangerous opponent anyone can face," Taylor advised Brady.

"Guess it's a good thing Claire's not big on love," Brady said.

"No. She's too selfish for that. That worries me," Taylor admitted

"All due respect, you just said that she would be more dangerous if...."

"At least if she had some ties we would have a trail to follow, Brady," Taylor explained.

"What about Anderson?" Brady asked.

"In Russia. Last he heard from Claire was the day of the attack." Michael Taylor picked up a piece of paper from his desk and perused it for a few moments. "Leave Claire to me," Taylor said. "I have a few ideas. I have something else I want you to concentrate on."

"And what might that be?" Brady inquired.

"Follow Agent Fallon," Taylor ordered.

"You suddenly worried about Fallon's loyalty?" Brady wondered.

"Just do it. He questioned O'Brien. Joshua Tate had to have approved that. See what our good Agent Fallon is up to these days. Who he is spending time with at the FBI when he is there."

"What do you hope to find?" Brady asked.

"I hope I find nothing, Agent Brady. But, better to know if there is anything to find."

***

Ian Mitchell squatted in front of the fireplace, poking at the logs mindlessly in an effort to break the tension in the room. It was approaching midnight, and there had been no word from Jonathan Krause. Alex was sitting on the sofa in the center of the cabin with her head back and eyes closed. She had been silent for hours. Eleana studied the two older agents thoughtfully. Occasionally, Alex would massage her temples with her thumbs, and Eleana noticed the slight grimace that accompanied each stroke.

"He'll make it," Eleana broke the lingering silence.

Alex gradually opened her eyes and leaned forward to regard the younger woman. "I know," she said.

"Something else is bothering you," Eleana guessed. Alex forced a smile.

"It's the curse of attachments," Ian Mitchell offered, prompting Alex to turn her attention to him. "Am I wrong?" Mitchell looked up from his task to capture Alex's gaze. "Attachments always pose a risk."

"No," a voice answered. Jonathan Krause strolled into the room and nodded to Alex. He was soaking wet and obviously exhausted. Alex immediately hopped to her feet and ran to retrieve a towel. "Attachments are not our weakness, Ian," Krause said, accepting the towel and a knowing smile from Alex.

"You look like shit," Alex told her friend.

"Thanks," Krause replied lightly.

"Trouble?" Ian asked.

"Nothing I couldn't handle," Krause assured him. Alex was walking back toward the sofa when Krause noticed her favoring her left leg. "What happened?" he grabbed her arm in concern.

"Nothing I couldn't handle," Alex winked.

"Alex?" he implored her.

"I'm fine. Ran into an unexpected guest at ASA," Alex said. Krause waited for her to continue. "Marcus Anderson," she explained.

"What the hell was Anderson doing at ASA?" he asked. Alex shrugged. "So, that's who I should thank for your limp?" Krause asked his partner.

"It's just a graze, Pip," she told him.

"Yeah? Show me, then," he challenged her.

Eleana noted the frustration in Alex's eyes and the concern in Kraus's voice. "It's not that bad," she supported Alex. "It didn't go in that deep. I sutured it when we got here. It'll be sore for a few days, though."

Krause looked at Eleana and back to Alex. "That son of a bitch stabbed you?" he asked furiously.

"I'm fine," Alex repeated. "At least no one shot me this time," she joked.

Krause did not respond to his partner's attempt at levity. His expression remained severe. "I'm going to go find something dry," he muttered as he walked briskly from the room.

Alex was completely perplexed. They had been in worse situations, and both of them had suffered injuries in the past. "What the hell was that about?" she pondered his behavior aloud.

Eleana started in Krause's direction. "I'll talk to him," she said softly.

Krause heard the footsteps as they entered the bedroom. "What do you want Eleana?" he asked.

Eleana slowly made her way behind him and placed her hand on his muscular back. "You need to tell her," she said gently. She felt him take in a full breath and hold it. "Jonathan, she has a right to know."

Krause hung his head, shaking it continuously. "How am I supposed to tell her?"

"Tell me what?" Alex asked as she entered the room. Krause and Eleana swiftly turned to meet Alex's confused stare. "Pip? What can't you tell me?" Alex implored him.

"I'll leave you two to talk," Eleana said. She leaned in and kissed Krause on the cheek, taking the opportunity to whisper in his ear. "You love her. I can see it. Tell her." She pulled back and stopped briefly in front of Alex, offering her new friend a compassionate smile before exiting the room.

"Pip? What's going on?" Alex asked nervously.

"Alex, sit down," he suggested.

"I don't want to sit down," Alex responded bluntly.

Krause let out a heavy sigh. "All right. Then I will."

***

Cassidy rolled over and picked up her cell phone, still groggy from sleep, but eager to hear Alex's voice. "Hey."

"Cassidy?" the voice questioned.

"Huh?" Cassidy was caught momentarily caught off guard by the unexpected voice. "Chris?" she asked.

"Yeah....Don't hang up," he practically begged her.

"What do you want?" Cassidy asked. Her head was already begging to throb.

"What happened to us, Cassie?" he asked quietly.

"Are you drunk?" Cassidy asked him seriously.

"Maybe. I still want to know," he told her.

Cassidy rubbed her eyes forcefully. "You can't be serious," she sighed in exhaustion.

"I am. Look at us. How did we get here?" he asked, sipping the whiskey in his hand.

"Christopher, it's after two o'clock in the morning. What do you want me to say?" she responded.

"Did you ever love me?" he asked her. His voice was strained from the alcohol clouding his brain.

Cassidy continued moving her hand over her face in a futile attempt to wipe away her frustration. Part of her was inclined to hang up the call, but something deep within her was surfacing. The past needed to be put in the past. Her past needed to be set in the past. Her conscience appealed to her to offer the man she once shared her life with the truth if for no other reason than to make peace with it herself. "Did I love you?" she repeated his question.

"Yeah. Did you?" he asked her again.

"I don't know, Chris. I loved who I thought you were. I loved the idea of us. I don't know that I ever truly was in love with you," she confessed.

"I loved you," he told his ex-wife.

Cassidy took in his words and accepted them at face value. For all of Christopher O'Brien's monumental faults, Cassidy was certain he believed the words he was speaking. "I think.... if you are completely honest with yourself, Chris, you'll find it was the idea you fell in love with; not me," she said honestly.

"Maybe," he admitted. A measurable pause ensued before he continued. "I never meant for you or Dylan to get hurt," he said. Cassidy detected the tears he was beginning to shed and closed her eyes. She was at a loss for how to respond. It didn't matter what his intentions had been. Christopher O'Brien had put himself first in every moment. He broke his commitment to their marriage more times that Cassidy dared to count. He broke his son's trust. Even if Cassidy could forgive all of the pain he had caused in their lives; she would never forget it. "Cassie?" he called to her. Cassidy remained silent. "He really isn't mine; is he?" the congressman asked. There was a tinge of despair in his voice, and Cassidy felt the warmth of a tear grace her cheek.

"No," Cassidy answered.

"Probably better for him," O'Brien said. Silence lingered for long moments before he continued. "Are you really happy?"

Cassidy closed her eyes and pictured Alex. "Yes, I am," she said assuredly.

"Good," he barely whispered.

"Chris," Cassidy began, "you know it's never too late to change."

Christopher O'Brien took a deep breath and released it in a sad chuckle. "Take care of yourself, Cassie," he said as he disconnected the call.

***

"What is going on?" Alex demanded an answer from her partner.

Jonathan Krause looked up from his seat on the small bed and inhaled a breath for courage. "Did you ever think it's strange how we seem to be able to read each other?" he asked.

Alex shrugged. "We think alike," she commented.

"Yeah. We do. But, didn't you ever think that it was strange? I mean, how quickly we fell into a groove?" he asked Alex.

Alex knew it would be a lie to tell her friend that she hadn't puzzled over their natural chemistry. She knew that her ability to anticipate Krause's actions and his ability to understand her motivations was not something that frequently occurred between partners; at least not in such a short period. "Of course," she admitted. "But, some things you just can't explain, Pip."

Jonathan Krause chuckled. "That's what I thought too," he hesitated before continuing. "Alex, I…."

"Jesus, Krause! Just spill it already!" Alex cried in exasperation.

"I was never close to any of my brothers. I was the oldest. We just never seemed to like the same things. John was my brother, in every way that mattered. I trusted him. When I lost him I knew I would never have another brother; not really….I never thought I would be that close to anyone else," he said as he recalled his best friend. Krause looked directly at Alex. She was watching him closely, and his expression softened. "Until you came along," he said honestly. Krause watched Alex's face contort in a mixture of confusion and gratefulness. "I wondered why that was," he mused. "Then Edmond showed me something. I didn't know if I should believe him. Then in Stockholm, that note John left. I think he knew. He knew," Krause said as he closed his eyes. "Viktor too..."

"Knew what?" Alex asked. "Pip, what are you so afraid to tell me?"

Krause nodded and sighed. "I was wrong. Seems I do have another brother....and a sister," he told Alex. Krause waited for her to respond. Alex just stared blankly at her partner. He braced himself for her outburst of anger, but it never came.

Alex covered her face with her hands and took a seat beside her friend on the bed. She struggled to quell the emotions and thoughts that were spiraling like a Ferris wheel within her. Her first clear thought was that she wished Cassidy was with her now. She had no doubt in the veracity of the claim that Jonathan Krause was making. Alex grabbed the bridge of her nose and swallowed hard; another secret kept for more years than she could fathom. It pained her, and yet, in some way she felt a sense of relief. She loved the man beside her. It was something she had difficulty comprehending and accepting. Cassidy had seen it. Cassidy had implored Alex to accept what Jonathan Krause had come to mean to her; to their family.

Alex grasped Krause's hand and spoke quietly. "Why didn't you tell me sooner?" she asked.

Krause shook his head. "I don't know. Part of me was afraid it wasn't true," he said. Alex looked at him curiously. "And, I wanted it to be," he admitted.

Alex let a knowing chuckle pass. She was acutely aware of the loneliness that often accompanied the work she and Krause engaged in. Alex had never realized how lonely her life had become until she met Cassidy. She'd spent years viewing attachments as dangerous vulnerabilities. Loving Cassidy had taught her many things, not the least of which was that greater strength was found in loving than in solitude. "Do you doubt it now?" Alex asked Krause.

Jonathan Krause shook his head. "No."

"I guess you really are Uncle Pip, then, huh?" Alex poked at him.

"Alex, I know this is..."

Alex tightened her hold on his hand. "Don't. You don't need to explain. I feel better knowing."

"Are you still up for France?" Krause asked.

Alex nodded. More now than ever she wanted to see Edmond Callier face to face. She was tired of the secrets and the lies. She wanted answers, not cryptic clues, not fancy rhetoric; facts. "I think he owes us some explanations," Alex said flatly. "We can't ask our father,"

"Are you prepared for that?" Krause asked.

"If there is one thing we both know, Pip. The truth always comes to pass. Avoiding Edmond won't change that," she said. Krause agreed. "I assume Eleana knows?" Alex asked.

"It populated in my file on Ivanov's database," Krause explained.

"Pip, what is the deal with Eleana and Claire?" Alex asked cautiously.

Jonathan Krause frowned. "They were best friends."

"Like you and John?" Alex led him to answer.

"Not exactly," Krause quirked a brow.

"I see," Alex reflected her understanding. "You trust her? Eleana?"

"She loves Claire, Alex. Really loves her. Always has. But, she knows who Claire is. Frankly, I think it's why she wanted in on this life. Some part of her hopes Claire changes," Krause said.

"Not likely," Alex chuckled. "It's more than that. You have feelings for her," Alex guessed.

"I'm not in love with her," he replied honestly.

"No, but maybe you could be," Alex said with a pat to his shoulder. "Sometimes you can't see what's right in front of you," she reminded him. "It takes someone else showing you the obvious."

"Speaking from experience?" Krause asked with a grin.

Alex winked at the man still seated on the bed. "Just keep your eyes open," she told her friend. "Farsightedness runs in the family. Another well-kept secret; our father wore glasses," she told him as she took her leave.

***

Saturday, January 24th

Cassidy emerged from the bathroom looking a bit gray. Rose pondered her daughter's sluggish pace and the weariness in her eyes. Cassidy was not a morning person. That became evident when Rose had to start waking her daughter for school when she was a child. This morning, fatigue emanated from Cassidy in every motion and expression. Rose realized that the battle Cassidy's stomach had been waging against food over the last few weeks explained a great deal of her daughter's exhaustion. She had also mastered deciphering Cassidy's moods long ago, and it seemed evident to her that Cassidy was on edge. She poured her daughter a mug of tea and took a seat beside her at the kitchen table.

"Didn't sleep?" Rose guessed.

"Not well. I got a call in the middle of the night," Cassidy explained.

"Everything all right with Alex?" Rose asked.

"I don't know. It wasn't her," Cassidy said.

"Who called you in the middle of the night?" Rose questioned curiously.

Cassidy traced the rim of her mug with her finger and sighed. "It was Chris."

"What the hell was he calling here for?" Rose asked. The venom in her voice made Cassidy shudder.

"He'd been drinking; I think. I think it's just catching up with him," Cassidy said regrettably. "I don't know though, if he'll ever realize that he created this life for himself," she said.

Rose had always considered herself a compassionate person, but she had no tolerance for her daughter's ex-husband. For many years, she tried not interfere in Cassidy's life; never offering unsolicited advice. It pained her to see the emotional toll that Cassidy's marriage to Christopher O'Brien caused for so long. In the past year, Rose had witnessed the true depravity of her former son-in-law. Cassidy had more than enough on her plate without Congressman Christopher O'Brien's emotional baggage weighing her down.

"Don't you give that egotistical bastard one more second of your time, Cassie," Rose instructed her daughter. Cassidy's eyes flew open at her mother's directness. "What?" Rose asked. "Don't ask me to keep my mouth shut anymore where he is concerned. I did that for far too long. You are my only daughter. I will not tolerate seeing you victimized in any way by that jerk. And that is what he is, Cassie. He is nothing more than a pompous ass. The only thing he is full of is himself. So, don't you spend one ounce of your energy on his shenanigans."

Cassidy's eyebrows shot up. "Shenanigans?" she poked at her mother.

"I am not fooling around, Cassie," Rose's mood remained sober.

"I know," Cassidy said tacitly. "I just feel awful."

"Awful?" Rose was astounded at her daughter's statement. "What do you have to feel awful about?"

"I've never hated anyone," Cassidy said. "I don't know... he shot Alex, Mom....he's dragged Dylan through hell and he wants me to feel sorry for *him*?"

Rose sighed. "You have every reason to feel the way you do," she told her daughter.

"Maybe," Cassidy said. "I just never wanted to be that person."

"Mom!" Dylan's voice beckoned his mother from upstairs. Cassidy could tell whatever Dylan needed; he was agitated.

"I'd better go see what he needs," Cassidy said.

"I'll go," Rose offered. "Stay here. You need to eat something...anything," she observed.

"I can't right now," Cassidy said.

"Mom!"

Cassidy shook her head and reached for the back of her neck. "I'll be back....Hold your horses, I'm coming!" she called back to her son.

Rose picked up Cassidy's mug and noted that it was still more than half full of tea. She tapped a spoon on the table repeatedly, mulling over what her daughter had said. There was no reason for Cassidy to feel any guilt over loathing Christopher O'Brien. She huffed in frustration as she looked out of the room toward the pathway Cassidy had just taken. "Oh, Cassie," she muttered when a crash startled her.

"Grandma!" Dylan's voice rang out through the house.

***

Edmond Callier reached for his phone in the hopes of hearing his daughter's voice. "This is Callier."

"Edmond?" a woman's voice questioned. Edmond Callier jumped at the sound. "Edmond, I need your help."

"Anything. You know that," he responded sincerely.

"Do you know where Alexis is?" she asked.

"Why would I…."

"Edmond, please don't think me a fool. I realize how many years it has been, but I am not that naïve. She is with Jonathan. Can you reach her?"

Callier stroked his chin thoughtfully. He had not spoken to the woman on the line in nearly thirty years. He did know that she would not have made the call without a pressing reason. "No, not at present. What's wrong?" he asked.

"It's Cassidy."

***

Alex looked ahead at the faint lights in the distance. She could tell that the home they were approaching was expansive. She glanced at the younger woman seated beside her. Eleana had her eyes closed. This was a familiar ride to the young agent. Alex looked across to Krause with the raise of her brow. He offered her a solemn smile. She pondered what the man who was awaiting their arrival must be feeling. Alex tried to imagine what it would be like to wait for one of her children to come home; to know that one of her children was in danger. The thought sent a shiver up her spine.

"You okay?" Krause asked.

"Yeah, just thinking," Alex said.

"Care to share?" he smiled.

Alex paused for a moment to take in the grandeur of the building as it grew larger. "I was thinking about what he must be feeling," she explained.

"Edmond?" Krause asked.

"Mm. I can't tell you that I agree with all of these secrets.... all of these lies," Alex groaned. "I don't. But, there is a part of me that understands."

"Understands all this deception?" Eleana asked without opening her eyes.

"No," Alex replied flatly. "I don't understand the deception. I understand the fear."

Eleana opened her eyes to regard Alex. "Fear?" she asked.

Alex nodded. "I can't imagine....if it was one of my children," Alex's thought trailed off. Her lips began to curl into a smile as she considered the motivation in her statement.

"Alex?" Krause called to her softly.

"Yeah," Alex smiled in earnest. "I'm still here," she chuckled. "Guess I was just thinking about that....my children," she explained. Krause nodded.

"I'm clearly missing something," Eleana interjected.

Alex laughed. "With all the excitement and recent *revelations*," Alex looked at Krause, "I haven't had much time to think about home. I guess I'm missing my family."

"You mean Cassidy and her son," Eleana surmised.

Alex nodded. "I mean Cassidy and our son, yes," she corrected her friend. "Haven't talked to them in almost a week. Never been that long. Just hoping that they are all right, and Cassidy is feeling better."

"Is she sick?" Eleana asked.

Krause turned to look out the window to hide his knowing smirk. "No," Alex answered. "She's pregnant," she said with a smile.

Eleana's surprise was evident. "Congratulations. I assume it was planned," Eleana said lightly.

"Well, if it hadn't been I'd have been a lot more surprised than you were just now," Alex joked.

The car pulled in front of the grand stone structure. Alex shook her head at its extravagance, musing silently that the inside must be something spectacular to behold. As the door opened, she noticed the figure swiftly moving down the stairs. Alex had yet to meet Edmond Callier in person. She had wondered if the Frenchman was deliberately avoiding such a meeting. After hearing Krause's news, she was certain her assessment was correct. Eleana's pace increased as her father approached. Alex could not stop the swell in her heart when she saw Callier embrace his daughter gratefully. It made her ache for home.

"*Eleana. Je souhaitais que vous choisissiez pas cette vie* (Eleana. I wish you would not have chosen this life)," Callier spoke softly to his daughter as he held her tightly.

"*Je vais bien, mon Père* (I am all right, Father)," Eleana reassured him. Callier stepped back and regarded the woman his daughter had become. Eleana was no longer a child. She was a beautiful, intelligent, and capable woman. He touched her cheek affectionately and turned his attention to Krause and Alex.

"Edmond," Krause greeted the older man. "We have a great deal to talk about," he motioned toward Alex. "My sister and I have some questions," Krause raised his brow.

Callier nodded his understanding to the younger man and then turned to Alex. He took her hand and looked into her eyes compassionately. "We have much to discuss," he agreed, "but now is not the time."

"Edmond!" Krause interjected.

Callier kept his gaze on the young woman in front of him. "Not now, Jonathan," he cautioned. "*Ne faites pas nos même erreurs* (Don't make our mistakes)," he told Alex. Alex studied him carefully as he continued. "You have a plane to catch, Alexis."

"I don't…." Alex began.

"Your family needs you now," Callier said. "Cassidy…"

"Cassidy? What's…." Alex's asked desperately.

"Stop," Callier spoke gently. "Call home," he handed Alex his phone.

Alex could feel hear heart racing as she waited for Cassidy's soothing voice to answer. The voice that greeted her was calm, but it was not her wife's. "Mom?"

"Alexis," Helen greeted.

"Where is Cassidy?" Alex asked as a wave of panic began to take hold.

Helen let out a detectable sigh. "She's at the hospital with Rose," she explained.

"Why? What happened? Is Rose…."

"Rose is fine, Alexis," Helen said. "It's Cassidy." Krause watched as Alex became unsteady and stepped in to support her.

"Mom?" Alex begged fearfully.

"She's all right. She collapsed earlier. You need to come home, Alexis," her mother said firmly.

"The baby?" Alex's voice cracked.

"They are both all right, Alex. Cassidy is not fine though, and neither is Dylan. They need you here more than you need to be saving the world," Helen said a bit more sharply than she had intended. Alex could only nod. The lump in her throat seemed to prevent any speech. Krause took the phone from Alex's quivering hand.

"Helen?" Krause asked.

"Jonathan," Helen answered him bluntly. "She needs to come home. Now."

Jonathan Krause knew a parental demand when he heard one. "She'll be on the next plane," he assured the older woman.

"Thank you," Helen said earnestly.

"Helen..." Krause began.

"Cassidy will be all right, Jonathan," Helen assured him. "You take care of my daughter right now. Alexis likes to think she can carry the weight of the world. She can't."

Krause looked at Alex and smiled. "I understand," he said.

"Good. I'll see you both soon," Helen told him.

"Alex," Krause directed Alex to look at him.

"Jonathan...." Alex tried to make the words come. "What have I done?" she whispered.

Edmond Callier stepped between them. "Alexis, stop this. I have my plane waiting. You'll be home by morning," he told her.

"I should be home now," Alex scolded herself. Krause looked to Callier helplessly. "How did you even find out?" Alex asked the older man.

"That's not important right now," Callier said. "Jonathan, will you be accompanying Alexis home?"

"No," Alex answered for him. "You and Eleana need to follow up on what we gathered at ASA."

Krause knew a protest would be futile. "All right. At least let me ride with you to the plane," he said.

Callier watched the exchange between Krause and Alex and motioned for his daughter to follow him inside and give them some privacy. Eleana looked at her father curiously. "What is it?" she asked him. Her father's eyes glistened slightly in the faint light that surrounded them. She had seen the genuine affection and concern cross his face as he spoke to Alex.

Edmond Callier looped his arm around his daughter's. "You and Elliot were never that close," he said.

"No," Eleana admitted. She and her brother were drastically different people. She would've liked to say that their distance bothered her, but that would have been a lie. She had not missed his presence in her life. Elliot's primary interest was in lustful pursuits of any kind. He seldom visited home and when he did she recalled the arguments that erupted between her father and her brother. "I sometimes wondered if he was really my brother," she confessed.

Callier laughed. "He was. He had more of his mother in him," Callier said. "Those two," he glanced back at Krause and Alex, "they are kindred spirits."

Eleana followed the direction of her father's gaze. She had only just met Alex, but she had known Jonathan Krause for many years. He softened in Alex's presence. It was as if Alex somehow smoothed the rough edges of his life. Eleana smiled. "Do you think it's good for them? Working together?" she asked.

Callier nodded as he led his daughter inside. "I think it is what was meant to be."

***

"Claire has gone missing." Assistant FBI Director Joshua Tate said.

"Missing?" Agent Fallon asked.

"Apparently," Tate answered.

"What does that mean…exactly?" Fallon asked for clarification.

"It means she's off the grid entirely," Tate explained. "No one has had contact with her since last Friday."

"Coincidence?" Fallon asked. "She disappears the day the embassy in Moscow is attacked. I doubt that is by accident."

Tate nodded. "I don't imagine it is, Agent Fallon. It is not what you are thinking," Tate said. "I suspect her absence is of a personal nature."

"I don't follow," Fallon said.

"Imagine learning that you were involved in killing the one person you were close to," Tate said. Fallon's confusion was unmistakable. Joshua Tate pulled a photo from his jacket pocket and handed it to Fallon.

"I don't understand," Fallon admitted.

"Claire spent Christmas in Belarus with a friend; an old friend. I would say her only friend; a Spanish national on the CIA's payroll," Tate explained.

Fallon looked up at the assistant director in disbelief. "You're telling me that the translator killed in the embassy attack was agency?" he questioned.

"That's not something you find very surprising; is it, Agent Fallon?" Tate mocked him slightly. "What's more surprising is her choice of companions," Tate offered.

"You think that this Eleana Baros was complicit in the attack?" Fallon asked.

"No. I don't. I think she was a fixture in Claire Brackett's life. I know that Claire had a hand in orchestrating the attack. That Cesium she and Anderson absconded with last spring is playing a leading role in the propaganda machine. That is not a coincidence," Tate said.

"I'm still not following you," Fallon shook his head.

"Agent, if you unknowingly were complicit in the death of someone you loved…if you believed the people you worked for betrayed that personal trust; what would you do?" Tate posed the question to his agent.

"You think she is going to go after Kargen and Ivanov?" Fallon asked knowingly.

"I do; among others," Tate supplied.

"So…what does that mean for us?" Fallon inquired.

"Check in on our old friend the congressman," Tate instructed.

"You think she'll go to O'Brien? What can he do? He's due in court again on Tuesday," Fallon reminded his superior.

"Just check in on him," Tate repeated his direction. "You don't seriously think the only money Christopher O'Brien squirreled away all these years was in Cheryl Stephens' accounts?"

"Holy shit," Fallon groaned. "You think she wants him to finance her." Tate just smiled. "She'll never be able to get him out of the country," Fallon said.

"She may not have to," Tate chuckled. "If she chooses to, believe me, Claire Brackett has more than enough connections to get Christopher O'Brien anywhere she chooses. He is just foolish enough to botch her plans without knowing. If her father and Taylor don't know where she is....we follow O'Brien."

"Don't you think they will do the same thing?" Fallon asked.

"I'm counting on it."

***

Chapter Seventeen

Sunday, January 25th

Alex looked out of the tinted glass as the car slowed its pace. She stilled herself as her eyes swept over the place she called home. She accepted her bag from the driver and flung it over her shoulder, keeping a steady pace toward the front door. The faint caress of snowflakes tickled her bare hands and nose, and she took a deep breath when her fingers reached the door handle. This moment reminded her of another time she had come home to the woman she loved. That was less than a year ago. Alex had left early that morning to travel back to Washington D.C. Only a few hours later, Cassidy had been taken against her will. Alex remembered the note that Cassidy had enclosed in her bag along with a photo of the two people she loved most in her life. The myriad of emotions running through her now was eerily familiar; anticipation, relief, anxiety. Only the sight of the woman who held her heart would serve to quiet the competing sensations and emotions.

Alex stepped through the doorway quietly and removed her coat. She was struck by the silence that in its own way was deafening. She closed her eyes for a moment. As she opened them, a presence made itself known in the distance. A shimmering green gaze captured her attention. Cassidy stood perfectly still in the doorway to the kitchen. Alex was certain she had never seen anything so magnificent. She dropped her bag and began to slowly close the distance between them.

Cassidy's eyes shut instinctively just as Alex reached her. The feeling of Alex's hands tenderly cupping her face sent Cassidy's emotions crashing. As she opened her eyes, she saw an expression that she was certain mirrored her own. Tears spilled over Alex's cheeks as blue eyes sought to convey every thought and feeling that coursed through Alex's being. Cassidy reached for Alex's hands and held them as they continued to caress her cheeks gently. She felt Alex's lips brush against her forehead and the release of a breath that she knew signified the relief they both felt.

Alex lifted Cassidy's chin to look into the eyes that she had grown to adore. She wasn't certain how it was possible to become completely lost and found in one perfect moment. Alex was convinced that looking into Cassidy's eyes was the closest thing to perfection that could exist. They told a story. They whispered unspoken secrets known only to these two souls. They were the doorway to home; Alex's home. She captured Cassidy's lips with her own tentatively and lovingly; a promise without words. As Alex pulled back, Cassidy's lips curled into an understanding smile.

"I missed you," Cassidy whispered. The pace of Alex's tears increased as she continued to marvel silently at the woman before her. Cassidy sensed Alex's fear and guilt and set out immediately to quell it. "I'm all right, love," she said.

"Never again," Alex whispered. Cassidy wiped a tear from Alex's cheek with her thumb. "I'm so sorry, Cass."

"Stop. You're here now. You're safe. And you are holding me," Cassidy said. "That's all that matters." Alex closed her eyes again, reveling in the tenderness and compassion her wife always offered.

"Alex!" an excited voice broke through their private moment. Within seconds, a lively little boy crashed into Alex's hip.

"Hey, Speed," she welcomed his embrace and lifted him to her waist. "Did you behave while I was away?"

"Yeah," he answered. "Mom was sick," he told her.

Alex sighed and fought the surfacing tears she feared might be endless. "I heard," she said softly. "I'll bet you took good care of her, though."

"Yeah and Mackenzie too," he said. Alex looked at Cassidy inquisitively. Cassidy just chuckled.

"Mackenzie?" Alex asked.

"Yeah, my brother," Dylan said as if she should know that.

For the first time in hours, Alex felt a sense of lightness wash over her. She smiled at her wife. "Guess we have some catching up to do," Alex surmised. Cassidy just arched her brow.

Helen stood at the top of the stairs listening to the conversation below her. She wiped a falling tear from her eyes as the sound of laughter that had been absent for many days began to filter through the house. Rose came up behind her and smiled.

"Guess she's home," Rose said.

Helen nodded. "I hope she realizes just how lucky she is," Helen said softly.

"She does," Rose patted her friend's shoulder. "Come on. I think our daughters could use some family time. You, me and a good bottle of wine," Rose suggested.

"Sounds perfect," Helen agreed. "Who's driving?" she laughed.

"Alex still has her penance to do. We'll call her if we need to," Rose joked.

Helen followed Rose down the stairs, listening as Dylan prattled on to Alex and Cassidy about his name and Mackenzie excitedly. "Oh, Alexis," Helen thought to herself. "Don't waste a single minute," she prayed silently.

***

"Have you lost your mind?" Christopher O'Brien screamed in disbelief. "Jesus, Claire, you have me in their back yard for God's sake? What the hell are you thinking?"

Claire Brackett ignored her companion's tirade. She found the congressman's constant complaints aggravating. He was very much like a spoiled child and children were not something that ever interested Claire. She ran her hands over the mantle that held several frames, stopping occasionally to study the faces behind the glass. "Relax," she told him.

"Relax? Claire…."

"It's perfect," Claire bragged. "No one will ever look for you here, believe me. No one knows about this place. It may just be my best kept secret."

"You'll forgive me….I never pictured you enjoying the comforts of small town New England," O'Brien said sarcastically.

"And, how have you pictured me?" she inquired. O'Brien was not amused by her banter, and that made Claire all the more delighted. "You are such a baby," she told him. "Since you are so curious…I went to school not far from here. This… this place was our escape," Claire explained.

"You think staying in one of Daddy's homes is a good idea?" he asked.

Claire scoffed at his assessment of the situation. "My father has no idea this exists. No, this was a rundown old farmhouse when I used to come here," she told him. Claire stretched out in a large chair and sighed as she examined her surroundings. "She was amazing," Claire whispered in admiration.

"You have lost your mind," O'Brien observed. "What are we here to rekindle your lost childhood? I thought we had an agreement."

Claire closed her eyes and relaxed her body. She had not been to this home in several years. Life had conspired to keep her apart from much of her past and that included this place. It was the first place Eleana had kissed her. It was the sanctuary that they had created to avoid the demands of expectant fathers and academic pressures. It was, Claire began to realize, the closest she had ever felt to 'home'; whatever that was. Claire had traveled in luxury her entire life. Somehow; whenever she and Eleana found cause or opportunity to escape to this place; Claire felt comforted. She chuckled at the memory of sleeping bags and camping gear, Pop-Tarts and warm soda. It had been heaven. The first time she made love to Eleana they were here, in this room. Eleana swore she would make this a real home one day. Claire thought it was the naïve fantasy of youth. She opened her eyes and shook her head at the simple yet elegant room. How could she have ever doubted Eleana's commitment to that dream? Eleana never failed to deliver on a promise to Claire; never; until now.

"This is the safest place I know," Claire said, her voice crackling with uncharacteristic emotion. "You can be certain of that. No one will look for you here. This is a small town, Christopher. Stay here for now. I will make certain you have everything you need before I leave."

"You don't seriously expect me to stay hold up in this place; do you?" he demanded.

Claire rose from the comfort of her seat and led him several rooms away to a large kitchen. She directed him to look out the window. "It's beautiful, isn't it?" she asked him.

"What is wrong with you?" O'Brien asked her. Claire was behaving so strangely that he was beginning to wonder if perhaps she had actually lost her mind.

"Just look out," she repeated. "There is no place in the world I can take you right now that you are not at risk of someone recognizing you. It's not forever, Christopher. Think of it as a new adventure," she suggested.

"Looking at trees and snow?" he ridiculed the suggestion sarcastically.

"Life is all about perception. How many times do I have to tell you that? You must not have been a very stellar student," she insulted him. "I need some time to shift your problems. I have a plan. I always have a plan," she assured him. "Now, be a good boy and go pour us some wine. Merlot sounds perfect. I have no doubt you'll find an ample selection in the dining room," Claire told him.

O'Brien smirked slightly. He was not pleased with his current circumstance, but there were advantages. He was not in a county jail cell with common thugs. He was not the center of a courtroom spectacle, and Claire was ready for some wine. Wine inevitably led to activities that would ease his tension dramatically. "So, you'll keep me safe. I recall something about meeting all of my needs," he breathed in her ear. "I'm feeling a bit tense," he explained.

Claire's attention never deviated from the landscape outside the window. She nodded. "I'm certain you are, Christopher. Wine always helps me." O'Brien ran his hands up Claire's sides slowly, anticipating her usual aggressive response. Claire remained still and closed her eyes. "Wine, Christopher," she said flatly. "Get the wine."

***

"How are you feeling?" Alex asked Cassidy. "Honestly?"

Cassidy took a deep breath, inhaling Alex's presence and all that came with it. She shimmied closer to her wife and let all of her stress fall away. "Relaxed," Cassidy finally answered.

"What happened?" Alex asked tentatively.

Cassidy knew that the question was inevitable. They had spent a quiet day together with Dylan, opting to forego any conversations that might produce anxiety for any of them. It was time that all three were in dire need of spending together. Cassidy had fought her exhaustion for hours, admittedly avoiding any risk of deeper conversation. She toyed with Alex's sweatshirt as a momentary distraction.

"I passed out," Cassidy explained.

"I know that. Why did…"

Cassidy pulled Alex closer and finally spoke. "Oh, Alex….I just got rundown. Not being able to keep much food down didn't help. You were way. Dylan had a horrible week at school. Then Chris called in the middle of the night…."

"Wait. O'Brien called here?" Alex could not believe that the congressman would have the audacity to intrude on their lives yet again.

"He did," Cassidy tried to speak calmly. She felt Alex's body become rigid with anger and pulled herself up to look into Alex's eyes. "You need to calm down," Cassidy warned her wife. "I know you are angry and I know you are upset. I need you..."

Alex nodded and gently pulled Cassidy back against her. "I'm sorry. Go on."

"His call isn't important, Alex. He was drunk and he was feeling sorry for himself. I thought it was you when the phone buzzed. I just wanted to hear your voice. He took me completely off guard. For a minute I thought I was still sleeping," Cassidy recalled the conversation with her ex-husband. "After I hung up....I just couldn't sleep. With so much going on....I just needed to slow down," Cassidy admitted. "I didn't slow down. I was dehydrated and over tired. Dylan was shouting for me, and I ran up the stairs too quickly. That was the straw that broke the camel's back. I remember feeling dizzy and then nothing until the paramedic was over me."

Alex stroked Cassidy's back and placed a kiss on her head. "I'm sorry I wasn't here," she apologized.

"You can't be here every minute," Cassidy stated the obvious and felt Alex's head shaking.

"I also can't be away so much," Alex voiced her realization. Cassidy didn't want to admit that she was relieved by the statement. She wanted to support Alex fully in her career. The last week had been trying. Cassidy was beyond tired emotionally and physically, and she craved Alex's strength. She desperately tried to respond, but words failed her.

"Cass?" Alex called gently.

"I want to tell you that I'm fine," Cassidy said.

Alex chuckled softly. "But, you're not fine," she said. "It's okay, Cass. You don't have to be."

"I don't want you to feel like you have to be here taking care of me," Cassidy said in frustration. "I don't want to be that...."

"Be what?" Alex asked. "Cassidy, when I heard my mother's voice on the phone....Look, I know that you want to take care of everyone. That's why I say you are like everyone's mom. You are. You have to let us take care of you sometimes. You have to let me..."

"I know." Cassidy took a deep breath. Before she could stop herself, she confessed exactly what had been on her mind. "I needed you this week. I just needed to hear your voice. Dylan wanted to be a Toles and nothing I said seemed to make him feel better. I spent so many hours on the bathroom floor I started counting speckles in the tile. If it wasn't Chris on the news, it was all about Russ and the embassy. I didn't know where you were. I don't want to do this alone," Cassidy rattled off her thoughts like a freight train.

"It's okay," Alex comforted her wife. "I know. I promise, you are not going to do any of this alone. I promise," Alex repeated the words over and over until she felt Cassidy begin to relax. She rocked Cassidy gently and was content to allow a peaceful silence to hover.

"Alex?" Cassidy broke the stillness.

"Yeah?"

"I want to do the paternity test with Jonathan. I know I should care about the consequences in the future...the lie... But I........"

Alex sat up against the headboard and pulled Cassidy along with her. "I agree," she said.

"You do?" Cassidy asked.

"Yeah, I do. Dylan needs to feel safe. He needs to believe he is an equal part of everything. I know you are worried about keeping the truth from him. I am too, but we have to do what we believe will keep him safe, and that includes emotionally. Honestly, I think Dylan will be fine when the time comes to tell him the truth. And that time will come," Alex said.

"I know," Cassidy's voice shook.

"Listen, Cass. Before we do that.....Things are....I don't know how...There's something I have to tell you," Alex sighed.

"Did something happen while you were gone?" Cassidy asked fearfully.

"A lot happened, actually. Some of it might be along the lines you are thinking, but none of that is important. Jonathan and I....well, he knew for a while...I...."

"What? Alex....you're scaring me," Cassidy said.

Alex chuckled nervously. "He's my brother, Cassidy."

"What are you talking about?" Cassidy said as she moved to sit up fully.

"My father....My father is Pip's biological father," Alex said.

"You're not joking; are you?" Cassidy looked at Alex quizzically. "Alex? This is not a funny joke."

"It's not a joke. He is. Jonathan Krause is my half-brother. Uncle Pip is actually, literally Dylan and Mackenzie's uncle," Alex explained. Cassidy's mood immediately shifted. Alex could tell by the signature arch of her wife's left eyebrow and the way Cassidy was struggling to conceal her smile. "What's so funny?" Alex asked.

"Mackenzie?" Cassidy questioned her wife. "Did Dylan bribe you while I was in the bathroom or something?"

"No," Alex said indignantly. "He made a lot of good points," Alex defended her stance. Cassidy pursed her lips to stem her laughter. It amazed Cassidy how the simplest sentiment could dispel all the stress and sadness in life. Time with her family always reminded Cassidy that she was happier than she ever imagined possible; happier and completely in love with the woman next to her. Cassidy listened intently as Alex continued to argue Dylan's case. "And, besides...Mackenzie will work either way. Less work for us," Alex offered her reasoning.

"Less work for us?" Cassidy asked curiously.

"Well, let's be honest. I think we both know you would rather it be a surprise. Am I right? So, either way…boy or girl, Mackenzie is it. One and done," Alex beamed.

"Uh-huh. What about a middle name?" Cassidy raised a new question.

"Eh. No one needs a middle name. It's just something your mom can use to threaten you when she's mad. Everyone knows that," Alex said. With that final statement Cassidy lost all desire to hold back and erupted into laughter. There were many moments when she could swear on her life that Dylan somehow came from Alex. She was certain Dylan would agree with the entire argument Alex had just waged.

"Maybe you should have been an attorney," Cassidy poked.

"Does that mean we win?" Alex opened her eyes wide for effect.

"I wasn't aware this was a competition," Cassidy said firmly. She watched as Alex's excitement deflated a degree and rolled her eyes. "Yes, Alex. Mackenzie it is."

"Oh good," Alex sighed. "I was worried."

"Worried that I wouldn't agree?" Cassidy wondered.

"Nah. I would have been fine with whatever you wanted," Alex admitted. "I just hate calling him, the baby. Seems so impersonal."

Cassidy leaned in and kissed Alex's cheek. "Him? You are adorable," Cassidy said as she moved her kiss to Alex's lips.

"Really? Adorable, huh?"

"Yes…when you aren't being annoying," Cassidy tried to act serious.

"I'm not annoying…..Am I? Cass….Am I annoying?"

Cassidy giggled and captured Alex's lips again. No, love. You really are adorable."

"So, what do you think about Pip?" Alex asked.

Cassidy sighed. She was curious how Alex discovered that Jonathan Krause was her brother. She was even more intrigued by the possibilities that surrounded this new information. Somehow, she didn't find it all that shocking. She looked at Alex for a moment and realized it made sense. Cassidy adored Jonathan Krause from the moment they met. She understood his feelings ran along a different path than her own. To Cassidy, her friend Pip was the big brother she never had. She placed her forehead against Alex's and spoke softly. "I don't want to talk about your brothers, either of them, right now," Cassidy whispered.

Alex felt her heart skip at the sensual tone in her wife's voice. She had missed Cassidy. "Cass, are you sure you are up to this? I mean…" Alex felt Cassidy's weight above her and moved her hands to Cassidy's hips.

"Alex, I told you. I need you. Right now I don't want to think about siblings or parents. I don't even want to think about Dylan or Mackenzie. I love them all. I just want you," Cassidy implored her wife.

Alex kissed Cassidy slowly, her hands tracing circles on Cassidy's back. The feel of Cassidy against her caused the fear Alex had suppressed over the last day to surge like a storm. Alex's body reacted with a shudder as she recalled the desperation she felt to get home to her family. Instinctively, she pulled Cassidy closer to her, needing to remind herself that Cassidy was safe. Cassidy felt Alex's kiss become more insistent and pulled back slightly. "Cass?" Alex asked in concern.

"Slow down, Alex. I'm not going anywhere," Cassidy promised.

"I'm not either," Alex responded as she attempted to swallow the lump in her throat. Alex closed her eyes. Within moments, Cassidy felt another shudder pass through her wife's body.

"What is it?" Cassidy asked.

Alex opened her eyes. She kissed Cassidy softly. "I want to you give you what you need. I know you want it to be just me and you….but I……"

Cassidy suddenly understood how those hours Alex spent traveling home must have felt for her wife. She laid back down and placed her head on Alex's chest. "Tell me."

Alex brushed her lips across Cassidy's head and attempted to find the right words. "I don't know how to explain it. First, I thought something happened to Rose, then when Mom said it was you....I thought I would...I was so afraid. She said you were all right. It wasn't even a second...not even that long that I felt relieved and then I stopped breathing again....wondering if the baby..."

"Oh, Alex....I'm sorry," Cassidy said with a squeeze.

"You are with the baby every minute. You are with Dylan every day. That's how it works. I get it. You need just to be Cassidy. I think I get that....But, I need to..."

"I understand."

"You do?" Alex asked hopefully,

"I think so. Just hold me. Hold us. You'll feel better," Cassidy assured her wife.

"I already do," Alex said as her eyelids grew heavy. "This is much better than squishy you," Alex grumbled.

Cassidy snickered. "Mm....I will remember you said that in a few months." Cassidy was ready to needle Alex some more when she realized that Alex had already drifted off to sleep. It was one of Alex's natural abilities that Cassidy secretly envied. Alex was like an infant. She could be babbling one second and sound asleep the next. "I wonder if that's a Toles' trait or a Pappas' quirk?" she mused. "What do you think, Mackenzie?" Cassidy smiled and let her own eyes fall shut. Alex's arm was draped around her protectively, and Cassidy realized that she was truly at peace. "I love you, Alex," she whispered as sleep finally began to claim her. She felt Alex's embrace tighten gently. "We all love you."

***

Monday, January 26th

"What are you doing up already?" Helen asked Alex.

"Mom, I'm always up this early," Alex reminded her mother.

"I guess I just thought you would want to stay in bed this morning," Helen said. "How is Cassidy?"

"Resting. I think maybe I should be asking you and Rose that question," Alex admitted with a sigh as she gratefully accepted a cup of coffee from her mother. "You know Cass," Alex said.

"I think I do," Helen responded.

"So?" Alex asked. "How is she....really?"

Helen pursed her lips and leaned against the counter behind her. "She's tired. It's not easy having no control over so many things in your life," Helen explained.

"What do you mean?" Alex asked.

"I mean that she has no control over most of what is happening right now. Her body is not cooperating. There's all this craziness with Dylan's father, and..."

Alex finished her mother's statement, "and I am missing in action."

Helen released a deep sigh. "Yes. She knows it comes with the territory," Helen said. Alex looked at her mother with a deep sense of regret. "It does come with the territory," Helen said flatly. "That doesn't make it any easier." Alex watched as her mother's fingers played nervously over the coffee cup in her hands.

"You called Edmond," Alex verbalized her suspicion.

"Yes."

Alex reached for her temples. "How do you know...."

Helen looked up from her coffee cup to her daughter. "He's your godfather, Alexis." Alex looked at her mother in disbelief. She wiped her hand over her face as if to sweep away the entire exchange. "Why is that so surprising to you?" Helen asked pointedly. Alex bit her lip in frustration and Helen nodded. "Your father and Edmond were friends before I even met your father," Helen explained. She watched as confusion played across her daughter's face. "Alexis, I may not be a genius but I lived with your father for fifty years. You don't honestly believe that I have no idea what it is that he did."

"He told you?" Alex asked.

"No. He did not. My mother gave me some idea," Helen told Alex.

"I know I did not hear that correctly," Alex responded.

"Yes, you did," Helen assured her daughter. "Do you want to have this conversation now?" Helen asked. Alex stared blankly at her mother. "All right then," Helen agreed and directed Alex to sit. "You have always taken after your father....before you start arguing with me, listen. You would create challenges for yourself just to prove you could master them. Every time you mastered something you had to find another, more difficult one to overcome. Sometimes it was building bicycle ramps, other times it was in school. You were always moving. Nicky is more like me. I think that worked for you because he became a project too."

"Nicky is not my project."

"Mm-hm....he was, in the best of ways. You were able to teach him and protect him, and you thrived on that," Helen said proudly.

"What does that have to do with YaYa?" Alex asked in frustration.

"Everything. One thing you have never mastered is patience," Helen observed. Alex sighed and nodded for her mother to continue. "Jonathan is just like you," Helen said.

"You knew?" Alex's voice grew cold.

"That Jonathan was your brother? No. I didn't. Not until I spoke with Edmond the other night. That you had a brother? Yes, Alexis, I knew."

"Why didn't you tell me?" Alex pleaded.

"And what would that have accomplished?" Helen asked. "Part of me didn't want to believe it. I suppose I thought if I ignored it, somehow it would not be true. It hurt me, Alexis; more than you can imagine."

"But you stayed with him," Alex said.

"I loved him," Helen said. "I married him. It was my...."

"Duty?" Alex asked.

Helen laughed. "No, it was my choice."

"I don't know what to say," Alex admitted. "What about Dad and Edmond?"

"They went to Harvard together," Helen said. "They were roommates when your father was in law school. That didn't happen by chance. Their parents ensured it."

"Why?" Alex asked.

"All of our parents met during the war," Helen said. "They served together."

"Grandpa Pappas and Edmond Callier's father?" Alex asked. "Grandpa was in Greece, Mom. He didn't serve in World War II."

"No, Alexis. Your grandmother and Edmond's father did."

"What the hell are you talking about?" Alex asked.

Helen sighed. "Your grandmother was not Greek, Alexis. You do know that?"

"Yeah. She was French," Alex said.

"Richard is French. That was not her original name," Helen said. "It was Kaufman."

Alex pressed her temples firmly. "What are you telling me? YaYa was German?"

"YaYa was a German Jew, Alexis," Helen explained. "She changed her name."

"To avoid persecution," Alex surmised.

"Partly. Only partly," Helen said. "She worked in an office in Rastenburg."

"Are you telling me she worked for the Nazis?"

Helen nodded. "They thought so," Helen smiled. "She worked as a stenographer, Alexis. You take after her as well. She had an aptitude for language. Did you know that?" Helen asked. Alex studied her mother. She was growing more curious and more anxious with each second that passed. "YaYa spoke Greek, French, German, English, and Russian fluently," Helen told a surprised Alex.

"She was a spy," Alex said in disbelief.

"In a manner of speaking," Helen confirmed. "She sent information about banking transactions to the allies. Specifically to a contact in France. A young French officer named Rene Callier."

Helen watched as Alex attempted to process the story of her grandmother's life. It was a fanciful story, but every word of it was true. Helen remembered the long conversation with her mother one stormy Sunday afternoon. Alex's father had been away for nearly a month, and a very pregnant Helen was growing weary. She could not understand what business could manage to keep her husband overseas for such extended periods. It was a pattern that repeated throughout the early years of their marriage, and Helen was beginning to wonder how many mistresses her husband had. Her mother's revelations seemed preposterous to Helen. As she listened to her mother, Helen came to embrace the idea that fiction is always born of truth. Helen looked at her daughter now and saw a familiar expression reflected back to her.

"It was no accident that I met your father," Helen said quietly. "Your Grandfather Toles was stationed in France during the war."

"Yes, I know," Alex said.

"Your father, Edmond….even me….we were born into this life, Alexis. We did not find each other by accident. It was carefully orchestrated. Not unlike like you and Jonathan. Your father and Edmond….they were not given much choice."

"There is always a choice," Alex responded swiftly.

"Is there?" Helen challenged her daughter. "Maybe there is. Maybe it's just part of who they were; just like you."

"You think I am like Dad and Edmond? Do you have any idea the things they have done?" Alex chastised her mother for her assertion.

"I don't need to know what they have done," Helen said. "I do know that neither of them wanted his children to follow in his footsteps. And yet, you have."

Alex shook her head. "I never wanted to be part of this, Mom. Not this," Alex said.

"And you think they did?" Helen asked pointedly.

"It was their choice," Alex offered her opinion.

"And, it is yours," Helen responded in kind. "You are very quick to judge," Helen reprimanded her daughter. "Particularly, when you don't seem to know all the facts."

"Are you defending them?" Alex asked. "They have financed warlords, drug dealers, sold weapons to terrorist. Jesus Christ, Mom...they've had people assassinated! What do you think killed Dad? A heart attack?"

"That's enough, Alexis," Helen demanded.

Anger and confusion poured through Alex's body. Helen closed her eyes to calm her frustration. She pulled herself from her seat and made her way to her daughter. Helen pulled Alex's hands away from their task of digging into her temples. She directed Alex to look at her and softened her tone. Gently, Helen pushed back her daughter's hair just as she did when Alex was a child.

"I didn't tell you this to hurt you, Alexis. It's part of who you are; where you come from. You tell me that your father made choices. Edmond made choices. That's true. I made choices. We all do. You chose to marry Cassidy. You chose to have this baby with her." Helen began.

"I love her," Alex said.

"Yes. I know you do. Your father loved me. He was always torn, Alexis; torn between what he felt he had to do, maybe even what he enjoyed doing." Helen struggled to complete her thought as a myriad of memories flooded through her mind. "And, with being present for the people that he loved. He did love you, Alexis, but he was never very good at showing you that. He was gone so often, and when he was home, he was preoccupied with whatever would take him away next. So, yes.... we made choices. Now, you have to make some of your own. You think chasing the ghosts of the past will make your children's future better?" Helen asked.

Alex's eyes betrayed her doubt as she answered the question. "I don't know," she admitted.

"They are that, Alexis....ghosts. They will haunt you if you let them. You have to decide now; what do you want? The past will always repeat itself unless you choose to stop it."

"That's what we are trying to do," Alex defended her actions.

"Is it?" Helen questioned Alex. "You and Jonathan; you want to change the future? Or do you think somehow you can change the past?"

Helen's frank question cut through Alex like a knife. "I..."

"The future is upstairs right now," Helen said. "Not just your future....our future. So, now it's your turn to decide how committed you really are to that. You can uncover all the secrets of the past. I'm confident of that. You might find some satisfaction in that, but you will never be able to change it."

"What am I supposed to do?" Alex asked helplessly. "I have to protect them. I need to know..."

Helen smiled and patted Alex's cheek. "You talk about choices, Alexis, and yet you see everything as right and wrong; absolutes. Only you can decide what choice is right and what choice is wrong. I can't do that for you. In the end, it comes down to what you value most," she said. "Talk to your brother," Helen suggested.

"You think I should tell Nicky...."

Helen stood and shook her head. "I didn't mean Nicky," she said.

"Mom?"

Helen offered her daughter a smile. "I'm sorry," Alex said

"What are you sorry for?" Helen asked.

"Everything. Disappointing my family...disappointing you," Alex shook her head. "Dad...."

"I've made peace with my choices," Helen said. "It allowed me to make peace with the past. I forgave your father long ago for his shortcomings. I never loved him any less because of them. Disappointment? You've never disappointed me, Alexis.

As for Cassidy and Dylan…they will love you no matter what choice you make. Disappointment is your own demon, honey. Once you learn that, you'll be much happier," Helen advised her daughter.

Alex sat silently for a few moments, pondering her mother's advice. She was surprised that she felt no anger or sense of betrayal in this new found information. Alex watched her mother as she puttered about the kitchen in a routine that was timeless. She'd never given much thought as to what it must have been like for her mother all those years. Helen was a homemaker. She was 'Mom'. Alex suddenly realized the wisdom that came with that role. She looked to the ceiling and chuckled before beginning the short trek back upstairs.

"Where are you going?" Helen called to her daughter.

"I think I've had enough of the past for one day," Alex explained as she left the room.

Helen watched her daughter leave and smiled. "Maybe there is hope yet," she whispered softly.

***

Chapter Eighteen

Friday, January 30th

Cassidy headed into the kitchen wishing she could indulge in a strong cup of coffee. Alex was sitting at the table with the newspaper in front of her, sipping her cup of exactly what Cassidy was craving. "What are you doing?" Cassidy asked her wife.

"Good morning," Alex greeted her.

"You didn't answer my question," Cassidy said.

Alex's eyes drifted to the mug beside her. "I would think that would be obvious," Alex answered.

"Don't be cute, Alex. You know exactly what I am referring to. Why aren't you working?" Cassidy asked.

"Who says I'm not working?" Alex responded.

Cassidy sighed in frustration. "You've been home all week. I'm fine, Alex."

"Hey, being the boss has certain privileges," Alex said. "Why are you so grumpy? I thought you were feeling better."

"I am feeling better and you know why I am grumpy."

Alex smiled and nodded. "Sit down," she suggested to her wife. Cassidy rolled her eyes but followed Alex's suggestion. "All right," Alex looked at her wife to ensure she had her full attention. "I know that you are okay, Cass. I won't lie to you, knowing that O'Brien is out there, God knows where and God knows doing what….well, I feel better being close."

"You don't think he would try and come here?" Cassidy asked nervously.

"No, I don't. You might be feeling better, but be honest; you and Dylan have both been nervous with all the news surrounding O'Brien. There is no way to shield Dylan from all of that, or for me to shield you. We both know that he feels safer with me here, even if he has no reason to be afraid."

Cassidy sighed. Alex was completely on point. Cassidy had been shocked and shaken when the news broke that Christopher O'Brien had failed to appear in court. He was now America's most wanted man. She couldn't fathom how such a public figure could maintain any anonymity. Congressman Christopher O'Brien's face was everywhere. "I know. The truth is…I feel better with you here too," Cassidy confessed.

Alex smiled. "Look, I do have some work I have to do later, but I can do that here," she said. Cassidy nodded. "I want to be here as much as I can right now; for both of you. Unfortunately, I have to go to Natick next week for a few days," Alex said. She knew that Cassidy would understand, but she hated delivering the news that she would be away so soon again, even for a few days. Cassidy offered Alex a small smile and nodded again. "I have some meetings, and I have to conduct them there," Alex explained.

"It's all right, Alex. I understand," Cassidy said honestly.

"I know you do. Pip is going to meet me there," Alex told her wife. Cassidy waited for Alex to continue. "He'll have some things that I need."

"When are you leaving?" Cassidy asked.

"Tuesday evening. I'll be back Saturday," Alex promised.

"Staying at your mom's?" Cassidy asked.

"That's the plan; yes. I have some things I need to deal with there as well," Alex said with a sigh. Alex confided in Cassidy the story that Helen had told her. Alex was rattled by all the revelations of the last week. They did not shock her, but she was not satisfied with only knowing the cursory details.

Cassidy was sure that Alex intended to dig deeper into all that she had learned on this short trip back to Massachusetts.

She understood Alex's need. She wanted to know the same answers, no matter what they were. The plain truth was that their children would be born into the same cycle that Alex and her parents had been. There was little doubt in Cassidy's mind that Alex sought to break that cycle somehow. She moved from her seat and plopped herself in Alex's lap, placing a kiss on her wife's nose.

"What was that for?" Alex asked. Cassidy shrugged. "You feeling okay?" Alex asked lightly.

Cassidy scrunched up her face playfully. "Actually, I'm feeling hungry."

"Really?" Alex was delighted at the simple statement.

"Yep. So, Agent Toles, how about you make your wife an omelet for breakfast and your wife will make you those tacos you've been craving for dinner?" Cassidy offered with a suggestive wink.

"I'm not sure that's a fair trade," Alex contemplated the offer. "Your tacos are much better than my omelets," she complimented.

"Throw in a lesson on the pool table," Cassidy whispered, wrapping her arms around Alex's neck, "and we'll call it even."

"You are feeling better," Alex grinned.

"So, deal?" Cassidy asked.

"I still think I got the better end," Alex admitted. "I'll figure out a way to make it even somehow."

"Is that so?" Cassidy flirted.

"It is. Now, get off my lap," Alex demanded jokingly. "My wife is hungry."

Cassidy put her hands up in mock defeat and removed herself from Alex's lap. "Please, I wouldn't want to upset your wife," she agreed.

"Me neither," Alex said as she headed for the refrigerator. "Nothing gets between me and my tacos." Cassidy's soft snort quickly turned into a fit of laughter. "What's so funny?" Alex pretended to take great offense in her wife's sense of humor. "There is nothing funny about tacos," Alex declared.

Cassidy sidled up to her wife and placed her hands in the back pockets of Alex's jeans, continuing to laugh softly. "Je t'adore," Cassidy said.

"*Tu m'aimes seulement pour mes omelettes* (You only love me for my omelets)," Alex huffed.

"*Ce n'est pas vrai. J'adore aussi tes leçons de billard. Maintenant, nourri moi avant que je sois grognon de nouveau.* (Not true. I love your billiard lessons too. Now feed me before I get grumpy again)," Cassidy ordered her wife with a gentle swat.

"Yes ma'am. I live to serve," Alex promised Cassidy with a kiss.

***

"Anything stand out for you?" Tate asked Brian Fallon.

"No, not really. It doesn't appear that he took much; wherever he went," Fallon answered.

"No evidence of any visitors?" Tate inquired.

"None," Fallon responded. "Look, Tate, everybody and his brother is looking for O'Brien right now, not just us. His failure to appear in court put him more on the radar than he ever has been. He can't possibly get that far, even with Claire Brackett's help."

"Under normal circumstances, I would agree with you. These are not normal circumstances. Keep digging," Tate told him.

"What am I supposed to be looking for?" Fallon asked.

"If I knew that I would tell you. Anything; anything that might lead to Taylor or Claire. Anything that leads to where he might have that money hidden. Just look." Fallon ran his hand over the top of his head in frustration as Tate continued. "Agent Fallon, if you see no evidence that anyone was there, then trust me, someone was."

"You mean, Claire."

"Probably, but I am guessing someone beat us to the punch this time," Tate said.

"NSA?" Fallon asked.

"Perhaps," Tate said. "Just look....look in the unexpected places, Fallon. Look in his sock drawer."

Fallon laughed, understanding the humor intended in Joshua Tate's directions. "Tate?"

"Yes, agent?"

"How many cartons of cigarettes do you think a person normally stocks?" Fallon asked.

"Depends on the smoker," Tate replied.

"O'Brien doesn't smoke. It's probably his only redeeming quality," Fallon explained.

"Cheryl?" Tate suggested.

"Yeah; she did. Thing is; there is no evidence she ever existed in this place. None. You think she would have left that behind?" Fallon interjected. Brian Fallon made his way to the towering stack of cigarette cartons that had been placed at the back of Christopher O'Brien's pantry. He delicately extracted one from the middle and pulled out his pocket knife to unseal the wrapper. "Son of a bitch," he muttered.

"What?" Tate asked.

"He's been squirreling away more than money," Fallon said.

"Fallon....make sure you weren't followed. Do it right now," Tate ordered, suddenly feeling apprehensive about Brian Fallon's whereabouts.

Fallon maneuvered the townhouse quietly. "I don't think so," Fallon said. "Sir...." Fallon turned around and met the icy stare of a familiar face. "You...."

"Fallon! Agent Fallon! Answer me! Fallon!" Tate screamed into the phone.

***

Christopher O'Brien paced through the large farm house, sputtering off a long list of complaints to himself. "She thinks I'm her pet hamster," he muttered. Claire Brackett had been gone for several days and O'Brien felt the suffocation of boredom pressing in on him. He made his way into the kitchen and poured himself a glass of whiskey. The smell and stench of the alcohol made him wince. He hated whiskey, but it seemed his best companion these days. O'Brien swirled the yellow liquid in his glass, watching it ripple in small waves. He sipped it slowly, wrinkling his nose as the size of each swig increased. Never stopping his love-hate relationship with the drink in his hands, he made his way to the bathroom. One final gulp and he set the empty glass on the sink. The congressman looked up into the mirror and groaned in disgust. "You look like shit, O'Brien," he told his reflection.

Several days of neglect had quickly transformed the congressman's usual clean-cut appearance. He stroked the growth on his cheek and smiled. "I don't even recognize me," he said. His declaration sparked an idea. He offered himself a sly smile, winked at his reflection, and headed back towards the kitchen. "Yes, yes....there you are," he said. He looked across the room and sighed with satisfaction before pouring himself another drink. He downed the glass quickly and retrieved the set of keys that hung by the door on a small hook. O'Brien donned his jacket, opened the back door, and made his way to the barn that served as a garage.

"Well, Claire...she certainly had good taste," O'Brien beamed in delight at the three cars in front of him. He was tempted to slip into the sleek red Porsche. "Too conspicuous," he admitted in disappointment. "No matter," he said as he slid into the silver Jeep. "Time to take a spin," he gloated.

***

"You son of a bitch," Fallon's loathing of the man before him was transparent.

"That's no way to speak to your superior," Michael Taylor smirked. "So, who'd you call, Agent Fallon? Was that Alex? No? Tate perhaps?"

"Fuck you," Fallon shot.

"You know, that is insubordination," Taylor shook his head. "You couldn't be content to be the inconspicuous FBI agent, huh? Had to get involved. You should have listened to Alex."

"So, this is all about drugs?" Fallon asked, referencing the open carton now on the floor.

"Hardly," Taylor laughed. "Gave you more credit than that," he said.

"Why don't you enlighten me?" Fallon told the NSA Director.

Taylor laughed. "I'm afraid our time is too limited to give you all those details," he offered his insincere apology.

Fallon was unwavering. He faced the gun that was pointed directly at him as if it was a simple toy. "She saved your life. How could you?" Fallon asked. He found the presence of the man before him revolting.

"Alex, you mean?" Taylor shook his head. "I suppose she did. Although, if she'd been paying more attention to what was going on around her instead of pining after that Iraqi girl....well, maybe we wouldn't be here now," Taylor admitted. He sighed and shook his head. "Alex could never leave well enough alone. And now, look at all the people she's dragged down with her."

Fallon scowled at Taylor and chuckled. "You are disgusting," Fallon said.

"I have a job to do," Taylor said.

"Yeah? Murdering people? Selling arms to terrorists? Running drugs? Quite the resume," Fallon responded.

"Oh, you are just like her. Pious. Give me a break, Agent Fallon. What did you think you were getting into?" Taylor said. "For whatever it is worth, I am sorry it has come to this. I can't have anyone knowing I was here. And, I have things I need to take care of. With the congressman away....well, you understand," Taylor explained.

Fallon took a deep breath and nodded. He felt his heart skip several beats as Taylor moved around him and placed the gun at the back of his head. He scoured his thoughts for a way to disarm the NSA Director, but he knew he would never be able to react quickly enough. Fallon closed his eyes and thought of his wife and children, silently begging forgiveness of all the people he felt he had failed.

"It'll be quick," Taylor promised. "You'll appear a hero. I'll make sure of it."

"Just do it," Fallon demanded. There was no sound. Fallon felt something hot running down the back of his neck. It took several seconds for him to realize that he was still standing.

"Don't move, Agent Fallon," a voice instructed from behind him. Fallon held his breath again. "You walk straight out of here. Don't turn around. Don't breathe. Just walk out the way you came in, slowly."

"I don't understand," Fallon stuttered.

"Trust me, agent....you do not want to be here with a dead NSA Director. I have work to do. Just get out of here...."

"Who...."

"You just tell Toles that there are people looking out for her interests. Pick up your phone and get out of here. Now," the voice ordered.

Fallon's nod was almost imperceptible. He took a deep breath and made his way deliberately for the front door and exited the congressman's townhouse. Stepping into the cold January air, he reached for the back of his head and felt the blood that soaked his short hair, grateful it was not his own. The falling snow had kept the streets clear, and Fallon said a silent prayer of thanks as he slid into his car and lifted his phone.

"Jesus, Fallon! Where did you go?" Tate blared.

"Director Taylor is dead," Fallon told his boss.

"You killed Michael Taylor? Shit....where are you now?" Tate asked.

"I didn't," Fallon said.

"I don't understand," Tate replied. "Who..."

"I don't know. Sir, there is enough cocaine and heroin in that townhouse to keep all of Washington D.C. high for a month," Fallon said.

"Listen to me Fallon; get in the car and drive to the lot where I had you take Cheryl," Joshua Tate instructed Fallon."

"Sir, I am a mess....literally," Fallon answered.

"Fallon, trust me....just do it. Get out of there right now," Tate ordered.

"What about calling in...."

"Fallon, by the time anyone gets there it will be too late. Just go," Joshua Tate repeated the order to Fallon. He disconnected the call only to place another one immediately. "It's Tate. No....It's Agent Fallon.....No.....There's been an unexpected development......Fine.....No, I understand. You make that call...all right. Where? Are you certain? We'll be there."

***

"Where the hell are you?" Claire Brackett's voice blared through the phone.

Christopher O'Brien fumbled with the device in his hands. The snow was beginning to fall more steadily, and the fog of whiskey seemed to make the road in front of him fuzzy. He was preoccupied with the hand that was insistently massaging his inner thigh, and Claire's interruption did nothing except irritate him. "What do you want?" he slurred.

"Where are you?" she repeated.

"Got lonely," he whined. "Not lonely anymore."

"Are you a fucking idiot? What the hell is wrong with you?" she screamed. "Get back to the house. Now!"

"Exactly what I am doing," he assured her.

"Are you alone?" she asked.

"Mm...no...." his reply came as a slight moan of pleasure.

"You are the stupidest person I know. You're going to get us both killed before this over. Who is she?"

"Shanna? Shana?" he glanced to the seat beside him. "Whoaaaa..." he chuckled.

"Get back to the house," Brackett repeated.

"On my way," he chuckled again. "That's........hey...oh..."

"O'Brien?" Claire heard what sounded like a scream in the background.

"Shit........" Christopher O'Brien's voice trailed off with a sudden bang.

"O'Brien! Shit...."

***

"Jonathan?" Eleana's voice came through the phone.

"Eleana, I didn't expect to hear from you until later this week," Jonathan Krause answered.

"Where are you?" Eleana asked.

"Just heading to my hotel in Boston," he answered.

"Good, you aren't that far. I need you to meet me," she said urgently.

"Now? Why? Eleana...."

Eleana Baros looked at the tire tracks that were fading quickly in the falling snow. "I think I know where Claire took the congressman," she said.

Nothing more needed to be said. Jonathan Krause's reply was simple. "Send it over now. I'm on my way."

***

Brian Fallon paid little attention to the direction in which Joshua Tate was driving. He had been surprised that the assistant FBI director had remained silent. Fallon was thankful for what he knew was sure to be only a brief respite. It allowed him to close his eyes and order the images that were scattered throughout his brain. Fallon was sure that he would be called upon to recall every sound, sight, scent, and even taste that he had experienced while in Christopher O'Brien's townhouse. He felt the car gradually reduced speed and opened his eyes. He watched as Joshua Tate pulled the vehicle into an underground parking garage.

"Where are we?" Fallon asked. Joshua Tate's only response was a reassuring smile.

Fallon followed Tate to an elevator only a few steps away. Normally, the FBI agent would have been full of questions and assumptions. Fallon felt confident that wherever they were headed, he would both be safe and expected to produce information. The elevator doors opened to reveal the corridor of what looked to be an office building. Fallon studied the building curiously. "No security?" Fallon asked; his question more of an observation.

Tate kept moving forward. "They see us," he assured Fallon. Tate led the way to another elevator. Fallon watched at the older man pressed several buttons. Within seconds, the small box carried them away again. When the door opened, Fallon nearly stopped breathing at the face that greeted them.

"Agent Fallon."

"Mrs. Merrow?" Fallon responded weakly.

Jane Merrow winked at Joshua Tate and took Brian Fallon's hand. "You look like you could use a drink, Agent Fallon," she observed. Fallon numbly followed her lead. He had played through many scenarios in his mind about who might be greeting him. The former first lady was nowhere on that list. "Go get yourself cleaned up," Jane said. "You'll find everything you need down the hall."

Fallon stood shell shocked for a moment. "I just...I don't understand...."

Tate removed his jacket and made his way to a chair in the corner of the large penthouse. "That's the most he's said in an hour," Tate said lightly.

Jane Merrow looked at Brian Fallon sympathetically. "Agent Fallon, I promise that I will explain things to you. I would prefer to do that without the..." she pointed to Fallon's blood stained coat and person. "Well, I would prefer that we all be as comfortable as possible. You have questions. I understand. Go on," Jane encouraged him. "Take your time."

Fallon nodded his agreement and followed Jane's simple directions to the bedroom at the end of the hallway. He regarded the clean clothing that had been laid out on the bed before heading into the spacious bathroom. Blood was an odor that Fallon's stomach never tolerated well. He had learned how to mask his queasiness while on the job with years of practice. Not even his wife had discovered his secret; that his stomach eventually always made its displeasure known. Fallon discarded his soiled clothing and leaned over the toilet, retching violently. He wondered how many hours might have passed before he was able to gain the strength to reach his feet and turn on the shower. Fallon stood under the scalding flow of water, desperate to cleanse his body and mind of the last few hours. Any relief would be short lived. Fallon washed away the grime on his body, but his soul still felt putrid. He groaned softly, taking a few more moments to don an air of control before making his way back to Joshua Tate and Jane Merrow.

"Well, Agent Fallon; you look refreshed," Jane Merrow said warmly. She directed the FBI agent to have a seat and offered him a drink.

Agent Brian Fallon had crossed paths with the former first lady several times over the last year on a personal level. He had observed the closeness that Jane Merrow shared with both Alex and Cassidy. Alex had told him that Jane worked within the agency, but Fallon had been led to believe that Jane Merrow took more of a passive role in the CIA and The Collaborative. He chanced a quick glance to Joshua Tate and saw the relaxed nature of his mentor. "I'm sorry if I seem," Fallon began.

"Confused?" Jane finished his thought. She handed him a glass of scotch and took her seat. "You look like you could use that," she smiled. "Listen, Agent Fallon....There are many things you don't know. There are many things Alex does not know. The fact is....there are many things Joshua and I don't know. When John died, he passed some things on to me. He entrusted me with them. Do you understand?" she asked.

"I think I might have an idea," Fallon said.

"You already know that John suspected Michael Taylor of a different agenda than his administration's for a long time. It's why he initially wanted Alex to stay at the Pentagon rather than work directly under Michael. But, Alex...well, she is determined, and there were advantages to having her at the NSA and close to Director Taylor," Jane explained.

"So, why encourage her to go to the FBI?" Fallon asked. "And, what does that have to do with today?"

"It has everything to do with today. There was no mistake in her assignment to Joshua at the FBI. He trusted Joshua; so do I," Jane said. Fallon looked at Tate again. Assistant FBI Director Tate's expression gave little away as to his thoughts. Jane Merrow watched Fallon carefully as she continued her explanation. "Michael Taylor has been a money man for years, Agent Fallon. There are very definite advantages to having a license to invade an individual's private conversations and a corporations' public records at your whim. Taylor leveraged that for years. The question that we still haven't answered is on whose behalf."

"Maybe his own," Fallon suggested.

Tate took the opportunity to intervene. "No question that he benefited, Agent Fallon. None at all, but Michael Taylor was not always at the National Security Agency. He didn't start there. The CIA has been watching him for years. Just like Taylor used the NSA to watch those people who might compromise his efforts...all of them," Tate explained.

"The issue now," Jane took over, "is who saw fit to bail you out, Agent Fallon."

"I've played the voice in my head over and over. It was vaguely familiar, but we see agents, we listen to conversations every single day. I can't place it," Fallon said, frustrated by that reality.

"Forget the voice for now," Jane said. She moved to sit beside him on the small love seat. "What did Taylor say?"

Fallon combed his memory of what he had thought was going to be the last moments of his life. "Taylor...he didn't say much. Said he couldn't have anyone knowing he was there. Told me he'd make me a hero. Oh, and he called Alex pious," Fallon seethed in disgust.

"Did he? Interesting," Jane said.

"Why is that interesting?" Fallon asked.

Jane ignored the agent's question and urged him to continue. "And the other man; what did he say?"

"He said to get out; he had work to do. Then he said to tell Alex there were people looking out for her interests," Fallon repeated the words as he remembered them.

"See? Interesting. Interesting he is worried about something that he perceives as Alex's interests," Jane observed.

Tate broke into the conversation deliberately. "Agent Fallon, this creates on opportunity for us."

Fallon pondered Tate's statement and found himself perplexed. "Opportunities?"

Jane Merrow chuckled. "There've been some other developments, Agent Fallon. We believe that Taylor was working with Viktor Ivanov. You are already aware that Michael Taylor orchestrated my husband's assassination," she inquired as a matter of assumption. Fallon nodded. "Yes. So you know that he was also complicit in the attack on the embassy in Russia." Jane watched as Fallon conceded that knowledge as well. "What you don't know is that Assistant Director Tate and I have come to believe that there is another partner in both affairs."

"Who?" Fallon asked.

"The president of the united states," Jane Merrow answered.

"Strickland?" Fallon startled slightly.

"The political propaganda is not a mistake, agent," Jane told him. "The Russians tie us to terrorists. We call the Russians liars, and Strickland makes the claim that pro-Markov entities in Russia attacked us. He denies the United States has any ties to terrorists formally and accuses Markov's government of failing to secure our interests in the region. And, the spin begins," Jane said flatly.

"To what end?" Fallon asked. "And Taylor…"

"Michael Taylor is the perfect accomplice. He has access to everyone, quite literally. He was John's friend publicly. Strickland knows that Taylor is partially responsible for putting him in The Oval Office….To what end? You can only run guns and drugs so long, Agent Fallon. That makes a few people a great deal of money. What can stimulate an entire nation's economy, boost patriotism, and empower those already in power even more?" Jane put the questions to Fallon.

"You think they are seeding a war?" Fallon asked. "That's what all of this is about?"

Jane Merrow shook her head. "No. There is not one war that has been waged in more than seventy years that has improved the economy of any nation. Nor has it bequeathed leaders with more power. It has done the opposite. War lines the pockets of a few players, many of whom you have become familiar with. Carecom, Technologie Applique, ASA, among others. But, no, Agent Fallon, not a war…a Cold War."

Fallon looked to Tate and back to Jane Merrow. "And Taylor's death? How does that create opportunities?" Fallon asked as he attempted to process what he was hearing.

"We create a different story, Agent Fallon," Tate said.

Jane smiled at the FBI agent. "Brian," her voice dropped to a whisper. "Get yourself together. Call your wife. You'll be away for a few days," she said.

"Where am I going?" Fallon asked apprehensively.

"We are going to see a friend," Jane said as she began to make her way out of the room. "I am expected elsewhere. Get some rest," Jane suggested. "A car will be here in the morning."

Fallon stared blankly at Tate for a moment. "There's more to this…"

Tate gave Fallon's shoulder a squeeze. "There is always more. Get some rest, Agent Fallon. You are going to need it."

***

Eleana Baros stood outside her car at the side of the road. From her position, she could see the rescue crews working franticly to put out a fire. Something drew her to come back to Connecticut. Something told Eleana that Claire would seek her out in their special place. Eleana hadn't had the opportunity to decide if she was relieved or disappointed when she found her home empty. Her personal thoughts about Claire had immediately transformed into professional inquiry when she saw the empty bottle of whiskey on her counter, men's clothes strewn throughout her bathroom, and her Jeep missing. She had just reached the garage when her phone rang. Eleana was, quite literally, frozen in place now. She heard a car pull closer, saw the faint glow of parking lights as it came to a stop, and heard the door close, but she did not move. She could not take her eyes off of the nightmare that was unfolding below her.

Jonathan Krause made his way to stand beside his friend. "What happened?" he asked.

Eleana shook her head and turned to Jonathan with tears in her eyes. "I don't know. I don't know if it's her."

Krause looked back toward the scene unfolding in the woods below. He scratched his chin thoughtfully. "You think that's Claire? Eleana why would Claire be here?"

"I went home. Not Belarus; home. Here. No one knows about it, Jonathan; only me...and Claire. I thought she might be..."

Krause sighed. "How did you end up here, Eleana?"

"She wasn't there. Whiskey bottles, men's clothing...but not her....my Jeep was gone. I know her, Jonathan. It makes sense. I realized she had brought O'Brien there. It makes sense," Eleana barely managed to speak the words.

"Why do you think that is Claire? Wait–you think Claire and O'Brien were in that wreck?" he asked.

Eleana took a deep breath a nodded. "It makes sense....I came...The Jeep is registered in New York to Maria Colone....I got a call..."

Krause recognized the name. Maria Colone was one of Eleana's aliases. "They called to report the accident?"

"Yeah. Someone took the plate number. I didn't answer; just listened. If I had answered... I don't have any credentials to use here, Jonathan. I can't get close enough. All I could get close enough to hear, without risk of compromising myself, was that they had one female victim thrown from the vehicle; assumed to be a passenger," Eleana choked out the words.

Krause put his hand on her shoulders. "I'll get down there. Where is the house, Eleana?" he asked her. "Eleana...go back to the house. I will meet you there."

"Jonathan..."

"Maybe Claire is there," he tried to comfort his friend. Eleana looked down at the scene below and closed her eyes. Krause noticed the quivering of the young woman's body and pulled her to him. "It's cold and you are in shock. Go and wait for me," he said gently. "I don't know who that is. It's not Claire Brackett," Jonathan Krause whispered.

Eleana pulled back slightly and shook her head. "It makes sense...How can you know that?" Eleana desperately wanted to believe Krause's assessment, but logic did not support his statement.

Krause brushed Eleana's frozen bangs off of her head and kissed her cheek. "It's not. Claire would never settle for being O'Brien's passenger," he whispered as he pulled away. "She'd insist on driving." Jonathan Krause led Eleana back to her car and turned her key in the ignition. "Go. I'll find out. Get warmed up..."

"I'll see what I can find there," Eleana began.

"I'll be right behind you," he told her. "Now, go." Krause shut Eleana's door and watched her drive away. "Well, Congressman," he mused as he started his car, "let's see if it's two for one day."

***

Chapter Nineteen

Saturday, January 31st

Alex rolled over and fumbled for the phone on her bedside table. "Hello?

"Alex?"

"Pip? What the hell time is it?" Alex yawned.

Cassidy rolled closer to Alex and grumbled inaudibly. "Tell him to go away," she whined.

Alex looked down at Cassidy, who had claimed her chest as a pillow and kissed her wife's head. "This had better be good," Alex said through the phone.

"It's four in the morning and I'm not sure this qualifies as good. Eleana and I are about thirty minutes from you right now," Krause told Alex.

Alex gently extracted herself from Cassidy's grasp and wandered into the bathroom. "What the hell do you mean you are thirty minutes from here?"

"Alex, it's O'Brien," Krause said.

"Did you find him?" Alex asked anxiously. A heavy sigh came over the phone. "Pip?" Alex asked. When Krause did not immediately respond, Alex lost her patience. "Jonathan?"

"There was an accident, Alex. I wanted to get to you before anyone got up in the morning....before Cassidy sees the news," Krause explained.

"What kind of accident?" Alex asked skeptically.

Alex's boisterous tone had awakened Cassidy. She stumbled into the bathroom in concern. "What's going on?" Cassidy asked, still wiping the sleep from her eyes.

"Still trying the figure that out," Alex said softly. "Go back to bed," Alex told her wife.

Cassidy collapsed gently into Alex and shook her head. "No," she answered.

Alex sighed. "Okay, before my entire family is awake.... what's going on?" Alex asked.

"Nutshell version? There was a car accident. Two victims. The passenger was thrown fifteen feet through the windshield. The driver was trapped. The car caught fire. They haven't determined why it ignited. It sailed right over the guard rail and into the woods. Had to be going fast. There's not much left, Alex," Krause said.

"Jonathan," Alex said carefully. Cassidy stepped back immediately. Alex rarely called Jonathan Krause by his first name. Cassidy's apprehension grew as Alex continued. "Who was in the car?"

Krause took another deep breath. "The woman appears to be local, Janice Rodgers. The driver...I can't say for certain, Alex. I can't. They found a wallet outside the car; it's O'Brien's."

Alex did not respond verbally. She closed her eyes and massaged her temples forcefully. Krause waited patiently for her reaction. "Was it him?" she asked.

"I don't know. They'll need to do tests...Alex, I...."

"Best guess," Alex implored him for his opinion.

"If it isn't him...someone is going to a lot of trouble to make it look like it is. I can't imagine why anyone would waste that energy now. Not even Claire," he said honestly.

Alex took a moment to process the information. "I need to talk to Cass before you get here. Is there anything else I should know?" Alex asked pointedly.

"There is, but I would rather tell you in person," he responded.

"Tell me now," Alex demanded.

"Michael Taylor is dead," Krause said plainly.

Alex felt a sudden wave of dizziness. "Alex?" Cassidy stepped closer and steadied her wife.

"How?" Alex asked.

"Longer story," Krause said.

"All right," Alex finally agreed to wait for more answers. "I'll put on the coffee."

***

"Is it done?" Jane Merrow asked as she crossed her legs and sipped her glass of wine.

"It's done," the reply came.

"Traceable and believable?" Jane asked.

"It's done," he repeated his response.

"Make certain you have covered all of the bases. I want the admiral and Strickland taken completely off guard. Do you understand?" the former first lady asked. "I want that asshole roused from his dreams and thrown into the lion's den. He'll have no choice but to call in Admiral Brackett and then...well...Then we will know where William Brackett's loyalties lie," she said.

"What next?" he asked.

"Timelines have changed. I am headed east in a few hours," Jane said. "They have issued the protocol to call in Sphinx."

"Unexpected," he responded.

"No," Jane replied. "Just premature. It changes nothing."

"You want me to find Sparrow?" he asked.

Jane took another sip of her wine. "Not necessary. I have a feeling that will be taken care of for us. You need to stay under the radar. Stay where you are and make certain our assets are secure," she instructed him.

"How long?" he asked

"As long as it is necessary, Agent Brady," she responded.

***

Cassidy sat on the edge of the bed with her face in her hands. Alex watched her wife intently. Cassidy had yet to have any verbal response to the news that her ex-husband was in all likelihood dead. "Cass?"

A heavy sigh came from deep within Cassidy as she finally looked up to Alex. "I'm supposed to cry; right?"

Alex looked at her wife compassionately. "I don't think you are supposed to do anything," she said.

Cassidy nodded. "They'll be here any minute," she said. "You better make that coffee you promised," Cassidy told Alex.

"Cass, I...."

"I'm all right. I just...I need a few minutes. Telling Dylan.... How do I tell Dylan?" Cassidy asked. The uncertainty in Cassidy's voice broke Alex's heart. "I know he's angry, but Alex, Chris is the only father he has ever known."

"We'll tell him together," Alex promised.

Cassidy looked at Alex as tears began to fill her eyes. "I remember that; my mother kneeling in front of me."

Alex sat beside Cassidy on the bed and pulled her close. So much was happening she hadn't stopped long enough to connect the obvious dots. No matter what had transpired in their lives, Cassidy had spent many years with Christopher O'Brien. Alex knew that even within the instability of that marriage, there had to have been happy moments. She had even seen glimpses of those brief times between Dylan and the congressman when she first met Cassidy. Christopher O'Brien was a selfish, egotistical man, but Alex could not deny that he remained a valid part of her family's life; even if his place existed in a chapter of its past. What hadn't occurred to Alex until this moment, was how the unfolding event would conjure memories of her wife's past. Cassidy had lost her father in a car accident when she was only ten. Now, she would have to deliver that news to her son. Again, history seemed to repeat itself.

"I'm so sorry, Cass," Alex said genuinely. "You know that I am here for you; both of you."

Cassidy stroked Alex's cheek and smiled sadly. "I know. I'll be all right. Honestly, I will. I just need a few minutes alone before every…."

"Say no more," Alex said. She quickly threw on a pair of jeans and a sweatshirt. "You come down whenever you are ready," she told Cassidy.

"Alex?" Cassidy called to her wife as she was about to leave the bedroom.

"Yeah?"

"Alex, Michael…you must be…."

"I'm okay," Alex said flatly. "I mourned the loss of Michael Taylor already," she said.

Cassidy nodded her understanding. "I'll be down…."

"Take as long as you need," Alex assured her wife. "I'm sure Pip and Eleana have more information that I need to hear. Take a shower. Do whatever you need to do; all right?"

"I want to call my Mom. I don't want her to wake up and hear it on the news," Cassidy said.

Alex smiled. "Why don't you ask her if she can come stay here for a few days?"

"Do you think you'll be leaving?" Cassidy asked.

"I don't know," Alex replied honestly. "There will be a lot to decide; for all of us. It couldn't hurt to have her here."

Cassidy nodded. "Thank you," she said softly.

"You never need to thank me for anything," Alex said. "Call Rose. I'll make the coffee."

***

"Sir, I'm sorry to disturb you, but this is pressing," a voice roused the president.

"Isn't it always?" President Lawrence Strickland replied caustically as he slipped into his robe. "What the hell is so pressing that you have to wake me at four in the morning? Someone brew the decaffeinated coffee again by mistake?"

Jeffrey Mansfield had assumed the role of President Strickland's Chief of Staff two days after John Merrow's death. It was an appointment envied by many and a position he was ready to rid himself of as soon as possible. Strickland had always been a difficult personality to manage. Since assuming the role of Commander in Chief, Lawrence Strickland had become insufferable. He was dismissive of advisers and staff; he scoffed at the importance of most matters, and Strickland seemed convinced that as president, he answered to no one. Mansfield pressed down his growing disdain for the man seated before him.

"Mr. President," Mansfield began, "they located Congressman O'Brien."

"And you needed to wake me for that because?"

"He's dead, sir," Mansfield said.

"Well, that will save the judicial system a few bucks," Strickland chuckled. "One problem solved."

"That may be," Mansfield admitted. "Unfortunately, there is a bit more to it."

"What did O'Brien do this time?" Strickland asked. "Besides get himself killed?" Mansfield looked at the President curiously. Strickland laughed. "Well, don't tell me the weasel had a heart attack or something. As many people as hated him, somebody must have gotten their wish," the president guessed.

"It was an automobile accident," Mansfield explained.

Strickland roared. "Oh, that is fitting. How glamorous," he continued to laugh.

Jeffery Mansfield fought the urge to reach across the room and throttle the president. "I suppose not. You might find Director Taylor's death more interesting," Mansfield snapped.

The blood drained from President Strickland's face rapidly. "What are you talking about?" he demanded forcefully.

"The FBI made visits to both of O'Brien's homes upon notification of the accident. Protocol," Mansfield said.

"What does that have to do with Michael Taylor?" Strickland bellowed.

"They made a few discoveries; over 150 kilos of cocaine and heroin in his D.C. townhome, among other things that are still under investigation," Mansfield began to deliver his news.

"How is that possible? The FBI, the CIA, Federal Marshalls, and the NSA all swept that residence when he failed to appear in court. It was sealed for Christ's sake!" Strickland slammed his hand on the arm of his chair.

"I would suggest that you direct that question to Director Taylor, but that might prove difficult now. They found his body in that residence as well," Jeffrey Mansfield said bluntly.

President Strickland's expression was vacant. He spun the words around in his head a few times before speaking. "So, what are you telling me...exactly?"

"Just what I know to be the facts. I already called in the team. The earliest wires are suggesting that Michael Taylor and Christopher O'Brien were dealing in more than just drugs and questionable campaign funding. It may be a stretch, but you know the press. They love to speculate, and they are already insinuating a possible hand in the embassy bombing," Mansfield explained.

"That's preposterous!" Strickland hopped to his feet. "There's no evidence of that at all. None! Michael Taylor had an impeccable record of service!"

Mansfield contained his smile. The president was growing more agitated as the minutes ticked by. It confirmed some of Jeffrey Mansfield's suspicions. Recent events caused a few of President Lawrence Strickland's closest advisers and staff to begin to question the real motivation behind the attack on the U.S. Embassy in Moscow. Strickland had reacted uncharacteristically cool and calm when the news of the bombing had been delivered. The president was a politician, not a military leader. Strickland was considered a master orator and speech writer. That was the persona that the public was allowed to see; the prepared and composed President Lawrence Strickland. Lawrence Strickland seldom responded to stressful news calmly in private. His handling of the situation in Moscow had garnered him plaudit after plaudit from the press. Privately, many of those closest to him had begun to wonder if President Strickland might have had some prior knowledge of the attack.

Mansfield allowed the president a moment before continuing. "I am aware of Director Taylor's official history of service. It doesn't change the facts. Michael Taylor was found with a bullet to the head in the kitchen of Congressman Christopher O'Brien's home, not even an hour ago. It appears he'd been dead for some time. The FBI, ATF, DEA, and the Department of Homeland Security are already on site," Mansfield said.

"Jesus Christ," Strickland groaned.

"The working theory is that Taylor had been operating outside the fray for years. He threw O'Brien to the wolves; O'Brien retaliated," the president's chief of staff stated the facts as he knew them.

"Like Christopher O'Brien could ever outwit the NSA? Come on, Jeffrey," President Strickland waved his hand in dismissal. "No one will ever believe that."

"People will believe almost anything they hear; if they hear it enough," Jeffrey Mansfield answered.

President Strickland's jaw became visibly taut. "I want to know the minute everyone arrives. Get William Brackett here as well," he ordered.

"Sir?"

"It's not a request, Jeffrey. Just get him here," Strickland barked.

"Yes, Sir," Mansfield agreed.

"And you make certain that Bob starts the spin cycle yesterday," Strickland called out.

Jeffrey Mansfield left the president's quarters continually shaking his head. His gut told him that if he didn't jump off President Lawrence Strickland's ship soon, he would sink along with it. He picked up his phone and dialed the Chairman of the Joint Chiefs of Staff. "General Snyder," Mansfield greeted.

"I'm on my way, Jeffrey," General Snyder replied.

"I am certain. He's requested Admiral Brackett's presence," Jeffery Mansfield explained.

The Chairman of the Joint Chiefs snickered. "Well, that *is* interesting. An unofficial player called to an official meeting."

"I agree," the president's chief of staff replied.

"Well, he is the Commander in Chief. I'll make the call," General Snyder said. "I'd suggest a lot of coffee and maybe a Valium or two at the ready," the general joked.

"I'll take it under advisement," Mansfield laughed. He made his way through the corridors of The White House without incident or conversation until he felt the buzz of his phone reverberate again. "Mansfield," he answered.

"Jeffrey," a woman's voice greeted him amicably. The president's chief of staff stopped in his tracks. "How's it feel to be the second officer on the Titanic?" she asked.

"Jane..."

"That's what I thought. You see the iceberg ahead?" Jane Merrow asked. Mansfield did not respond. "I want you to head straight for it," she told the man.

"You don't know what you are asking," Mansfield said hoarsely.

"I do," Jane assured him.

Jeffrey Mansfield struggled momentarily to catch his breath. He'd been in this business most of his life. John Merrow had told him once that there was no escape. When you signed on at the agency, it was for life. You might simmer on the back burner for a long while, but sooner or later things would boil over. It was inevitable. "What do you need?" he asked.

"Delay an official statement as long as possible," she said. "Let the wheels turn a bit."

"You know that won't be easy," Mansfield said.

"That's why you make the big bucks, Jeffrey," Jane reminded him.

"I understand," he answered.

"I know you do. I'll be in touch. And, Jeffrey? Let me know how Bill Brackett responds to this situation; will you?"

***

Alex listened to Jonathan Krause intently. She sat continuously pressing on her left temple with her thumb, absently lifting her coffee cup to her lips again and again. Krause had explained the details of both Michael Taylor's death and Christopher O'Brien's car accident as he understood them. Alex was not only curious as to who Brian Fallon's savior might have been; she was worried about the motivation behind that action. Great pains had been taken to link NSA Director Michael Taylor directly to Congressman Christopher O'Brien. Alex did not find relief in any of the knowledge she had gained, but rather concern. "You and I both know Taylor was not running drugs, and neither was O'Brien," Alex said.

"I know. Someone wanted Taylor compromised, Alex. Someone. My best guess is that they were in the process of setting up O'Brien, and he just made their plan all the more easy and attractive. It timed perfectly. O'Brien's accident feeds directly into the scenario," Krause said.

"But why?" Alex wondered.

"I don't know," Krause admitted. "It wasn't me. It wasn't Edmond who made that call to take out Taylor. And, trust me, I would like to take the credit."

"The admiral?" Alex guessed.

"Maybe. Maybe not. I don't know. We need to push up our meeting," Krause said.

Alex nodded her understanding just as Cassidy entered the room. "Guess that answers the question of your leaving, huh?" Cassidy tried to seem unaffected. Alex grimaced.

"Cassie," Jonathan Krause stepped forward and hugged his friend. "I'm sorry," he whispered. "For everything."

Cassidy sighed heavily and pulled away. "It's all right, Pip."

"There is some good news," Krause offered.

"Really?" Alex made no effort to conceal her sarcasm. "By all means, enlighten us!"

"Well, for one thing you will be gone Monday morning, but home Monday night," he said. He turned to Cassidy. "Neither of us will be traveling anywhere far soon, Cassie."

Cassidy was perplexed and looked to Alex to explain. "It would send up too many red flags," Alex said. "We're grounded; indefinitely," she said.

Cassidy still did not completely understand. She just nodded softly to indicate her acceptance of the statement. Cassidy could not deny the truth; the news that Alex was "grounded indefinitely" lifted a weight from her shoulders. Cassidy realized that might be selfish, but at the moment she didn't care. She looked at the stranger seated across from her wife and offered the younger woman a smile. "I'm sorry," Cassidy said apologetically. "You must be Eleana."

Eleana nodded. "It's nice to meet you. I am sorry about the..."

Cassidy shook her head. "No. No more apologies today from any of you," she said.

"Did you get your mom?" Alex asked.

"Yeah. She'll be here in a couple of hours. Alex, I want to see the news before Dylan gets up," Cassidy said.

"Are you sure?" Alex asked. "Cass, Pip and I can fill you in on what we actually know."

Cassidy held up her hand. "Not now, Alex. I need to know what Dylan might hear, not what you have discovered."

Alex sighed heavily. "All right, fair enough."

"We'll leave you two," Krause began to offer his goodbyes.

"No," Cassidy stopped him. "No. Dylan needs all of us," she said. Cassidy looked at Alex and recognized her wife's silent thanks. "You're part of this family too, Pip."

"I should go," Eleana pulled out her chair.

"Not you either," Alex scolded the younger woman. "Eleana, we are all in this one together. Jonathan was family long before I knew he was my brother," Alex admitted. "You've been through enough today," Alex said. "You both need some rest. We have the room. And, I can't believe I am going to say this, but maybe you should call Claire," Alex suggested. Three sets of eyes fell on Alex in stunned disbelief. Alex rolled her eyes. "Jesus! I don't like the woman!" Alex exclaimed. She looked at the pained expression on the younger woman's face and sighed. "I'm sorry, Eleana. I am. I don't trust Claire."

"I know," Eleana said. "I wouldn't expect you to understand."

Alex huffed slightly. "I didn't say that I didn't understand. I said that I don't trust her. I don't trust her actions not to hurt my family or my friends," Alex admitted. She watched Eleana's eyes fall shut in resignation of the truth. "That includes you," Alex continued.

Cassidy studied Alex as she spoke and squeezed Jonathan Krause's hand. Alex had filled Cassidy in on some of her observations of Eleana Baros. Alex had shared with Cassidy that she detected an emotional connection between Edmond Callier's daughter and Jonathan Krause. Alex might have little use for Agent Brackett, but she was growing fond of Eleana. As Cassidy listened to her wife address Eleana, she was reminded that Alex was incapable of hate. Cassidy and Alex shared the same feelings about many things. They loathed people's actions. They struggled to comprehend the level of pain that selfishness could inflict, but neither of them could hate another person. Cassidy glanced at the friend beside her. Jonathan Krause was listening with great interest to the conversation just inches away. It did not escape Cassidy's notice that his focus drifted back and forth between the two women with a similar expression of admiration.

"Call Claire or don't," Alex said. "It's your decision. No matter what happens going forward, Claire will always be a part of you," Alex said. "The sooner you accept that, Eleana; the sooner you can actually let her go." Alex motioned to Cassidy to follow her into the other room.

"I love you, Alex," Cassidy said as they walked into the family room. Alex tipped her head in confusion at the endearment. Cassidy chuckled. "Have I not said that lately, or something?"

"No, I just wondered where that came from," Alex admitted.

"No place in particular," Cassidy said. "I just do. Now, come on; let's get this over with. Dylan will be up before we know it."

Alex clicked on the television. "Cass, for whatever it's worth....I know he will always be a part of your life in some way. I am sorry," Alex said honestly.

"That's true. Chris isn't my future," Cassidy said. "I hope Eleana takes your advice."

"You do?" Alex asked.

"Yeah. You have to let go of the past before you can see the future that is staring you right in the face," Cassidy observed.

Alex chuckled and took her wife's hand. "You sound like my mother."

"Smart woman," Cassidy said, taking a deep breath as Alex increased the volume on the television.

Cassidy braced herself for the images and words she was about to confront. She felt Alex squeeze her hand in encouragement. "You know, they say you always marry a woman like your mother," Alex whispered. She heard Cassidy's soft snicker. "I promise, I'll make sure we all get through this," Alex said confidently. "I'll do whatever I have to do so that Dylan feels safe and happy. Anything."

"I know you will," Cassidy said. "That's why I married a woman just like my mother."

***

"Dylan, honey....sit down here; okay?" Cassidy guided her son to the sofa. "Alex and I need to talk to you about something."

"Are you going away?" Dylan asked Alex.

Alex could see the fear in her son's eyes. "No, Speed. I'm not going anywhere."

"It's not about Alex, Dylan. It's about Daddy," Cassidy explained softly.

"Is he in jail again?" Dylan asked.

Cassidy's skin was tingling with nervousness. This moment was a moment she prayed would never come in her lifetime. The memory of her mother sitting almost exactly as she was right now, telling a ten-year-old Cassidy that her father had died, was seared into her consciousness. Cassidy had worshipped her father. Her heart broke in that moment. A piece of it remained forever lost in that memory. It would be different for Dylan. Cassidy understood that. Dylan had grown increasingly distant from Christopher O'Brien. Her son did not trust the man that he knew as his father, but that did not change the facts. Christopher O'Brien, to Dylan, was still Daddy. Losing a parent was always devastating. Cassidy had thought a great deal about Dylan's reaction the previous year when his father had been injured in an accident. Dylan's reluctance to spend time with his father had already made itself known. Even still, she recalled the fear and the sorrow in Dylan's eyes when he thought his father might die.

"Dylan, sweetheart," Cassidy's voice cracked. "Daddy had a....it was very slippery last night in the snow...he had an accident...."

"Is he dead?" Dylan looked directly at his mother.

Cassidy sucked in a ragged breath. "Yes, sweetheart," was all she could manage.

Dylan sat still for a moment. Cassidy tried to read the emotions as they played across his eyes and lips. He seemed to be thinking very intently and then his tears broke forth. He was not sobbing, but his pain had finally begun to surface. It was not his tears that stabbed her heart. It was the weight of the words he spoke. "He never loved me," Dylan said. Cassidy was at a complete loss. It was not the reaction she had expected.

Alex intervened. "That is not true, Speed. I know things with your dad have been pretty upsetting, but that is not true.

Your dad loved you," Alex told him firmly, surprising herself at the conviction in her voice.

"No, he didn't," Dylan cried. "He always leaves. Everyone says they will come back. They don't. Parents aren't supposed to leave."

Alex closed her eyes for a brief second. Dylan's declaration was not lost on her. His tears finally came forth in a wave of uncontrollable sobs. Cassidy pulled him to her and rocked him. Alex watched helplessly, berating herself silently for being away so much the last few months. Finally, she knelt beside Cassidy on the floor and placed herself in between mother and son. "Dylan," Alex began. Dylan jerked away from her touch. "Dylan," she called to him again. Alex finally managed to get him to look at her. "I want you to listen to me, okay? I understand. Mom and I understand. We do. When my father died.... well, Dylan, I was very angry with him. I still loved him. He was my dad." Cassidy wiped away her tears and listened to Alex confess a painful truth to their son.

"But, your dad loved you," Dylan said.

"I didn't think so," Alex said honestly. Dylan looked at her quizzically through his tears. "But, yes, he did. He did love me, even if he didn't do what I thought he should do."

"Do you miss him?" Dylan asked.

"Yes," Alex confessed. "I do. Sometimes, I do."

Dylan looked at Cassidy and started crying again. He threw himself into his mother's embrace. Cassidy made her way to the sofa and pulled him onto her lap. "It's all right, baby. I know it hurts. I know. Alex is right. Your dad loved you. A lot of people love you," she assured him. "Alex and I love you more than anything."

"Do you miss your dad?" he asked his mother.

"Every single day," Cassidy said. "I wish he could be here to see you. You would have loved him. He would have made you laugh," she told her son.

"But, you never had another dad," Dylan observed.

"No, that's true," Cassidy said.

Dylan looked at Alex and whispered something in Cassidy's ear. Cassidy pulled back from Dylan's firm grip and placed him beside her. She directed Alex to sit with them. "Dylan, there is no limit on the people that you are allowed to love. Do you understand that?" Cassidy asked her son cautiously. He did not respond. Alex suddenly realized what was troubling him the most; guilt.

"Hey, Speed…" Alex pulled Dylan onto her lap. "Can I tell you a secret? A secret that hardly anyone knows?" He nodded. "Well, I have two brothers." Dylan looked at Alex in shock. Cassidy smiled inwardly at Alex's confession.

"You do?" Dylan asked.

"Yes, I do," Alex told him. "I didn't always know my older brother. The truth is, Dylan…Uncle Pip and I have the same father. That means he really is your Uncle Pip." Alex watched as Dylan's eyes grew wide. "And, you know what?" Dylan shook his head. "I don't love Uncle Nick any less because I have Uncle Pip now." Cassidy listened as Alex continued. "Do you remember when I asked you if I could marry your mom?" Alex asked.

"Yeah."

"I gave you my Saint Alexander medal; remember? I told you I never thought that I would have a son or daughter to give it to, but then I found you and your mom," Alex reminded him. "Pretty soon we'll have Mackenzie with us too. I already love Mackenzie, but I will never love you any less. Just like I love Grandma as much as I love YaYa. Each person is different. That means you get to love them all as much as you want to," Alex said.

Cassidy looked at Alex and mouthed the words, "thank you."

"I won't ever see him again," Dylan said.

Cassidy kissed her son's forehead. "It's not the same, sweetie, but you can see Daddy anytime you want to. You just have to remember him. And you can talk to him too. I talk my dad all the time," Cassidy said.

"You do?" he looked to his mother hopefully.

"Yes, I do," Cassidy said.

"Dylan, it's okay to be sad. It's even okay to be angry. Just remember that we love you," Alex said.

"Alex?" he asked hesitantly.

"Yeah, Speed?"

"You won't leave me, will you?" he asked her.

"Aww, Speed. No one can ever promise you that; not the way you want them to. But, I will do everything I can to make sure I am here for a long time to come. I promise you that," Alex said. "And, I would never leave if I could help it."

Alex and Cassidy comforted Dylan the best they could. He had questions. He had fears. They listened to each one until he finally let out a small sigh. "I never said goodbye," he said.

Cassidy smiled and gave Dylan a kiss. "The thing about loving someone, Dylan, is you never have to say goodbye. You tell Daddy whatever you need to, just in your heart. He'll hear you," she said. Dylan accepted his mother's advice gratefully.

Alex sensed that Dylan was in need of a diversion. It had been an emotional morning for all of them. There would be more to face in the days and weeks that would follow. Grief had no particular timeline. Alex had learned that. Sometimes, the only thing you could do was find something else to think about for a while. "You know, Uncle Pip is in the rec room. Last I saw; he was napping on the couch. Maybe you should go wake him up," Alex suggested lightly.

Dylan brightened slightly. "He'll tickle me," Dylan smiled.

"Huh," Alex said. "Tickle him back," she encouraged her son.

"He's not ticklish," Dylan pouted.

"No? Hmm....Try his feet. It's a Toles thing," Alex whispered conspiratorially. Dylan hopped off the sofa and headed out of the room.

"Hey!" Dylan turned back to his parents. "My feet are ticklish."

"I know. I told you," Alex said. "It's part of being a Toles." Alex and Cassidy watched Dylan as he left, noting that his step still lacked its usual bounce. "He'll be all right," Alex said, partly to convince herself.

"He will," Cassidy agreed. She placed her head on Alex's shoulder. "But, I don't think you realize you just gave away your Kryptonite," Cassidy winked.

"What are you talking about?" Alex asked.

"Dylan may not have put two and two together that Uncle Pip's ticklish feet are part of being your brother. I guarantee you when he tries that on Pip; Pip will explain it to him," Cassidy said.

"I'm bigger than he is," Alex reminded Cassidy.

Cassidy kissed Alex lightly on the nose. "Yes you are. For now."

***

Chapter Twenty

Sunday, February 1st

"This was not what we prescribed," Sergei Kabinov reprimanded President Lawrence Strickland through the phone.

"Are you certain of that?" Strickland shot back.

"Of course!" Kabinov retorted.

"The admiral seems to think that you might need to have a conversation with Mr. Ivanov," Strickland told the Russian prime minister.

"What are you insinuating?" Kabinov demanded.

"Come now, Sergei. We both know that neither Michael Taylor nor Christopher O'Brien dealt in drugs. That is far too small time for either of them; cocaine and heroin to street dealers?" Strickland chuckled. "If my people did not conjure up this lunacy; then who did?" Strickland indirectly pointed the finger.

Sergei Kabinov remained undaunted. "No. We held up our end of this perfectly. All you had to do was toe the line," Kabinov said.

"Well, the line seems to have changed," Strickland observed.

"Perhaps you do not know who you have working for you," Kabinov suggested.

President Strickland looked at the occupant of a chair across from his desk. "Perhaps. I would suggest that you take that under advisement as well," he offered. "This could work to our advantage," Strickland said. "If we play this correctly."

"The international media have begun making Michael Taylor a scapegoat," Sergei Kabinov said. "That does not play into our plans. It manifests a conclusion where we require an open end," he told Strickland.

"Let this play out, Sergei."

"We will do what is necessary," Kabinov replied.

"Is that a threat?" President Strickland asked.

"No. It is a reality," Kabinov said.

***

Cassidy was resting on the couch in the rec room when Rose entered with a cup of tea. "Sorry, I know you'd probably prefer wine," Rose admitted. Cassidy snickered and accepted the cup with a smile. "How's he doing?" Rose gestured to her grandson who had fallen asleep in his favorite bean bag chair.

Cassidy shrugged noncommittally. "He's hurting. Having Pip and Alex spend the evening with him last night helped," Cassidy said.

"How are you doing with all of this?" Rose asked.

"I'm all right, Mom," Cassidy answered. She could see the doubt that clouded her mother's eyes and she smiled in reassurance. "I'm worried about him," Cassidy confessed. "It's not an easy thing."

Rose swallowed hard. "I know how hard this is, Cassie. I remember."

"Yes, but no matter what Dad's faults were; I didn't know about those when he died. To me, he was a hero. In some ways that made it easier for me; I think," Cassidy said.

"How so?" Rose asked.

"Dylan….you know, no matter how angry he has been, some part of him loved Chris," Cassidy said. "Chris was Daddy. He may have been an absent father, Mom, but he was still Dylan's daddy for seven years."

"I know," Rose sighed.

"The thing is, Dylan; he loved Chris because that's what he always knew. With Alex, Mom, he loves her so much. He beams whenever she walks into the room. She might not be the person he knows as Daddy but...."

"I think I understand," Rose interrupted. "He's feeling guilty because he wants to be with Alex and you, and now his father is gone."

"Yeah," Cassidy said.

"I understand," Rose repeated.

"Mom?" Cassidy looked at her mother inquisitively. "How come you never remarried? I mean, you never even dated that I remember?"

Rose kept her eyes on her sleeping grandson as she considered how to respond. "Oh, Cassie...at first...well, at first I couldn't even think about that. Things were not perfect between your father and me. That doesn't mean that I didn't love him. I did. It hurt. My life became you. I loved that life," Rose answered honestly.

Cassidy suspected there was something more to the story than her mother was offering. "You never wanted to replace him for me. That's it; isn't it?"

"Partly; yes. It took time, Cassie; for both of us to heal. You were happy. I was content. I saw no need to rock that boat," Rose explained.

"Content? What about your happiness?" Cassidy asked.

Rose smiled. "My happiness comes from seeing you happy," she said earnestly.

"You know what I mean," Cassidy rolled her eyes.

"I do," Rose admitted. "I was never lonely; if that is what you are wondering."

"And now?" Cassidy asked.

"Lonely? With this brood you've got going? Cassie, life with you is never lonely or boring," Rose poked.

Cassidy laughed lightly at her mother's good-naturedness. "Seems like this family grows daily," Cassidy laughed.

"I'll assume we are talking about Jonathan here, and this is not your way of telling me that you and Alex are expecting twins," Rose looked suspiciously at her daughter.

"Very funny. I was thinking about Pip; yes. But also Jacob and Mackenzie," Cassidy said.

"Mackenzie?" Rose raised an eyebrow.

"Yeah. Like it? Dylan's idea. Just so happens Alex seemed to hop right on board Dylan's name train," Cassidy chuckled.

"How are you doing with all of that?" Rose asked.

"I'll assume you mean Pip and not the twins," Cassidy winked at her mother.

"Cute, Cassie," Rose responded. "You are joking about that?"

Cassidy laughed harder. "About Pip? No. Pip really is Alex's brother. And, to answer your question, I am happy for her." Rose lifted her brow a tad higher. Cassidy swatted her mother's leg. "And, as for twins; I hope I am kidding."

"What do you mean; you hope?" Rose asked.

"Well, Grandma Curious, the doctor only heard one heartbeat. So, I am going with just a little Mackenzie. But, we will know for certain this week," Cassidy said.

"Ultrasound?" Rose guessed.

"Mm-hm."

"Alex must be on pins and needles," Rose winked.

"She doesn't know," Cassidy winked back.

"What do you mean? You didn't tell her?"

"Nope. I was going to this weekend. Everything blew up. I thought we'd bring Dylan along. There's been enough death. A little glimpse of life might help," Cassidy explained her reasoning.

Rose patted her daughter's leg. "You are one hell of a mother, Cassie," Rose tried not to tear up.

"I learned from the best," Cassidy said honestly.

"I've been thinking," Rose said, looking over at Dylan.

"About?" Cassidy wondered.

"Moving closer."

Cassidy directed Rose's attention back to her. "Are you sure you would want to do that? I mean, Mom...you have a whole life in New York."

"No. I have friends in New York. I'm not moving into the convalescent home, Cassie. I can still drive; you know?" Rose lightened the mood. "I'm here all the time anyway. Besides, who else are you going to get to babysit Alex?"

"Good point," Cassidy conceded. "You know, I would love it. So would Dylan and Alex. Any ideas where?" Cassidy asked.

"Now that you mention it, your wife had a few suggestions," Rose snickered.

"I'll bet she did," Cassidy giggled. "Care to share?"

"There's a nice ranch not far from Dylan's school," Rose said.

"You're serious about this," Cassidy observed.

"Serious enough that there is an open house this afternoon I want to attend. I was hoping I could coax you and Dylan into checking it out with me."

Cassidy smiled. "He'll want you to buy it right then."

"Stranger things have happened," Rose replied.

"Really?" Cassidy joked. "Mom? Can I ask you something?"

"Of course," Rose answered.

"What do you think Dad would have said?" Cassidy verbalized a question that Rose was certain she had been mulling over for a long time.

"About?" Rose sought to clarify.

"All of it," Cassidy answered truthfully.

Rose took a deep breath and released it. "Cassie, your father thought that you hung the moon. If you are asking what I think...I don't think he would have liked Chris much. He certainly would have had a hard time keeping his mouth shut about a lot of what happened in your marriage, and since." Rose saw Cassidy's breathing grow shallow and uneasy. "If you are asking about Alex....well, I don't know for certain, but I'd bet my pension that he would have approved," she told her daughter. Cassidy's surprise was evident. "What? Do you think your father was a bigot or something? He was not. He would have cared that you were happy, Cassie; happy, safe, and provided for. He was adamant about all three. He wanted to make you happy, protect you, and he was determined that you would have everything you needed; always. Sound like anyone else you know?"

"Thanks, Mom."

"Don't thank me, Cassie. Just do me a favor and slow down on the new additions for a while. I want to buy a raised ranch with three bedrooms. At this rate I'll need a cattle ranch just to fit the relatives at the holidays," Rose complained playfully.

Cassidy kissed her mother on the cheek. "No worries, Mom. Helen's got plenty of room," she whispered before rising to go cover Dylan back up.

"Wise ass," Rose mumbled under her breath.

Cassidy smiled. "I heard that. Told you, I learned from the best."

***

Alex walked side by side with Jonathan Krause. Very little had been said between the two as they traversed the woods behind Alex and Cassidy's home. Alex had noticed Krause's constant fidgeting at the kitchen table and made the suggestion that they get out of the house for a bit. She was feeling on edge as well. Dylan had finally fallen back asleep after some nightmares. Cassidy was exhausted and needed rest. Rose was still in bed. Eleana had left early in the morning, and both Alex and Krause had grown restless in the quiet.

"Thanks," Alex finally broke their mutual silence.

"For?" Jonathan Krause asked.

"Being here for Dylan and Cassidy....and me," Alex admitted quietly.

Jonathan Krause nodded. He followed Alex to a large log that had been placed by the stream and sat beside her. "I still can't believe it," he said.

"What's that?" Alex asked. "That O'Brien is dead? That Taylor is gone? Or, that I'm your sister?" she asked.

"Maybe all of it," he confessed through a nervous chuckle.

"Do you believe it?" Alex asked.

"Which part?" Krause poked.

"Touché," Alex replied.

"I'll feel better when the autopsy results come back on O'Brien," Krause confessed.

"Do you have some reason to doubt that it was him?" Alex's voice rattled in concern.

"No, not really. Just overly cautious," he explained. Krause picked up a rock and cast it out toward the water, cracking the thin ice.

"Who do you think made that call?" Alex asked. "If it wasn't Edmond or even the admiral; who? Ivanov?"

"To remove Taylor?" Krause asked for clarification. Alex nodded. "I wish I knew, Alex. That's what worries me the most. Think about it. You know there have to be more files at Carecom, your father didn't just keep that information in an old photo frame."

"Yeah, I know. I've been thinking about that too. And, Edmond swears that he doesn't know who this Sphinx is?" she asked.

"Edmond claims that no one knows who Sphinx is; unless Sphinx divulges it willingly, or is called in through some protocol," Krause explained.

"Doesn't make sense to me," Alex offered her assessment. "Edmond has part of The Collaborative's personnel list, Brackett, my father, Ivanov; who else? And none of them are Sphinx? If I didn't find it so far-fetched already, I'd …"

"I know," Krause chimed. "John had quite the map going of The Collaborative. It makes me wonder."

"You don't think John was Sphinx?" Alex asked.

Krause shrugged. "Not really. I'm not even certain there is a Sphinx," he said.

"A huge bluff? A ghost created to keep them all in line; one that never existed," Alex followed Krause's train of thought verbally. "That's an interesting theory."

"It's only a theory," Krause said. "And, I don't know what to believe right now. I just want to know what we all have to do with this. What role did they intend you and me to play in this whole thing? I mean, what is the end game here?"

"Money," Alex suggested.

"Yeah, but it is more than that. I agree. Let's face it Carecom, ASA, Technologie Appliqué....Callier, your father, Ivanov, Brackett, Daniels, O'Brien, Taylor...even John....I mean let's be honest, they all have enviable financial means, positions of power. Sure, but why rock that boat now? We're missing something here. The Collaborative was established after the Second World War; right?" he asked. Alex nodded. "We still don't know to what end. What changed? Why do you think Ivanov wants to break off now?"

"My best guess is still money," Alex said flatly. "Taylor became an exposure risk. That's my guess."

"I agree with that assessment. I still think we are missing something," Krause said. "Have you noticed the personal tone..."

"Yeah," Alex interjected. "People's families are involved; their children...it is personal, Pip."

Jonathan Krause shook his head in frustration. "I guess you would understand that a little better than me," he admitted.

Alex smirked. "Oh, I don't know. I think you understand it more than you care to admit," she goaded him. "But, yes, I do understand. You're right. Dylan has been hurt enough in all of this. He's just a little boy. He didn't ask for this craziness. He should be playing soccer and going to birthday parties, not funerals."

Krause released another sigh. "I don't want them to inherit this either, Alex."

"I know that," Alex said. "You and I both know what that might mean; for us."

"Yes, I suspect we do."

"Pip? I'm not certain who we can trust," Alex confessed.

"I know. I'm skeptical myself," he said. "Do you trust me?" he asked her pointedly.

Alex looked directly at the man seated next to her. "You know, it's strange," she said. Alex pinched the bridge of her nose for a moment before continuing. "The truth is, Jonathan, I have no reason to," she said. Krause nodded. "But, I trust you more than anyone in my life; other than Cass."

Jonathan Krause let a small smile creep onto his face. "Eleana?" he inquired.

Alex laid her hand on her brother's knee. "You are falling in love," she said.

"I trust her," Krause said assuredly.

"I know you do," Alex replied.

"You don't?" he asked. "Because of Claire?"

"I trust her more than I do most of the people surrounding us," Alex said. "I like her. That goes a long way," Alex winked. "Cassidy likes her. That goes even farther," she laughed. Alex watched as Krause cast another stone into the water.

"Are you worried about Eleana seeing Claire?" Alex asked Krause.

"Worried that Claire will harm her? No. Not physically anyway," he answered.

Alex let the statement lie for a moment. "She has to let go, Pip. She cares about you. I can see it."

"She loves Claire."

"Yes, I can see that too," Alex said. "Everyone has a past, Jonathan. Everyone. Someone recently urged me to think more about the future."

"The future, huh?" he sighed.

"Yep."

"When John and I were kids we used to do this," Krause recalled.

"Do what?" Alex asked.

"Sit on a log and throw stones in the water," he laughed. "When John wasn't trying to build an airplane out of them."

"He built airplanes out of logs? Or stones?" Alex asked.

Krause laughed. "He built airplanes out of everything. That's all he ever dreamt about; flying."

The pair sat in companionable silence for a long while, each occasionally casting a stone over the water. "What about you? What did you want to be?" Alex asked her brother curiously.

"A pirate," he laughed.

"Of course," Alex joined in his laughter. "I wish I had known you then," she said a bit sadly.

"Me too," he said. "What about you? What did you dream of doing? Flying? Sailing the high seas?" Alex grew extremely quiet. "Alex? Hey, I'm sorry…"

"No…no, don't be. I never thought about that much until lately. When I was really young, I wanted to be a doctor," she said. Krause studied Alex as she continued. "My YaYa, she was the greatest," Alex said. "She got sick when I was about five. I remember my mother crying one night in the kitchen. She asked my father why they couldn't fix her."

"What was wrong?" he asked.

"Cancer," Alex answered. "She had a brain tumor; inoperable."

"I'm sorry," Krause said.

Alex shrugged. "Anyway, I asked my father that night why they couldn't fix YaYa."

"What did he say?" Krause asked.

Alex chuckled. "He told me doctors were like detectives, first they look for all the clues to find what's wrong and then they put them together. But, he said, sometimes they just can't find all the pieces in time."

"Interesting analogy," Krause said. "And that made you want to be a doctor?"

"I wanted to fix things," Alex said. "I guess I still do."

"And here I just wanted to be a pirate," Krause poked.

"Pirates are cool," Alex winked. "Jonathan, I…."

"Don't say it, Alex. We'll see what Edmond and Jane offer tomorrow and go from there. One way or another...your kids will choose whatever they want to follow for themselves. I promise."

"Yeah…what happens when they want to be pirates and detectives?" she tried to ask lightly.

Jonathan Krause took his sister's hand. "Then, we will make sure they know everything there is to know so that they can be the best pirates and detectives there are. They might just surprise you, though," he said.

"You think?" she asked.

"Yeah. Your kids have a whole lot of Cassidy in them. You're likely to get teachers and doctors," he suggested.

"One can only hope," Alex said.

***

Eleana Baros walked quietly in through the backdoor of her home. She stopped in her tracks at the faint sound of approaching footsteps. Her breath caught in her chest at the sight that quickly unfolded before her. "Claire," Eleana flew across the room.

Claire Brackett heard the back door open and close softly. She retrieved her pistol from her jacket and headed directly toward the sound; expecting to find one of Ivanov's minions or one of Taylor's goons. She shook her head to clear the vision that greeted her. "Eleana?" she called out, falling to her knees slowly.

"Claire, Claire," Eleana repeated. "Look at me. Look at me."

Claire Brackett looked up into a pair of bright, hazel eyes and stuttered. She reached her hand to touch Eleana's cheek. "You're dead," she whispered.

The bewilderment in Claire's eyes broke Eleana's heart. "No," she said. "I'm not."

"You…how can you be here?" Claire began to cry like an infant.

Eleana fell to the floor and wrapped her arms around Claire. "I'm not dead, Claire. It's okay."

"I thought you left me," Claire wept in her lover's arms.

Eleana held Claire close. She was positive that no one would believe that Claire Brackett was capable of so much emotion. Underneath Claire's brash exterior, there still resided a hint of innocence. It was the part of Claire that Eleana had fallen so deeply in love with all those years ago. As she felt Claire cling to her now, she realized that she always would love her. "It's all right," Eleana assured Claire. "Come on," she helped the weeping woman to her feet. "Let's go sit down."

It took several minutes for Eleana to get Claire settled and composed on the sofa. She took a moment to remove her coat and brought Claire a glass of water. "Here," she handed Claire the glass.

"How about something stronger?" Claire asked.

Eleana offered her lover a weak smile. "We need to talk," Eleana said.

"I don't understand," Claire replied. "Marcus told me. It was on the news…Eleana, I saw the building…I went to…"

"I know what you were doing," Eleana said. "You were going to take down Dimitri; right?"

"You were not supposed to be there," Claire said.

"What about all the other people who were, Claire?" Eleana asked softly, prompting an anxious expression from Claire. Eleana sighed deeply. "Twenty-one people, Claire. No, I didn't die. Only because of Russ. Twenty-one people did. How could you be a part of that?" she asked. Claire did not answer.

"Oh, Claire. Is it true?" Eleana asked.

"What?"

"You are the one who killed Elliot?" Eleana's pained expression brought on another wave of Claire's tears.

"It was an order," Claire tried to explain.

"I see. What about me?" Eleana asked. "Did you stop and think about me, Claire? Even once, in all of this...When did you stop and think about me?"

"I think about you all the time," Claire said honestly.

Eleana looked to the ceiling and closed her eyes. "You think about this...about then," Eleana said. "Is that it? You think about us; what? Having sex? Tell me, Claire...I need to know. What do you think about?"

"I....Eleana...no....I think about you...."

"Claire....you brought O'Brien here? To our place?"

"I wanted to be close to you. You were gone!" Claire defended herself.

"You made love to him in our bed!" Eleana shot back.

"I never made love to him. Never....never to anyone but you," Claire declared.

"What about my brother? That was just sex? Then you killed him? My brother, Claire!"

"It wasn't...."

"I know what it wasn't," Eleana said. "What were we?"

"What do you mean; what *were* we?" Claire asked.

"What is this?" Eleana gestured to their surroundings. "What does it mean to you?"

"Everything," Claire said. "It's the only place I have ever felt....home."

Eleana's tears began to fall. She looked at her lover compassionately. "Yes. It was. It was our home. I thought eventually... that would be enough...this place. What it meant to us."

"It is," Claire reached for Eleana.

"No. It isn't. We are not the same people we were, Claire. We've chosen different paths," Eleana said as her tears picked up their pace.

"Don't you love me?" Claire asked.

"Always," Eleana answered. "That has never been a question."

"I love you," Claire spoke the words and placed a kiss on Eleana's lips.

Eleana allowed herself one last indulgence. She slipped her hand around Claire's neck and brought her closer. She could feel the depth of Claire's emotion. This was the only way that Claire could connect to that. It was always visceral, primal for Claire. As Eleana faded into her lover's kiss, she realized that she required so much more now than Claire could offer. Part of her screamed to give in to Claire's needs. Reluctantly, she pulled away and cupped Claire's face in her hands. "I have to go," she told Claire.

"Where are you going?" Claire said. "You just got back.... you..."

"This isn't my home anymore," Eleana said. It was a realization she wished she could deny. "You stay," Eleana kissed Claire's cheek.

"I need you," Claire grasped for Eleana.

"Maybe. I needed you, Claire; all of you....or maybe that is just what I wanted; I don't know," Eleana confessed. "You have to decide what you want."

"I want you."

"I know, but you will never be able to commit to that," Eleana said.

"I'm here," Claire argued. "I'm always with you."

"Until the next time," Eleana pointed out. "And, where was I when you helped Dimitri blow that building?"

"I didn't...."

"You didn't press the button. I know. Where was I when you killed Elliot?" Eleana asked.

"Where were you when I thought you were dead?" Claire shouted.

Eleana nodded. She was tempted to take the bait and argue passionately, but something deeper was calling to her. "This is your home, Claire. That's what I always intended. It's yours."

"It's ours," Claire said defiantly.

"No," Eleana said as she reached for her jacket. "Not anymore."

"Eleana, wait!" Claire caught hold of her lover. "Please, stay. Tell me what you want? Do you want me to quit? Walk away; what?"

"You can't quit being who you are," Eleana observed. "We're different. We always were. Just, now....You still live in the past. What your father wants. What you need to prove. Even this place...."

"Eleana, please...."

Eleana smiled. "I love you."

"I love you," Claire said. "I should have said it...."

"I know," Eleana smiled. "I've always known. But, there's no future for us. I don't want to live in our past any longer." Claire closed her eyes. And felt Eleana's lips tenderly brush over hers. "Be careful, Claire. It's hard enough losing you once."

When Claire Brackett finally opened her eyes, Eleana was gone. She closed her eyes again and leaned her head against the door. It felt to Claire as if the only solid thing in her life had just been washed away. They had argued many times. This had been different. There was a finality in Eleana's kiss that Claire could not deny. She took a deep breath and centered her thoughts, looking back at the home surrounding her. "She'll be back," Claire whispered. "Everyone goes home."

***

Monday, February 2nd

"This is getting out of control!" President Lawrence Strickland screamed. "Jeffrey! Where the hell are our people on this? It's only been days, and already there are people calling for my impeachment! Jesus! Is this an investigation of a God damned witch hunt?"

"Mr. President, with all due respect, I do not control the international press," Jeffrey Mansfield said.

"Then you'd better create a damn good counter-offensive," Strickland ordered. "Who the hell leaked information about Merrow's inquiries into Taylor? No one knew that but the people in this office! I want to know who it was, and I want a viable story to debunk it."

"Mr. Mansfield," Admiral Brackett interrupted carefully. "Can I have a moment with the president, please?" Jeffrey Mansfield threw his hands in the air and left the Oval Office. "You need to calm down, Larry," Brackett advised. "You are pouring gasoline on the fire."

"Well, what do you suggest?" Strickland asked angrily.

"Calm. I suggest calm. You need to be the eye of the storm if you hope to survive it," Brackett said. "Plenty of people knew about John's suspicions. I've told you before; this is not a small network. You think because you are sitting in that chair that you are running the show. You aren't. Not even close. It took almost seventy-five years to build The Collaborative into what it is today. You are just a dot on the map, Larry; a dot that can be easily erased. If Viktor wanted you gone; you would be. Someone does not like the game you and Viktor have been playing," Brackett said.

"And you, Admiral Brackett? Do you approve? Or are you simply here to watch the show?" Strickland asked.

"I've navigated the intelligence arm of The Collaborative for twenty-five years. It's in my best interest to preserve it," Brackett said.

"So, you have a suggestion?" Strickland asked.

"Simple, you cross Ivanov."

"What?" Strickland asked.

"I thought that was pretty straightforward even for you, Larry. You cross Ivanov. Take a hit in the press. Throw Michael Taylor and Christopher O'Brien under the bus. Implicate others. Take them to task and throw away the key. Make examples of them. Become the janitor that you are...and clean house," Admiral Brackett told the president.

"I take it you have some thoughts on who these sacrificial lambs might be?" Strickland asked.

"Look in your backyard first, Larry. Mr. Mansfield for instance."

"Jeffrey's not........."

"Jeffrey's not who you think he is," Brackett said flatly.

"And then?" Strickland urged.

"There are plenty of lambs to be led to the slaughter. We just have to find the right ones," Brackett said. "Starting with those who were closest to John Merrow."

***

"Cassie, who was that?" Rose asked.

"Eileen," Cassidy said softly.

"O'Brien?" Rose gently urged.

"Yeah. They're planning a service next Thursday in Southampton," Cassidy said.

"Are you going to go?" Rose asked.

"Yes."

"And Dylan?" Rose wondered.

"I need to talk to Alex and Dylan about that. Eileen has always been good to Dylan, Mom. It's not her fault Chris turned out the way he did," Cassidy observed. She had never been close to her former mother-in-law, but she did not dislike the woman. "I did make it clear that if we attend; Alex will be accompanying us."

"How did she respond to that?" Rose asked.

Cassidy shrugged. "If she wants to have Dylan remain in her life in any way, she'll have to accept Alex."

"I'd like to be there," Rose said.

"I would appreciate that," Cassidy admitted.

"Are you going to call Alex?"

"Yes. For some reason, I think she'll want to know," Cassidy said.

"Do you think it will be a big affair?" Rose asked.

"She said private; family and friends. I don't know how much of either he has left," Cassidy sighed.

"How was Dylan when you dropped him off at school?" Rose asked.

"I don't know. I didn't. Alex and Pip took him," Cassidy said. "They could convince him of just about anything; I think."

"Probably so," Rose admitted. "I'll leave you to call Alex. I have an appointment to get to."

"Are you headed home?" Cassidy asked.

"In a way," Rose winked. "I'll see you later."

Cassidy waved goodbye to her mother. "Always so cryptic," she laughed as she dialed Alex. "Hey, got a minute?"

***

"Any changes?" an older man asked.

"None; everything is secure," Agent Brady replied.

"Well, Agent Brady....I'm sure this is not what you imagined your reward would be," the older man chuckled slightly.

"I'm afraid you have me at a disadvantage," Brady said.

"That is both a fair assessment and a significant understatement," the older man said with a smile. "It's not the most exotic place for an assignment, but it won't be forever," he said.

"Forever can be defined different ways," Brady responded evenly.

The older man laughed. "I can see why she chose you," he said. "Come on, Agent Brady. Let me buy you a cup of horrible coffee. We'll get to know each other."

***

Chapter Twenty-One

"What did Cassie say?" Krause asked as he and Alex rounded the corner of the hallway.

"O'Brien's mother called. Wanted Cassidy to know about the service they are planning," Alex explained.

"I hadn't even thought of that. Probably be pretty bare," Krause said.

"Oh, I don't know. You know how curious people can be, "Alex replied. She led Krause into an elevator and pressed the button for the basement. "I'm more curious about this meeting," she said.

"Yeah, well....we'll see what Jane and Edmond bring to the table," Krause replied.

Alex stepped out of the elevator with Krause following closely behind. They walked through a wide corridor, passing through several doors before Alex stopped. "I still can't believe this place sometimes," she said as she pressed several numbers into a keypad and then lifted her thumb to it. "How did he even build this without anyone knowing?" Alex wondered aloud. The pair passed through the door into a small room. Alex stepped forward again and placed her eye in the appropriate position. Krause followed suit. A panel finally rolled upwards, revealing a long tunnel. "Have you spoken to Eleana yet?" Alex asked as they continued their trek.

"No, but I'm certain she will be here," Krause said.

"I hope so," Alex admitted. She stopped abruptly and turned toward the wall. A few seconds passed and a screen appeared. Alex pressed her thumb to it. Within seconds, a door was revealed and opened. She stepped through first and nodded a silent greeting to the room. "I see you all made it safely," Alex said.

Jane moved to Alex and embraced her. "How are Cassidy and Dylan?" she asked.

"As well as can be expected," Alex answered truthfully. She turned her attention to Brian Fallon. "Glad to see you in one piece, Fallon. Welcome to my humble abode," she said sarcastically. "Let's sit and skip the pleasantries. Pip and I have some questions, and no one is leaving this room until I am satisfied we have some answers," Alex said bluntly. "So, who wants to start? How about we start with who made the call to remove Michael Taylor and plant drugs in Christopher O'Brien's townhouse."

There was no pause. "That's an easy one. I did," Jane said flatly.

***

"Hi," a small voice said.

Dylan looked up from the paper he was coloring. "Hi, Jamie," he said.

The little dark haired girl took a seat beside him. "I'm sorry about your dad," she whispered. Dylan just shrugged. "I don't think you're a villain," she told him.

Dylan smiled at his friend. "Thanks."

"Are you sad?" she asked him.

Dylan shrugged again. "Kind of. Sometimes he played video games with me and stuff."

"Yeah. I never see my dad. He left when I was a baby," Jamie said.

"But I see your dad all the time?" Dylan looked at her in confusion.

"Oh yeah; you mean Jimmy. He's my mom's boyfriend. He's nice," she said. "He picks me up sometimes and he even reads to me. He doesn't live with us, though. Maybe someday."

"Alex lives with us," Dylan said.

"Yeah, so is she like your dad then?" Jamie asked innocently.

Dylan laughed. "No, she's a girl," he stated the obvious.

"Yeah, but isn't she like married to your mom?" Jamie asked. "That's what my mom said."

"Yeah?" Dylan was confused now himself.

"So then, what is she?"

"My mom," Dylan answered.

"But you have a mom," Jamie pointed out.

"Yep. I have two. I have two uncles too…and two cousins," he said.

"That's cool," Jamie said. "I have a brother, but I've never met him…at least that's what my mom says."

"How come?" Dylan asked.

"He lives with my dad, and she doesn't know where they are," Jamie said.

"I wouldn't like it if I didn't know Mackenzie," Dylan said.

"Who is Mackenzie?"

"My brother. Well, Mom says Mackenzie might be a girl, but I don't think so," Dylan said. Jamie looked at Dylan as if he had two heads. He laughed. "My mom is having a baby. He's not here yet," he explained.

"Which one?" Jamie asked curiously. Dylan wrinkled his nose in confusion. "Which mom?" she asked him.

"Oh…Mom, not Alex," he giggled. Jamie nodded. "I can't wait to meet him," Dylan said.

"How come you tell everyone your name is Toles?" Jamie asked.

"I don't know," Dylan looked down at his paper. "Cause Alex is my mom, and she lives with us. Mackenzie will be. My mom is a Toles too."

"I think that's cool," Jamie said.

"You do?" Dylan asked.

"Yeah. I have my mom's last name," she told him. Dylan smiled. "You're lucky," Jamie said a bit sadly.

"How come?" Dylan asked his friend.

"I don't know. I don't have a dad, or any uncles or brothers. I just have my mom…and sometimes Jimmy, if he's not working," she explained.

Dylan looked at his friend and smiled. "You can share mine if you want," he offered.

"Really?"

"Sure. We're friends; right?" he asked her. Jamie nodded. "Alex and Mom say you can love as many people as you want to. Do you like video games?" Dylan asked.

"Sure," she said.

"Do you like tacos?" Dylan questioned his friend.

"Yeah, but my mom hates them," Jamie complained.

"Maybe you can come over when my mom makes them. They're the best," Dylan said proudly.

"Which one?" Jamie asked. Dylan shook his head "Which mom makes tacos?"

Dylan laughed. "My mom…not Alex. Alex makes cereal and eggs. YaYa says she's missing a gene."

"Who's YaYa?"

"She's my grandma. I just call her YaYa," Dylan explained. "It's Greek, like Alex."

"Wow. You know a lot of people," Jamie said wide eyed.

"I guess," Dylan said. "I'll ask my mom about the tacos."

"What are you making?" Jamie asked, looking at Dylan's picture.

"I was making it for Alex and Mom, but you can have it," Dylan said.

"Really?"

"Sure, it's my family. I see them all the time. You take it. Then, you won't feel so lonely," Dylan observed.

Jamie accepted the picture and gave Dylan a hug. "You're the best friend I ever had," Jamie told him.

***

"Excuse me?" Alex said. "I missed something."

"No, you didn't miss anything," Jane assured her. "I ordered the cartons of cocaine and I ordered the rest of the evidence planted in O'Brien's apartment. Things did not go exactly as I had planned. Maybe better."

"I don't believe this," Alex said. "How could you…"

"Alex, it's time for you to wake up," Jane said.

"Did you have Cheryl killed too?" Alex asked furiously.

"No. I'm not in the business of having people murdered. I didn't plan on Agent Fallon confronting Michael Taylor in the townhouse. It was Brian or Michael. Which would you have preferred?" Jane shot back.

"All right," Krause broke in. "Let's calm down. We know O'Brien needed to fall, Alex. Taylor got in the way. It happens," he defended Jane.

Alex shook her head in disgust. She looked at Jane and sighed. Jane's expression was harder than normal. "Fine. Who is Sphinx?" Alex asked directly.

"No one knows that," Callier spoke up. "If anyone does know, they are not talking. Alex, Sphinx changes periodically. Usually upon death, but occasionally for other reasons. It's a safeguard. The only people who know the protocol to pass Sphinx on are the people who were Sphinx. There is a protocol to call Sphinx in; in the event that The Collaborative's hierarchy is threatened. I issued it. There has been no response."

"What does that mean?" Eleana asked her father.

Callier smiled at his daughter and then turned his attention back to Jonathan Krause and Alex. "It means one of several things. Sphinx is no longer an ally; Sphinx has some reason not to comply that we…"

"How about Sphinx doesn't exist?" Krause suggested. Callier remained stoic. "Is that a possibility?" Krause asked pointedly.

"Yes," Callier answered immediately, noting the sighs that escaped each member at the table. "But, not as you are suggesting, Jonathan. Sphinx is very real. However, if Sphinx were to die and fail to pass on…"

"You think my father was Sphinx," Alex surmised. "And he never passed that role on to anyone before he died."

"It's a distinct possibility, Alexis. It also makes sense," Callier said.

"How does it make sense?" Krause asked.

Jane took a deep breath. "He cut off funding to ASA; he closed accounts; Alex…your father started a shut-down of the pipeline he spent years building just before he died," Jane offered.

"You think he wanted to make The Collaborative unstable?" Alex asked. "Why?"

"Why else?" Callier sighed.

"To protect us," Krause interjected.

"If not me, who else would it be but your father? It is personal in nature, Jonathan. Surely, you have recognized that," Callier said.

"If you're right, that means he was shutting off more than ASA. That does not explain everything happening; the shift in loyalties. What if you are wrong?" Krause asked. "What if Sphinx is out there and is an adversary…Ivanov or Brackett?"

"Doubtful. Also a possibility, but unlikely," Callier said.

"Who has access to the database?" Eleana asked.

"Myself, Viktor, William, whatever Nicolaus left for Alex; that's it now; other than Sphinx," Callier said.

"What does that mean? Now?" Alex asked.

"It means that there were six of us. That has not been the case for many years," Callier said sadly.

"I see," Alex said.

"Not to break up this mumbo jumbo you have all cooked up," Fallon chimed, "but exactly what are we supposed to do now? Strickland might be involved; the Russians are making threats and accusations; Claire Brackett is MIA..."

"Claire's not missing," Eleana offered. "Although I'm not certain where she will travel next. It will either be back to her father or to Dimitri."

Krause and Alex both offered Eleana an understanding smile. "So, what do you suggest?" Alex asked. "Let me tell you where I stand. I just found out that I have a brother. Apparently, my father, my grandparents, all had a hand in creating this debacle you people call The Collaborative; this entity that has served to kill my best friend. It put my wife in danger, and it has put my son through hell. To what end? I still have not a clue. So, Edmond... you are no longer in charge of this little fiasco...Jonathan and I will take the lead. And, we will take the fall, if necessary. I will not have my children sitting at this table in twenty years. Not if I can help it. So, plans...what are they?" Alex asked.

Jane looked at Alex and addressed her directly. "Alex, if you are suggesting that what you want is to shut off The Collaborative, and you are positive that is your goal; I will support you. But, if you think that can happen without stepping in the mud..."

"Don't lecture me, Jane. I love you, but I'm very clear on this point," Alex said.

"So?" Krause said. "Alex and I have some ideas. You've obviously given this some thought, Jane. Let's hear it."

"Alex stays at Carecom. She shuts down the pipeline little by little, not all at once; make the company shiny and new...and into new acquisitions. Carecom expands, buys out some of the smaller entities. Alex assumes the media role; the hero, starting with attending O'Brien's funeral. God knows the press love her and Cassidy. We need a façade. Eleana comes out of the shadows. She tells her story; how she survived the attack. That is was Russ who saved her. How Russ had been working with John all along to root out Ivanov and Markov's plans. Eleana implicates Daniels subtly. Get people questioning Strickland even more."

"Are you crazy?" Callier barked.

"*Laisser la finir, Père*(Let her finish, Father)," Eleana called across the table.

"Eleana is safer in the open, Edmond," Krause supported Jane's stance. "Continue."

"Jonathan, you go on board at Carecom; work with Eleana on the database. Determine who knows they are Collaborative and who is in the dark. Help Alex and Edmond begin to strengthen our corporate side and weaken Ivanov's and the admiral's. We take control of as much of the resource pool as possible, slowly so as not to draw too much attention from any one corner. Joshua will be promoted out of the FBI. I've called in a dormant asset in Strickland's administration that will be able to help," Jane explained.

"You're suggesting we pit the Russians and Strickland against each other?" Fallon asked. "Isn't that playing with fire?"

"We are already walking through fire, Fallon," Alex said. "What Jane is suggesting is that we flush the drain and see what washes out. We use finesse. We use the media to our advantage to gain leverage. They'll put pressure on Strickland's administration to clean house. At the same time, we eat up all the little fishies The Collaborative left prey in the pond. Am I right?" Alex asked. "We use the assets that have been left dormant and shift the power to us, slowly."

"What do you mean assets?" Fallon asked.

"She means you," Tate finally spoke. "She means the people who have no idea The Collaborative exists. They work for the government, Carecom, a host of other organizations and companies, and have no idea that those entities have any nefarious or secret agenda. That's what she means," Tate clarified.

"Doesn't that just create a new conspiracy?" Fallon asked, feeling a bit bewildered.

"You don't understand, Agent Fallon," Jane said. "The Collaborative has penetrated every industry and government. It's how they stay in control. The only advantage we have is that it is so vast, they have left more holes than they ever intended. This is not a network of ten or twenty or even fifty-thousand people," Jane told Fallon.

"There's no other way, Brian," Alex conceded. "They are Goliath. It's going to take more than a slingshot and a rock to shut it down, or at least change its course. Sometimes you have to become the thing you despise in order to destroy it."

"You realize what you are saying?" Fallon asked.

Krause saw the tension in Alex's temples. "She knows, Agent Fallon....What about Sphinx? If he does exist..."

"Then we hope to flush him out as well," Callier said. "And hope he sees it our way."

"It's a different tactic," Krause said. "A more subtle approach."

"Yeah, but safer," Fallon surmised.

"No," Alex chuckled. "Far more dangerous. It might seem safer for a while; only for a while. There will be a response. There always is. And, then....then it will be more dangerous for all of us than it has ever been. This is far from over."

"Alex, you and Brian have families," Tate said. "No one would blame you if you stepped away."

Jane looked to her friend. "He's right, you know."

"I would blame me," Alex said. "What do I leave them? Who will do this if it isn't us? Do you want Stephanie and Alexandra dealing with this one day? I may not have created this, but I will not walk away from it. What do I tell Cassidy and Dylan... Mackenzie...if I walk away?"

"That you love them," Krause said softly.

Alex smiled at her brother. "I can't walk away."

"I know," Krause said.

"So, if anyone wants to bail…and I mean if you are not fully committed, now is the time. It might seem comfortable for six months, a year…but when it comes home to roost it will be a shit storm like you have never seen. Ivanov and the admiral will look for a way to exploit us. When that happens, we will have to react; expose them and cut off the head of the monster. We all know that will mean choices none of us wants to make," Alex said.

Silence lingered. "Whatever you need," Callier said first.

"I'm in," Eleana said.

"Are we going to be all right?" Jane asked Alex.

"We're good," Alex said.

"All right; I'm in," Jane said.

"No question," Tate nodded.

"Me too," Fallon promised.

"All right," Krause said. "It does not leave these walls. It remains between the six of us and Edmond. None else knows the details; only what they need to know. Agreed?" The agreement was a foregone conclusion.

Jane approached Alex before leaving and smiled. "I'm sorry, Alex. I did what I had to do."

Alex nodded. "No secrets, Jane."

"There are always secrets, Alex," Jane replied. Alex just nodded. "I'll see you at the funeral," Jane said. Alex offered her friend a half-hearted smile.

"You two okay?" Krause asked.

"She's not telling us something," Alex said.

"I know," Krause said as he watched Jane leave the room. "But, whatever it is…she has her reasons. She would never endanger Dylan or the girls," Krause said.

"Not intentionally," Alex agreed. "Why don't you go save Eleana from Edmond?" Alex suggested.

"You okay?" Krause asked.

"I've made my choice. I just want to go home," Alex said.

"Sorry," Brian Fallon interrupted. "How are Cassidy and Dylan?" he asked Alex.

"They're okay, Fallon," Alex said. "Are you sure about this?"

"Yeah. I am. I don't know how much help I will be…"

"I trust you," Alex said. "So does Pip. I'll be in touch," she said. "Go spend some time with Kate and the kids." Alex turned her attention to Joshua Tate. "Any ideas on who might replace Taylor?" she raised her eyebrow knowingly.

"No," Tate laughed.

"I don't know that you'll love that promotion," Alex said. "For all the chatter, NSA is kinda quiet. Not like the FBI at all." Fallon looked at Alex and Tate and shook his head. "Meet your new boss, Fallon, or should I say your old boss in a new place," Alex told her friend.

"Let's just hope it's the right move," Tate said. Alex shook Tate's hand. She watched as he explained the entire interaction to Brian Fallon on their way out the door and chuckled.

"Alex, Eleana and I are going to go grab something. Want to come?" Krause asked.

"Thanks, no. I want to talk to Edmond for a few. Try to get home for dinner," Alex said.

"Understood," Krause said with a smile.

Alex made her way to the last occupant of the room and stood confidently before him. "Tell me, Edmond….Why now?" Alex asked.

"Why have I decided to help you; you mean?" he surmised. Alex tipped her head in acknowledgement. "What makes you so sure I haven't been helping you all along?" Callier asked.

"What? By lying to all of us? Keeping us from the truth? Explain to me how you and my father have helped, Edmond?" Alex asked him.

"Alexis," Callier sighed. "You are so much like your father."

"That's debatable," Alex said.

The Frenchman laughed. "Ah, and like your mother too. Why are *you* doing this now?" Callier turned the question around on her. "Dylan? This new baby? Cassidy? Jonathan? Am I wrong? But, the truth is you couldn't walk away even if it were just you to consider. It's not how you are built, Alexis. You just have different commitments now. That's your answer," Callier told her.

"Not much of an answer," she said.

"You understand more than you pretend not to know, Alexis. I don't expect your forgiveness. Neither would your father. I hope you never have to ask it of your children," Callier said.

"I already have," Alex acknowledged.

Edmond Callier put his arm around Alex's shoulder and guided her to the door. "The truth is Alexis, none of us can walk away from who we are; we can only walk toward who we choose to become. Go home to your family. Take this time and hold onto it. I already lost two men I considered sons, and three that I called brothers. I suspect they will not be the last," Callier said sadly.

Alex looked at the older man intently. "He won't let anything happen to Eleana," she said quietly.

Callier smiled. He had recognized the growing affection between his daughter and Jonathan Krause. "I believe you are right," he said. "But Alexis, I would mourn any one of you as I did Elliot. You may not believe that. It is the truth," Callier told her. "*Les familles ne sont pas seulement trouvé dans le sang. Je pense que vous devriez le comprendre plus que la plupart.* (Families are not only found in blood. I should think you would understand that more than most)."

Alex turned back to the empty room and allowed her eyes to roam freely. It was a fortress. She thought silently about the friends she had already lost; John Merrow, her father, Russ Matthews, even Michael Taylor. She closed her eyes as her thoughts traveled to Dylan, so much he had lost as well; the only father he had ever known, and a father that would never share his life. "No more," she said. It was a silent commitment to the future. "No more."

***

Friday, February 6th

"Alex, stop fidgeting," Cassidy laughed. "Why are you so nervous?"

Dylan looked up to Alex and waited for her to answer his mother. "I'm not nervous," Alex said. Cassidy raised her eyebrow and shook her head just as the doctor walked into the room.

"Well, the entire Toles family today," Dr. Allison Bartlett greeted the room. "You must be Dylan," she said.

"Yep. So, when do we get to see Mackenzie?" Dylan asked the doctor.

Dr. Bartlett looked between the two women in the room. "That was fast. Mackenzie; excellent choice; only need one."

Alex stood next to Cassidy gloating and received a slight smack to her arm for her cockiness. "Yeah, yeah," Cassidy groaned. "I was outnumbered," she told her doctor.

Dylan and Alex both offered the doctor a toothy grin. "I can see you have your hands full," Dr. Bartlett joked.

"Yeah, let's hope this one has some of my genes," Cassidy laughed.

"YaYa says Alex is missing a gene," Dylan told the doctor.

Dr. Bartlett looked to Alex and pretended to study her carefully. "Which gene are you missing, Ms. Toles…Calvin or is it Levi…"

"Do you know Cassidy's mother by any chance?" Alex asked the doctor suspiciously.

"No, can't say that I've had the pleasure," Dr. Bartlett answered. "So, what do you say we take a peek here and see if we can find Mackenzie?" she winked at Dylan.

"Yeah!" he exclaimed.

"Cassidy, there is a possibility I might be able to see the gender. Some things we can't tell for certain, others are a little more....obvious," Dr. Bartlett said.

"We'd rather it be a surprise," Alex said. Cassidy smiled at her wife gratefully.

"But, if anything make itself known," Cassidy raised her eyebrow, "that would be fine too."

Dr. Bartlett set about her tasks, explaining each thing she was doing as she went. "How can you see him from out here?" Dylan asked.

"Actually, Dylan, this uses sound, but so high that you can't hear it," Dr. Bartlett explained.

"Can Mackenzie?" he asked.

"No, Mackenzie can't hear it either, but Mackenzie should be able to hear your mom pretty soon," she said.

"Really?" Alex asked.

"Yeah," the doctor smiled at Alex's enthusiasm. "Okay, here we go. Let's just...oh...see; right there," Dr. Bartlett pressed a button on the machine and then moved the wand again. "Right there," she pointed to the screen. "See, there are Mackenzie's hands."

Cassidy looked at the screen, relieved to see the life within her. She looked up at Alex and lost her breath. Alex was completely captivated by the image. Her mouth was slightly open, and her eyes were moist. "Cass..."

"Alex! Look!" Dylan bounced on his heels. "Is he waving?" Dylan asked.

Dr. Bartlett tried not to laugh. "Maybe," she said. "But you see; right there, Dylan...those are Mackenzie's feet."

"Be careful," Dylan warned the doctor. "Kenzie's feet are ticklish." Cassidy looked at Alex and started laughing.

"How do you know that?" Dr. Bartlett asked.

"We all have ticklish feet; even Mom. It's a Toles thing," Dylan told her.

"Let me snap a few good ones for you," Doctor Bartlett said. "How are you feeling now, Cassidy? Any nausea left?"

"Nope. None," Cassidy said.

"Good. Alex, why don't you take Dylan out into the waiting room while we finish up here?" the doctor suggested. She made a few notes on the pictures and handed them to Alex. "First photo," she winked. Alex just nodded a bit dumbly and led Dylan from the room.

"You could tell; couldn't you?" Cassidy asked her doctor.

"Not a hundred percent," Dr. Bartlett smiled. "Do you want me to give you my best guess?" she asked.

"No," Cassidy said as the doctor wiped off her stomach and continued the exam. "I already have a pretty good idea."

"Sixth sense?" the doctor asked.

"Sounds silly, huh?"

"No. Not really. I knew what all four of mine were going to be," Dr. Bartlett said. "More accurate than the ultrasound. I wouldn't be surprised if you felt some movement soon," she told Cassidy.

"I already have," Cassidy confessed.

Dr. Bartlett smiled. "I'm not surprised. Haven't told Alex?"

"No. They are just little flutters. Started this week and not all that often. She'll drive me crazy for the next few weeks until she can feel it if I tell her now," Cassidy laughed.

"Well, Mackenzie is right where Mackenzie should be," the doctor assured. "Everything looks good, Cassidy."

"Thanks. Thanks for letting Dylan be here," Cassidy said.

"How are you doing; emotionally, I mean?" the doctor asked.

"I'm okay. Today helped....all of us," Cassidy said with a smile.

"I'm sure. I'll let you get dressed. Just....Cassidy...make sure you take care of yourself too."

"I will," Cassidy promised.

***

Thursday, February 12th

Dylan sat between Alex and Cassidy in the pew of a small church, toying with the button on his jacket. Dylan felt his mother tighten her grasp as music began to play. He followed his parents' lead to stand. The cherry casket at the front of the church was covered in a spray of yellow and red roses. Dylan stopped and looked at it. He kept his parents' hands in his own and approached the casket. He'd seen people do the same thing when Alex's father died. Alex leaned over into his ear. "Do you want us to give you a minute?" Dylan shook his head no. He wanted to talk to his father, but he wanted Alex and Cassidy beside him.

"I just want to talk to him," Dylan explained.

"Go ahead, sweetie," Cassidy said. "We're right here."

Dylan stepped up and put his hand on the wood. It felt cool and smooth. He smiled slightly at the way the lights reflected off the perfectly shined wood. "Hi Dad," he said. "I'm really sorry that you went away. Santa brought me a cool new video game for Christmas. It has Batman in it. I think Alex asked him to. She can never beat Mom at racing."

Cassidy choked back her tears and smiled at her son's innocence. She looked at Alex who was watching Dylan protectively and reached for her wife's hand as he continued.

"I'm sorry that you won't meet Mackenzie too. He's my brother…or my sister; I guess. Anyway, thanks for playing those games with me. And, for the beach. I hope you won't be mad, but I am going to be a Toles now. Mom says I can still love you even if I have a different name." Dylan started his slow retreat and then turned back abruptly and dropped his voice to a whisper. "I almost forgot. Can you find Alex and Mom's dads and tell them they say hi? Me and Kenzie too. I think that would be nice. Thanks, Dad," Dylan said. He looked up to Alex and then to his mother.

"Ready?" Cassidy asked. Dylan nodded. "Okay, let's go."

***

"I can't believe how much press was there," Cassidy said.

"Yeah, well...he's a big story," Alex replied.

"Alex, what now? I mean, do you even know where Agent Brady is?" Cassidy asked.

"No. And, that isn't my concern," Alex smiled as she climbed into the bed next to Cassidy.

"What about President Strickland and..."

"Cass?" Alex called to her wife gently. "Let it go," she said softly.

Cassidy turned slightly on her side and gave Alex a peculiar gaze. "What is going on?" Cassidy asked.

"A lot and a lot of nothing," Alex answered.

"I don't follow," Cassidy confessed.

"Nothing has changed, Cassidy...and yet, everything has changed. I don't know how else to explain it. There's going to come a time when I will have to be away again; maybe on a moment's notice..."

"I know that," Cassidy conceded.

"But, that won't be for a while. My focus right now is restructuring Carecom and this family; not in that order," Alex said.

"Mmm...Dylan handled today better than I did, I think," Cassidy changed the subject.

"He is something," Alex said proudly. "I think he told every person he met he was going to have a brother," Alex laughed.

Cassidy looked at her midsection and shook her head. "Well, Mackenzie?"

Alex put her hand on Cassidy's stomach and started talking. "You in there?" Alex asked. "You know; your brother thinks you are a boy, Kenzie. Are you?" Cassidy shifted slightly and giggled. "What? Did I tickle you?" Alex asked.

Cassidy smiled sweetly and brushed Alex's hair aside. "No. I think Mackenzie is telling us he is a boy, or *she* is telling us we'd better prepare her brother," Cassidy explained.

"You felt him?" Alex pulled herself up. Cassidy nodded. "What did it feel like?"

"A flutter, but a pretty big flutter this time," Cassidy said.

"Wait....you felt him before?" Alex asked.

"Very little, Alex. Very little...until just now," Cassidy explained.

Alex ran her hand over Cassidy's belly lightly. "Ask him something," Alex said.

"What?" Cassidy laughed.

"Dr. Bartlett said he can hear you. Ask him something," Alex encouraged her wife excitedly.

"She didn't say the baby could understand me," Cassidy laughed harder.

"He can. Come on. Ask him something."

"What do you want me to ask *her*?" Cassidy inquired.

"Ah! I knew it! You think it's a girl!" Alex exclaimed.

"What if I do?" Cassidy answered back smartly. Alex put her head on Cassidy's abdomen. "Alex, what are you doing?" Cassidy giggled.

"Kenzie, are you a girl?" Alex asked excitedly. "No? Um... are you a boy? Well, come on...inquiring minds want to know."

Cassidy started laughing so hard she became short of breath. "Oh my God, Alex...stop...you are going to make me wet the bed."

"Well, if you'd ask, maybe he would answer!" Alex said indignantly.

"Fine," Cassidy agreed. "Mackenzie....tell your Mommy here that you are our little girl," Cassidy said.

"Haha! See...she didn't move. She is a he!" Alex said.

"You are worse than Dylan," Cassidy chuckled again. "Your mother and your brother are insane, Mackenzie," Cassidy said and then smiled widely.

"Cass? Moved again, huh?" Alex guessed. Alex kissed Cassidy's belly. "See, our son doesn't like it when you call Dylan and me crazy."

"Yes, love. I'm sure Mackenzie was defending your honor."

Alex stroked Cassidy's stomach for another minute before pulling herself up for a kiss. "I don't care, you know?" Alex said honestly.

"About?" Cassidy wondered.

"If it's a girl or a boy. I don't care at all," Alex grew serious.

"I know that," Cassidy said with a smile. Alex captured Cassidy's lips in a fiery kiss. "What brought that on?" Cassidy asked.

"I was thinking about Pip and me....and Nicky. About Stephanie, Alexandra, and Dylan. I just want to make sure Mackenzie knows from day one who we are and that we all love him...or her," Alex said.

"She will," Cassidy replied.

"I knew it," Alex said.

"You're serious about being home more; aren't you?" Cassidy asked. Alex nodded. "Promise me that you know I support you no matter what..."

"Cass...stop. I know. I have things I have to do," Alex said with a sigh. "Pip and I, we're sitting at a table I don't want to be sitting at." Cassidy listened quietly. She knew exactly what Alex was referring to. The idea that Alex and Jonathan Krause, Eleana, Claire Brackett; were all born to fill seats at a table they did not choose. Cassidy offered Alex a comforting smile as Alex continued. "The truth is....I would like nothing better than to fill a whole table with our kids. The kind of table that they felel welcome to come home to when they want to; not one they feel obligated to stay at," Alex said.

Cassidy raised her brow and changed the subject. "Just how big of a table are you thinking here, Agent Toles?"

Alex shrugged. "One with leafs."

"You're impossible," Cassidy laughed.

Alex pulled Cassidy close and kissed her gently. She let her kisses slowly trail down Cassidy's neck until she heard soft sighs escape her wife. Alex felt Cassidy's hands run over her back tenderly, exploring curves and skin methodically and sensually.

She pulled Cassidy's sweatshirt off in one fluid motion and looked down at her wife in awe. "You are so beautiful." Alex barely managed to form the words when Cassidy pulled her down and kissed her. "No," Alex cautioned. "I want to make love to you....I just want you to feel me, Cass."

Cassidy threw her head back and closed her eyes. Alex's touch could set her on fire in an instant. Most nights she happily drifted asleep under Alex's gentle touch. But, there were moments when Cassidy wanted to be consumed by Alex. It often happened with just the brush of Alex's hand, or a loving expression that passed between them. "God, Alex...."

Alex's hands covered every inch of Cassidy. She left nothing untouched. Her kisses laid trails where here hands had just fallen, gently exploring and whispering the truth to Cassidy without any speech. Alex pulled herself up and looked into her wife's eyes longingly. "What, love?" Cassidy asked.

Alex leaned closer and claimed another deep, passionate kiss before returning to caress her wife gently. Cassidy felt Alex's hand trail along her thigh and pulled Alex closer. Cassidy's eyes revealed her need. Alex held her wife's gaze as Cassidy began to move her body in time with Alex's touch. "Stay with me," Alex pleaded.

Cassidy understood the dual meaning of the statement. She kept her eyes locked to Alex's as her body fell over the precipice that her heart had long ago willingly leapt off. She called out Alex's name, never breaking the connection of their eyes, and felt Alex's release travel through her at the same moment. Alex softly collapsed beside Cassidy and pulled her into her arms. "Thank you," Alex whispered.

"What on earth are you thanking me for?" Cassidy asked.

"Everything. You, Dylan, Mackenzie..."

"You're welcome," Cassidy said gently.

"And for understanding that is what I needed," Alex admitted. "Just to let me say thank you."

"Anytime," Cassidy said sleepily.

"Night, Cass," Alex whispered. Cassidy grumbled slightly. "Night, Kenzie," Alex said as she drifted off to sleep.

Cassidy felt another flutter and snuggled into Alex. "Night, Alex."

***

Chapter Twenty-Two

Five Months Later

Friday, July 17th

"Marta," Alex called her assistant.

"Yes, Ms. Toles?"

Alex giggled. It took her a year, but she finally realized that Marta would never succumb to informalities. "Is my two o'clock here yet?"

"No, Mr. Krause hasn't arrived."

"All right. Do me a favor and hold my calls until he does."

"Certainly, Ms. Toles."

Alex picked up the phone and dialed home. "Toles residence," a voice greeted her.

"Hey, Speed. Where's Mom?" Alex asked.

"Ummm…I dunno," he said unconvincingly.

"Dylan, where is your mother?" Alex asked a bit more forcefully.

"Okay…hold on…she's cleaning Mackenzie's room again," he said.

"How can she be cleaning Mackenzie's room?" Alex asked. "Mackenzie isn't even here yet."

"I dunno!" he said. "But, she was really serious about it."

"Dylan, go bring the phone to your mother," Alex ordered her son.

"Okay, but she won't like it…..Mom!" he called as he pounded up the stairs.

"Honestly, Dylan! Where is the fire?" Cassidy asked.

"Alex is on the phone," he said. "Bye, Alex..."

"Bye, Speed. I'll see you at soccer," Alex told him. Sensing that Cassidy had hold of the phone, Alex spoke. "What are you doing?"

"Cleaning," Cassidy answered abruptly.

"Kenzie making messes already that I don't know about?" Alex asked.

"Don't you have a company to run?" Cassidy asked a bit harshly.

Alex huffed. Cassidy's usual agreeable demeanor had been less than pleasant for the last few days. "Cass, why don't you just relax?"

"Relax? Relax? Alex, did you call home for some specific reason or are you just acting on behalf of the relaxation police?"

"I just called to check in," Alex confessed.

"All present and accounted for," Cassidy answered.

"I love you; you know?" Alex said.

Cassidy noted the hurt in her wife's voice and sat down in the rocking chair. "I'm sorry, Alex."

"It's okay."

"No, it isn't. I just...I'm tired, and I feel like a slug climbing a mountain. It's hot..."

"Cass, I don't know what it's like for you. I don't. Please, just try and relax–a little? Put the air on. Are you in the rocker?" Alex asked.

"Yeah, how did you know?" Cassidy was curious.

"Your breathing changes," Alex said. She heard a knock at her door followed by Jonathan Krause's face peering into her office. "Listen, Pip is here. I have to go. Just sit there for a while and take it easy. Please?"

"My breathing changes, huh?" Cassidy asked.

"Yep," Alex said. "Do you want me to pick you up for Dylan's soccer game or meet you there?"

"Meet us there," Cassidy said.

"You sure?" Alex asked.

"Yeah, I'm positive. Sorry, I'm such a jerk," Cassidy admitted.

"Tell Kenzie to behave. He giving you fits today?" Alex asked, shooting a smile toward Krause.

"Early this morning when you were talking to him…not too bad for the last couple of hours," Cassidy said.

"All right. If you want to clean, have at it, but I think Mackenzie has the cleanest diapers in the country, or at least changing table," Alex joked.

"Okay, point taken. I'll see you tonight. Tell Uncle Pip we say hello."

"Done. Love you," Alex said.

"I love you too," Cassidy said as she hung up the call.

"Everything all right?" Krause asked.

"I think so," Alex said as Marta entered the room with some coffee. "It's like living with Mary Poppins lately."

"Nesting," Marta said as she placed the coffee in Alex's hand.

"What?" Alex asked.

"Mrs. Toles….she's nesting. It's normal," Marta said.

"If you say so," Alex shrugged.

"Mm-hm," Marta smiled as she left the room.

Alex shook her head. "If I didn't know better I would think she ran The Collaborative….So, what gives? Not that I am not happy to see you," Alex winked.

"They're moving forward with the special prosecutor," Krause said.

"That's good. That was the hope; right? He should be impeached. Strickland is dirtier than a three dollar bill. Why he ever thought he could pull off this cleaning house scenario…."

"Yeah, Alex, but there is more. Sparrow surfaced in a small community outside of Lesosibirsk," Krause said.

"She is cold, but Siberia? What the hell is she doing there?" Alex asked.

"Strange, I know. I don't know. Eleana is making some calls. I have no idea. I haven't unearthed any Collaborative interests within a hundred miles of her location," Krause said.

"Why do I think there is more?" Alex asked.

"There is. Your play to acquire MyoGen has raised the bar," he said.

"I imagine it has," Alex smirked. "They don't want us in genetics and they don't want Technologie Applique in petroleum. Taking their market; such a shame," Alex feigned sincerity.

"If you succeed, Alex…it will likely tip the scales. Someone will react," Krause warned.

"That was the plan; wasn't it?" Alex said. "Look, Pip….that merger is at least another six months in the making. If you think that prompted Claire's northern exposure; then keep Eleana digging. They are feeling the squeeze financially; everywhere. The admiral and Strickland are probably in worse shape than Ivanov. He still has enough capital to grow whatever network he is building, but unless he is Sphinx, or has Sphinx in his court; he is at a severe disadvantage. We have my father's and Edmond's database. We have part of Viktor's and whatever John uncovered."

"I know. I just don't want you to get hurt," Krause said.

"You think they'll make a direct play for me?" Alex asked.

"No, maybe for Carecom," he said.

"Well, we'll just have to stay one step ahead until that time comes," Alex said. "Now, why else are you here?" Alex asked with a smile.

"Hoping you wouldn't mind if Eleana tagged along to Dylan's game tonight," he said in one quick breath.

"Why would I mind?" Alex asked.

"Nick going to be there?" Krause asked.

Alex nodded her understanding. "Nicky will not be there. And why are you avoiding him, anyway?"

"I don't think he likes me much," Krause said.

"God, for a man who is supposed to be so intimidating, you sure can be a wimp. Nicky's always been my mother's baby. It's not about you," Alex said. "And as far as Eleana goes, you know she's always welcome. Cass loves her, so do Rose and my mom. What's going on with you two anyway?"

"Nothing. I swear. Just friends," Krause said.

"With benefits?" Alex asked teasingly.

"No benefits," Krause snickered.

"Man, I might have to get that DNA test. No way are you my brother," Alex goaded him.

"Alex, seriously....just for a minute. Aren't you worried about Claire at all? I mean, who sent her there and why?" Krause changed the subject.

"Yes, I am. But, Pip...we knew when we agreed to take this course that this is what would happen. We can't run off after Claire. We have to keep our cool, let it play out until the right time," Alex reminded him. "We've learned more in the last five months than John had in years. Ivanov made poor choices; Taylor, Strickland, O'Brien...he's bound to do it again," Alex said.

"I just hope we aren't missing something," Krause said.

"We are. We always are. That's why we have jobs, Pip. You know that. If it worries you that much, we'll sit down next week and see what we can do. Maybe Edmond has someone he can get closer; take a peek at what might be intriguing Claire," Alex suggested. "Now, I have to go. I have a conference call with personnel about benefits."

"Sounds exhilarating," Krause chided Alex.

"Hey, it's still a company; a growing one. People like Marta have needs," Alex explained.

Krause started for the door. "You know, you are good at this. If we....when we get through this, you should think about staying here," he said sincerely.

"I don't know about that. Me and desks...just be back by five so we can make it to Dylan's game," Alex said sternly.

"Okay, boss," he scoffed at her.

"Screw you, Pip," Alex laughed.

***

"Dylan! Come on!" Cassidy called.

"Coming, Mom!" Dylan yelled back.

"Are you all set?" Cassidy asked.

"Yeah. Are you okay, Mom?" Dylan looked at his mother apprehensively.

Cassidy ruffled his hair and smiled. "I'm fine, sweetie. Mackenzie is just getting really big, and I'm a little tired," she explained.

"He playing soccer in your belly again?" Dylan asked.

"Not too much," Cassidy laughed. "Think he's resting up for your game. Get your bag. Alex is meeting us there." Cassidy shook her head as Dylan grabbed his bag off the stair and scurried out the front door. She barely made it through the door when she was startled by a sudden pain. "Behave, Kenzie," she gave a playful pat to her belly. "Your brother has a game tonight. Trust me, you'll have your turn soon enough," she giggled as she locked the door. "Ready?" Cassidy asked Dylan who was already strapped in his seat.

"To the soccer field!" he cried.

Cassidy glanced in the rearview mirror and caught Dylan in the middle of practicing his version of a celebratory dance move. "What are you doing?" she asked.

"Practicing my happy dance for when I score!!" he said. "Toles shoots and he….scores!"

"Oh God," Cassidy groaned. "She wants a table full?"

***

Claire Brackett stepped inside the small tavern and took a seat at a wooden table. She was grateful to be here in July and not in the colder winter months. "*Vy opozdali* (You are late)," a voice greeted her.

"*YA dumala, vy shutili o Sibiri* (I thought you were joking about Siberia)," Claire laughed.

"Good to see you, Sparrow," a young man said. "Your father was cryptic in his message. What is it that I can do for you?"

"I am looking for *spyashchego cheloveka,*" she said. "Have you heard of him?"

The man across from her narrowed his gaze to an intense stare. "The sleeping man?" he asked. "Everyone has heard of him. People hear call him *prizrak, kotorogo mozhno uvidet'* (the ghost that can be seen)," he explained.

"Do you know where I can find him?" Claire asked.

"He is a legend, Sparrow. Nothing more," the man dismissed her request.

Claire Brackett studied the man closely. "Yuri?" she said. "Tell me the legend."

"Just a tale, Sparrow."

"Humor me," Claire encouraged him.

"Well, the town people say that many years ago a man passed through here. He was pale and tired and looked like a ghost. It had been a difficult winter that year. There was a great deal of illness. Many people died, mostly children. This was a very poor town, Sparrow. With so much sickness few could make it to the larger cities for services. The man was worn himself. Some say with illness, others with grief. A local family took pity on him. They had a young daughter who fell ill and became very frail. The man spent hours in her company. Told her stories in other languages. The day that the man vanished, a team of Dutch doctors miraculously passed through the village on their way to Moscow. No one knows why they were here. They took the girl with them, refused any payment. Months later a different man returned with the girl. She was healthy; never strong, but healthy. She never spoke of her journey except to say that there are ghosts that can be seen and that some are angels."

Claire nodded. "Beautiful fairy tale."

"It is; I suppose. Yet, for some reason I suspect you think this ghost is real," Yuri guessed.

"No one speaks of seeing this man now?" Claire asked.

"If he did exist, he has been gone for many years," Yuri said.

"Anyone in this village that remembers him?" she asked.

"Yes," Yuri said. "A few. You can speak to them, but don't expect much. The man is a myth. You will hear many versions of what I told you."

"I can't wait," Claire said.

***

"Dylan! Left!" a voice called out. Dylan moved left up the soccer field, casting his glance from his teammates toward the goal ahead. He picked up his speed, determination evident in his eyes as he watched the ball sail toward him. A light bump of his chest and the ball fell at his feet. Quickly and deliberately, he maneuvered around an opponent and took his shot.

"Go, Speed!" Alex yelled across the field. "Yes!" Alex jumped up in celebration as Dylan's shot found its way to the goal. Dylan's excitement and pride radiated from him, even in the distance. He accepted the praise of his friends and jogged while doing his "happy dance" back to the middle of the field.

"He's good for eight," Krause said with a smile.

"Nah, he's just good," Alex beamed with pride and made her way to Cassidy to share her excitement. Alex was still bouncing when she noticed the flush in Cassidy's cheeks. "Hey. You okay?" she asked with growing concern. Cassidy had her bottom lip gripped between her teeth and just nodded. "It's hot out here," Alex observed. "Need some water?" she asked. Cassidy took in a shaky breath and shook her head. "Kenzie acting up?" Alex guessed.

Cassidy closed her eyes for a second and caught her breath. "I don't think Mackenzie wants to be left out anymore," Cassidy said.

"Well, I don't blame him. Having his own match in there?" Alex moved her hand to Cassidy's belly.

Cassidy gave Alex a tiny smirk. "I think we need to go," she said softly.

"Too hot, huh? Okay, you want me to take you home or have Pip..."

Cassidy shook her head. "No, love...I don't think you understand. I think Mackenzie is done waiting. We need to *go.*"

Alex's face turned pale. "Cass, Mackenzie isn't supposed to be here for almost two weeks."

"Tell that to Mackenzie," Cassidy said as another, slightly sharper contraction hit her. She saw the shock in Alex's eyes and couldn't help but giggle. "Alex, it's okay. Go tell Pip and Eleana, and I will call Dr. Bartlett. They can bring Dylan after his game."

"How can you be so calm?" Alex asked.

"I can't exactly back out now," Cassidy laughed as the contraction passed. "Go on. We'll wait for you; trust me," Cassidy winked.

Alex kissed Cassidy on the forehead and headed back to Jonathan Krause and Eleana. "He's talented, Alex," Krause said as he watched Dylan run up the field. He turned to Alex and grabbed her arm. "Whoa. What's wrong?" Krause looked over toward Cassidy, who was sitting on a bench. "Is Cassidy all right?" he asked, prompting Eleana's gaze to find Cassidy's location. Eleana smiled at Alex and headed to sit beside Cassidy. "Alex?" Krause asked again.

"Pip, can you stay with Dylan. Meet Rose at the house after the game?" Alex asked.

"Meet Rose at the house?" Krause was confused momentarily. "Holy shit, Cassidy's in labor?" Alex just nodded. "Yeah, of course. You okay? You don't look so great," he chuckled.

"I'm fine. Just wasn't expecting..."

"Well, it is your kid. I would expect the unexpected," Krause laughed. "Don't worry, I'll fill Dylan in."

Alex nodded her thanks and made her way back towards Cassidy. "Thanks," she said to Eleana.

"Alex, one of us can drive you…."

"No," Cassidy answered and handed Eleana her keys. "Take the SUV when you go. It's easier for me to get into Alex's car anyway," she said as Alex helped her to her feet. Eleana winked and took her leave. "Come on, Jeeves…take me to the palace," Cassidy joked.

Alex rolled her eyes and helped Cassidy to the car. "How bad is it?" Alex asked as they pulled out of the parking lot.

"As compared to what?" Cassidy asked with a grimace.

"I'm sorry," Alex said sincerely. Cassidy reached across the seat and took Alex's hand. "I think I am supposed to be the one comforting you," Alex reminded her wife. Cassidy just smiled. "How long have you felt the contractions?" Alex finally asked.

"A while," Cassidy confessed. "They were far apart, honey."

"And now?" Alex asked as she turned onto a short stretch of highway. Cassidy blew out a heavy breath. "Guess that answers that question," Alex chuckled nervously. "You just stay where you are for a little while longer Mackenzie," Alex ordered.

Cassidy laughed out loud. "I think your mother just put you in time-out," she said with a rub to her belly.

"Damn right, I did," Alex said. "Hope it works."

***

"Nothing yet?" Barb asked as she entered the waiting room with Helen.

"No," Rose smiled.

"Have you been in to see her?" Helen asked.

"Yeah. She's fine, well…as fine as you can be in labor," Rose admitted. "Alex is a wreck."

"Good Lord, she's been to murder scenes," Helen shook her head.

"Not the same," Alex's voice broke through.

"What are you doing here? She didn't have the baby?" Rose jumped up.

"No. They're giving her an epidural. Kicked me out for a minute," Alex explained. "I'm going to call Pip and have him bring Dylan."

"Is she that close?" Helen asked in surprise.

Alex smiled and shrugged. "Dr. Bartlett seems to think things will pick up quickly. She's six centimeters. She didn't want an epidural, but when the doc told her again that a little rest and relief might help…well, she caved. I'm glad she did. Why don't you go and say hello while I call Pip?" Alex suggested to Barb and her mother.

"I'll call Jonathan," Rose told Alex. "You look like you could use a cup of coffee."

"Come on," Helen grabbed her daughter's arm. "I'll buy. Let Barb and Cassidy visit for a few minutes." Alex nodded and followed her mother. "How are you doing?" Helen asked Alex.

"Nervous," Alex confessed. "I hate seeing her in pain," she explained. Helen smiled. "She's so calm; even when she's hurting. I don't know how she can be so calm," Alex said in amazement.

"It will all be worth it," Helen assured her daughter.

Alex brightened. "I know. I can't wait to see Mackenzie," Alex beamed.

Helen handed her daughter a cup coffee. "Do you want to sit for a minute?"

"No," Alex smiled at her mother. "I want to get back to Cass. I don't want to miss anything."

"I'm so proud of you, Alexis," Helen said.

"Of me? Why?"

"There are a lot of reasons. Watching you with Cassidy and Dylan these last few months…I think they are very lucky to have you," Helen said. "All of them."

Alex felt her mother's praise embed itself in her heart. "I gotta go," she said. "You sure you don't want to come and say hello? I'm sure Cass would be happy to see you."

"No. I'll see you when that baby finally arrives. This is your time. You go," Helen instructed her daughter. Alex nodded and headed off.

***

"So? Now what?" President Strickland barked at Admiral William Brackett.

"Calm down, Larry. You'll have a stroke before they can impeach you," the admiral laughed.

"If that's your idea of humor…."

"Relax. They'll never secure the votes for an impeachment. We just need a few assurances," Admiral Brackett said.

"Oh? Like an embassy bombing? That's what got me into this mess, Bill!" President Strickland reminded the admiral.

"There are other ways to create a crisis, Mr. President."

"I assume you have an idea?" Strickland guessed.

"Oh, I have several. Let's see what Claire uncovers on her trip," the admiral said.

"You have more confidence in your daughter than I do. What makes you think she won't jump right back into Ivanov's camp?" Strickland asked.

"Oh, she will jump somewhere. I'm counting on it," Admiral Brackett admitted.

"You want her to betray you?" the president asked in bewilderment.

"It's not a betrayal if you planned it all along. Claire will go where she sees the greatest benefit at the moment; for her. Viktor's plan was not as misguided as its implementation was," the admiral said.

"Are you suggesting we work with Ivanov?" Strickland asked.

"Not at present, no. We both know that Toles and Krause are up to something. I have my suspicions. They want us to react first. I intend to force their hand. Throw them back in the mix, compromise their....investments; Carecom and MyoGen. Imagine the fervor should some genetically engineered biotoxin end up in the hands of the Russians, or worse, effect some small, impoverished community. I'm not so certain Carecom would be considered the pillar of the corporate world," the admiral gloated.

"Carecom hasn't even merged with MyoGen yet," Strickland said.

"No, all in good time. For now, we plant the seeds. And we let them water them for us, without even knowing they are," the admiral explained.

"I hope you know what you are doing," Strickland said.

"If I don't....and we fail? Impeachment will seem like a picnic, Larry. Give it time. Trust me."

***

"Okay, Cassidy," Dr. Bartlett gently called to her patient. "Next one push, and push hard. I can see Mackenzie."

"You are doing so great," Alex said as she held Cassidy's hand. "Kenzie is almost here."

"Mackenzie better get a move on!" Cassidy demanded.

Within seconds, Cassidy heard the firm direction to push. Alex felt the strength in Cassidy's grip on her hand. She was almost positive that she would lose some permanent feeling from the repeated pressure her wife was applying. At one point, Alex found herself questioning how someone whose touch was so gentle could possess such strength. "Come on, Cass. One more," Alex encouraged.

"It was one more like ten minutes ago!" Cassidy yelled. Alex flinched at the hostility in her wife's voice accompanied by another vice like grip of her hand.

"Now," Dr. Bartlett ordered. Cassidy pushed for all she was worth, mentally urging Mackenzie to hurry up. She was so focused on the task that she almost missed the words as they fell out of the doctor's mouth. The sound of a cry suddenly registered reality and Cassidy looked up to see Alex crying. "You have a daughter."

"Cass, you were right," Alex said with a kiss. Cassidy just closed her eyes.

"Come on, Alex. You going to cut the cord here and let the little one into the world formally?" the doctor asked. Cassidy winked at Alex and watched her walk the few steps away. It was only seconds before Alex was beside Cassidy again, placing Mackenzie in her arms.

"God, she is beautiful, Alex," Cassidy said through her tears.

"Yeah, she is," Alex agreed as she ran her finger over the baby gently. "I love you, Cass."

Cassidy looked up at Alex. Alex was watching Mackenzie with such an expression of love that it took Cassidy's breath away. "Thank you," Cassidy reached for Alex's cheek.

"Thank me?" Alex looked to Cassidy in awe. "You…"

"I love you, Alex." Cassidy chuckled. "You'd better go tell Dylan," she said.

"I will. In a minute when they take her for all that fun stuff," Alex said. "Not until then. I doubt there will be many minutes for just the three of us ever again." Cassidy giggled at the truth and looked down at their new daughter. "Did you ever think of a middle name?" Alex asked Cassidy.

"Jane," Cassidy said. "Maybe it sounds funny. But, Jane has become…"

"No, it's perfect," Alex agreed. "Well, Mackenzie Jane Toles, welcome to the family."

***

"Well?" Rose shot up from her seat when Alex entered the waiting room.

Alex smiled and made her way to Dylan. Dylan's eyes grew wide in anticipation, and Alex chuckled. "Well, Speed; you have a little sister."

Alex wasn't sure how Dylan was going to react to that news. He had been so adamant about a little brother. He had his Big Brother shirt on, and his small chest puffed out immediately in pride. "I got one too, Uncle Pip!" he exclaimed. "Can I see her?"

Alex laughed. "Yes, you can, Speed. I know Mom and Kenzie are anxious to see you," she told him. She straightened to her full height and looked at the room. "I know you all want to know. At eleven thirty-eight, Mackenzie Jane Toles made her appearance weighing in at eight pounds even and twenty-one and a half inches long, with a head of hair that Cassidy says explains a lot. Whatever that means," Alex chuckled. "She's perfect," Alex declared.

"I'm sure she is," Helen hugged her daughter.

"How's Cassidy?" Rose asked.

"Tired," Alex admitted. "Happy, but tired, and anxious to see Dylan."

"Congratulations, Alex," Barb said. "Tell her we love her."

"You can all tell her yourself in a little bit. But, first I need to get Speed in there to meet his sister," Alex said. Dylan followed Alex from the room and down the hallway. He grew a bit tentative when they reached the door. "What is it, Speed?"

"What if she doesn't like me?" he asked.

Alex bent over and gave her son a smile. "I wouldn't worry about that, Speed. Not one bit," she assured him.

Dylan walked into the room and saw his mother in the bed holding the baby. "Well, look who's here, Mackenzie," Cassidy cooed. She looked over at Dylan and patted the bed. "Come on, come up here and meet your sister," Cassidy encouraged him.

Alex helped Dylan to get on the bed next to Cassidy and settled in to enjoy the sight before her. "She's teenie," Dylan said.

Cassidy chuckled. "I know," she said as she looked to Alex. "But not *that* teenie," Cassidy winked. Alex laughed at her wife's sense of humor.

"Hi Kenzie," Dylan whispered. "I'm gonna teach you how to play soccer and pool," he promised.

"How was the rest of your game?" Cassidy asked her son.

"Great! This is the best day ever!" he said. "I scored two goals and I got Mackenzie."

Cassidy kissed her son's forehead. "That is a pretty great day," she agreed. Dylan was excited, but Cassidy could tell he was tired. She placed a kiss on the baby's head and motioned to Alex. "I know they are all chomping at the bit to get in here," Cassidy said. "Why don't you take Mackenzie for a little while? Let Dylan lay here with me," Cassidy suggested. Alex accepted Mackenzie from Cassidy with a kiss. "Here," Cassidy pulled Dylan to her. "I don't know about you, but all this excitement wore me out," she said. "How about a rest?"

Dylan needed no further encouragement and put his head on his mother's chest. Alex sat in the chair beside the bed holding her new daughter. She saw Cassidy smile and close her eyes in contentment. "Well, M.J., I think I like that...What do you think, Mackenzie? M.J. is a cool nickname. You look like an M.J. Your mommy says babies look like babies. Shhh...don't tell her I told you that. Nah, you look like your mom."

"Yeah, sleepy," Cassidy called over without opening her eyes.

"Hey, no fair faking so you can listen in on our conversation," Alex scolded her wife. "See, your mommy is sneaky," Alex whispered. "You are gonna love it here. Speed even gave you his Batcave. He'll have you in action in no time," Alex continued her dialogue with the infant in her arms. "There are certain things you need to know, M.J. Like, tacos. Every Tuesday Mommy makes Tacos. It's a Toles thing."

Cassidy listened on, astounded by the abiding love she felt for the woman a few feet away. "You might want to tell her about the Kryptonite before you go giving her that cape," Cassidy interrupted.

"Shhh, she's just being silly," Alex whispered to her daughter. "Don't you worry; Mommy gets her superheroes confused. That's a Superman thing; he's an alien. Batman is human like us," Alex assured her sleeping daughter.

Cassidy chuckled. "All right, Alfred. Let the Justice League get some rest."

Alex snickered and kissed Mackenzie's forehead. She stood up and placed the baby in the portable crib and then kissed Dylan the same way. She moved to Cassidy and felt a hand reach out for her. "Get some sleep," Alex whispered. "Je t'aime," she said with a kiss.

"I love you too, Alfred."

***

"You wanted to know," a voice said through the phone.

"Yes, I did," a deep voice answered.

"A girl. A few hours ago," the voice told him.

The man's voice cracked slightly. "And how is...."

"Everyone is well," she assured him.

"Thank you," he said.

***

Epilogue

One Month Later

Saturday, August 15th

"Cass?" Alex called up the stairs.

"Yeah? I'm in Kenzie's room!"

Alex made her way up the stairs and down the hallway. "Man, she is a pooping machine," Alex laughed. Cassidy just rolled her eyes as she finished changing the baby. "You know, this will be the first time we've had everyone here since Mackenzie arrived," Alex said.

"I do know. Thank God, your mother likes to cook," Cassidy laughed. "No way could I feed all these people on my own."

Alex reached over and took Mackenzie. "That is not a Toles thing, M.J. Nope. YaYa can tell you anything she wants. That cooking thing is a Pappas thing. Uncle Nicky got that gene. Skipped right through me," she said.

"Doesn't mean it will skip right through her," Helen said as she entered the room. "I thought I heard you two up here. Now, give me that baby and stop filling her head with your silliness," Helen scolded Alex.

Alex started to hand over her daughter and pulled back. "Now, just wait a minute there, YaYa. One man's silliness is another man's truth. Isn't that right, M.J.?"

Cassidy extracted their daughter from Alex's grip and handed her to Helen. "Hey, she's yours," Cassidy shrugged and pointed to Alex.

"Yes, I know," Helen said as she left the room with the baby. "Missing a gene," she called back.

"Am not!" Alex defended herself. She turned to Cassidy, who was shaking her head. "What?" Alex asked. Cassidy just raised her brow. "And, anyway...I'm yours now...you are stuck with me," Alex reminded her wife. Cassidy stepped into Alex's arms and pretended to consider the statement seriously. "Second thoughts?" Alex asked lightly.

Cassidy's answer was a slowly deepening kiss. "No."

"How would you like to get away for a weekend; alone?" Alex asked. She could tell she had piqued Cassidy's curiosity. "Okay, well...maybe not a weekend, just a night. No crying, no pooping, no soccer games, just you and me," Alex said.

"Tempting," Cassidy admitted.

"But?" Alex asked. Cassidy shrugged. "You're not ready to leave them yet," Alex surmised the problem and received another shrug. "Yeah, I know the feeling. I hate having to be away when I'm at work. So, I am just suggesting a nice dinner on the water, a walk along the beach and a night with uninterrupted sleep." Cassidy raised her brow a bit higher. "Okay, well...maybe there won't be all that much sleeping," Alex confessed.

"And when would you like to take this little excursion?" Cassidy asked.

"Tonight."

"Tonight? Alex, everyone will be here in an hour for this barbeque you planned," Cassidy said in disbelief.

"I know, that's part of the plan. Keep the kids distracted. Mom and Rose will be here."

"Alex, I have to pump...and..."

"Yep...already thought of that. We don't leave until six. I promise, I will have you back home before noon tomorrow," Alex said.

"You are too much sometimes," Cassidy smiled. "What do I need to bring?"

"Already set. Just you," Alex said with a kiss.

"Out of curiosity; what prompted this?" Cassidy asked.

"I made myself a promise when we decided to have Mackenzie," Alex said. Cassidy was intrigued and looked to Alex to explain. "That I would not ever forget you and me. We've all lost a lot, Cass; all of us. Too much."

"Yes, but look at everything we have," Cassidy reminded Alex. "I wouldn't change it, not if it meant not having you or Dylan, or Mackenzie."

"I know. Our parents didn't always do such a great job of remembering each other; maybe even us. I know that we can't make things perfect, but I don't want to make their mistakes, Cassidy. My father put everything before his family and look where it landed him. Look at your mom…."

"Stop," Cassidy said. "I understand. For the record, Alex; you don't have to take me away anywhere for me to know that you love me."

"No, but I want to," Alex said.

"You've gotten good at this sales thing," Cassidy laughed.

"Nah, you're a willing buyer."

"Alex, are you happy? I mean with the way things are right now in our lives?" Cassidy asked.

"More than I have ever been," Alex answered truthfully.

"But you're worried when the other shoe will drop," Cassidy observed a bit sadly.

"It always does, Cass. We both know that. There will be another storm. It's not a question of if, but when." Alex saw the tinge of fear in Cassidy's eyes. "I just want to be certain we have our anchor. I have my anchor. That's you," Alex confessed.

"Always," Cassidy promised.

Alex led Cassidy down the stairs and smiled as Cassidy took hold of their daughter. She watched Dylan barrel through the kitchen and slide to a stop and wave to his baby sister. She wasn't certain when the storm would surface, but she was certain she could feel it brewing. Cassidy looked over and smiled at her wife. Alex felt her mother's hand on her shoulder. Helen read the thoughts in her daughter's mind. "It will be all right, Alex. No matter what; as long as you have them; it will be all right."

"I know," Alex said. "I'll make sure of it."

***

A tall, gray-haired man with piercing blue eyes opened the door and peered inside. "Well; how is the patient today?" he asked the therapist at the foot of the hospital bed.

"The same; disagreeable," the therapist answered.

"I see," the older man replied. He made his way next to the young therapist who was finishing his work. "Leave us," he said. He waited for the door to close and looked at the occupant of the bed. The patient kept his head turned away in a blatant show of disregard for his visitor. "You are a miserable son of a bitch, Congressman. I should think you'd be more appreciative of the efforts here. After all you were a mess," he said.

"What do you want?" Congressman Christopher O'Brien asked.

"That's an interesting question. The only reason you are here is that I happen to think you could be of some use to me. Meaning that you have information that might be helpful. Believe me, Mr. O'Brien, I have killed far better men for far less than you," the man said with a chilling smile.

"So, what? So kill me, then. I'm dead anyway."

"No, and there are fates far worse than death; trust me on this," the man said. He began to pace the room slowly as he addressed the congressman. "You know, when John sent Alexis to Cassidy....well, I never expected what would come next. Of course, I never understood how someone like you could manage to land someone like Cassidy either. Still, it was a surprise... but then my daughter has never ceased to amaze me," he said proudly. "You have caused her family a great deal of pain, Mr.

O'Brien. I don't appreciate that. So, don't mistake your life as any show of kindness. You have information that can help me. I expect you to be forthcoming as payment for your current accommodations."

"You think I care?" O'Brien seethed. "Fuck you. Who the hell do you think you are?"

The older man laughed. He made his way to a small panel on the far wall and pressed a button. "I've been called by many names, Congressman. Some you may have heard. Who am I to you? I am the man who can decide how comfortable or how.....challenging your time here is, Mr. O'Brien," he said as he pointed out a window. O'Brien looked out at the cement walls beyond his room. It was dark, but he could make out the steel doors that lined them. He shivered at his new reality.

"Where did you think you were, Mr. O'Brien?" The older man's eyes twinkled with mirth. "It was bad enough that you were a horrible husband," he observed. "A piss poor father, as well."

"What do you know about it?" O'Brien shot back.

"Everything. Everything about you, Christopher. I failed my daughter on many levels. I know that. I will never be able to forgive myself for that. I will not fail to protect her now, nor my grandchildren. You will help me achieve that. So, I suggest you reconsider your position. My penance is watching the people I love from a distance. You can share that fate and comply with my request, or I promise you; your penance will be more painful and enduring than you can possibly imagine," he said bluntly.

The door opened slightly, and the older man looked up from O'Brien's gaze. "Yes?"

"You have a call, Mr. McCollum."

"Thank you, Agent Brady," McCollum answered and looked back at O'Brien. Christopher O'Brien looked at the figure above him in stunned silence. James McCollum laughed. "I'll give you some time to consider my request," he said as he headed for the door. "Make no mistake, O'Brien; I died once to protect my daughter. I won't hesitate to kill for her either."

James McCollum left the room and leaned his back against the door. "Sir?" Agent Brady called to him.

"Storm's brewing, Agent Brady. I can feel it."

"You could always go in," Brady said.

"No, that time passed long ago, my friend," James McCollum answered.

"At least, they're all safe," Agent Stephen Brady assured him.

"No, but they will be, Agent Brady. They will be. I promise you that."

35576340R00233

Made in the USA
Charleston, SC
09 November 2014